More Bread
or I'll Appear

also by Emer Martin

BREAKFAST
IN BABYLON

Emer Martin

More Bread
or I'll Appear

HOUGHTON MIFFLIN COMPANY

BOSTON • NEW YORK 1999

For information about permission to reproduce
selections from this book, write to Permissions,
Houghton Mifflin Company, 215 Park Avenue South,
New York, New York 10003.

Library of Congress Cataloging-in-Publication Data
Martin, Emer, date.
  More bread or I'll appear / Emer Martin.
    p. cm.
ISBN 0-395-91871-5
I. Title.
PR6063.A7134M67 1999
823'.914 — dc21   98-49676 CIP

Printed in the United States of America

Book design by Robert Overholtzer

QUM 10 9 8 7 6 5 4 3 2 1

Grateful acknowledgment is made to *Notre Dame
Review,* in which "The Doubting Disease"
originally appeared, in slightly different form.

TO MY ORIGINAL FAMILY

Marguerite, Eamonn, Ciara,
and Daragh Martin

contents

irish
pronunciation

Siobhan: Shivawn

Aisling: Ashling

one

television, history,
and the church

Where I grew up there was a trinity evident from birth: television, history, and the church; death as entertainment, death as catalyst, death as salvation.

A plump, loving hand drove her away. Five sausage fingers waving. The corridor was long. A guard took her ticket and wouldn't allow her mother to come any further. There were adults huddled in the wind and rain, waving, their arms held up together like river reeds, pummeled by the gale force. All peering for a last glimpse of the young people leaving.

Walking sideways, she waved back. Her own fingers flickered in the subdued light of the tunnel, sending signals, wanting to return. She was not discarded, she was launched. Like a metal ball in a game. Lobbed through the air. One beloved child thrown to hit off the other child, who was out there, back turned. The steel kiss, the jolt back home.

The ship that sailed was loud and hot. Babies squalled and money fell in the slot machines. She went to the deck but was battered back in through the iron doors by the wind. She went to the window to catch the last glimpse of home. It trailed away, oppressed under mighty forces. Dark clouds, slanted sleet, though not yet noon. The people milled about the smoky bar in a welter of bravado. Before she lost sight of land she was already exhausted.

Her mother, Molly, had given birth to five children, one after another. Keelin was the youngest, the baby. There was only one boy. His father used to take him out to the betting shop. He would hide under the bed and Molly would have to drag him out by the heels, urging him to come to his senses and go with his father; her panicky tone made him dither, but he always went in the end, dragging his feet, five paces behind the crooked, shrunken frame of his father. His father had a cap pulled tight on his head, his behind sticking out from the tails of his jacket.

He was a stunted weasel of a man, their father. A veritable picture of reticence and brooding — short, shrewd, buckling with restrained venom. His wiry freckled arms reached out only to hound them away, to bruise off the sides of their heads, to lay waste any attempt to even feign interest. His brother and only companion drove a van. The smack of money on the table as he counted it, licking his thumb each time before he pounded it down. The father eyeing it, an educated poor man coveting the bounty of his artisan sibling. Keelin hated money; it smelt like traveling children. It made her sick. She could not hold it in her hand. Keelin remembered her father's brother pinching her cheek hard and forcing a coin into her hand. She squirmed away, dropping the stinking penny to the floor, rubbing her hands to rid herself of the odor. Money smelt of the poor.

Around this time Molly was learning how to drive. A short while after the third driving lesson she drove all the children to the west. She opened the door to a cottage in Connemara and they trooped in. The older ones thought it was a holiday but were dismayed to see some of their furniture already there. Their mother drove alone across the country, back to Wexford. She did not return for a week. Aisling, the eldest girl, took charge.

Keelin was four years old and Aisling jiggled her on her knee.

Aisling's shovellike hands squeezed the flesh on her youngest sister's belly till it rumpled like an old woman's thigh; she then pressed her lips down and blew. There were uproarious farting noises and unbearable tickles as she panted and struggled on Aisling's knee. Keelin felt an overriding helplessness when she saw her older sister coming: beaming, snatching her into her arms, turning her upside down, so that her skirt fell to the waist, rattling her and roaring with laughter, biting on her toes. Her playfulness was a kind of torture. Keelin would have stayed outside all the time, absorbed in meditative games of solitude with sticks and stones, but the weather was relentless.

The evening their mother came back Aisling lit a fire in the grate. Molly slumped into a chair after unloading heavy boxes from the car boot. That night the storm rose to epic proportions. The water flailed from the sea and waves doused the house, coming down the chimney and putting the fire out. They all knelt around their mother's double bed, reciting the rosary. Patrick wet his pajamas during the Joyful Mysteries. The next month they moved to another cottage, seven miles inland but still out in the wilds of the bog, at the mercy of the wet winds.

They enrolled in the local school, which had high ceilings, long arched windows, heavy wooden doors. The outside walls were pebble-dashed. There were only two rooms, or one small hall divided by a wooden partition. Lessons were given in Irish. Aisling and Orla were in the same class; Keelin was behind the partition with Patrick and Siobhan. The roof leaked, so they sat with orange buckets on the desks and the plip-plop of rainwater pacing their thoughts.

Connemara was orange, brown, and green, mountainous, rocky, and boggy. Sheep grazed loose with colored brands stamped on their wool, their corpses strewn all over the roads. The roads were twisted, flanked by steep, sodden ditches and full of gaping, rain-filled holes. The sea was ferocious and had battered a necklace of sandy beaches that stretched away, abandoned to the cold. Mists rolled in and wove landscape tapestries among the postage-stamp fields and stone walls. It gave a drama to their mundane existence that was lacking when they had lived, equally disgruntled, on the gentle slopes of Wexford.

Ireland became an island only when they left it. Before then, it was the center of the universe. It was vast and all encompassing. Its history was the terrible history of the world. Beyond the sea lay lands ravaged by earthquakes, tornadoes, hurricanes, poisonous snakes, deadly wild animals, tropical diseases, serial killers, skyscrapers consumed by towering infernos, Turkish prisons, wars bloodier than their own, armed police, capital punishment, and killer sharks.

Molly was preoccupied with the tyranny of everyday life, the task of directing five children through each day. She gave piano lessons, but she rarely played for pleasure. Her escape was to settle in front of the television with her feet up on a stool beside the stove. She toasted bread on a long black toasting fork, opening and closing the small iron stove door like a porter at the gates of a miniature hell. She was absorbed only in the eldest child, Aisling. The others did not get much attention, a cursory hug or kiss, a perfunctory talking to, a distracted slap on the back of the legs. Aisling read them bedtime stories and undressed them in front of the fire. She hung their clothes on the bar of the stove so that they would be warm in the morning. All the love Molly gave to Aisling filtered down to the youngest, becoming strangely more abundant as it passed through this generous vessel.

Molly had no camera. There was not one concrete image of the entire family together. The only family photo was taken before Patrick was born: the two eldest as babies in Molly's arms, their father posing stiffly, standing up behind her, his eyes slightly crossed. Molly was slim and her hair black; she was not the fat, gray Molly they knew. Later, whenever Keelin saw other people's family photos standing on casual parade on pianos or mantels, they appealed to her like the traces of ghosts, color shadows on paper, brimming with expectancy, pleadingly confident in their ability to invoke posterity. Those years were proven only by their arrival in the present, intact but unsure. She craved the assurance that her recollections were sturdy and not just dreams trapped in a sticky web of longing and misunderstanding.

Uncle Oscar took them for a walk along the cliffs. Keelin was the youngest at five and Aisling the oldest at twelve. Molly was grateful for the peace she could have only when her twin brother, Oscar, visited from America. He was a priest, and his black figure shepherded them along a narrow mud path a meter from the edge. They marched in single file, their cheeks whipped red by the battering wind. Rosy and ebullient, they trotted in order of seniority, with Oscar at the rear, scooping Keelin up every so often to swing her over a rock or tangled bush. She shrieked in delight, pedaling the air as he whisked her through the snapping wind. Nice kids, eager to obey and rapturous at the invitation to leisure overseen by an adult, a rare thing in their lives outside the school. Red and brown heads, five of them, and wide faces smothered in freckles. They raced along, open to the future, abandoning themselves to each turn of the winding path. Tiny hands pawing the air, little legs stamping the mud exuberantly, chubby fingers frozen at the tips, eyes streaming brightly in the wind, all different shades of blue.

Patrick walked too close to the edge; he strayed from the ramshackle line. The wind pummeled him and his feet were unsteady. He peered over the cliff, catching glimpses of the metallic sea that pushed against a slate gray sky. Oscar sensed the menace and with one leap seized the tiny, wind-embattled nephew who was hovering so close to catastrophe. He shook him and took him back to the path.

"Don't walk so close to the edge. This is serious — you could be blown over. I have responsibility for you all. Jesus, Mary, and sweet Saint Joseph."

Patrick's lip quivered. Oscar relented.

"Aren't you the only man among all these hens? We can't lose you."

They were subdued for the rest of the walk. Oscar carried

Patrick in his arms for a while and kissed his cheek and nuzzled his neck. They arrived in town at an Italian chipper. He gave Aisling ten pence to play the Space Invader machine. The Italians chatted to him; they were as likely to make a fuss over a priest as the God-fearing Irish. The children felt proud to be with him, so impeccably groomed, with his sparkling Yankee accent, decked out in black with his white collar, attracting favorable attention from all the town and countryside. Aisling pestered him for more coins, but he shook his head and wiped the grease from their hands with napkins.

"Well," he asked, "which part of the day did you enjoy the most? The train ride or the walk on the cliffs?"

Siobhan, a slow eater, still had the stained, slimy white bag in her hands. She dug her vinegary fingers in and fished out the last squashed chip. "If you don't mind me saying, Uncle Oscar," she faltered, "I think this is my favorite part now." She stuck the chip into her mouth as if stunned by her own audacity.

"No, Siobhan." Oscar smiled beatifically. "Of course I don't mind you saying so. I'm only glad you're enjoying yourself."

She smiled back weakly, a meek seven years old, her tiny, quivering body suspended in anticipation, perpetually lost in a clamor of siblings, the only conventionally pretty one in the brood. Patrick pointed to the statue of the pregnant virgin on a donkey — her skirt hoisted up, dust in the stiff folds; her bare plaster leg, yellowed by cigarette smoke, hanging almost casually over the beast's flank. Uncle Oscar tut-tutted, "There you have it!" he said genially. "That's the Italians for you."

Oscar and Molly sat on either side of the stove. He drank whiskey and she drank gin. Twin brother and sister. He put a little water in his and she put tonic, lemon, and ice in hers. He became loquacious when drunk and she withdrew. All of them turned to the black-and-white television, American cops and British comedies — TV not a mirror for their lives but a tantalizing window.

That night Orla, Siobhan, and Keelin slept as usual in the

same big bed. They put their woolly tights on their heads to pretend they had long hair. The legs dangling down were plaits that they would flick back and forth over their shoulders, and the bed was their carriage; they flailed the horses mercilessly and bounced up and down as the carriage leaped daringly over treacherous potholes. Though they never established a destination, they were in a great hurry.

Below in the kitchen, Uncle Oscar started to sing in Irish. They listened for their mother but could not hear her. Aisling, who was allowed up till all hours, sang along. She clapped and whooped and they could hear her heavy footfall thumping a jig on the linoleum. Oscar played a tin whistle and she danced in front of his eyes. They never knew what their Mother was doing. They only heard her shuffle off to bed at some point. Oscar remained in the kitchen teaching Aisling songs until early in the morning. They would be long asleep and never hear Aisling creep off to the bed she shared with Molly at the end of the hall. When they got up for school, Oscar was still drinking whiskey in the chair beside the stove. He reached out to squeeze them, bleary-eyed and full of melancholy affection.

As the years went on they trudged home along the bog road, the winters holding them down, the sick fields on either side stabbed by wind-bent trees. They neglected their homework and sat transfixed in front of the TV, thought extinguished, numb feet coming back to life to burn with chilblains. Molly was busy washing or baking, muttering abstractly, sighing inordinately, retreating finally to the armchair by the stove to toast her bread on the fork. She ate her toast burnt, with chunks of melting, yellow butter, and she drank her tea milky and lukewarm. Her varicose veins were like rivers flowing on a strange planet down her leg, a foul terrain under nylon. She dozed off, her mouth hanging open in an inutterable, vowelless lament.

They moved to Dublin, south to a town called Dun Laoghaire, when Keelin was ten and Aisling was seventeen. Aisling was starting college, and Molly said she had more chance of piano pupils in the city than in the depopulated west. In truth she was not ready to let Aisling go. They lived in a flat on the ground floor of a Georgian house close enough to the harbor. The children were delighted: in the west there were only two government-run stations available; now they could get all the English stations and one from Northern Ireland. Neighbor children asked them where their father was. The older ones avoided the stigma of admitting their parents were separated, said he was dead. They ganged together and sought out each other's company to keep things simple, for they knew their mother was odd and their father was missing. Aisling had courage, Orla was straightforward, Patrick said his prayers, Siobhan was pretty and timid, Keelin, the baby, was fussy and sensitive.

In this new flat Patrick slept in the living room and folded up his camp bed every morning. He had a drawer in the girls' room where he kept his personal belongings. Molly kept the curtains closed at all times to prevent the good couch and chairs from fading. Patrick was not allowed in the living room till it was time for bed. He would slide the bed out from the cupboard and unfold it, then return to the kitchen to fill his hot water bottle from the kettle on the stove. He slipped back into the room, closing the door behind him, climbing into the bed, flipping and tossing the hot water bottle with his feet under the covers. He slept each night in these mysterious surroundings, like an unexpected guest.

In this sitting room there were three pictures in frames: President Kennedy, the Sacred Heart, and De Valera. Jesus looked sad and pretty; his brown hair descended lightly to his shoulders, and his eyes followed all of them in a sorrowful quiz about the room. He held a strange pink heart entwined with thorns, as if he wasn't quite sure what to do with an organ so out of place. De Valera looked mean and judgmental; Kennedy looked well fed and uncomprehending. Molly arranged the pictures in the new flat as she had hung them in the old house. "Jesus should feel comfortable there, hung between two thieves," she said with satisfaction.

Molly and Aisling's room was at the end of the hall. The bed was high and Aisling slept by the wall. They shared the dressing table and there was an old chair always smothered in clothes; it had a white tin potty hidden beneath the seat. There was a dark green painting of all the doomed men who had signed the 1916 declaration of independence sitting about a table with an Irish flag draped in the background. De Valera had been spared because he was American-born. The proclamation itself hung over the bed beside the crucifix, a silver metal Jesus, suspended in an agony without respite. A weird Christ, the arms as long as the clumsily molded legs. Aisling and Molly lay among the relics and reminders, two husks in the bed, churning and turning through the dark nights.

Each of Molly's fingers was unique unto itself. Their linkage was tentative, each one molded and muscled from piano playing. They never touched but made their separate ways from the bones in the bulk of the hand. Individually, they looked nothing like fingers: lined, red, callused, sprouting hair, flat tops, translucent bitten nails, knotty bulges. They were not for stroking, for sewing hems, fixing cut knees, making star shapes in dough. Children trailed shyly in and out for piano lessons. They themselves were all taught to play from age three. Molly sat in the dark, curtained living room with her eyes closed, listening to her children play, sucking in the air through her teeth when they faltered on the keys.

When Keelin walked to school she touched each lamppost with her left hand, brushing her fingers on the wood, their tips black with sticky tar. If she thought she had missed one she was compelled to go back. Sometimes she was unsure, which was disastrous, since she might need to go back to her home and repeat the entire route again. Then there was always the chance of hitting one twice by mistake and upsetting the balance. It had to be done properly. The nuns scolded her for being late so often.

It was a convent school but they had lay teachers also. They spent the school week leading up to the pope's visit studying his life and looking at pictures of him. "Look at the special intelligence you can see radiating from him in his school pictures. Even as a baby his face had a gravity," the teacher told them earnestly. They all looked intently.

The day before the pope was to come was declared a national holiday. Siobhan was in the front garden and found a four-leaf clover; she pressed it in her prayer book. Patrick, Orla, and Keelin then spent the entire afternoon on their hands and knees, sifting methodically through the dense, rubbery patches of clover in the grass. Siobhan stood aloof, a new aura of saintliness about her.

"Maybe you have a vocation," Aisling jeered from the steps where she and Molly cradled mugs of tea. Molly snorted with laughter.

"A vocation is only a good thing for a man, not a woman," Molly said. "Patrick, you should talk to your uncle Oscar when he comes this evening. He's a grand life, that one. Always gadding about."

"The priest gets respect, power, a house, a housekeeper, a car. He can play his round of golf and can have a few drinks in the bargain," Aisling agreed.

"Yeah!" Orla stood up and brushed herself off. She was wearing her school uniform because she'd had hockey practice that morning. Her hair was red and spiked, and she wore her socks bunched at the ankles. Her skirt hung short over her stocky freckled legs and her school tie was askew. Though they weren't allowed to wear makeup at school, she had sneaked some blue eyeliner and mascara and smeared a cheap orange foundation on her face, giving her freckles a greenish hue. "Nuns can't do shite," she said. "They have one car between the lot of them, nobody likes them, and they have to live together like a bunch of lesbos." They all laughed.

"Now, now," Molly said, frowning. "None of this when your uncle comes."

"He's not going to be alone either." Aisling slurped noisily from her cup. "He's bringing his friends, the racy set of the Irish church."

Molly went inside and put a new picture of the pope on the mantel alongside a picture of an out-of-date pope. "He's a lovely, kind face all the same," she said to herself.

They were all enraptured and open to his love that weekend.

Oscar arrived in the evening. He had come from New York the day before, was staying at the Shelbourne Hotel, and had two other priests in tow. He was, as always, impeccably turned out, his clothes designer or tailored. He wore black silk trousers and a black suede jacket, but had made his priest's collar from a white strip of cardboard from a box of washing detergent. Keelin sat on his knee and twirled the collar in her hand in fascination; it still had some brand letters on the end. The three priests laughed at her.

"Not so mysterious after all, my child," Oscar said, grinning.

The three men sat like sleek black panthers around the wooden table in the large kitchen. Molly had taken down all the half-dried washing that hung in front of the stove and stuffed it damp into the bedroom drawers. They had all scrubbed, polished, and tidied the flat before the men's arrival. Molly served the priests and poured their tea; they complimented her homemade bread and thanked her profusely. She took their plates to the sink when they had finished eating. Aisling was nineteen years old then and she arrived back from the pub a little drunk. She kissed Oscar on his shiny forehead and shook the other priests' hands.

"It's only six o'clock. What were you doing in the pub so early?" he said, holding her hand.

"A friend of mine's going away to England to do nursing." She pulled her hand away. "Anyway, we had to celebrate his holiness's arrival. Raise our spirits on this spiritual occasion."

"I can see the kind of spirits you've been raising," Molly snapped, as she set a place for her daughter at the table with the priests. The other children, who hung about the kitchen eating from plates or lurking at the back doorstep, eyed her hallowed position enviously. Aisling was tall and broad, her thick bush of red hair bound in an enormous plait that ran down her back.

She had a round, freckled face and blue eyes with dark blue rims. Stabbing her food aggressively, she talked easily with the middle-aged priests. She didn't address them as "Father" but called them by their first names. Molly sat on her old armchair by the stove with one veiny leg tucked under her. She ate from a plate of white bread with huge chunks of butter on it and thick, pink, hairy slices of ham drowned in salt.

"You treat that girl like the man of the house," Oscar said to his twin sister later, when the priests were sipping whiskeys by the fire in the living room.

"Sure she'll be up and leaving me soon." Molly shrugged.

"Come in and play us an aul' tune, Molly," shouted one of the priests, who had been around with Oscar before. Orla went out with a boyfriend, but the rest of them gathered in the small living room. Aisling topped the men's whiskeys and poured herself one. Siobhan made her mother a gin and tonic and set it on the piano. Molly pounded the keys and the three priests took turns singing — no hymns, but rebel songs, famine songs, sad love songs, and funny songs. *And poor Wexford, stripped na-ked, hung high on a cross, and her heart pierced by traitors and slaves! Glory O! Glory O! to her brave sons who died for the cause of long down-trodden man.* The children, all teenagers now but Keelin, joined in, and they sat up till the wee hours of the morning. *Here's a piece of advice I got from an aul' fish monger, When the food is scarce and you see the hearse, You'll know you've died of hunger.* The priests were red-faced, drunk, and jolly. Molly was uncharacteristically gay, swirling the ice around in her gin, her bleary eyes glistening as her fingers idled on the keys between songs. Keelin moved closer to her and sat with her back against the side of the piano, feeling its soft, hollow vibrations. Patrick, fifteen years old, sat on the arm of his uncle's chair, filling up the whiskeys liberally. Siobhan, newly a teenager, dressed from head to toe in black, sat camouflaged between the two priests on the couch, joining in all the choruses in her earnest way.

"Aisling, pet," Molly urged, "'The Spinning Wheel.' Sing 'The Spinning Wheel.' You do it so well."

The three priests nodded. "Lovely, lovely!" they murmured.

Eileen a chara, I hear someone tapping.
'Tis the ivy, dear Mother, against the glass flapping.
Eily, I surely hear somebody sighing.
'Tis the sound, Mother dear, of the autumn winds dying.

The priests left at three in the morning, when the last drop of whiskey was gone. Oscar drove them, and they giggled like young girls in his rented car. Orla was walking up the dark road arm in arm with a lanky boy. She waved as she saw them weave past.

At the house, Molly was leaning against the doorpost. "Come in you — you hussy," she barked. "We have to get up at five o'clock tomorrow to go to the park and get a good place. Where have you been, anyway? The pubs have long been closed."

Orla let go of the young man and climbed the steps to the front door of the flat. "We went to a disco."

"I'll disco you! Are you drunk?"

"Not as drunk as you." Orla eyed her mother disdainfully as she went into the girls' bedroom, slamming the door behind her.

Siobhan and Keelin woke first and looked at the clock.

"Jaysus! Would you look at the time," Keelin said. Siobhan giggled. They poked Orla, in the bed beside them, and she snarled. Keelin swung out of bed and ran into the corridor.

"Mammy, Mammy, we're dead late, we are."

Patrick was up and dressed. "I can't wake them up. They've got hangovers," he sniffed piously. "I'm going by myself. I'm not missing this."

Molly appeared at the door, her eyes puffy and her gray hair wild. "You're not going anywhere," she croaked. "Now put on the kettle like a good lad and make us a pot of tea."

It was quarter to ten when they all straggled out the door with rugs, deck chairs, umbrellas, and bags stuffed with food.

"All my friends' families were leaving at five in the morning," Patrick pouted. "Some were even staying overnight at the park. We'll never get a place now."

"Ah whisht, will ye," Molly snapped. She, Aisling, and Orla limped along together in mutual sympathy.

A third of the country's population were in the park that day. A million and a quarter people. A huge white cross had been erected above the altar. The space in front was roped off into square lots, the lowest numbers being closest to the altar. Molly was given their lot number and color. Patrick snatched the ticket and looked disgusted, his face reddening and tears springing to his eyes. Keelin took it from him.

"We're 36C," she whined. "That's ages away; we'll never see anything."

"It might be the one chance you have of being 36C in your life, child of grace," Aisling said, and she, Molly, and Orla guffawed heartily. The three youngest looked puzzled.

They shared the lot with another family. Cheers went up when a helicopter flew over, but it was just the police. They stuck the umbrellas in the ground for Siobhan and Keelin to huddle beneath against the wind, then waited hours.

A ripple of excitement spread from the front of the crowd through the people at the back. They all stood up in the lot, unable to see if the pope had arrived, but running to the ropes all the same. Molly blessed herself, and Aisling grabbed Patrick by the shoulders excitedly when they heard his voice. His accent was thick and the loudspeakers clashed with each other, their timing slightly off. Gradually the people sat down, and after an hour of his words echoing in a holy jumble, Orla noted that the other family was eating a picnic behind their wind shelter. Molly shook her head.

"An hour's fast before Communion, Orla."

"But he's been talking for an hour already," Orla protested.

Patrick was on his knees with his rosary beads.

"What part of the mass are we at all, at all?" Molly asked him.

He opened his eyes. "I haven't the foggiest. I can't hear a word he's saying."

Aisling was already rooting through the bag. "We'll not go to hell for a cheese sandwich, surely?"

Wrapped in blankets, they ate their sandwiches and drank their flasks of tea during the brutal cacophony of the mass. Molly and Orla were arguing over who forgot to pack the clubmilks. Patrick clasped his hands in prayer and turned away.

A Vatican-colored yellow and white tent had been erected in the middle of the million-and-a-quarter-person throng. There was one toilet there. Orla and Aisling came back shocked.

"It was a disgrace," Aisling said.

"People shitting into holes, standing on planks, everyone together, and the smell!"

"Would you not think they'd have organized it a bit better," Molly tut-tutted. She took Siobhan and Keelin through the crowds to the riverbanks.

"Look, we're not the only ones." Keelin pointed to others furtively darting into bushes.

When the pope toured in his popemobile, he held a rose in his hand. Molly leapt up and down, waving her arms. The ecstatic children crushed to the side and got a good look at him. Aisling was nowhere to be seen when all the pandemonium was over. In the tangle of crowds, Patrick got lost as they shuffled out of the park, deck chairs and rugs under arm. Molly panicked and told the three girls to stay where they were while she went off to look. But the ebbing crowds buffeted them and they lost their place. Orla tried to find it, pushing her way back. Siobhan and Keelin stood on a wall and surveyed the crowd frantically until they spotted a school friend's family, who insisted that the two girls come with them. Siobhan hopped off the wall and threw herself to her new family.

"We were 12A yellow. What color were you?"

"Did yiz go to the toilets?"

"No, but we heard about them," Siobhan said.

Keelin, appalled by her traitor sister, slipped into the crowd with her deck chair and a bag of empty flasks. She needled through the dense pitch of people, tears pouring down her face, until a young man grabbed her.

"Are ye lost, child?"

She tried to squirm away.

"I'll take you to the place for lost children. Your mammy and daddy are probably there." He took her hand and she numbly followed him as he weaved in and out of the crowd with great agility.

"Where are we going? Where are we going?" she pleaded, suddenly frightened as they weaved farther and farther away through the furor of people.

Lost Children, the sign read, and the man smiled at Keelin and dodged back into the river of humanity. Molly screamed when she saw her. "I've been back and forth. Back and forth."

Double-deckers in a line rocked with the movement of the faithful. Families were split up and people grew cranky from the crushing. Molly and her little daughter kept their eyes peeled for the rest of their family.

United in the evening by the fire, they related their separate adventures. Aisling had bumped into Uncle Oscar. The newspapers and radio were full of outrage about the toilets. A man had fallen into one of the holes and had to be rescued and carted off to hospital. They watched all the pope's subsequent appearances on TV, and when he addressed a stadium full of young people in Limerick with the words "Young people of Ireland, I love you," there wasn't a dry eye in the house. The pope went to New York next. Women asked why he would not ordain them as priests. He angrily stated that there was to be none of that nonsense in the Holy Catholic Church.

"Typical of those yanks," Molly said. "We would have never thought to ask that question." But the girls felt betrayed by the pope's hostility. Despite Patrick's objections, Aisling took his picture from the mantel and placed it more obscurely on the bookshelf. The talk of toilets lingered on over the next few weeks.

"Funny," Aisling mused months later, "how the Pope's visit will always be associated with shite."

On the altar steps, like ravens on branches, was a group of men in black, allies winging among each other like old friends. Oscar sees Aisling stride through the crowd, an air of triumph, an unfeminine swagger. Her bushy red hair ringing her head like a mane. She sees him. Smiling, she approaches, her arms swinging, and he almost takes flight — swoops into the air, gasping in the compression of this crowded sky. He has a vision of her — a giantess, and as she walks the villages burn.

It was the beginning of Lent, Ash Wednesday six o'clock in the morning. Keelin had never seen an adult unclothed; she had pushed the door open thinking the toilet was empty. Aisling was brushing her teeth, stark naked. Keelin was frozen as her senses were flooded with gigantic pink saucer nipples on huge bell breasts, and massive power of thighs. Amid the expanse of white flesh sprouted an abundance of red pubic hair that snaked up her moonlike belly like a fox's tail. She closed the door abruptly and fled, mortified, her older sister's laughter flooding the air. *Monster! Monster!*

Gray light then washed away the dark dawn. Their family took up one whole wooden pew in the church. To be woken up in darkness and rooted out so early for all this gloom. The mass was an ordinary mass, and no one listened. But after Communion, as the priests stood with the bowl of ashes and the crucifix, they queued up once more. It was a big Dublin church, crowded with hundreds of people bundled in winter coats and half asleep. Alive in an eerie, suspended way, their routine broken for Ash Wednesday. *Ashes to ashes, dust to dust,* the priest murmured to each one of them in turn. A cruel reminder to humble themselves before the grim inevitability: the corporeal was fragile, all their organs and limbs and ever-growing nails and hair just borrowed machinery to propel them around this station on the way to oblivion. One by one the lips, chapped and unpainted, kissed the metal feet of Christ. The priest held him to each sleep-stunned face, the steel feet warm with nervous kisses. Another priest pressing a thumb of ash onto the foreheads, smooth, wrinkled, pimply, all imprinted with the mark of death.

"Ashes to ashes, dust to dust," Aisling whispered to Orla and Siobhan, who were standing in the line in front of her. "If the Lord won't have you, the devil must."

They giggled, and Molly turned and frowned ferociously. Patrick pulled his anorak down as far as possible: he had had an erection in the aisles. He trembled in terror and anticipation, dreading the forceful thumb, the poor sinewy feet of a man he thought he understood.

People spilled out into the broadening light of morning. The whole churchyard, the whole city, the whole country walked today, a strange tribe, a bruise on their pale foreheads, a target for death's sure arrow. Keelin watched as they milled about the car park shouting greetings, shaking hands, bustling their children into their cars to drive to work in the early morning frost. All of us alive will be dead in one hundred years. It was not a soul she had, it was fluid. She remembered Aisling's body, which would be hers soon. Blood and water and pus and sap, her heart, her brains, her lips, all tightly packed moisture, red and blue rivers running in circles. Panicking, she grabbed Aisling's hand out of nowhere. It was warm and enveloping. She could feel the slight pulse beneath the silky skin.

Aisling and Molly faced each other down at the kitchen table. Orla sat dejectedly between them, her head in her arms.

"She has to have an abortion."

"That's a sin," Molly said, narrowing her eyes.

"Fuck the church. This is her whole life at stake here."

"No grandchild of mine will be aborted. She made all her decisions when she lay down with the young whelp. Abortion is illegal here."

"So are contraceptives, so what do they expect? I'll take her to England with me. My friend is in nursing school over there. She'll know where to go. It's free you know."

"It's not the money."

"That's a change."

"The shame. The shame." Molly shook her head and thumped

Orla, who sprawled limp in her chair. "You little tramp, how could you?"

"Leave her alone," Aisling glared, "It's no use talking like that now. I'll deal with it. Listen Orla, what do you want to do?"

"I want the baby," Orla wailed. "Mammy's right — it's a sin."

"You fucking eejit," Aisling snarled. "You'll wreck your life."

Molly looked at her two daughters in disgust. She placed her chubby hands on the table and heaved herself up. "I'll go to the corner and ring Oscar. He'll know what's best."

"Why don't you go upstairs? They have a phone."

"I don't want anyone knowing my business."

When her mother left, Aisling poked Orla. "Straighten up for fuck's sake. Go pack your bag. We'll get the boat and go to England tonight."

Orla wiped her snotty nose and looked at her older sister in terror.

Orla fidgeted nervously with the safety belt on the plane and wondered if Uncle Oscar would be pleased to see her, the first of the family to come over. She couldn't imagine the two of them in the car together without cringing. Of all the children, Orla deferred to him least. Would he collect her in a car and drive her to New York? They would have to talk. She would be embarrassed. He would bring her out to a nice restaurant. He always ate out in Dublin. She would awkwardly fish for things to say, running out of news and family anecdotes. She tried to picture the priest's house, attached to a giant cathedral. Oscar was beloved in the neighborhood, helping the poor, feeding the hungry, pardoning sinners. And then herself, pregnant and transplanted so suddenly, unpacking her suitcase in her new surroundings.

Uncle Oscar met her at Kennedy airport and took her in a taxi to Manhattan. She couldn't look him in the eye. He had a small, two-bedroom apartment on the Upper West Side with

Persian rugs and a view of Central Park. She spoke only when spoken to and only in monosyllables. She was relieved to close the door of her room and be alone.

In 1980, Aisling left to spend a summer studying in France; she was twenty years old. The morning she left she sat Keelin on a stool in the kitchen. Ailsing pressed ice cubes to Keelin's ear lobes and held them. Keelin shivered but Aisling bade her be still. Aisling blindfolded her with her brown tights that were unwashed and host to a blizzard of skin speckles. They smelt of rust, heavy and tangy. She pierced the thirteen-year-old's ears with a needle. Leaving a safety pin in each ear to keep it open, she promised to buy gold studs and send them over. There was no fuss; she walked down the road with Patrick and Keelin. The sun was brightly shining, and she bought her two younger siblings ice pops at a corner news agent's. Patrick had shot up — at sixteen he was as tall as her, and he had soft fuzzy hair sprouting above his lip. He made a show of not wanting the ice pop and took out a pack of Major, offering Aisling a cigarette. She laughed.

"Wait till Mammy catches you at that."

He sniffed and cupped his hand around the tiny flame that licked the end of a wooden match. Aisling bent down to accept the light.

"Keelin, you can have two ice pops now, unless you want a fag too."

Patrick, in a fit of chivalry, offered to carry Aisling's rucksack. Keelin carried her tickets. Patrick slouched along, rucksack on back, smoking industriously.

"Are you getting the boat?" Keelin asked.

"No, the train to Wexford and then the boat to France. I wouldn't touch England with a ten-foot pole. Not while they're letting our hunger strikers die one by one, like animals. Now the French — they always helped us out."

"They just saw us as a back door into England," Patrick said, parroting the history books.

"I know, and it always ended in disaster." Aisling shrugged.

The boat was in, but she was not going to take it. It sat white and sturdy in the water, with its great poking chimneys fingering the blue sky and its jaw hanging open to let miniature cars drive up its tongue and into its ravenous mouth.

"I'll never take that boat," Aisling declared heroically.

"You have already," Patrick reminded her. "You bunked off school and went to Wales for the day."

"That doesn't count — that was just for shoplifting."

They strode with Aisling to the train station by the harbor.

"See you in three months," Aisling said, kissing Keelin.

"Bring me back a present," Keelin pleaded.

Ailsing hugged Patrick.

"Patrick's crying," Keelin blurted out in glee. Patrick punched her venomously in the arm.

"You're a crybaby," Keelin retorted. "I'm not even crying," she said, though she bit back the tears now, rubbing her arm.

"Stop causing trouble you," Aisling scolded, "and be good for Mammy, and wash those ears with whiskey every day."

When the train arrived, she gave them each a fiver from the money she had saved from working weekends at the supermarket. Patrick and Keelin walked on the platform parallel to their sister, who lugged her suitcase down the train aisle. They stood where she sat down and awkwardly kept waving as the train lingered in the station. Patrick lit another cigarette, which made Aisling laugh. Then the train left.

Patrick looked at Keelin distractedly. "Go home for your tea, young one," he said.

"Aren't you coming?"

"Things to do."

Patrick skulked off and went to sulk among the docks and watch the boat leave the harbor. He looked for friends hanging out in the bandstands on the pier. Keelin strolled home, dragging her feet and brushing the lampposts with her fingers; she faltered when she touched one too lightly and some of her fingers felt only air. She repeated the gesture, this time stroking it too hard. She walked up and down the road, questing for a symmetry, until it grew dark and she was satisfied. When she entered the flat she saw that her ham and eggs had been sitting on the table for hours. She walked into the living room; her mother smiled faintly from the armchair by the curtained window, bereft and old. Keelin ate alone in the kitchen, listening to news of the hunger strikers. They all would die and Aisling would never come home.

Keelin played Eric Satie's compositions over and over again. She perfected the obsessive sequences, followed his deliberate trail, not looking for anything but secure in the patterns and simple logic. The quietness of his agony, the order of his yearning, his mathematical trinity of despair. She pictured, as she played, his defection from festive Montmartre to the sullen suburbs, his meager belongings in a wheelbarrow. The twelve identical corduroy suits hanging in his wardrobe, the writing on the filthy wall when they finally ventured into his lodgings after his death: *the devil lives in this house.* His passion muted and constrained, tinkling peacefully and blankly in her own phobic brain. The melancholy pauses between notes, as if always unsure of the future's worth. She swam through the resigned sadness of *Gymnopédies* and *Gnossiennes* until her fingers cramped and faltered on the keys. Numbly she closed the polished piano lid, feeling the whole house sigh with relief in the silence left over by her relentless playing. The notes stuck in her head; she carried them away with her, in key but off-center inside her, pressing the white and black wooden parts of her brain with soft felt hammers. As she played she had the sensation that she was disappearing.

Patrick was the oldest altar boy at the church and spent hours there after class, brooding in the dark calm. When Uncle Oscar was visiting, the local priest took him aside and complained that the boy was going to confession too often. Patrick was so embarrassed that outwardly he appeared to calm down and go about his normal teenage duties. After graduating from secondary school he worked at McDonald's on the main street. When the country was whipped into a frenzy by numerous sightings of moving statues and alabaster effigies shedding salty tears, Patrick was again stricken with obsession. He was twenty-one. He stood vigil in the local churchyard, where there was a small grotto with Our Lady, blue and white robes lifted daintily to reveal her tiny bare foot crushing a lizard. Keelin and Siobhan trotted down at lunchtime to visit him.

"In America they've UFOs; here we have twitching virgins," Keelin teased.

"Have you seen anything, Paddy?" Siobhan asked, peeling back the tinfoil from a raw carrot. She wore a baggy jumper over tight denim jeans. She had left the convent a year ago and was on the dole. She lay about the house lethargically during the day or went for long walks on the pier. Keelin was in her last year of school and under intense exam pressure. She wore her uniform, which had been handed down so many times it had suede patches on the sleeves and the hem of the skirt was stapled where she couldn't be bothered to sew. She gave Patrick some cheese sandwiches, which he ate contemplatively.

"I've seen nothing, but I don't give a shite. I'm staying here. I get up to go sometimes, but when my back is turned I feel something and I have to stay."

"So you haven't seen anything," Siobhan repeated, nibbling on the carrot, scraping her teeth along the surface.

"Nah!"

"You'll have to hang a sign around her — Out of Order," Keelin said, and she and Siobhan rolled around laughing.

Patrick glowered. "I'm not doing this for the craic, you know. I don't want to. I can't leave."

"Well, you're not the only lunatic around," Keelin said, comforting him. "The whole country's at this racket. There's crowds down West where the two kids saw her weep. I saw it on the telly; they've set up hot dog stands to feed the pilgrims and the locals are complaining about the litter. They interviewed one guy with his binoculars trained on the statue and he said to them, 'She's moving well today.'"

"I feel like a right eejit." Patrick was close to tears.

"Come home with us," Keelin said.

"I don't know." He hesitated. "Maybe I could. The priest has threatened to set the dogs on me."

"Then come on, for fuck's sake. We're the laughingstock of the neighborhood, as usual." Siobhan twirled her dyed blue-black hair around her finger.

"I feel if I leave something awful will happen," Patrick said.

"Something awful *will* happen," Keelin retorted. "Life will go on as shittily as usual."

"I have to go, anyway," Siobhan said, shrugging.

"Got an appointment?" Keelin sneered. "She walks up and down the pier to burn off calories."

"This family is fucking creepy." Siobhan sighed. "Aisling and Orla had the right idea. I'm going to get out of this stupid country at the end of the month."

"Listen," Keelin said to Patrick, "take the statue with you. We could all carry it; I don't think it's attached, and it's small enough."

"What would Father Ryan say?" Patrick seemed to be seriously considering the idea.

"Just leave a sign on the pedestal saying Out to Lunch," Keelin said, and she and Siobhan cracked up laughing again. They managed to take Patrick with them and force him to abandon his lonely vigil. He seemed relieved.

Patrick left Ireland before Siobhan did. Keelin escorted him to the boat. Though apprehensive, he was in a rare good mood.

"Have you money?" she asked.

"Too much," he said.

"I must get a job so I can save. As soon as all these bloody exams are over."

"Ach, I spent most of me money down in the pub with the lads. I sort of borrowed from Ronald McDonald. He extended me a wee loan, so to speak. Now don't worry about your exams — sure aren't you always swotting? You'll do well and go to college. Since Aisling dropped out Mammy hasn't been herself."

"What is herself? She seems the same to me."

"Well, she's not."

Patrick finally took the boat he had watched so many times come and go in the harbor.

Keelin studied French her first year at college and used Aisling's books. She read the margin notes over and over again as if they would have some hint of Aisling's later flight. In Racine's *Phèdre* only two lines were circled in the entire play, and beside them was a note: "These are the two greatest lines in the French language."

> Ariane, ma soeur, de quel amour blessée
> Vous mourûtes aux bords où vous fûtes laissée!

Aisling had translated it in pencil:

> Ariane, my sister, wounded by such a love
> You died on the shores where you were left!

Keelin had seen Molly sit down at the table every Friday night to write Aisling her two pages in small, neat handwriting. Aisling had flooded them with postcards from different places — France, Israel, Egypt, Thailand, India, Nepal — and then nothing for the past year. Maybe they should have visited her when she pleaded with them; and once, when she wrote saying she was broke, perhaps she wanted to return and could not.

After the long absence of communication they received a postcard from Aisling with a picture of Hiroshima and an address in Tokyo. She wrote that she was standing at the Hypocenter where the A-bomb went off. She was giving English lessons in the Roppongi district in the capital. Keelin never got around to writing back, but she knew her mother would.

It was a dreary day, the gray blanket of sky pressed close to the earth. Keelin came home early from college with the prospect of two papers to write for the next day. As she mounted the steps and opened the red wooden front door, she bent down to pick up the mail that was lying in the hall on the floor. There was a letter addressed to Aisling in Japan with a return-to-sender stamp on it. It had made it all the way across the world and found no one. The journey home unread. This would break Molly's heart. I can't let her see this, she thought, and pocketed the letter. Better for her to believe some contact was made.

Keelin was writing papers into the night. Molly came home and Keelin had cooked dinner for her; she'd brought home pasta and rice to wean her mother off the potatoes and white bread of a lifetime. They had tea together frequently, and Molly had taken to sitting at the table, not on the chair by the stove. A bottle of wine with meals and sometimes salads, avocados for starters, and kiwi for dessert. They were becoming a part of Europe.

The letter she had hidden ate into her brain like a parasite. She left her desk and the unfinished second paper and rooted in her coat pocket for the unrequited missive. Without dwelling on it any longer, she opened it and began to read.

My dear Aisling

We were delighted to get your card and find you were well. It must be very exciting for you seeing all those places. The weather has been terrible here, rain, rain, rain. I had a touch of the flu but am all right now T.G. I can't remember what I told you in the last letter or if you got it so I might be repeating news. Patrick met some young lads on the boat to England and moved into their place. He says it is a squat but everyone squats in London. They helped him to get a job on a construction site. It is very heavy work and I hope he does not hurt himself. Siobhan went over to stay with him a few weeks later but they fought all the time apparently and she found her own squat on the other side of London. I hope she is eating; she sometimes forgets. Orla is still in America. She is working in a bakery in Yonkers, which is somewhere in New York City and has to get up at four in the morning. Can you imagine Orla getting up so early? She was never home by then when she lived at home. Keelin did well in her exams and is now in Trinity College and working very hard. Maybe you could come back and finish. You need qualifications. You could do a secretarial course and go off again with skills.

I had a breast removed last year and was told that I had high cholesterol and blood pressure. You must be careful, my mother died of the same thing and the nurse says it can be passed down by blood. The nurse gave me a chart and instructions to do monthly checks and I will put it in the envelope. I had to give up covering everything in salt. I was coaxed into taking up golf by our new neighbour, Blue Cone. She's very sporty — her father even called her after a horse. So now I go out a few times a week before piano lessons. Keelin is always complaining about all my golf advice books lying around the house. It's only ourselves left here and very quiet. We each have a bedroom after all these years. The springs are gone on Keelin's bed after all the girls bouncing up and down on it. Patrick and Siobhan came over last Christmas and brought us a CD and stereo. Orla arrived from New York with a huge collection of CDs, some classical and Irish traditional. It was a conspiracy and I told them. Oscar comes every summer and always asks for you — you were always his little girl. Maybe you could make it for one of the Christmases. We all miss you and sit down to Christmas dinner saying, If only Aisling was here. There is no more news — life is very quiet. We haven't won the Lotto yet. Keelin had a bit of a cold but it seems to have cleared up. I will get her to write to you when she comes in. I will stop here and send this off tomorrow. God bless, love and take care of yourself. We love you very much.

All the best, Mammy X X X.

Keelin put the letter back in the envelope with the breast self-examination leaflet and went out to the front steps of the house. It was dark and the grass was stiff with frost. She took a box of matches from her pocket and set the thin airmail pages and leaflet on fire. The wind picked up and blew out the flames. She tried again, this time hunkering down, shielding the flames against the wind. The letter burnt, the edges of the paper glowing orange and eating their way through the words.

A few years later Keelin was smoking a joint in her room one evening, sitting on the windowsill that looked out on the overgrown garden and the washing line, when Molly knocked on the door. Keelin was startled, for Molly never approached her; it was she who usually made the effort.

"Coming," she called, but Molly opened the door and came in. Keelin was left with the joint burning in her hand.

"I thought we'd go out for a jar."

"Now? Just the two of us?" Keelin raised her eyebrows.

"That's if you're not busy, that is."

Keelin couldn't help looking at the joint. She shrugged. "All right."

"I'll get my coat so," Molly said.

"Grand." Keelin stubbed the joint out in the ashtray and grabbed her jacket from the bed.

They sat side by side in the local pub, Molly with her gin and Keelin with a pint of Guinness.

"You'll be finished uni soon." Keelin cringed; her mother always called it uni.

"Have you put much thought into what you'll do?"

Keelin folded her arms, leaning back. "God, Mammy! It's not like you. Are you worried about my future?"

"I worry about all of ye," Molly said sadly.

"Ach, I don't know, I was thinking of teaching."

"Teaching who what?"

"I studied English and history. Then, if you recall, I hemmed and hawed for a bit before I decided to do the master's in English. I suppose that's what I'd be teaching."

"Some kids take a year off and do something."

"Yeah, like go on the dole."

"Or travel."

"Do you want me to stay? Is that it?" Keelin asked gently, touched by the idea of being the last left to take care of her mother.

"Ireland is a hard place, Keelin. There's no work here. Nobody stays."

"There's some. I want to live here. When I went those summers to work in London, it was grand for a bit but it didn't suit me. I like it here."

"You're a capable girl."

Keelin laughed. "And you're a good letter writer, Mammy."

"I don't have much to say."

"How's the golf?" Keelin asked. "Have they made you a member yet?"

"Women can't be members in Ireland. I'm an associate member."

"That'll change."

"All this change, I don't know if it's for the best."

"Jesus, of course it is. You've been listening to Uncle Oscar too much."

"He was very good to you all when you were little. Always sending you presents. Walkmans! Remember the year he brought the Walkmans? You were the first Irish children with Walkmans. He was so good to Orla."

"He made her give her child away."

"That was for the best. She's all right now. It wasn't easy on her, poor Orla. Times have changed, but not that much. Look at you, though; in my day a woman couldn't sit in a pub, let alone drink a pint."

Keelin took a few gulps, heartened by that notion.

"Did you read Siobhan's last letter?" Molly asked.

"Yeah, which one was that? The one where she's now an aerobics instructor?"

"She sounds happy. I didn't think training for being a chef suited her. She never liked food."

"She wanted to be a chef because she is obsessed with food, not because she likes it. Siobhan used to do three laps of the pier every time she ate an apple."

"The rest of us are too fat. She stands out."

"Yeah, right," Keelin said sarcastically.

"She must miss Patrick all the same."

"I don't know, Mammy. They never hung out. Only when I

came over — we'd all meet for a pint now and then. Sure, when he left for Boston you and I knew before she did."

"I don't like to think of him living there illegally. Do you think Patrick is O.K.?"

"He seems a bit lost all right. As long as he's still saying his prayers."

They both laughed.

"It's harder for a man."

"It is not," Keelin retorted.

"Girls can get married and be happy. A man should find good work."

"Ah, Mammy, you're still in the Dark Ages. Anyway, Patrick is working; he's a barman. A lot easier than the construction he was doing."

"I hope he's not drinking too much."

"From the horse's mouth."

They finished their drinks. Keelin stuck her hands in her pockets. "My round now. Do you want another one?"

"Sure, why not," Molly said. "I'll be dead long enough."

Molly and Keelin made it a habit to go to the pub every Thursday evening. One night, as they were finishing their third drink, Keelin asked a question she never thought she could ask.

"What happened to my father?"

Molly's face dropped. She toyed with the ice cubes in her drink.

"He got stuck in the door."

"What?"

"He always had a bit of trouble getting through doors."

"He wasn't fat. I don't remember that."

"No. He had to touch things, turn circles sometimes. Fierce particular he was. Then one day, when we lived down in Wexford, he got stuck on the threshold. Couldn't go forward or backwards, not for any amount of persuasion. Just stood looking up at the corner."

"Do you know where he is?"

"They put him in an asylum. We never were that close, your

father and I. I sent him letters but I never went to see him. His family didn't like me. They take care of him. I stayed away, God forgive me. His sister used to pull out her own hair. She had no eyebrows or lashes and always wore a wig. Bald as a coot she was. His brother liked me all right. Patsy. That's who Patrick is named after."

"He drove a van."

"Yes. Don't you have a great memory all the same? I have to be getting back now. You're an awful time waster, Keelin, just like your sister."

"Aisling?"

"Yes, yes." Molly pulled on her coat.

"What's the rush, Mammy? I need to pee."

"Me too. Well, come on. The golf will be on soon."

"God forbid we miss that." Keelin drained her Guinness and stood up.

Molly and Keelin had cooked Christmas dinner, 1993, and the family was now slumped, stuffed to the gills, in front of the fire, cradling Gaelic coffees and passing around a box of After-Eights. Patrick was a thin young man of twenty-nine with a little red mustache. His hair was thinning on the top. His freckles had faded on his pale face, and he had a small chin and bright blue eyes with lashes so fair they were invisible. Siobhan, her head shaved and her nose pierced, was gaunt and savage in a tight black dress and big, eighteen-hole Doc Martens. Orla wore beige leggings and a pastel green cardigan, her red hair permed, her face rosy and chubby. Keelin's auburn hair was long and wavy, her face pleasant, her demeanor placid. She had answered the door on Christmas Eve and found Uncle Oscar on the doorstep with a suitcase. He'd been drinking in a New York midtown Irish bar when the old songs had propelled him in a torpor of nostalgia to head for the old country. He stumbled home and got his passport and some clothes, then threw in his folder with the family tree information. He had to buy a first-class ticket at the airport, since all the planes were jam-packed with immigrants returning for the holidays. His hair was gray but he dyed it brown, which Keelin thought a strange yet harmless vanity for a priest. He wore a huge emerald ring and had a dissipated air about him. He said he was worn out with jet lag, but the others suspected it was the drink.

Uncle Oscar was unrolling the family tree parchment with the names filled in; he had sat with every old relative in the country, drinking whiskey and collecting stories. The younger generation sat at the fire now, listening to the same stories they had heard their whole lives. To come back to Ireland and be children again was a luxury. They fingered the threads that linked them to the darkness of history. Oscar always laced his narrative with condemnations of the British colonizers. The first light that shone was Bridie, born in 1826. Before her, the great yawn of the past had swallowed everything personal and their private history was indiscernible. Bridie had been born a peasant in County Mayo and had lived through the famine while all her family had starved or fled the country on leaky coffin ships. She had eaten seaweed and nettles while the corn was being shipped out of the country to England. In 1860, when she was thirty-four, Bridie died giving birth to her third child, Kathleen.

Years later, when the mass of evictions took place, the British soldiers came to their little hut and dragged Kathleen's family out. Her brother resisted and they took him away. Her other brother went to Cork and boarded a ship to America. Nobody heard tell of either again. Kathleen left western Ireland and went to Ulster to work as a seamstress for a Catholic tailor. They had ten children before he died from drink in 1894, causing the children to scatter to England, America, and Australia, or to work as laborers on nearby farms.

Oscar's whiskey eyes grew misty as he began to talk finally of his own mother, Bridget, Kathleen's daughter. She was four years old at her father's death and had lost all her hair. This time Britain was not to blame but scarlet fever. When Bridget was twelve she was minding pigs on a farm. She was fourteen when they told her that her mother Kathleen had died in a workhouse. Bridget was to marry Jim Kelly, the third son of a poor farmer.

She and Kelly prepared to leave for America, but he joined Paidrig Pearse and the young De Valera in Dublin for the Easter Rebellion of 1916. British gunboats floated up the Liffey, annoyed at being distracted from the real history of the world. Kelly was shot in the chest in the ensuing battle. Bridget met Kelly's cousin, Malachy Lydon, at Kelly's deathbed and grimly returned to Ulster and married him instead. He worked for a mill. Her new husband was a gambler and a drinker; she took the pledge to spite him. They fought tirelessly, but he taught her to read and write and keep the accounts.

Bridget had twelve children; Molly and Oscar were the last to be born, in 1930. Molly was the elder by five minutes. They were so poor their father wrote to the newspapers that his family had to eat grass in free Ireland. This was of no end of amusement to the local people — not that the family ate grass, but that the father was literate.

Bridget skimmed the cream off the milk for the boys and fed the girls on their scraps. The girls had to stand and give the boys their chairs when they entered a room; they had to wait on them at the table, wash their clothes, and cut and comb their hair. The girls were sent off at age nine or ten, but the boys were kept till they were twelve or thirteen and had finished primary school.

The triplets, Conner, Brian, and Paidrig, were split. Conner was far away in County Tyrone working for a tyrant farmer. Molly and Oscar returned from school one afternoon to find their brother dead on the kitchen table and the old farmer asking for another child. He had hanged himself in the cow shed. Paidrig and Brian got wind of the news on the farm where they worked, outside Shercock. Because it was harvest time, they were refused permission to go to the wake. The two thirteen-year-olds took a rowboat out on the lake and split the bottom with a hatchet. The water slopped in the little wooden boat behind a wild, muddy islet; in the fog, the children sank.

Oscar was the beloved. Bridget pampered him and Molly was his servant. His father taught him to play the tin whistle and carried him about on his shoulders. He was the only child to whom Malachy paid any mind. Malachy had been in his late fifties when the last twins were born; Bridget had been forty. The other men scorned Malachy for coddling his son, but Bridget was satisfied and determined to keep and educate the child. Oscar teased and tortured his twin: he made her eat primroses, which caused her face to swell; he tormented her with stories of the devil as they delivered milk down the lightless back roads to isolated houses; he told her each night that she would be sent at dawn to the same farmer who had carried Conner to the cottage in his arms, his small neck ringed with a red wedge inches deep. She adored him in return, was his devoted slave, and played his every game.

Oscar was inconsolable when his acolyte was sent to work for a Protestant woman in County Down. He and his sister were ten years old. The woman was not cruel, and there was a housekeeper and a cook. Molly rose at five in the morning, said her prayers, set the fires, and did her chores. When the woman rose at seven, Molly carried her tin potty down the carpeted stairs and emptied the stinking piss into the outside toilet. Molly flooded Oscar with letters, but he never replied. She spent the cold winter evenings at the piano under the tutelage of the old woman. The long summer evenings were whiled away smoking cigarettes with the cook under the elm trees in the yard behind the big ivy-covered stone house. Five years later her father, Malachy, died of a heart attack in the local pub, as drunk as he had lived. The woman reluctantly let her young servant go back home.

There were only five of her twelve children left to stand at her husband's grave. The triplets were dead, and Kitty, one of the girls, had died of pneumonia when she was thirteen and working as a clerk in a solicitor's office in Cavan town. Her father was buried beside her, the three boys, and a baby who'd been stillborn. Two had already emigrated; one daughter had not the money to come back, and a son was somewhere in Australia and never wrote. The graveyard was on a hill, stone crosses cowering around a little white church. The fields rose and sank, infinitely bending and bowing away from the encircling mossy walls. The stony soil opened in a rectangular gasp. All stories end here in the hole. The gravedigger, a ragged man caked in wet clay, eyed them crookedly and sneered.

"Are youse the family that ate the grass?"

The family laughed, as they always did at this point. Patrick and Keelin made everyone drinks.

"There's nothing on the telly," Orla complained, flipping through the guide. "Crap! Crap! Crap!"

"To hell with the television!" the priest cried from his corner.

"Well, you do have the authority," Keelin quipped.

"Did you ever hear tell," said Molly, "of a man by the name of George Armstrong who went off to Australia and only came back with thruppence —"

"And he weighed so little" — Orla finished it for her — "that his mother had to put him in a basket and keep him by the fire."

"That's a good one." Oscar slapped his thigh. "Mammy used to tell that one."

"Sounds like Siobhan." Patrick smiled and opened a can of draught Guinness.

"I'm drinking Guinness tonight, not Perrier." Siobhan raised her glass toward him.

"You're an Irish anorexic, so." Patrick clinked his can with her glass, and she made a face at him.

Molly shook her head. "All these young girls, starving themselves."

"There are many kinds of famines," Keelin said.

"And hunger strikes," Patrick added.

"When are you getting yourself a boyfriend?" Oscar squeezed Keelin's arm.

"When are you getting yourself one?" Keelin retorted.

Molly was shocked. "That's no way to talk to your uncle." The others howled with laughter.

"They're getting very cheeky," Oscar said. He frowned and muttered into his drink.

"I'm thirty-one now, Uncle Oscar." Orla grinned. "None of us are spring chickens. I'm exactly five years older than Bridget was when Kelly got his comeuppance in 1916. What a thought! She was already burying one and marrying another, and I can't even get one to take me to dinner."

"His comeuppance?" Oscar was aghast. "If it wasn't for those brave men we'd be just like Scotland or Wales now."

"*The sea, the sea,*" Molly sang. "*A gra geal mo chroi, it runs between old England and me; Oh pity the Scots they'll never be free, but we're completely surrounded by water.*"

"These nationalistic wars," Keelin mused, "are fading in significance. Since we'll all be ruled by Brussels, what does it matter if London holds the north?"

Oscar recited wearily,

> They weighed so lightly what they gave,
> But let them be they're dead and gone.

"Things are not so cut and dried for them as they were for us," Molly said, to placate him.

"What a grubby generation." Oscar sniffed in disdain.

"At least we're not murdering people in their beds," Orla snapped.

"Did you go back to the Protestant woman?" Keelin asked her mother. She knew the story well but she wanted to deflect the argument.

"It may be solved by the conference table," Oscar said, glaring at Orla, "but, by God, the IRA brought the British by gunpoint to the conference table."

Orla looked at Oscar with contempt. "All these generations you're so proud of, but the first of the next one is given away to an American family."

"Oh, Orla!" Molly pursed her lips. The others threw their eyes up to heaven.

"Your mother and I thought it was for the best," Oscar faltered.

"You were only seventeen." Molly shook her head.

"There must be something on the telly," Patrick said, raising his eyebrows. Siobhan got up and went to the door.

"Where are you going?" Molly called after her.

"Just getting some more salt to pour in everyone's wounds," she shouted from the hall.

"She's gone to vomit up the Christmas dinner," Patrick said.

"Ah, not the Christmas dinner," Molly said, sighing.

When Siobhan returned, Molly resumed her part of the story. "I went back, all right. What else could I do? Oscar was the only one my mother could keep. She scrounged and saved to send him to boarding school. Everybody else finished after primary. I never went to a class after I was ten. The old woman got me to read to her. I've read all the classics countless times, countless times. I was happy enough there, though she had to let the housekeeper and cook go and I was the only one keeping that big house from falling apart at the end. Just me and the old woman, who got weaker and bedridden. She never left the house, wouldn't even let me wheel her under the elm trees and breathe some fresh air. I was reading her Swift, *Gulliver's Travels,* when I looked over and she was dead. Her mouth opened and her hairy face fallen out of shape. I had seen enough corpses to know. Poor woman. I was fond of her, I suppose, though I can't say I missed her much. I got a job in Belfast city. I was seventeen, it was 1947. I worked in a little café. I had a room with two other girls on the premises. Ah, it was grand. We'd go to the dances and I had a bit of money of my own, but Mammy called me back."

Oscar nodded. "I was starting in Maynooth. My studies for the priesthood. Mammy got cancer. I came to see her every chance I got. To be by her side."

"Mary was in Dublin and had a family. The other twin boys, Malachy and Seamus, were men, and it was a woman's lot to take care of the old and sick."

"Poor Mammy," Oscar intoned.

"Poor Molly," Keelin said.

"I missed the city. To leave Belfast and be stuck in the wilds of Cavan! The mill was abandoned at that stage, and she had the little cottage beside it where we grew up. There was nobody around."

"She was a wonderful woman," Oscar told the children.

"I never knew if she liked me; she only talked of the boys, especially Oscar. I longed for his monthly visits. We'd sit on the river walls by the ruined mill and smoke and talk. Remember you used to stop off in town and get a bottle of whiskey? You had no money, God love you. You were very good to come up all the time. I don't know what I'd have done. Gone round the bend. Mammy wouldn't let drink in the house, you know. She tried to beat me with a stick when she caught me smoking. Poor Mammy, God rest her soul, she'd had a miserable life. She talked about the boys all the time. She had fond memories of them. Even the dead triplets; it was sad to hear it. The boys were the pride and joy, but only Oscar ever came to visit. Mary came a few times, mind you, with her children, which was a diversion, but it was the lads Mammy loved."

"That's awful," Keelin said.

"That's the way it was back then — nobody thought it could be any different. We paid it no mind. It was the same for every family."

"Just my luck," Patrick grumbled. "Born a generation too late to be irrationally worshipped."

Oscar patted Molly on the hand. "I was arrogant when I was young, but I came as much to see you as her."

"I missed having a piano." Molly sighed.

"Mammy was a great storyteller," Oscar said. "She'd have you transfixed. I wish I'd written it down or recorded it. She loved the radio. She sat the whole war with her ears glued to the big wireless in the kitchen."

"On the side of the Germans, of course," Molly said, smiling. "Any enemy of England was a friend of hers."

"Poor Mammy," Oscar said. "When she heard about the

atrocities afterwards. The camps. And she gunning for the Nazis all along."

"She hated them all, " Molly said. "Both sides. She was like a woman possessed. She would read and listen to any news about it. The Dresden bombing, the A-bomb in Hiroshima and Nagasaki, the death camps. Any horror she could get her hands on."

"I remember all that," Oscar said. "She told me once, near the end, 'The real plague is in our hearts.' She was adamant I'd be a good priest and help people. Good against evil. She was idealistic in that way."

"It broke my heart to see her eaten away by cancer," Molly said. "She was in so much pain. By the time I got her to the hospital she was riddled with it, and they sent her home with me to die."

"A slow, terrible death. She suffered," Oscar said. "She wanted to see Ireland a free country before she died. In her lifetime, that was her wish."

"It's a good job she didn't see the mess it's still in now." Orla said.

"She took long enough to die," Molly continued. "It was November 1953, five years after the diagnosis. I was twenty-three years old. I laid her out and put on her favorite wig. I should have left the country then, when I had the chance. But she had left the house to Oscar, and I had nothing, not even the fare. I worked in a chemist in Cootehill after that. Your father's uncle owned it. That's how I met him. He was working there during his summer holidays. He convinced me to come down to Wexford where his family lived. I was actually seeing a guard at the time. Should have married him, would have had tall children. But I liked the sound of Wexford and I wanted to get out of Cavan and see a bit more of the world. His family owned another chemist in Wexford town. He wanted me to work there. He had a degree, he was an educated man, and I had not met many of those. His family thought I was beneath him. He almost backed out, and there I was, down in Wexford without a job and running out of my few pounds saved. I got a job cleaning the cinema. He dithered for years, and I was thirty-one by the time we got married. There was an awful feud because of it and they cut him off. Refused to even come to the wedding. They didn't speak to his brother either — Patsy. Patsy was the best man at the wedding and would have nothing to do with the family from an early age, for what reasons I can't fathom. I had Aisling a year later and was forty when I had Keelin — same age Bridget was when she had Oscar and me."

"So our father's family has money?" Siobhan perked up.

"Oh yes, they had money, sure enough. I never saw any of it."

"We should have kept in contact," Siobhan said. "Maybe we could inherit something."

"They're an odd shower," Molly told her.

"That's putting it mildly." Oscar grinned and sipped his whiskey.

Patrick took his camp bed out from the cupboard that night and went to the kitchen to boil a kettle for his hot water bottle. Keelin and Siobhan were clearing up. "Where's Uncle Oscar going to sleep?" he asked.

"Why don't you take the couch and give him the camp bed?" Keelin said.

"Yeah, all right. Jesus though, his snoring is something else."

"You won't have to worry about that," Siobhan said. "He'll be up all night playing the tin whistle."

Patrick winced. "Or singing one-hundred-verse ballads about the famine. What rhymes with British oppression?"

"Recession," Keelin said.

"Depression," Patrick said.

"Obsession," Orla added.

"Talking of obsession," Keelin said, "Patrick, I saw you turn off the lights with your elbows and keep your hands curled up close to you. Remember the moving statues? Have you ever had that looked into?"

Patrick looked as if he were about to cry or run. They were all silent for a second.

"Keelin's sleeping with Mammy." Siobhan dried a glass. "I'm in with Orla."

"She snores too," Patrick added quickly.

"What a charming family," Keelin said, laughing.

"I think Mammy in her old age thinks you're Aisling." Patrick looked at his youngest sister. "You look most like her. A shorter version."

"Where is she? It's been almost fourteen years." Siobhan frowned. "Why won't she come home?"

They were silent.

"I think it's eating Mammy alive," Keelin confided. "She keeps singing 'Oh, Danny Boy' to herself."

"That bad, huh?" Patrick groaned.

"When are yiz heading back?" Keelin asked them.

"I have to sign on next Tuesday," Siobhan said.

"You're still signing on? I thought you were teaching aerobics," Patrick said.

"Just twice a week."

"I quit my job at the bar," Patrick said. "I think I'll go down to Miami. I've a friend who promised me a job on a cruise ship. That's if immigration lets me through. It's getting harder and harder. I've so many entry stamps on my passport. Every time I go back me heart is in me mouth."

"Orla's in the same boat," Keelin said. She went into the living room to say goodnight to Oscar. The twins were sitting by the fire, ruminating on the past, the dead who were once so close.

Aisling had slept in the same bed as her mother until she was twenty years old. Such abnegation of privacy horrified Keelin. On this Christmas night she lay stiffly by the wall as Molly breathed laboriously beside her, smelling faintly of gin and turkey. Her beefy arms, sticking incongruously out of the frilly night dress, grasped the covers to the wiry gray hairs that sprouted from her chin.

"Aisling," Keelin said aloud. Her mother, sunk in sleep, hummed blissfully at the sound of her first child's name.

> A chi vive in angosica il tempo e zoppo.
> Fallacissima speme, speranze on piu verdi ma canute.
> All' invecchiato male non promettete piu pace o salute.

The mournful aria penetrated Keelin's morning sleep. She put on slippers and a dressing gown and shuffled down the hall to the kitchen. It was a Saturday noon in January 1994, and the sky lay like a gray slab outside the window. Molly had been up practicing her golf swing in the back garden. Her clubs were lying on the floor. Last night's dinner dishes were congealing in the sink, and the next-door neighbor's cat was pawing insistently at the glass.

"Do you want a cup of tea?" Keelin shouted.

"Lovely," Molly's voice rang back.

It was freezing in the sitting room. Molly sat on the armchair in her tracksuit.

"Going to golf?" Keelin asked.

"Women can't play on weekends."

"I'd blow up the clubhouse if I were you."

Keelin flipped through the paper and Molly closed her eyes and listened to the CD. The fireplace was heaped with gray ashes, still faintly warm.

> Torna il tranquillo al mare,
> Torna il zeffiro al prato.

"The wretched cat has left paw marks all over the window again," Keelin said.

"Have you got a steady teaching job yet?"

"I've an interview on Monday up at the convent."

Molly laughed. "They used complain about you being late every day. They'll surely not give you a job."

"Thanks!"

"It'll be fourteen years this summer since your sister left."

"Time flies."

"You have to go and find her." Molly said suddenly. "Something has happened. She won't come home by herself, and I'm not getting any younger."

"Why me? Ask one of the others. I'm the only one with a life."

"You can pick up where you left off. You're the only one I can rely on."

"That's ridiculous. I wouldn't know where to start."

"You like to travel. You used to travel after working all summer. I have the postcards. Greece, Yugoslavia, France."

"I'm getting dressed. This is getting out of hand." She stood up.

> Tornan le brine in terra, tornano a centra i sassi
> E con lubrici passi torna all' oceano e rivo.

"Turn that music down. My head is addled," Keelin fretted.

"I've never asked you for anything," Molly said.

"And I've never asked you."

"I'm begging, Keelin. I'd go myself but I'm frightened. I've never left the country. I want to go. I've prayed for the strength all these years but, God forgive me, my spirit fails. She's in trouble."

"What trouble. She's just selfish."

"No! No! That's not her at all. That's not her nature. She was a good girl. Very giving. You read so much in the papers. AIDS and drugs, all sorts of things."

"So Aisling's a crack head. What am I supposed to do about it? I have shite to do here. I could still have safety pins stuck in my ears for all she ever cared."

"I talked to Oscar and he said he'd send you some money. He said it was a good idea. If you ever have children, Keelin, you'll understand why I have to ask you."

"What about you? You'd be all alone."

"There's not a moment when I don't think about her. I haven't heard from her since Japan. Just tell her we love her, see if she's safe —"

"I don't know where she is!"

"Her best friend, Aine, in London. Talk to her. Go to England."

"The telephone's been invented, you know."

"Keelin, I'm old. This is a lonely time, January. I look forward to Christmas when everyone comes back. I mightn't make it. We're the only ones who care. She was like a mother to you. I was so busy. When you get older you'll understand what I'm asking. What do we Irish know more that any other people in the world? All the sad songs we've been singing for years? That life, in the end, will break your heart."

"Talk about melodrama." Keelin slumped back in the chair.

Tu sol del tuo torna perdesti il giorno.

"I think about her too. I miss her as well."

There is a rope that binds, a rope that swings, a rope that pulls, a neck that chokes. For every rope a neck that chokes, a knot that tightens.

Keelin stood at the gate and watched the children. They were playing the same games she had played on the other side of the country years ago — one child at each end of a long skipping rope and two or three other kids waiting to jump in. *Vote! Vote! Vote! for De Valera*, they all sang, and a girl came in on cue, her face gripped with fierce concentration. *In comes Aisling at the door, aye-oh!* That name, always. *Aisling is the one, who will have a bit of fun, and we don't want De Valera anymore, aye-oh!*

Molly fussed with the door keys. She clutched her giant black handbag against her shabby white winter coat, the buttons straining around her plump midriff. *Vote! Vote! Vote! for De Valera! In comes Sinead at the door, aye-oh! Sinead is the one* . . . Keelin swung her rucksack onto her back, and she and Molly left the Georgian house, walked down the familiar road. In the fog the children sank.

"You look like some crazed doctor in that get-up," Keelin told her mother. "Off to an assisted suicide, no doubt."

Molly smiled at her. "It's a terrible day to be sailing. The wind is picking up and the glimpses of the sea between the houses . . . I don't know, it looks choppy."

"Maybe I should turn back. Try again tomorrow," Keelin said ironically. Her mother marched on, one pace ahead. The sky broke and the rain began to fall heavily.

"Aisling would never have taken this boat to England. If I am to follow in her footsteps I should sail to France."

"She's not in France. Although she might be."

"Well, it was worth a try."

They were shouting through the wind, the rain pelting their heads, blasting in their faces, soaking them.

Molly bit her lip, fighting back tears. "I never came to see any of the others off. I couldn't bear it. It's too much."

"Thanks, Mammy. I appreciate it."

"It was you who went with every one of them. But there's no one left but me."

"I won't be long. I'll find her and come right back."

"Write to me. Sure I might get a phone."

"Typical. You modernize when I leave. It'll be central heating and an electric cooker before we know it."

"Tell her to come home and see me. I want the whole family together next Christmas. Give Siobhan my love."

"O.K., O.K.! Watch your cholesterol."

"Yes, yes. And you examine your breasts every month."

"Jesus, Mammy!" Keelin glanced about. "Do you have to announce it to the whole pier?"

Molly fumbled in her handbag and extracted a breast examination leaflet. She thrust it into Keelin's hand. The ship, standing staunchly in the hungry rain, could afford to be patient. People embraced and made promises.

They hugged each other outside the entrance, and Molly pushed Keelin gently but firmly into the tunnel. She watched her mother closely; walking sideways, she waved back. *Not discarded but launched.* At the mouth of the tunnel the adults, their arms held up together like river reeds. Keelin turned a corner and mounted the iron gangway. The water lapped, licked the boat with a frosty tongue. She thought of her young uncles long ago in Cavan. They brushed the murky bed and floated up. A hunter found a body bloated in the rushes.

Keelin sat in the smoky bar, watching the land recede. Television, history, and the church; Rome kept their souls, England took their language and their land, and now America had captured their imagination. She knew that it was a different Ireland that Aisling had left well over a decade ago. Dublin had been derelict, boarded up, bushes growing out of buildings. Now this *fin de siècle* Ireland had opened its heart to the European continent. There were contraceptives available, the church's austere power was fading, censorship was relaxed, highways built with EC funds were crisscrossing the country. An area by the Liffey River had been renovated and was packed with bars, Italian restaurants, nightclubs, and art galleries. If you stepped a street away from the thriving, buzzing, youth-packed city center, though, the rows of crumbling, boarded-up Georgian buildings waited, in silent testament to the dormant past. More of an Eastern Europe than a Western one, a history more African than Northern, the capital more a Budapest than a Los Angeles.

Molly and Oscar's lives clung to this century. They might leak over, but they belonged here in the twentieth. They would go halfheartedly into the new millennium, not belonging. Keelin was apprehensive about leaving her country, leaving this century. The Pol Pots, Idi Amins, and Hitlers of the century, and the Genghis Khans and Cromwells of the millennium, would fold over, be mirrored, and come again in the next. She thought. I come from a country where the enemy never left, where every war was fought but no war won. The movement is history itself, and we are all only cells. We have borrowed our lives from history. A burgeoning population ill at ease on a depleted planet. The famines unended, the concentration camps still open for business. She had to find Aisling before it was too late for Molly. The ship lurched in the rising storm, drinks spilled, bottles fell and smashed behind the bar. People were sent scuttling to one side, and then they let out a cheer and carried on drinking and singing and shouting and gambling.

two

lotto and lumps of cancer

IN MIAMI, Patrick's roommate pulled a gun on him, sticking the hard cylinder to his temple. He was an angry man in his thirties who had a Third Reich flag pinned to the wall over his bed and stacks of porno magazines piled all around him. He slept two feet from Patrick's mattress. Patrick didn't ask the man why he was trying to kill him, but the man gibbered on about the Mexicans with whom Patrick had been drinking and Patrick's personal habits.

"Cubans," Patrick stammered. "Anyway, you have a Mexican girlfriend."

"She's Hawaiian." He put the gun down. "Not Mexican."

"Mexican," Patrick corrected him. "And I'll clean the bathroom if it bothers you so much."

"You're crazy," his roommate said. "You need help."

Patrick hadn't gotten the cruise job he'd been promised, and he left Miami in a hurry. It was noon when he crept out of the apartment, leaving his homicidal roommate sleeping, bristling with dreams of revenge, surrounded by airbrushed paper women. Since Patrick hadn't so much as touched the beach in his time in Miami, on his last day he walked over the sand, hot and grainy under his tender soles, and dipped his toes in the warm Atlantic. Then he lay down in the shade and looked up at the sky.

The next day on the plane he applied thick white greasy

cream to his feet. He had fallen asleep under the palms with his shoes and socks off, and the sun had moved and burnt his feet. Somewhere over Georgia, rubbing on more cream, he wouldn't stretch out his legs under the seat in front of him, as he felt sure the whole row would collapse and slam down on his blistered feet, crushing the bones into the red skin. In fear he pulled his legs onto the seat and sat miserably huddled all the way to New York.

Patrick was still thin, and he had grown a small red goatee in an attempt to adopt a more thoughtful look. His pale eyes were unprotected under his invisible eyebrows and lashes. One leg jiggled as he sat in the armchair in Oscar's New York apartment. Oscar thought Patrick looked as if he were about to burst into tears. He felt bewildered by his fragile, obsessive nephew, his crooked, wafer-thin teeth, his brown freckled eyelids as soft as bruises on apples, his savagely burnt feet shining with thick grease.

"It's time you settled down, Patrick."

"I know, I know," Patrick hummed uselessly.

"I'll pay for your college if you apply. I've told your mother I would."

"Thanks, but I was never much of an academic."

"Well, you have to learn a trade."

"You mean like plumbing or something?"

"Anything. What about computers? All the boys your age seem to love them."

"Maybe." Patrick half smiled. "I'm thirty years old, Oscar."

"If you find out about a course, just let me know."

"Well, I was thinking of learning to play guitar."

"What took you to Miami?"

"I heard about a job on a cruise ship, but I ended up working as a bellboy in a big pink hotel."

Oscar smiled. Patrick said, "I'll try Orla again. I keep getting the machine."

"They're a terrible invention." Oscar shook his head.

*

The next day, Orla and Patrick sat in a bar in the Bronx. The door was open but the hazy sunlight didn't enter the grimy establishment.

"Everyone's Irish in this neighborhood," Patrick noted.

"Yeah," Orla said, nodding. "It's great. Just like home."

"Better weather."

"So what do you think of Mammy sending Keelin off to look for Aisling?"

"It's daft, it is."

"She was just about to get a permanent teaching job. It's a disgrace."

"Aisling was Mammy's favorite."

"That was a long time ago. Keelin and Mammy have been thick as thieves for years in that house." Orla lit a cigarette with her stubby fingers. She had grown fatter and now looked more like Molly. "Mammy was afraid one of us might do well."

"Ah, now, that's unfair," Patrick said. "She's so worried about us all. I get a letter from her every week."

"Me too. Lotto and lumps of cancer."

"What?"

"I have a cold; Keelin has just got over a cold. We didn't win Lotto this week. And a breast inspection leaflet." Orla rolled her eyes. "Same every time."

"That sounds about right. I don't get the cancer, but I get told to get a decent job. Oscar is hassling me the past two weeks since I arrived."

"I only see him Easter Sundays and Thanksgiving."

"He's not a bad oul' sort."

Orla shrugged. "He bullied me into giving my son away to some horrible Christians."

"Do you ever see him? What age is he now? Fifteen?"

"I used to, but they'd rather I didn't now he's older."

"Let's go out and see him," Patrick said, signaling to the barman for two more drinks. Orla lit up, smiling for the first time that afternoon, her radiant, chubby, face framed by a fuzzy bush of red hair.

"The two of us together?"

"Sure. Why not."

"It would be the first time anyone in the family saw him. I send Mammy photos, but she probably throws them away."

There were a thousand bubbles of air in the stale glass of water left on Patrick's bedside table, their number and position corresponding to the thousand discontents he felt in himself. Oscar came home in the evening and found his nephew still in bed, his head turned to the messy bedside table. His clothes, strewn about the room, seemed no more than rags, strips of torn T-shirts and jeans and sweatshirts. Oscar stood at the door of the room, but Patrick was focusing on a glass of water.

"I told you no smoking. If you can't abide by my one rule . . ."

The next evening Patrick slouched in front of the TV, remote control in hand, watching a talk show. There was a full ashtray on the cushion.

Oscar counted out a few twenty-dollar bills and gave them to his nephew.

"This is to tide you over. So no computer course?"

"Nope."

"Patrick, what are you going to do with yourself?"

"I don't know."

"What would you like to do?"

Patrick shrugged.

"Are you going to get any kind of job?"

"I'm just catching my breath here. I've been on the move for a good while. I'm thinking of heading out West. I'll get some kind of bar work. Maybe Vegas."

"Look, Paddy, you can stay here as long as you want, but I need to see you do something productive while you're here. Is that too much to ask?"

Patrick pocketed the money and nodded noncommittally.

Orla grew pensive as they got closer to the station in New Jersey, then businesslike as she arranged for a taxi to the house where her son lived. Orla had lived here while she was pregnant. Where once there were fields and woods, now there were rows and rows of newly built wooden houses, all painted in the same pastel peaches, blues, and yellows. Almost every house had an American flag drooling over the porch.

"Do you think Keelin is a virgin?" Orla asked her brother in the taxi.

Patrick laughed. "Jaysus! Where did that come from? I don't know. Probably not. She's too old now. She must have met someone in college or on her teaching jobs. Just no steady boyfriend."

"She'd never bring anyone back to the house to do it. Too scared of Mammy."

"Scared? They get on like a house on fire."

"I always wondered about that expression," Orla mused glumly. "I guess I was the slut of the family. Aisling had sex before she left Ireland but I got caught."

"Sex in Ireland — what a thought!" Patrick laughed again. "Orla, you're something else."

When they arrived, the adoptive mother reluctantly invited them into the living room, offering them no refreshments after their journey. Her blond hair was cut in a neat bob, and she wore an electric-blue silk pantsuit.

"My husband will be home soon." Her tone was pleading.

Patrick sat awkwardly on a chair, looking from woman to woman. He had worn his good clothes for the occasion — black Levi jeans and a green cotton shirt. His matchstick freckled arms stuck out of the short sleeves. Orla was cold and staunch. On the wall were a cross and a framed picture of Ronald Reagan.

"Sure I just wanted to see him. I came to his first few birthday parties, after all."

The woman pursed her lips, composed herself, smiled grimly. "I know, Orla. It must be hard, but we agreed it would be too much as he got older . . . all the questions. We send you photos."

"Not for three years," Orla said quietly. "Not since he was twelve."

"When he's eighteen, and if he wants to. I don't know how to say this." She fretted, glancing at the Christ, whose head hung down, self-absorbed, then at Reagan, as if in supplication. "You have to go. My husband will be home shortly. He won't be pleased." She stood up, switching to the offensive. "I mean really. No phone call, you just arrive. You can't see him anyway. He's off at his grandparents. Please go."

Patrick stood and walked to the door.

"Come on, Orla," he said gently.

Orla stared at the woman, as if in a trance. She got up and followed her brother, who was relieved at her compliance. The woman closed the door so quickly behind them it banged Patrick's heel.

"I thought that went well," Patrick said.

"Shut up, Patrick, will you." Orla seemed upset. "Let's get back to New York. Whose idea was this, anyway? Jesus Christ, I'm not all in it. Have we lost the run of ourselves?"

The shine had not yet gone out of the day. Large houses stood bunched in a circle around a clump of green; white parking lines radiated from the grassy mound like stretch marks. Orla had breastfed the child here for the first month and had left their house shortly after. Birds sang, people came home from work in nice new cars, children too young to be her son stumbled around on rollerblades, hands reaching out, grasping for balance.

Suddenly the woman came running out of her house. They stopped and waited for her. Patrick thought he saw a face in the upstairs window of the house.

"Shawn's been acting strangely lately. Otherwise, maybe . . . Look, write to us and perhaps sometime . . . Now he seems to be going through a phase. I don't want him upset."

"Is he sick?" Orla asked sharply.

"No, no. Just puberty. Something like that. It's a bad time."

"I'll write to you so." Orla nodded curtly and walked away.

As they turned the corner onto a wider road, Patrick looked back and saw that the woman was still standing in the circle, her expression frantic.

"Sean?" he said. "I've always wondered about that. Was that your choice?"

"No. They're Irish-American," Orla said scornfully. "They spell it S-h-a-w-n."

Patrick laughed. "I suppose you're lucky it wasn't a girl. They'd have called her Colleen or Shannon."

"It's easy to laugh at the Americans, but at the moment they own the world."

Shawn plucked himself apart with deft, exacting fingers. He pulled the wool from his sweater and rolled it into a ball. So that was his real mother down there. He hovered at the stairs, his head cocked like a bird. Was she sick too? He'd read of the deer that ran fast on the western American plains. Evolved to escape. The deer were running too fast now, because the ancient predator had long died out. But the herd ran from them forever. The fright was in the genes. An atavistic mess. He had a photo somewhere of a woman at his birth, holding him and smiling ear to ear. But she left. He waited for his mother to call. He went back to the room and combed his hair in anticipation, then he took the hairs from the brush and snowballed them into the lint from his sweater and opened his closet door. In the closet was a beach ball of lint and threads and hair; he crunched the new stuff into it. When it grew too monstrous his mother would destroy it and he would have to start again. Like a squirrel gathering stones for winter as if they were nuts, knowing they weren't.

Back on the landing, his feet touched the top stair. When guests were over he couldn't come down unless called; it was a rule of his father's. His father was a producer for a big TV station in New York. Shawn's sweater was tattered, and his dethreaded buttons had fallen from his shirt. They were leaving, and he ran to the window to see them, to maybe wave. Ghosts from the past. If he slowed down, the herd would surely trample him, the ghosts devour him. His blond mother was running after them and she saw him at the window, but they didn't look up. Their backs were to the house. His mother's face warning him away from the window. He heard the door slam and her mounting the stairs.

"Shawn, look at you. Your new sweater and shirt. Your father said he'd dress you in plastic if you can't keep your clothes for more than a few days."

"Was that my mother from Ireland?"

"She left her address. You can write if you want, but I'd rather you didn't. You can see her when you're eighteen — not until then. We'll discuss it with your doctor." She opened the closet door. "This is going out right now. Please don't tell your father about this visit. He's under pressure at work, and you've given him enough heartbreak."

The speed misjudged on the plains. Fear did not stop in the blink of a millennium. He had to think back geologically to stop this, to understand what clicked then that did not matter now. A brain not listening to itself needed to be reset. They thought he was stupid because he was mostly silent, mostly occupied with control — caught in a battle between past necessities and present impulses that collided horribly. Maybe the Irish mother knew how to fix it.

He must change something before he picked himself apart. Nightmares of his hands finding a loose thread in his skin and pulling it through and his body falling open but the hands not stopping, finding loops of intestines and pulling and unraveling, and his eyes like threadless buttons, popping soundlessly from the sockets. His father hated him, would dress him in plastic. It had not always been like this. Years ago there was a time when the needle in his brain was not stuck. His other mother might get him back, or at least let him continue in peace. He held her address in his hands and read it like a prayer.

Patrick felt that his tongue was too large for his mouth. Huge and ill-fitting it spread over his teeth, and at night he didn't know where to put it. The tongue, throbbing, constricted, bunched and curled behind closed teeth. In the mornings he woke with it clamped between his crooked molars. During the day he browsed through his uncle's belongings as he experimented with tongue positions, asking himself where was the safest place to keep it when moving, when sitting. He rooted furtively through the medicine cabinet, which was host to a plethora of pills that Patrick popped at random. In a bedside drawer he found a photo of his eldest sister in Nagasaki standing between two sculptures in a park. Aisling was smiling broadly, wearing sunglasses and a suit and tie, with her hair either cut very short or greased back in a ponytail. He thought of keeping the photo to show Orla.

There was a book from the Hiroshima museum which Aisling had inscribed for Oscar's birthday. He flicked through pictures of the exhibits. Oscar's bookshelves were overflowing with literature, and there was a painting of Wagner on the wall. He had countless CDs and albums, all classical and opera, but Patrick found a small collection of sentimental Irish music hidden in a cupboard. Beneath this messy pile were some gay porno books and magazines. A complex man, Patrick thought as he flicked through one of the paperbacks. *Since you've been away my butt has ached with emptiness.* He laughed.

Oscar's key turned in the door. Scurrying back to the study, he hurled himself on the couch and grabbed *The New Yorker,* pretending to be engrossed. Oscar sniffed the air for traces of telltale smoke. He was a little drunk. Patrick smiled at him in greeting.

"How was your day, Oscar?"

Oscar laughed. "Oh Patrick, what will we do with you?" He went to the kitchen and chose a bottle of red wine. When he came back he handed a full glass to his nephew.

"I had a letter from your sister."

"Which one?"

"Aisling."

"Oh yeah? So the dead arose. Where is she now?"

"Japan."

"Still?"

"Uh-huh!" Oscar nodded, filling a second glass for himself.

"Do you have an address?"

"She's staying with a friend. I have that address."

"So we can write and tell her to come home, that Molly has sent Keelin and all that rubbish. Let Keelin go home and get on with her life or come over here, like she told me she might. I talked to her a few weeks ago. There's trouble with Siobhan, Keelin said. She wants to get her away from London."

"Keelin, she's a cute one, all right. No flies on her. I talked to her on the phone when you were out last night, and she's only been in London three months and already got driving lessons and a license. She's also got a part-time teaching job. Would you believe it?"

"Keelin is the ambitious one in the family."

"The most together, I would say." Oscar cleared his throat. His face was flushed and he was sweating. The crown of his head was bald, but the bit of hair he had was neatly cut and he still had an energized, youthful air about him.

"Look, we know Aisling won't come home. God knows why, but if anyone can get her Keelin can. Keelin is a capable, industrious, and intelligent girl. She has good sense. I'm sending her out to get her sister for once and for all. This is the first time we have a concrete address. Molly is beside herself with worry and her health is not holding up. She loved Aisling too much."

Patrick was incredulous. "Keelin gets to go to Japan? Just like that?"

"Well, she didn't want to go. She liked her job in England. I told her to take Siobhan and she said she'd think about it."

"Siobhan too! Oh, for God's sake." Patrick gave a low whistle. "Where do you get your money?"

Patrick carried his suitcase up the stairs to Orla's apartment in the Bronx. He was moving in. There were five other Irish people staying there, and some slept shifts in the same bed. He sat by the wooden table, smoking and blinking. Perhaps he had lost his sight, he thought. He opened his eyes very wide, then shut them; when they were shut he felt that maybe they were really open and he couldn't see, so he opened them again. When they were open he thought he might be dreaming the washed-out green of the kitchen wall, so he shut them to see if they had been open. Now that they were shut, he thought they were open and he was blind.

the frog in the toilet

SEA AND SKY consumed the loose ends of Tokyo. Above, a smoky red sky striped with dark and clouds; below, black fingers of land speckled with light crawling out into the sea.

Siobhan sat on the plastic green seats in Narita Airport watching Coca-Cola ads on a big-screen TV. "I want it to feel different. I want it to be so strange. I need that culture shock buzz. When is it going to feel different?"

Keelin counted her newly exchanged money and separated it into the compartments and pockets of her clothes and luggage.

"Like landing on the moon," Siobhan said, slouching languidly over the seat. She stared at an immaculately dressed airport guard walking the length of the area, slapping his gloved hand with a truncheon.

"We're not even out of the airport yet. Calm down!" Keelin told her, handing her a wad of yen. "Put this somewhere safe in case we lose each other."

"Lose each other?" Siobhan gasped. "What makes you think we'll lose each other?" She stood reluctantly and swung her huge rucksack onto her back. A strange creature: tight silver capri leggings on stick-thin legs, big clunky platform patent leather boots, a yellow fuzzy sweater. Her long, scrawny neck was ringed with a shell choker and her small head was recently shaved and now covered with a thin fur of newly grown dark hair. Her face was potentially beautiful — she had large, icy blue eyes, fine symmetrical features, a small, budlike mouth, sharp cheekbones — but the sunken bluish flesh was draped over an obvious skeleton. All her bones were prominent and readable, her biology bared, her wrists so thin you could almost see the joints slide as she fidgeted with a red satin neck purse.

"The woman at information showed me Tsukuba on the map. It's not in Tokyo but it's not too far, either," Keelin said. "That's the only address we have. She rang ahead and booked us for two nights in a hotel. All we have to do is get the bus at exit eighteen."

"She spoke English?" Siobhan asked.

"No. I got all that in Japanese." Keelin made a face.

On the bus Keelin was surprised when Siobhan slipped her long frail hand in Keelin's smaller but sturdier one. Siobhan could be spontaneously affectionate at times and at others as distant and unconnected as a bird in flight. Her older sister was mired somewhere a little beneath the surface, preoccupied, without energy. Keelin often felt magnified and coarsely animated in her presence. She stroked her hungry sister's listless hand like a nurse wooing a patient from under anesthetic.

The two sisters gazed out the window with fascination. The road was narrow and dark, flanked by cement walls. They peered into the winter night, hoping for some distinct image that would begin to unfold Japan. Tiny blank cement houses, garages with parking lots stuffed with identical new cars, a few signs in Japanese writing. Rows of giant, shabby rosettes on wooden pallets like huge paper carnations flapping in the wind outside some gray, unremarkable buildings. But they saw no life, no people, barely any moving cars.

"These trees are Japanese trees," Siobhan whispered. "That house has Japanese people inside. Those shops will sell Japanese food. Those traffic lights are Japanese lights; those dusty bushes are Japanese bushes covered in Japanese dust; that's a Japanese pile of tiles at the crossroads . . ."

Their trance was broken after an hour when the bus stopped in Tsukuba. Tsukuba, Science City, a sign read in English. On a large bilingual map they found their hotel clearly marked. Keelin got her bearings and led Siobhan out of the bus station, through the fiercely windy streets, then along a busy highway to their hotel. The hotel was big but cozy. It had a fifties feel to it — brown decor and ugly frosted lamps. Japanese dining rooms with cushions and low tables faced out onto an elaborate garden constructed in the parking lot. There was a bar near the reception desk full of western middle-aged men greeting one another in a jovial manner, as if it had been awhile since they had gathered.

"Are you here for the science conference?" a smiling receptionist asked, in stilted, but perfect, English.

"I took home economics instead of science in school," Siobhan told her. Keelin told her their names, and they were given a key with a room number. The lift was small and the long brown corridor was dimly lit. Their room had two single beds, a TV, and a desk. The tiny bathroom was up a step; bath, toilet, and sink were all one piece of plastic. They had two robes in the sliding wardrobe, and when they slid the white paper shades to the side and wiped a hole in the condensation on the window they faced a highway stabbed with signs for McDonald's and Kentucky Fried Chicken.

"Oh great!" Siobhan huffed.

Keelin laughed. "You're going to have to try harder."

They went to sleep almost immediately. Aisling flooded Keelin's dream with water and swam close to her, unclothed — big and enveloping, an absorbent creature engulfing coral, shell, and stringy weed. Then, still looking at her, Aisling floated toward her other little sister, her large hands squeezing on Siobhan's flat, naked chest, two thick thumbs snapping simultaneously on her rubbery dark nipples as if flicking a switch. Siobhan gasped and twisted in the sheets, falling into her own dream.

The relentless wind shook the windows with ferocity, but the room was overheated and stuffy, which comforted Keelin when she awoke in the dead of night. She saw her sister gasp and turn.

Keelin's sense of time was confused. She was not sleepy anymore, and she felt odd and unnerved. The white paper screens seemed so foreign, and she felt a frisson of alienation, a wet rub of culture shock that Siobhan so longed for.

Siobhan woke Keelin up at ten.

"You should have woken me earlier."

"I thought you were jet lagged. You were drooling on the pillow."

"We have to get to that address. I don't want to spend another expensive night in this godforsaken place. Did you ask at the desk?"

"No, I just went down for breakfast."

"I wish you'd woken me. Was it good?"

"I didn't really eat . . . I just wanted to see what food they had."

Keelin crawled out of bed and slid the paper screens to the side. She saw the main road, the fast-food signs, some messy, plowed patches of land, a mountain of car tires.

The receptionist told them the town on the address was at the foot of the mountain by the cable car. She wrote it in Japanese for them. In the bus station they showed the ticket woman the names; she gave them a large white map in Japanese and circled the places where they had to change buses. They showed the map to a bus driver and he nodded, smiling, indicating that they sit down. The passengers eyed them discreetly.

"It's like being handicapped," Keelin muttered, to Siobhan's amusement.

Soon they were in the countryside. A bright, crisp December day, and nothing grew nor bloomed. Nobody was in the fields, and the town where they switched buses appeared abandoned. The houses were tiny; they had traditional curling tile roofs and flimsy wooden walls or gray cement facades with paper windows. The street was empty. A plastic rack with old yellowing seed packets stood outside one house. There was a steaming gutter at the side of another house, with a stone frog crouched on a rusty iron altar. Siobhan and Keelin wandered the streets, then entered a hardware shop. There was no one behind the counter so they browsed guiltily, as if they were intruding.

"We'll miss our bus," Keelin said, breaking the frozen silence. "Let's go wait in the wee station."

At the foot of the mountain there were a few deserted souvenir shops selling paper dolls, plastic swords, bizarre, unrecognizable pickled food in plastic packets, and hundreds of ceramic frogs of all different colors and sizes.

In a hotel gift shop a polite woman scrutinized the address, frowning thoughtfully. Finally she shook her head and pointed in the air, speaking to them in Japanese. They shrugged and shook their heads. She took the girls by the arms and pulled them outside.

"Keburuka . . . Yama! Yama!" She pointed up the mountain.

"That's where this is?" Keelin asked. The woman was panicky and exasperated; she glanced from side to side. Keelin pointed to the address. "This?" and then up the mountain, "there?"

The woman broke into a smile, nodding eagerly. "Hai! Hai!"

"Arigato," Siobhan said.

"Arigato goziamasu." The woman bowed several times, fleeing hastily into the safety of the hotel. Keelin looked at Siobhan, and Siobhan held up their phrase book.

"I was studying all morning while you were getting your beauty sleep."

After walking up a steep flight of steps they came upon a small temple and a group of stone Buddhas, crudely carved, with white lichen smothering their faces and bright red bibs tied around their necks. There were several wooden sticks poking out of the soil and a plastic Mickey Mouse on a spinning top in a Mexican costume, his head tilted perkily, holding two green castanets. Moving on, they came to a bigger temple with monks scurrying about and a shiny red fire engine parked outside. The truck was beautiful; it had a curled gold hose and sparkling brass bells on top. Several giddy firemen in pressed uniforms lined up in front of the shrine while the chief took their picture.

Keelin and Siobhan mounted more flights of steep stone steps; a tiny old woman bounded up past them with grace and alacrity.

"She looks as if she could outdo you in aerobics," Keelin panted.

A tram pulled them slowly up the steep mountainside through a density of quiet woods. Maple trees were shades of burning orange and red. On top of the mountain stood a three-story tower.

"Konichiwa!" Siobhan sung gaily as they entered the tower. There was a makeshift shop selling strangely shaped items in airtight packets. A middle-aged woman took their address and consulted a man sitting on the floor fixing a radio. Without looking up he spoke to her, and she pointed to an iron spiral staircase in the center of the room. Keelin took the address and they climbed the stairs.

The second floor had glass walls. There were low tables on the floor on tatami mats and hard cushions. They were the only people present. As soon as they sat a woman appeared with two cups of hot green tea on a tray, as if she had been expecting them. Belatedly taking their shoes off, they sipped the tea and gave her the address. The view stretched in a dark brown expansion of bare crumpled mountains, dense forests, layered fields, and a flat valley with an orderly patchwork of fields all shades of brown, beige and tan. Wind hurried small groups of white and black clouds through a deep blue sky, but the earth encircled them for miles and miles, motionless.

Another woman then appeared and knelt beside them with their piece of paper in her hand. "Musuko. Mai son."

They looked puzzled. She pointed to the paper. "Kyoto."

A young girl in a navy school uniform, her hair in two long perfect plaits, came to the rescue. "Our brother's address. Post come here. He move place and place."

"Where is he now?" Keelin inquired, her nail scratching the letters on the tiny teacup.

"Kyoto." The girl bit her lip and spoke to her mother, who droned on in a low voice, like a lament.

"We are looking for our sister," Keelin said. "Aisling." She raised her hand. "Big girl. Red hair like this." She clutched her own hair.

The girl shrugged. "Gomemmasai, we sorry . . . not know . . . never see . . . send post to Kyoto."

"Can you give me the address?"

She and the mother conferred.

"Box," the girl said. "No home we know. Box number."

"Can I have that?"

The girl spoke sharply to the mother and the mother scurried off to a tiny kitchen in the center. The girl smiled at them shyly.

"Your English very good," Keelin complimented her.

The young girl blushed and lowered her head, pleased.

There was a sound of feet padding and they turned to see the mother approaching, waving a piece of paper with Japanese writing. "Kyoto," she said, smiling, and gave it to Keelin. They stood.

"How much for the tea?" Keelin asked.

"No. No. No." The woman shook her head vigorously, her eyes cast to the floor in embarrassment.

"Good-bye! Thanks so much!" The girl said. "Thank you very much. Thank you."

Siobhan went first down the green spiral steps and out the door. A gust of wind caught her at the bottom and she was blown a meter to the side; her neck looked as if it were about to snap. Keelin raced over the rocky ground and caught her.

"Are you trying to fly away?"

Siobhan's cheeks were streamed with tears.

"Are you crying?" Keelin held her sister.

"It's the wind. The wind."

They stood by a stone wall. The wind died down for a moment and the valley gathered silently at their feet, the mountains folding out onto the misty horizon, the clouds stalled.

"Well, at least we have a P.O. box number. That's something."

"And to think she has never even been here," Siobhan shouted over the wind, which had picked up again. "No one has even seen her. Everything I had touched I was thinking she had touched too."

The spry old woman who'd been at the foot of the mountain sliced through the wind toward them and handed Siobhan a matchbox. Keelin watched her disappear behind the row of closed shops.

"What is it?"

Siobhan scrutinized it.

"It's from a bar in Kyoto."

The following morning they took a bus to the Tokyo train station and bought tickets for Kyoto. Keelin bought a wooden box of sushi. Everywhere, in windows, were beautifully displayed plastic models of the food available, with the prices beside each item. This made it possible for them to eat. They would coax a waitress outside, point to a plastic bowl of noodles, then wait to see what they'd get.

"Everyone is so slim," Siobhan marveled. "We must look like monsters."

"You have no idea what you look like, do you? Anyway, I've seen a few fat young people," Keelin remarked, as they got two sodas from a machine.

"Too many Big Macs. They should stick to sushi."

When they boarded the train and sat on the wide, comfortable seats, Keelin flipped the trays down. Siobhan read the guidebook aloud. "You can't eat or drink while you're walking down the street. If you get a drink from the machine, you have to stand there and drink it on the spot. You can't swing your legs while you sit and you can't blow your nose in public."

"What else?" Keelin opened each layer of the pretty, multi-packaged box of sushi.

"The first train journey was from Tokyo to Yokohama. The dignitaries took their shoes off and were astonished, when disembarking in Yokahama, that their shoes were not there."

"I know the feeling."

The train pulled out on the dot of eight-thirty. Keelin offered

Siobhan some sushi, and Siobhan took a roll as if it were a grenade with a loose pin. She placed it on a napkin and picked the grains of rice off the side, sucking each one individually. Keelin cracked open her can of soda and took a thirsty gulp.

"Ahh!" She winced.

"What?"

Keelin looked at the silver can. It had a big lemon on the side; the writing was in Japanese.

"Taste it!"

Siobhan opened hers and sipped. "Gin and tonic!" She beamed.

They clicked cans.

"Slainte!" Keelin toasted.

"Kanpai!" Siobhan countered, pouring it greedily down her throat.

Tokyo's concrete sprawl unraveled outside the window. Siobhan soon fell asleep, but Keelin woke her to see Mount Fuji, beyond patches of winter fields. Siobhan smiled faintly at the magic mountain and slipped back to sleep. Keelin read all she could about the ancient capital of Kyoto. American scholars begged the military to spare it from bombs; they could replace people but not temples. She leafed through Siobhan's fashion magazines and was struck by the fact that the women pictured bore a resemblance to her scrawny sister beside her. She felt guilty that she was enjoying the trip too much.

The area around the station was modern, but they were to discover that Kyoto wrapped its present around its past and that both elements were, at least to the passing visitor, in harmony. They found a Ryocan Inn down a small alley just over Schichijo bridge, where they were told that the bar on the matchbox was a forty-five-minute walk through the city. The bar turned out to be an open indoor area with a half dozen counters serving different types of Japanese food. Siobhan pushed her rice around her bowl with her chopsticks and took twenty minutes to swallow one piece of sashimi. Keelin, to make up, moved from counter to counter, drinking copious amounts of cold sake and trying every new food in sight. The place was crammed with young people drinking, smoking, and talking animatedly. They handed the Japanese address that they'd been given at the teahouse to each chef, who in turn shook his head. Finally, at the sushi counter, a young man nodded.

"He come tomorrow, Kenji."

"Kenji? That's his name?"

"Hai, Kenji."

"He work here?" Keelin sometimes found herself more easily understood if she imitated their English.

"No. No work. Customer."

Every night for two weeks they were told he would come, but Kenji never appeared. They plodded about in the rain between temples. Suddenly, at night, modern Japan became beautiful. There were narrow streets crammed with bloated red lanterns and neon signs stroked with colored script. Geishas in traditional dress scurried to work, over bridges in thick white socks and wooden shoes. White lanterns hovered and swelled like globular distended bellies from each forbidden house. The indecipherable writing blinded reason and comprehension, the unknown language left them deaf. Like infants they drifted, looking at colors, neon strips sweeping up sides of buildings, shallow canals with overturned bicycles mired in the sodden muck. A plastic life-size statue of a boy ran with a bag of food, ensnared eternally by a white dog pulling his pants, exposing his genitals to the flesh and blood night.

They glided as ghosts through the cold thin alleys, water dripping from gutters, each leaky street narrower than the last. Two ghosts tracking a dream of a sister. The sake was cold and slipped down their throats like heavy water. They got drunk every night, choosing from the plastic food, glazed clusters of noodles frozen in the air, entwined around a suspended fork. The invisible devouring the inedible.

They stayed in a two-story concrete inn. A pile of muddy shoes in the hall and a bowl of bruised, dried-up satsumas in a yellow plastic basket. Tea and trays beside the linoleum-covered stairs. Their room was the size of eight tatami mats. A low mahogany table and a coin-operated TV were the only furnishings. The light rice paper screens opened onto a little balcony overlooking an overgrown yard with a giant tree.

Keelin's black winter coat hung forlorn from a hook in the wall. She crouched beneath it. For a moment it seemed the coat was the living being and she had slipped out, piled misshapen and empty on the floor. The coat had substance and purpose, but she might crumble and blow away. Siobhan was in the room, her presence barely tangible, escaping consciousness on the rolled-out bed, her fragile body trapped under a smothering of thick blankets. Her head was cranked awkwardly on the rock of a pillow. Her mouth fell open and a glistening run of saliva crawled down her cheek, gelling on the wool covers. Not one lost sister but two. Keelin was frightened.

Boys in navy military school uniforms with golden buttons raced across the gravel stretch of a shrine. Orange wood, bright green curling roofs surrounded by pine trees, and a sky as white and bright as a flash of light. Trees were tied with paper fortunes. Women in kimonos and tiny little girls, so serious in the gardens, looked at the two ghosts with momentary curiosity.

There was a story Keelin told Siobhan on the philosopher's walk. Down in Connemara, when she was six years old and Patrick ten, Molly had taken them to the house of a recently deceased neighbor. She had been asked to keep an eye on it for the son in Dublin. Neglect hung thick in the air. The curtains were closed. The kitchen still had dishes on the draining board, the rims of the cups stuck to the metal. Molly opened some windows and went to run the taps, but the water had been shut off. The air was suddenly punctured by Patrick's scream. They ran into the bathroom and he pointed down the toilet bowl. A green frog crouched on the steep ceramic walls. The toilet was dry and its throat caked with flaky brown mold and rot. "Saints preserve us!" Molly cried out, snapping the lid shut.

Siobhan walked along dragging her feet, minor stumbles over

minute cracks in the pavement, her hands deep in the pockets of her brown suede jacket. She laughed at "Saints preserve us," prompting Keelin to end her story, laughing too. Contemplating the frog, they reached Ginkakuji, the Silver Pavilion. Keelin sighed as she took out her purse to buy two tickets: "Every time I see a monk I reach for my checkbook." White dust rose against the drizzle over smooth mounds that pushed out of raked gravel.

They could not stop filling the wet December days with temples and shrines. It was off-season. The sites were moderately empty, and they had nothing else to do. Sixteen days had passed in Kyoto. Siobhan bought ink and a bamboo pen and began sketching the gardens and buildings in notebooks she had bought from the monks. Keelin walked with her around thousand-year-old artificial lakes, with the autumn trees breathing a mass of mixed color. She read modern English novels and Japanese history books, sent lack-of-progress reports to Oscar, phoned him once. He urged her to stay, to go stand in shifts by the P.O. box where Kenji collected the mail. She mailed a card to Kenji instead and wrote long letters to Molly, and talked of her all the time to the patient Siobhan.

It was mid-morning, and a busload of schoolchildren were taking photos of one another with disposable cameras in front of the Golden Pavilion.

"I miss Ireland," Keelin said.

"I don't want this to end." Siobhan looked away. "I have nothing back in London. This is the best time of my life. I've never done anything interesting until now."

"Come back to Ireland with me," Keelin said. "You can live with Molly and me."

"Oh God, you've got to be kidding. I can just imagine Mammy's face. What would I do there? There's no work. The dole in London is one thing, but Dublin and Molly, no way."

"Why don't you go to art college?" Keelin stopped and turned to her. "I'm serious. I've seen all those ink drawings you make everywhere. They're great. What have you got to lose?"

"Really?" Siobhan flushed. "You think they're nice?"

Women were clapping and throwing money into tiny Shinto shrines, impatiently ringing bells to get their deaf or inattentive gods to pay more heed to their earthly woes. An eerie mist floated just above the ground, weaving calmly and deliberately among the foliage. There was a curious immobility to the scenes before their eyes as the sun penetrated the still canopy of lime green trees. Everything had a frozen quality, beyond time, behind glass. The light conveyed an aching unreality, as if they were witnessing something distant, yet too close, like images on a screen or a landscape painting. Every detail near or far seemed meticulously clear, vividly discernible. The world was flat, but not without dimension. Each drop of rainwater was apparent, clinging to each tiny leaf. Magic was palpable among the trees. When Siobhan sank to her knees on the spongy carpet of moss and laid her head against the deep brown bark of a tree, Keelin felt that her sister had fallen prey to a spell.

"Siobhan." She knelt beside her older sister. "Siobhan," she whispered, "you must start eating or I'm afraid you'll not have the strength to go on living."

That night, when they walked into the hall of restaurants, everyone was excited to see them. "Kenji, he here!" one chef gushed, and all the other chefs, behind their counters, grinned.

Kenji was a slim young man about thirty years old. He wore black, jeans and a polo-neck. His hair hung in a long fringe to the side of his face, and he sported a small mustache, neatly combed. He stood when he saw them and offered his hand. "You look like Aisling," he said to Keelin, "but smaller."

They sat down in relief. It was exhilarating to hear their sister's name mentioned at last. He offered them a cigarette. Siobhan took one; she only smoked when people offered. Keelin had always been too much of a good sensible girl to smoke.

"So. How you find me? You wait two week, they say." He poured them some sake and ordered sushi.

"We saw your mother in Tsukuba. Then an old woman gave us this address on a matchbook."

He laughed. "Was she fast old woman?"

"Fast? Yes, and strong. She was quicker than us going up the mountain."

"That my grandmother. Mother of mothers."

"Do you know where Aisling is now?"

He frowned. "She was here. We live with her." Then he looked at them nervously. "Toru, I, and sister. Live like friends," he assured them. "Why women come look for bad sister? Why not men in family sent?"

"You should see the men in our family," Siobhan muttered.

"Why you say bad?" Keelin inquired.

"No, not bad." Kenji downed another sake. Keelin drank hers in the same manner, without taking her eyes off him. "Aisling and Toru . . . Aisling friends with African girl . . ."

"Toru is African?"

He howled with laughter. "No. No. Toru is man, is Japanese. Fatima African. Fatima love Sadao. Japanese boy. Aisling teach piano and English — "

"Piano!" Siobhan almost choked on her sake.

"She go with Toru to Hiroshima, his home place, when Fatima and Sadao leave Japan to go America to Fatima brother. Aisling very sad. Toru bring Aisling to Hiroshima."

"I'm sure that cheered her up no end," Keelin said.

Kenji told them no more about their sister, but he rang Toru in Hiroshima to see if Aisling was still there. Toru said that she had left for Tokyo. He told them to come down to Hiroshima and they would all go to Tokyo together to find her. Kenji treated them to dinner and brought them to an old sake warehouse called Taku Taku. There was a punk band playing.

Keelin sat at the bar, having broken, drunken conversations with various broke, drunk students. Siobhan and Kenji danced, and when Keelin looked over at one point they were leaning against the wall kissing. Siobhan was running her hands down his back and ass, her upper body leaning back, her belly button and concave stomach exposed by her little woolly red sweater. Keelin was taken aback by her sister's sexual aggression; it was not what she would have expected. Nonetheless she was pleased to observe it, for any kind of appetite conveyed hope.

Keelin's sex life had been desultory. Pragmatic as ever, she had invested in a vibrator in London to satisfy herself without complication. A cheap orange plastic thing, with no fixtures or gimmicks. She was attracted to men but not altogether impressed with them. Siobhan, on the other hand, was too self-absorbed for romance, but she had had an affair with a professional comedian in London. She confessed to Keelin one drunken night that he used to beat her up and was now stalking her. She was still afraid of him when they left for Japan, which was one reason Keelin had decided to quit a cushy teaching job in Croyden and go with Siobhan to search for their bad sister.

It struck Keelin, as she sat at the bar guzzling sake at an alarming rate, that the voracious sexual impulse she guessed was felt by Aisling, and was so apparent in Orla, had petered out as it came to the younger ones. A horseshoe of lust, with Patrick as an unknown entity at the middle. She was the last, the opposite of Aisling, and strangely satiated by her battery-operated plastic penis. Hiccupping emotionally and swaying slowly to the screeching of the ludicrously sprayed, painted, and torn Japanese band, she was momentarily flooded with tenderness for her mother, uncle, and siblings. The real passion, she guessed, lay just there.

Toru had a perm. He speared the center of his spiral curls with his finger and pulled lightly, letting the hair spring back. Toru's aunt had microphelia, a condition caused by being radiated in his grandmother's womb at 8:15, August 6, 1945. She would be fifty next year and had lived an extraordinary amount of time for a pinhead. His family usually kept her tucked away in the confines of the house, locked her in a room when guests came, but his grandmother and father were now dead and his mother sick, and he had taken to shaving his aunt's head to accentuate her narrow, pointed skull, leaving a spray of hair at the peak. He paraded her about Hiroshima shamelessly. She was timid at first, after so long in hermitude, but he had coaxed and cajoled and started her off with little jaunts up and down the local street. They bounced a tennis ball back and forth in the alley.

His mother had not always hated him. When Toru was young she had fed him with cream to fatten him up and sang songs to him in the park. She had been five when the bomb dropped, and talked of the light and heat, but she didn't remember much except the typhoon that hit the town in the following months, killing many more and flattening their makeshift house on the smoldering ruins. Her elder brother had been ten and doing war work on buildings in the city center. They'd found only his lunchbox with the charred remains of food inside. There were curled black fingernails beside it, and his grandmother had kept these in a bag to give to his grandfather when he returned from the war in China. Toru's mother had brought him and his sister and brother to the river every year to float lanterns for the dead. They loved to do this; it was beautiful to see all the lights glowing and floating downriver. But Toru, the eldest of her children, had been a great disappointment to his mother and father. He passed his time in Tokyo, Kyoto, and Hiroshima, pliant as a reed under the tempest of maternal scorn.

His sister had married a salaryman and his brother was a salaryman. But there was Toru, strolling hand in hand with his retarded aunt through Peace Park at the age of thirty-four, searching for tourists to practice his English on. His aunt adored Aisling, his western friend, and she had liked his aunt, and he had worshipped Aisling. She was a woman, so fierce, a predator, a force. She could have gobbled him and his aunt up and shat them out, but instead she had been all hugs and cuddles, and she found a piano in a bar and played them a piece of Lizst that sounded as if she had three hands. His mother would not let this monstrous friend in the house, so Aisling had slept in cardboard in the alley until she smelt of cats. Now her sisters were coming in her wake, and Toru had got his lank perm refizzed in anticipation of their arrival.

Toru tried to conceal his disappointment. One sister was like her, but short and staid, and the other was barely alive, a skeleton draped in skin. Where was the roar of the big sister that made him tremble and brought goosepimples to his skin? These dishrag children could barely wipe the snot from his aunt's ever-dripping nose. And when he brought them to the piano bar the short replica played not demonic Lizst but a weak, slow, grinding music that turned in on itself over and over again. The starving one had not eaten a morsel of food all day.

A day later, in the museum of Hiroshima, they saw a step where a person had been waiting for the bank to open and at 8:15 A.M. had been vaporized. A human stencil. Nothing left but a shadow on a stone step. There were bed sheets hanging that were streaked with black rain. Siobhan could not resist touching things that had been touched by the bomb. Toru was wearing a skimpy gold miniskirt, with his balls and cock strapped tightly out of sight, a purple silk blouse, and slingback heels. His face was layered with a delicate shade of foundation, brown and green matte eye shadow, rose streaks of blusher tastefully blended, waterproof jet-black mascara and eyeliner, his mouth blood red, like an open wound. He wore a fake diamond choker, bracelet, and earrings, astounding them in the hotel that morning. They didn't recognize him from the previous day, when the only incongruity had been the ridiculous perm. Siobhan and Keelin had been lounging about in their hotel dressing gowns with embroidered H's on the pocket. They were addicted to Japanese TV. Then Toru had sauntered in, perfectly secure in his alarmingly high heels, and offered to show them around town.

"Hello chickens, it's Mother!" he had shrilled on his entrance. But he gave them no information about Aisling, except that she had slept in the alley beside his house because his parents were afraid of her. Keelin didn't believe him. While they fumbled for clothes and got dressed, he sat at the foot of the bed, his slim legs crossed primly. He flicked through the channels, shrieking strange things about all the actors and dramas. Finally settling on an old dubbed Hollywood movie and winking at Siobhan, who was drying her hair with a towel, he pointed the remote to a redheaded screen siren and proclaimed, "Rhonda Fleming! Married eight millionaires and died of leprosy."

"Do your parents know you dress like that?" Siobhan asked shyly.

"No, no. I dress elsewhere, my darling."

"You know, you actually could look pretty if you didn't dress like such a slut," Siobhan said, zipping up her platform boots.

Toru shrugged. "Then what's the fun?" Keelin appeared from the bathroom fully dressed; she grabbed her bag and the town's tourist brochure from the bed. *Hiroshima, the town famous for Japanese pizza,* it read.

"So what *is* the fun?" Keelin asked.

"Fun? Fun? Oh, today we go to the Holocaust Museum, a stroll through Peace Park to the A-Bomb Dome, the only surviving monument, and then drinks. Tomorrow Miya Jima, beautiful sacred island with monkeys and temple on the water, and next day Tokyo and painting the town red with your sister Aisling."

"No Nagasaki?" Siobhan said.

"We're not tourists, Siobhan, for Christ's sake. Let's just find Aisling and get her home."

"Your sister could not fit inside a home," Toru sniffed.

"Listen, Toru, I appreciate your offer, but I'd prefer to go to Tokyo today. I don't want to hang around. Maybe just the museum. It would be a shame to miss that."

Toru shook his head firmly. "No. You must see my town. Hiroshima is a very important place to see. Aisling would want it."

"Then tomorrow, for definite," Keelin told him.

"Two days," Toru said petulantly. "Then I'll take you the third day. You waited three weeks for Kenji. You will give me two days."

Keelin pursed her lips. "All right, Toru. We've no other choice. We're in your hands."

"What about Nagasaki though?" Siobhan pleaded.

"Forget it." Keelin scowled.

"Poor Nagasaki!" Siobhan sighed. "Always second fiddle."

On the tram, Toru fingered his hair distractedly and said, out of the blue, "My mother is bald from the bomb."

Keelin looked at him. "My grandmother was bald."

He nodded. "Scarlet fever." Keelin and Siobhan glanced at each other and smiled. Now they were sure he had been close to their sister.

"Scarlet ribbons, scarlet ribbons, scarlet ribbons for your hair," he sang to the old Irish tune. And then he sang the chorus to show off, because it was one of many Aisling taught him to perfect his English: "I looked in to say good night, And what did I see lying there? Scarlet fever, scarlet fever, scarlet fever for her hair."

In the museum there was an old watch stopped exactly at 8:15. There were roof tiles blistered, melted with the nightmares of the human race.

Aisling had stood and seen the pictures of the keloid scars on arms and backs and a photo of the Hiroshima maidens on the steps of a jet plane, off to America. American surgeons were shown in other photos trying to treat wounds that had set solid. Delivering the risen flesh into the arms of the men who had burnt them. Doesn't the battered woman always go back? Waving on the steps, smiling. The Californians donated a children's library in the shape of a mushroom to the city. The Americans moved in for a decade, forbidding talk of the bomb and experimenting on the Hibushka, those who survived. More photos of trams through the toxic, smoking rubble, corpses burnt beyond recognition, still unburied. Aisling had looked at the videotapes of the survivors, at pictures of children who came to the flattened city center to scour the rubble for their parents. They were eventually rounded up and put in orphanages, the little notice read in neat type, only to die of cancer.

"I carry future generations in my belly," Aisling had said.

"That's my function. I want to save the earth for my walking, talking discharge. Well, it won't work. You men are pregnant with the bomb." Toru had laughed softly and held her hand. She wore a suit and tie, smelling of the alley, and he a red dress and Chanel No. 5.

"The bomb was the last machine that mattered," Aisling told him. "We lost the very world we lived in."

"Your sister, you see," Toru explained to them, "saw everything. She was mad all day long. You could not mention a subject without her bringing up the political angle. So Fatima moving to America nearly killed her, the North Americans being the world's biggest bullies."

"When did this all happen?" Keelin asked.

"Nineteen forty-five."

"No — I know that. I mean Aisling being here."

"Oh . . . A year ago, maybe."

"A year? Jesus — how long ago was Aisling here?"

"I don't know. I'm bad with time. Ten months."

"Are you sure she's in Tokyo?"

"Yes. I can find her. Don't worry."

In Peace Park, Toru took them from monument to monument, and they took photos of one another under the shadow of the A-Bomb Dome. It was a grim, green ghoul of a ruin surrounded by great stark trees, almost enough to satisfy such lusty voyeurs as themselves. The monument for the ten thousand unlucky Koreans who were in Hiroshima as forced labor and died in the attack was just outside the park. "Who do they consider killed them?" Aisling had asked. "The Americans or the Japanese? And why is it not inside the park with the other memorials?"

Toru took a photo. "We spent time in Nagasaki too."

"How many times was Aisling here?" Keelin looked at him. "We got a post card years ago from here."

"Maybe it was years ago."

"Kenji seemed to suggest it was recently," Siobhan said, turning over the camera in her hand and inspecting it.

"Kenji is a fool." Toru glowered. "He knows nothing. His English is bad."

Keelin glared at Toru's gaudy necklace and wondered if it would hold throughout the entire strangulation. "I'm going back to the hotel. I have to get to Tokyo," she shouted at him. "You're wasting my time, you little faggot freak."

Tears welled in Toru's eyes.

Siobhan held Keelin's arm, which was raised in a fist. "Calm down. He knows where she is. We don't. He's trying to help us."

Keelin felt the rage curdle, her stomach bunched into frustrated knots. "Is there a toilet in any of these damn monuments?"

"Why don't you just shit on me," Toru said, his face bright red. "Shit on Japan."

Keelin ignored him.

"One last monument. Oh, how sad — it's the children's one." Siobhan looked at her map. "Then the Hypocenter, then home."

"Lunch?" Toru's voice wavered. "You can buy me lunch?"

"She doesn't eat," Keelin hissed. "Remember? She's too fat. Look at her. FAT. FAT. FAT."

The three walked through Peace Park, Toru sulking, Siobhan stunned quiet by her sister, and Keelin's fingers itching for the little red button.

"There was a little girl with radiation sickness," Toru told Siobhan. "She believed that if she made one thousand paper cranes, she would get better. She died making the 964th." They had to laugh at this, which broke the ice somewhat. The monument was shaped like a bomb, with a stone girl at the top, her arms reaching out and a crane taking flight above her.

"The crane is a Japanese symbol of longevity and happiness." Poor Toru was the consummate tour guide.

Thousands of multicolored paper cranes made by schoolchildren were draped around the area — in wreaths, in big glass jars, wet with rain, sodden in a dazzling pulp. They watched an old woman walk to the shrine and, without glancing at them, bow and pray. She wore western dress and was almost doubled to the ground. Her face was leathery, her eyes bleary. She took from a cloth bag two bananas and left them in front of the monument.

"Her children?" Keelin whispered. Toru sighed and shrugged, and when the woman sludged off slow as a snail, he turned to go. Keelin followed him. She was hungry and still needed a toilet.

"Look, I'm sorry, Toru. O.K.?" she said in exasperation.

"I miss Aisling," he said.

"I know. We'll find her. What trouble she causes for everyone. All her politics — she could've thought about my mother. What a fucking hypocrite."

"Where is Sive — how do you say your names?"

"Shiv-awn," Keelin said. "There's an old joke: knock knock."

Toru lit up. He loved these. "Who is there?"

"Siobhan."

"Siobhan what?"

"Siobhan *who*," Keelin corrected, ever the teacher.

"Siobhan who?" He was excited.

"Siobhan your knickers; your mother's coming."

"Knickers?"

"Underwear."

"Oh! Ha ha! But why Siobhan?"

"Shove on your knickers."

"Oh, yes, yes! Ha ha!" He was delighted and took her hand. She reluctantly conceded to let him hold it as they went back to look for Siobhan. Siobhan was standing amid the multitude of paper cranes, eating both bananas.

It was Christmas Day on the island of Miya Jima. Traditionally, no one was allowed to give birth or die on the island. The mothers returned after labor on a little boat; the sick were banished to the mainland. Miya Jima was sacred, not to be sullied by the frantic comings and goings of mortals. The giant, sixteen-meter torii rose like an elaborate doorframe out of the sea, a watery threshold. Sacred deer walked everywhere, their antlers hacked off; they came into the train station and snatched Siobhan's sandwich out of her hand, just as it seemed she might actually eat it.

"Sacred venison." Keelin protectively kicked them away.

Keelin wanted to ring Molly and wish her Happy Christmas. She wanted to talk to Patrick and Orla, who might be home. Who knows, even Aisling. They would all be gathered by the fireside, telling stories. But she stalled, confused. Was Ireland a day ahead or behind? What was the time difference? The uncertainty froze her intent, and she could not clear her head of Japan for an instant to figure out the global puzzle.

Toru led them to the chair lifts. Snow monkeys washed their food in the hot springs. The night before they'd gotten drunk in a tiny bar in Hiroshima, a corrugated tin hut flung up for the evening with a solitary red lantern outside. The woman behind the counter had smiled and bowed repeatedly, and she gave the sisters an ugly, brown-flecked ceramic cup as a souvenir. Siobhan passed out, her head on the bar. The woman stroked her short fuzzy hair and cooed in consolation.

Toru had brought his aunt to the island today, and the four glided up the mountains on chairs. Last night they had carried Siobhan home. Toru turned off the light and kissed Keelin. She had stood, a statue, eyes shut, barely breathing as he undressed her. He had released his genitals, marked and red. Aisling, where are you taking me now? she murmured. When he heard that name, he put his hand tightly over her breast and eased her onto the bed. Her mind coasted through the dark drunkenness, and her toes sparkled with haywire nerve endings. She opened his silk blouse and rubbed his flat chest. He groaned in fright as she wrenched his tight skirt down, binding his thighs. In a surge of rage, she grabbed his head and pushed his protesting face between her legs. She kicked his back with her heels and she wanted to scream out in frustration, hatred, despair, and shame.

His aunt laughed and swung her legs in delight to see the

monkeys shoulder-deep in the hot springs. The night before, Keelin had stumbled to the bathroom in the middle of the night and stuck her head under the tap, dehydrated, drinking desperately. Her face looked swollen and blotchy in the bathroom mirror. Should she drink the water in Hiroshima? She groped in the dark for a long T-shirt, and, pulling it over her head, she got into bed with the comatose Siobhan. That night she lay awake, appalled with herself. She had become too distracted by the journey. She would grab Aisling and drag her home to Molly.

Light was fading and the sky brooded above the four as they walked down the mountain path and over a red wooden bridge. A giant stone frog squatted on the bank of the stream. The island was closed, shops and restaurants dark and shut. A man was burning a pile of rubbish on the tiny beach, and they walked down the steps toward the flames. Along the promenade were rows of stone lanterns with electric bulbs, unlit. Keelin could not bear to look at Toru or his aunt. She vowed never to drink again. Wind blew the flames as darkness wrapped around them like a burden of sorrow. Aisling had walked on this very beach in the lively summer season, when couples strolled arm in arm and groups of teenagers sat on the walls taunting one another. Laughter had swayed the hot night, and parents had children dancing in giddy circles around them as they bought ice creams. Every shop and restaurant was open, throbbing with vacationers till the wee hours. Now they stood mesmerized by the fire, their backs cold as the wind-whipped flames grasped toward them. Brown, mangy deer appeared, and soon there was quite a menacing gathering. They nuzzled roughly at the aunt, smelling food in her pocket. Her face collapsed in fright. She held onto Toru, who tried to shoo the pests away. The electric bulbs came on along the dark empty promenade, and they all fled to catch the last ferry and train to Hiroshima. The sacred deer trailed after them like a police escort.

more bread or i'll appear

PATRICK WAS FLYING HOME to Ireland from New York with rubber hands: he wore surgical gloves on the plane. There was a plastic bag full of them in his carry-on. I'm as mad as my father, he thought. Forever stuck on the threshold. That was how he remembered him, hovering on the piece of wood nailed to the floor, long long ago. Looking up into the corner of the open door: panicked and stuck.

The family had picked up their belongings and fled to the West, where there was a grocery shop down the road. Two petrol pumps outside and people gathering there on Sundays after mass. Rhubarb tarts cooled on the window ledges and the cats lay curled on the pastry for warmth. Many times Patrick and his sisters would spot a face in the upstairs window of the little two-story shop. It was said to be that of Sive, the grocer's daughter. Legend had it that she was mad and her parents kept her upstairs out of shame. Anytime her parents had company that ventured farther than the shop front, she would shout, unseen, from the top of the stairs, "More bread or I'll appear." These were the only words she was ever heard to have said, and in the wild, gaping landscape that dwarfed and barely tolerated the grocery store, she had only ever been seen looking out the grimy window above the shop. A face and a voice, nothing corporeal. An image in a vacuum. Nobody.

Aisling, his missing sister, had always waved at Sive but got no response. What was she doing sending books from Hiroshima as birthday gifts? Was she as mad as that face in the window? Patrick ran from the bomb in his brain, far away from where it first dropped. He also knew the pull of the bomb. The relief of the mushroom cloud finally rising after a life of anticipation. The satisfaction of tearing the planet to shreds like a child smashing a sandcastle. If we kill it, we will beat it before it beats us.

To his mind, there were no delusions, no momentary lapses. Everything was apparent and cruel. There were words strung up in sentences like ropes over rafters. *To feel the fear I felt before.* In this involuntary mantra fear was a driving force, and it was fear that kept a sack of gloves at his feet. And then he heard the story told by his friend Thomas and again by someone else. Across Ireland were mad children gathered at tops of stairs threatening. More bread or I'll appear. If he had no bread, how could he silence them? What would they say when they all came down? All over the world he hated to glance at upstairs windows. Afraid to catch the eye of Sive. Already cursed by the first sighting.

Patrick, poor Patrick. Affection-starved. A shadow on a stone. A face in a window. There was a parasite and it ate his dreams. There was a worm and it tied knots in his soul — little pulpy, throbbing knots of compulsion. To open his brain, press both temples to break seal, then lift lid. He can listen to a million conflicting reasons, read booklets with addresses listed in the back, and help groups and phone numbers and membership fees. But he couldn't afford a doctor. Treatment was expensive and had to be maintained for a lifetime.

To feel the fear I felt before.

Sive in the shop. Her face at the glass. Was her hair long or short? They had imagined long, with yellow, curling fingernails, but it could have been she was well looked after and bathed and combed and groomed and even loved. Love? In Ireland? And who might be there to administer such a deluge of emotion?

Patrick, little tadpole, little sperm, awash with fear on a DC-10, protecting himself from germs. The infection of a filthy century. Ah, my poor father! Stuck. Always on the verge but without power to look behind, to go forward.

In Dublin, Orla opened the door and hugged Patrick. Then she drew back, wrinkling her nose.

"Paddy! Jesus tonight! What are you wearing them gloves for? Can you not afford the real thing?"

"I've a skin infection."

"Yuck! Is it contagious?"

"Orla, will ye let me through the door. I've just flown the Atlantic."

"You mean the pilot did. You just sat on a seat."

Going home for Christmas was a pattern worth keeping to. A stump around which to tie his tether.

"Mammy's taken to the bed," Orla said with a sigh, as soon as he dropped his suitcase in the living room.

"Since when?"

"She's been there the whole week I've been home. She's not herself at all, at all. I even feel sorry for her."

"Is she sick?"

"Ach! She drives me up the walls. She says she's been under the weather for a few months."

"Did ye call the doctor?"

"She says, Sure once you let yourself into the clutches of a doctor you'll never get out. They'll always find more wrong with you. She says, I have a wee bit of a stomach infection. So I call a doctor anyway and she gives in. He says she has to go in for tests and a D&C."

"DNC?"

"Her stomach, Jesus wept. Ah, Paddy, sure I almost died —"

"What?" Patrick was alarmed.

"It wasn't her stomach at all. The doctor was in there for ten minutes before she could tell him it was vaginal. And she didn't have a word for it."

"For what?"

"The vagina. She still keeps saying, down there, my lower tummy."

"I never thought vagina was a good word anyway." Patrick lit a cigarette. "Aisling once told me it was the word for sheath, for a sword. Pussy, cunt, box, snatch. What do you expect — they're all awful. She's old, too."

Orla looked baffled. "Patrick, what are you on about? Are you even paying a whit of attention to what I'm saying? I'm going to have to stay. Until Keelin comes back. She needs looking after. She shouldn't be alone."

"She's stronger than you think."

"What have I got over there? I'm sick of getting up at three in the morning six days a week to go to the bakery. My son doesn't give a shite. I lost night's sleep with the embarrassment and shame of what I did to his other mother. Honest to God, what were we thinking at all? Barging in on her like that."

"You've changed your tune. I thought you were great. I felt an eejit meself, but you were so cool."

She rubbed his arm affectionately, "It was looking at Mammy sick. I got to thinking —"

"Where is she?"

"She's asleep. Why don't you put your clothes in the girls' room. I cleared out a drawer. You'll be back on your camp bed, if it's not all rust and mold. She'll be delighted now to see you. She kept talking about us all when we were wee ones."

"Nothing good, I bet."

To feel the fear I felt before. Where did he get that? Was it the time he read Plato by mistake? Picked up a slim book in Oscar's apartment and flicked through to get the gist of it. Maybe not, but he associates that sentence with the philosopher. It was a connection he made when he kept having to say it over and over. A casual glance through a book and now one sentence stuck like a splinter in his brain. And they wondered why he didn't want to study. How could he tell them that he was tortured by words? that they pursued him like an animal? Would they understand in a country like this, where an entire language was stolen from their mouths?

Molly lay in bed amid fluffed pillows. Orla had put Christmas cards on the windowsill, which was wet with condensation. Already the cards were soggy. Molly eyed Orla skeptically as she bustled back and forth, her ministrations more matronly than angelic. Molly's face was yellow and her skin hung loosely from her arms and skull. Her elbows and chin jiggled with extra flesh. She was shrinking inside her fat body. On the bedside table were a big box of tissues, a glass of water, rosary beads, and some books on golfing technique.

"If it's the will you're after, Orla, sure I've nothing to leave any of you except grief."

Orla smiled sweetly. "Mammy, honestly, you're getting your old spirits back." She carried the tea tray into the kitchen.

Molly raised her eyebrows and squeezed Patrick's hand. He had kissed her forehead when he entered.

"Are you sure she's not putting the last nails in my coffin out there in the yard?"

"She's worried, Mammy. I'm worried."

"There's not a bother on me. A little bit of a flu and a tummy infection," Molly sniffed. "Tell her to go back to America and to her job. She won't find work here, and it does a body harm to sit around all day. Sure half the reason I'm down is from worry about ye all. At least I don't have to look at any of ye, wasting your lives in my own house."

"Did you sit around all day?" Patrick asked.

"Keelin's not long gone. I had my golf up till a few months ago."

Patrick was silent. *To feel the fear I felt before.*

"Orla told me you had a waiter job."

"I jacked it in."

"Or did they jack you in?"

"No," Patrick lied.

"It wouldn't be because you've taken to wearing rubber gloves, now, would it?"

"I'm illegal; they wanted to see my papers."

"Orla got the Morrison Visa in the lottery."

"Yeah, she's been acting so superior now that she's legal. Strutting around the Bronx like she owns the place. I applied but I didn't get it."

"Take those gloves off, they're giving me the willies."

"I've an infection."

"I'm not as green as I'm cabbage, you know. " Molly's looked sad and weary. The wind howled outside, and it was dark at four o' clock. "Basically, Patrick, I think your life is over."

Patrick stared at a string of tinsel taped above the bed. He withdrew his hand from hers and she offered no resistance. Finally he spoke gently, matching her exhausted tone. "That's a terrible pronouncement to a man of thirty."

Orla swept into the room. "Time for your medicine, Mammy." She read the label and vigorously shook two tablets into her palm.

"Open wide. There's a good girl."

Molly, still looking at Patrick, threw her eyes up to heaven and made a face as she swallowed the pills with the stale water. Patrick laughed noiselessly and patted his mother's leg through the blankets.

Patrick slotted himself like a copper coin back into the bar scene in town. Brian Malone, a freelance journalist who had a habit of pushing his glasses up his nose, never had a penny in his pocket or a word in print. His friends had to torture him until he bought them a round to make them stop. He was a man in his early thirties, eyes permanently bleary, greasy brown hair parted in the middle, and skin that looked as if it had been scoured with sandpaper. He always wore a shirt and tie with a waistcoat and his collar buttoned up.

"Look at him cradling that Coke. Are ye off the drink, Brian?" Thomas McGee asked him.

"Just for Christmas, is it?" Garrett Conroy sneered.

"Tell me something, Brian," Thomas said. "If you're off the grog, why come in here bothering us?"

"My flat is too small. Sure this is like my living room," Brian answered meekly, looking about for an escape route that wouldn't look too much like flight.

"Flat my arse. Where's this mythical flat?" Thomas folded his arms, a leer breaking out on his freckled, narrow face. "I heard tell you've moved back in with the Mammy."

"She's taken to the bed," Garrett chimed in. "He brings her tea and toast with the *Irish Times* on a tray every morning." The group laughed at this.

"Mammy, is it a dab of milk and two lumps of sugar, is it?" Thomas imitated Brian's nasal voice, pushing imaginary glasses up his own long bony nose. "I grilled the rashers and sausages, sure you'll be up and about in no time. Ten years is a long time to be in bed, Mammy, ever since I failed me leaving. Mammy, will I open the curtains for you? Sure isn't it a lovely day and you can see the pigeon house from the window. Let me just prop you up on those pillows till you catch a glimpse. I'm going out tonight, Mammy, to see a fellow about a job. Could you lend me a few bob to buy him a drink? Or else I'll have to steal the bus fare from your purse. Ah thanks, Mammy . . ."

The others howled. Brian tried to smile, pretending it was just a joke for him too.

"I heard he massages her feet every night with lanolin," Garrett said through the laughter.

"What's with the surgical gloves, Paddy?" Brian tried to deflect the derision.

Thomas leaned in and said, "He's performing rectal examinations later tonight. We thought you'd be first in line, seeing how close you are to the Mammy and all."

"Why in bejaysus are you wearing those shagging yokes?" Garrett asked Patrick.

"It's all the rage in Miami."

"Miami," Thomas snorted. "A little fairy told me you were in the Bronx. Miami my arse."

Thomas had taken a communications course in Rathmines years ago and called himself a film director. He then wrote a screenplay and got money from the Irish film board. The pilot had been shot in the West, but he hadn't managed to raise the money to edit it. That was three years ago. He'd see some of the actors and cameramen in the dole office on Tuesdays, and they always demanded their pay, knowing he hadn't two pennies to rub together. He had the wide-eyed look of a child.

Brian bought the table a round of pints and shorts. It cost a quarter of his dole check, but he placed the drinks in front of each man as if it were an appeasement.

"Here you go, Garrett."

"Ah, thanks, Brian, thanks."

"Patrick."

"Good man yourself, Brian. I'll stand the next one, so I will."

"Thomas, there you go. Last but not least."

"What are ye having yourself? Another bloody Coke?"

"I'm all right. I'm on the wagon," Brian said, sweating. "Sure you know yourself."

"No! I wouldn't know, Brian." Thomas poured the whiskey rapidly down his throat. "It wouldn't be anything to do with those gin blossoms currently in bloom all over your face. I hear alcohol exacerbates that particular condition."

"Ah, leave off him," Garrett said, a mustache of Guinness cream on his upper lip.

"W. C. Fields, I believe, had it. A genetic condition. Steer clear of spicy foods and alcohol, they say. Without treatment the nose can be hideously deformed with lumps . . ." Thomas expounded, as the others sniggered guiltily. "What's it called again?" He said, egging them on.

"Rosacea, I believe," Colm said. Colm was a mild man in his mid-forties; he wore a suit and tie and carried a briefcase. It was said that he worked for the government in the ministry of forest and fisheries.

"Rosacea. Sounds religious," Patrick said. "Our Lady of Rosacea."

Thomas grinned ear to ear, looking at the others, and turned to Brian. "He could be the rosacea poster boy."

Brian stood abruptly, leaving his Coke on the table, and sidled out of the bar into the lounge. The men clapped and roared.

"Poor bastard . . . why can't you leave him alone," Patrick said, making sure to smile.

"He's a fucking eejit," Thomas snorted, draining his pint. "What's the shyster coming in here to drink Coke for?"

"Company," Patrick shrugged.

"It's your shout, Dr. Benway," Thomas said to Patrick. "Spread around some of those big bucks you must be raking in stateside."

"Jaysus," Colm said. "When I was in San Francisco for the summer I was making seven hundred a week working as a waiter."

"That's nothing, boy." Garrett shook his head. "I was working three jobs in Boston — construction, bartending, and night doorman. Raking in the dough. Thousands."

Unlike most of them, Thomas had never done a stint in America and was consequently virulently anti-American. "When I was making my film about the racehorse, the Yanks came over and we were trying to milk them, you know? So says they to me, but what about the love interest? Where's the lead actress? There's no woman in the film. Well, says I, that's where you're wrong. Sure isn't the horse a female?"

Patrick headed to the bar to order another drink. An old man with a long white beard grabbed him by both arms and started to growl at him. "You can't say every third Irishman is a shyster, me lad. We have suffered eight hundred years of slavery. Sure we're just finding out who we are now. I'm a poet. My ancestors were Firbolgs. Here before the Celts. To those of you shower of Normans and the like who didn't come till 1142, I say to you, Welcome to my country."

Patrick squirmed free and wriggled in between two women at the bar.

"Are you a doctor?" one of them said, leaning drunkenly into his face. She wore big hoop earrings and two rings through her nose.

The other, a bleached blonde with short, spiky hair and leather trousers, laughed. Patrick ordered a round for the table.

"Why don't you join us?" He nodded toward his group.

"You're not with that pack of losers, are you? Those bowsies prop up the walls in here. And you can tell that Thomas McGee he can fuck off regarding the other night."

"Ah, sure he never means what he says," Patrick said. "He's a decent skin. He just likes to take the piss."

"Is that what's it's called in this day and age? Attempted rape is more like." The nose-ringed one sniffed.

Patrick dodged away, stretching his fingers around a bunch of pints. The old poet came to the table and stuck out his empty glass. They all obliged, pouring a bit of their drinks into his until he had quite a cocktail. He drained it in an instant. As half cascaded down his beard, he stuck out his glass.

"Ah, go away out of that, boy," Thomas told him. "Ye got your share." He turned to Patrick. "What were you talking to those two slappers about?"

Patrick shrugged. "I was enticing them to join me, but when they caught wind of the company I keep . . ."

Thomas smiled. "I owe the blond bitch money. Deirdre. She sells ecstasy. I got a few on credit the other night and she came dancing in Ri-Ra's with me. Listen, we went back to her flat in Temple Bar. She's an artist. Nice fucking place — ugly sculptures everywhere."

"She seemed to suggest it was attempted rape."

Thomas smiled slyly. "I was out of me head on E's. I thought she was enjoying it until she kicked me in the bollocks."

"She had you in the house all doped up and horny," Garrett said. "Was she fucking with your head or what?"

"I thought you've been going out with Kathleen for years," Patrick said.

"I have. What's Kathleen got to do with this? We're only engaged."

"When are ye going to tie the knot?" Patrick asked. "Who's going to be your best man, the rosacea poster boy?"

"She wants me to give up the drink and show some responsibility. She doesn't understand filmmaking is my life." They all laughed at his facetiousness.

"She's a lovely girl," Garrett said solemnly. "Works in the bank."

"Too good for the likes of me," Thomas admitted.

"She works?" Patrick said. "You've got yourself a laying hen?"

Cian came in through the side door, a good-looking young man. Black hair hanging over his blue eyes. He glanced around the pub and, spotting the lads, went over, nodding to acquaintances and friends on the way.

"I'm gasping for a drink," Cian said, placing a stuffed black plastic bag at his feet. "Oh, hello Paddy. Back for Christmas, is it?"

"Who's in the bag?" Thomas asked.

"I have to move back into the ancestral mansion in Dundrum."

"Who's left in your house now?" Patrick asked him.

"My parents. They sleep in separate rooms." Cian kept looking over his shoulder

"An Irish divorce, so to speak," Colm said.

"Yeah, something in that order. Then Aine is back from Australia, and Cliodhna has left Patsy and the kids and moved back in."

"All back to the roost, one way or another," Patrick said.

"They're a close family, so they are." Thomas noisily slurped the last of his pint.

Colm stood, reaching into his pocket. "I'll get the next. What's your poison Cian?"

"Guinness, thanks very much."

"Have you taken root in that spot, Thomas?" Garrett looked at him skeptically.

"I can't go up. I've a tab in this dump. They'll hassle me for it."

"That's convenient," Garrett grunted.

"Listen, are any of yiz up for some stuff tonight?" Cian whispered, narrowing his eyes. They all shifted in their seats without looking at one another.

Thomas cleared his throat, lowering his voice. "O.K., but don't let on to Colm there."

They handed him some money, and he disappeared out the door.

"He'll not be back," Patrick said.

"He left his bin liner," Garrett remarked.

"He probably just picked it from the outside bins for a prop. Give us a look." Thomas gestured to Garrett, who handed it to Thomas, who peered inside. "Just as I thought, women's underwear . . . I always knew the little maggot was a shirt-lifter." Colm returned with the drinks.

"Time, gentlemen, please." The barman scooped all the empty glasses from the table.

"Where's that little cunt Cian, and I after buying him a drink," Colm complained.

"What does he do now, Cian?" Patrick asked.

"He went to Trinity years ago. Ah, sure he says he's a publicist. Well, that's the latest." Colm shrugged.

"Half this bar says they're bloody publicists," Thomas said. "All the celebrities have fled the country and left us with the publicists."

"Time, ladies and gentleman," shouted the barman. A young woman approached Garrett and curtly handed him an envelope before leaving with her companions.

"Is that a check?" Colm asked hopefully.

"I very much doubt it." Garrett turned it over warily in his hand.

"Time to go, ladies and gentlemen," the owner shouted again with exasperation over the din and clinking of glasses. A group sang emotionally and swayed in the corner, on the verge of tears. "I am vile, I am wretched, but I am morally perfecting myself," the poet howled at the barman, who pushed him gently out the door.

"Must be a summons so," Thomas said, grabbing the envelope from Garrett and opening it savagely. Garrett snatched it back and read the official-looking letter.

"A summons it is." Garrett was downcast.

"For what? Whose little boy have you been interfering with of late?" Thomas snatched the letter, tearing it in half.

"It's for a bank loan I never paid." Garrett looked dourly at the torn half letter and dropped it on the floor, pushing it under the table with his foot.

"Who would loan you money?" Thomas asked.

"Time I went to the States. I took it out for the plane ticket."

"So what about all those millions you made?" Patrick was triumphant. Cian came back.

"Oh look. It's head-the-ball," Thomas said, perking up.

"HAVE YE NO HOMES TO GO TO," the barman screamed at the impassive throng.

Outside, the air was cold and the street empty. "We can't go home to my place. Kathleen would have a fit. I told her I was visiting the Mammy," Thomas told them.

"I live out in Dun Laoghaire. My mother's sick, though, and Orla would be there"

"I'm not going near that bitch," Garrett said. He had always had a crush on Orla but was terrified of her. The bleached blonde stumbled by, arm in arm with her friend.

"Hey Deirdre — any chance we could come back to your place? We have some goodies."

"Fuck off, Thomas McGee," she shouted, without looking back.

Patrick laughed softly. "You know, the great thing about you, Thomas, is that you've never been ruined by failure."

Thomas smiled. "That goes for all of us. Well, the ones who stick it out in this shitty."

Cian stood in the shadows shivering. "Jesus, lads, let's find somewhere quick."

"Look at your man bugging out. " Thomas stared at him in amusement.

Colm hiccupped. "I don't know what youse lot are up to and I don't want to know. I'm off to Ri-Ra's. Are any of yiz coming? Full bar?"

"No, no. I'm sick of that place." Garrett looked at Patrick significantly.

"Suit yourselves. I'm off. See you tomorrow." Colm sauntered off with big goofy strides, briefcase in hand.

"Would you look at him," Thomas sneered. "He must have got an E out of Deirdre of the Seven Sorrows when he was up at the bar. Off to boogie his tight little arse off."

"Colm's discovered the rave scene at forty-five," Garrett told Patrick. "He was in the POD the other night jiving with all the nineteen-year-old UCD students in his suit and tie, with the briefcase on the floor in front of him."

"A wolf among lambs." Thomas shook his head.

Cian's teeth chattered. He looked nervously over his shoulder. "What about your place, Garrett?"

"I've been sleeping in the office."

"Let's go there," Thomas said.

"I've got the keys. I suppose we could."

"Let's go so." Cian hopped about. "I've some tinfoil."

"Does your father not know you sleep there?" Patrick asked.

"My father doesn't know I work there." Garrett shrugged. "He's on so much medication."

The five men walked abreast up the street.

"I didn't know your old man was sick," Patrick said.

"The fucker's always been sick."

"He's a manic depressive," Thomas told Patrick.

"Well, we're waiting for the maniac side to surface after all these years," Garrett said, sighing.

"What kind of medication? Anything good?" Cian asked.

"Oh, here we go!" Thomas groaned. "Cian is going to go on one of his searches. He'll be rooting around all night now."

"Prozac?" Patrick asked.

"Yeah, that and everything else."

"Jesus," Thomas said. "Everybody's on Prozac in this bleeding country. Everyone but me, that is. It's an outrage, that's what it is. I've been waiting my turn for years."

Orla picked up the phone in the hall. "Hello? Mammy?"

"No, it's Orla. Aisling?"

"Keelin. Aisling? Has she been in touch?"

"No. You sound alike. I was hoping. Happy Christmas. We miss you."

"I miss you too. How's Mammy?"

"She's sick. Has to go in for tests."

"Is it serious?"

"We'll have to wait for the results. I'm going to stay with her until you come back. What's taking this long?"

"Yeah, you stay with her. Don't talk to me about this mess. I'll tell you all the suss when I'm home, which I hope will be soon. A few days. Put me onto Mammy, will ye? I don't want to waste any more of Oscar's money than I have to. He's been so patient and concerned. Is Oscar there?"

"Just Patrick."

"Keelin, pet, how are you?"

"Fine, Mammy. I heard you were sick."

"Ah, I'm all right now, love. Where are you?"

"We've just arrived in Tokyo. In the train station with a friend of Aisling's. He says he knows where she is."

"Ah, that's fantastic. Do they have Christmas there at all?"

"They have a few decorations, but it's not a big thing for Buddhists. My money is running out, Mammy."

"Mammy? Happy Christmas! This is Siobhan. We're in Tokyo. It's great."

"Siobhan, love. Get Aisling and come home for the new year."

"We will. We're going to get her tonight. What day is it there?"

"It's Christmas Day, pet. Get your sister. Tell her we love her and want her for Christmas and then she can go gadding about all she likes. We just want to see her."

"It's the twenty-sixth here, a day ahead. We were trying to work it out. It's great that you got a phone at last."

"Oscar forced the wretched thing on me. Sure I never use it, but it's worth it just for this. I thought you'd all be home in time for Christmas."

"Mammy, this is Keelin again. We got to go. The money is running out and we have to get Aisling. Believe me, I thought we'd be home too."

"O.K., pet. Happy Christmas. We miss you."

"You too, Mammy. Bye!" The phone clicked off.

"I wanted to say hello," Patrick said, pouting.

"They didn't have any more money."

"Why didn't you get their number and call back?"

"Sure I wouldn't know how to call Tokyo, and it's on the other side of the globe. It would cost an arm and a leg. They'll be home in a few days, she said."

Patrick threw his eyes up to heaven.

"We have to go over to Aunty Mary's for a wee Stephen's day gathering tomorrow," Molly said when they were all gathered in the living room.

"Aunty Mary?" Orla exclaimed. "Are you friends with her now? I thought we just saw that lot at funerals."

"She's old now. Sure her grandkids are almost grown. She's my only sister in the country. I thought I should make the effort. I was only close to Oscar — none of the others felt like family. I can barely remember them growing up. We were all sent away."

"Why doesn't Oscar visit them?" Patrick said. He sat on the couch beside his mother.

"He does when he wants to milk them for family-tree stuff," Orla said. "He doesn't like them much."

"Why not?" Patrick asked.

"Ah, they're teetotalers," Molly said. "I used to go over there with Aisling. None of the rest of you liked them. Never a drop to drink in that house. All her kids took the pledge and stuck to it. Lawyers and doctors the lot of them, or married to accountants and bankers. What am I going to tell her about my lot? None of ye married and not one of you working, either."

"Keelin was a teacher," Patrick reminded her. "Until you told her to go."

"She didn't need much prompting. And then she got to London and got a job and showed no sign of going after your sister," Molly said softly. "No, she certainly didn't need much prompting. She was out of here like shite from a goose."

Standing in the kitchen ironing, smoking, and listening to the radio, Orla was even bulkier than usual in Molly's pink dressing gown. She wore the furry slippers that Molly had bought her for

Christmas. Her red hair was frizzy, her face deathly pale without makeup. Molly shuffled in her old tatty slippers, dressed for the first time since Orla had come home.

"Mammy, you're dressed!"

"Morning, pet. Make us a cup of tea, would you, like a good girl."

"Wait till I finish this blouse."

"Better practice well. It's all you'll be doing for the rest of your life."

"Never miss a beat, do you?" Orla stuck out her tongue in concentration as she ironed between the buttons.

"What age are you now, Orla? Patrick says he's thirty. It gave me an awful shock. I thought he was about twenty-three."

"I'm thirty-two."

"You should get married and have a family."

"You should get an annulment from Daddy and go out and find a man."

Molly guffawed loudly. "At my age. I've one foot in the grave. I won't make it till next Christmas."

"You've been saying that for fifteen years now. Every Christmas."

"Does Patrick have a girlfriend?"

"I don't know. He could be queer for all I know. I work shifts, you know. I only see him the odd time in the flat. We have to share the bed. I'm up at three in the morning and that's about the time he crashes."

"You poor ol' sagosha."

"Why?"

"All your life sharing beds with your sisters, and now that big galoot Patrick has moved in on top of you."

"He's not staying long. I like to have some family around. Anyway, Mammy, I'm not going back. He can have the bed all to himself."

"Go back to the life you've made. Sure you'd hate it here. It would be very dull altogether. You even speak like a Yank."

"I do not." Orla flushed with anger.

Patrick suddenly appeared, wearing tracksuit bottoms and a sweater.

"Well, well, the dead arose and appeared to many," Molly said.

"Manny McKutchen." Orla smiled and stubbed out her cigarette.

"Wha?" Patrick rubbed his eyes.

"Remember Manny in Connemara? We used to always say that. The dead arose and appeared to Manny McKutchen."

"Ah, whisht with your blathering." Patrick waved his hand dismissively.

"Excuse me! Who's had a rough night? You didn't come back till six in the morning and now you're like a bear with a sore head. Don't take it out on me. I was saving meself for New Year's tonight." She held up her blouse and inspected it. With a look of satisfaction, she put it on a hanger and reached into the ironing basket for a pair of jeans.

"I don't feel well. I'm going back to bed."

"Are you going out with all your horrible friends tonight?"

"No. I hate New Year's. The pubs are too packed, you can never get a seat — or a bus or a taxi, for that matter. Celebration is forced, it's always an anticlimax. What do I care about the Roman calendar?"

"God, would you listen to Scrooge here." Orla winked at Molly, who got up to put on the kettle.

"I'll sit in and keep Molly company," Patrick said.

"You needn't bother your head. I'll be in bed asleep at ten."

"Where are you going?" he asked Orla.

"The Lep Inn."

"Where in God's name is that?"

"Leopard's Town, beside Foxrock."

"Why do you want to go all the way from one suburb to another? At least go into town."

"They've a bar extension till two and, as you said yourself, you can never get a ride out of town."

"Jesus, Orla, I always knew you were a bit of a square, but this takes the biscuit. Are you looking for a rich husband?"

Molly swirled the water around the teapot and laughed. "It's good to have yiz home all the same. A bit of craic."

"Where are you going all dressed up?" Patrick said. "Don't tell me you're going to the Lep Inn as well."

"I thought I'd catch Mass. Why don't you come along? You used be a great one for the religion."

"No, no. I got over it, thank God."

"It's not a disease. I had high hopes for you, you know."

"That he'd become as pious as our dear uncle?" Orla snorted.

Molly shrugged. "I raised a bunch of heathens."

"I have to dress up here just to go to bed." Patrick looked at his feet, with their two pairs of socks. "Without central heating I'm perished alive. How can you stand it? There's frost on the inside of the windows every morning. I can scrape it with my nail."

"I'm surprised you can do anything with those rubber gloves on." Molly poured the tea through the strainer into mugs.

"No wonder you stay in bed, Mammy," Orla said. "You're too weak to light a fire and clear it out and carry the coal scuttle to the shed. I worry about you. I noticed you've gone back to your old eating habits. A big casserole dish of bread pudding in the fridge. And you with high cholesterol. Honestly! At least Keelin kept you eating properly."

Molly cast her eyes down. "God save me from my children," she muttered.

"Orla is going to stay until Keelin comes back," Patrick said.

"That could be weeks for all we know. She'll lose her job."

"Fuck the job. I hate the shagging job. Jobs are two a penny over there. I can get another one in a jiffy. It's not exactly a career."

"Patrick, would you ever convince her to go back?" Molly said. "Don't leave me with Sporkin Reilly, here."

"Sporkin Reilly!" Orla narrowed her eyes. "Don't you fucking call me that, Mammy. I'm trying to take care of you and all you can do is call me names."

"Who was Sporkin Reilly, anyway?" Patrick asked.

"He was a mean little git in Cootehill near where she grew up. I don't see why she calls me that."

Molly sipped her tea ruminatively. "It's the classic case of the Irish parent. All the chicks returning to the nest like big fat cuckoos."

Orla sat in the jam-packed bar at the Leopard's Town Inn among her old friends and their husbands and wives, drinking Bacardi and Cokes. She must have been on her twelfth. At midnight, everybody joined hands and sang and kissed. Paper streamers and balloons buffeted back and forth. She pushed her way through the crowd and flew out the door. In the parking lot she found a quiet spot and, full of self-pity and booze, she wept. After a moment she took out her pocket mirror and touched up her streaked makeup, then walked back to the bar. She weaved through the crushed mass of bodies and sat down at the table. Her friend Trich put her arm around her.

"Are you all right?"

"I just went out for a bit. I was gasping for some air."

"Feeling queasy?" Trich leaned drunkenly toward her.

"No."

"I am."

Orla laughed. "Don't get sick on me, will ya?"

"Any word from Aisling?"

"Oscar got a letter from Japan. Keelin's gone to get her."

"You must miss her. You were so close."

"That was years ago. I haven't seen her in ages."

"It must be great to travel like that. I feel like such a bore. Staying in Ireland. Fair play to both of you."

"Ah, Trich, to tell the truth, you were lucky. I wish I had stayed." Big tears plopped from her eyes. Trich, surprised, gave her a hug.

"Orla, it'll be all right. Don't cry. Mick, get Orla another Bacardi, will ye? She's in dire need."

*

Aisling could be dead. Patrick looked at his mother, who was sitting with her eyes closed, listening to a Samuel Barber string quartet on CD. She would find this out soon, he thought, and it would break her heart. Oscar had been so cagey about the letter he received from Japan. What if it was news of Aisling's death, and he was just stalling until Molly died to break the terrible news? Adagio: slow and mournful. Patrick did not like to be manipulated by music. Those violins and cellos could pull at his heart, and their bows could scrape his private sorrows raw. He preferred the dissonances of the modern composers because they weren't indulgent; they repelled him and pushed him away and did not tinker with his propensity toward sentimentality. If Aisling were dead, they would scatter her ashes on the train tracks by the harbor, or cast them under the feet of emigrants so they might move more swiftly away from their own history.

"Put on what you like, Patrick," Molly murmured. "You can see what's on the telly."

"I'm all right. This is nice."

"Oh! Young Thomas rang earlier. Are you going out?"

"I might go to the pub for a good-bye pint. I want to spend the evening with you, though."

"Go out, Patrick," Molly said, sighing. "You're like a hen on a hot griddle."

"Maybe I will." Patrick stood up and walked to the living room window. He looked at the opposite row of Georgian houses. "I'll go and pack so."

"You haven't much to pack." Molly smiled at him affectionately. "You're a nice man, Patrick. You're probably the kindest out of the whole bunch."

Patrick crossed the room and, sitting on the arm of the chair, kissed her.

"Are you worried about immigration?" She patted his rubber hands.

"Sure, if they let me in, well and good, and if they don't, they don't."

"You know what he said in the thirties or forties?" Molly nodded to the stern picture of De Valera on the wall. "'No longer shall our children be raised like cattle for export.' Sometimes I am here on the street and I notice a slowness and wonder have we lost our best."

"I've heard all that crap before. Who cares? The ones who left left because they had nothing. I don't think humans sort themselves out according to merit, Mammy. Life is a lottery. You of all people should know that. A genetic, economic, historical lottery. All those little sperms and eggs. We won one lottery to become alive, so how could we win another? The laws of probability don't make it likely."

"The Lotto," Molly purred. "The drawing's tonight. Two million. What would you do with it, Paddy?"

"Round up the family and relocate to Hawaii. Start all over again in the sun, not the wind and fog and rain. That's why I'm going to try Las Vegas next. I want somewhere bright. Full of lights."

"I could never leave Ireland. Never have. I'm used to what I've got. I'd like to get the windows replaced, though. All the frames are rotting and the bathroom needs re-tiling. Or I'd buy a wee place of my own and give the rest of the money to you all to start businesses, so I wouldn't have to worry. That's what has me sick, you know. Poor Aisling — what could have got into her?"

"Be careful, Mammy. Aisling might be a lost cause. Don't lose Keelin for her. Don't throw good after bad. Siobhan has nothing better to do, but Keelin does, and she's very sensitive. She might get sucked under. Siobhan had to starve herself into an identity, but Keelin needs stability, I think. Even if she doesn't find Aisling, let her come home now."

"She'll find her. I know her — she won't come home till she's done. That's why I sent her. Aisling hadn't a bad bone in her body. The years are passing and you're all forgetting but I think of her every day. Such a child, always laughing and chatting and singing. Everyone loved her; she was so bright. That reminds me

— I'd get that piano tuned if I won. We've had it a long time. It's part of the family, but it's gone — sure I never play it at all now. I'm on the dole like the rest of the country."

Molly went to peel off Patrick's gloves, but he snapped his hand back and stood abruptly. She shrugged. "I'll leave you alone, Paddy. I'm sorry. But you should go to a doctor over there or that infection will spread like leprosy all through you, and then you won't know where you are."

"It's not like here. Doctors aren't for poor people."

"I know all about America," Molly said. "I read Conor O'Cleary's column in the *Times*. I also check the temperature in all the cities yiz are in. When I can keep track, that is. I wish I knew where Aisling was." She reached over and chose another CD.

"Mahler's Ninth? Mammy, you're really in a mood."

"I'm old, Patrick. My life is over. I need hints."

"Is that why you still go to Mass and keep the picture of the pope?"

"Just in case," Molly said. "Just in case. Like the Lotto."

"What do you do, Mammy? On all these long evenings."

"I practice my chipping in the garden, and I listen to music and watch the telly and read through the books. My mind is getting so bad I can read the classics over and over again and still forget the endings. She did me a great service, that old Protestant woman I worked for, making me read all those books. Listen to me now, sure I'm probably as old as she was then. She'd make me learn whole parts of it by heart."

"Do you remember any?"

"I can't remember where I left my glasses. I must have Alzheimer's."

"Would you stop announcing diseases."

A strangely lovely fervency, a yearning
Drove me to stray in fields and forests far
And when my heart was loosed, and tears came burning
I neared the threshold where no sorrows are.

"Go on," Patrick said to Molly.

"Ah, Patrick, I forget, I forget. Go for your drink — you're addling my head. We have the book if Keelin didn't take it with her. Aisling and Keelin were the ones who took to reading —"

"Is that the end of it? The poem?"

"No it's not, Patrick. It's a play, not a poem."

"It's a bit too much for me."

"I told you, Patrick, when you're my age you have to get hints. I'm thinking of compiling a book and CD collection called *Go Out with the Greats*."

Patrick raised his eyebrows. "You'll be awfully disappointed if these tests come back negative."

Patrick sat on the top of the bus on the way into town. This route was so familiar he felt the banality would shatter him. Orla was to follow in his footsteps next week. He was surprised that after New Year's Eve she'd conceded to return to the Bronx. Molly had been obviously relieved. Emigration is good training for death, he thought. If one of us dies far away, the rest would all be used to living with their absences.

The bus pulled in at Stillorgan. Aisling, this was your city too, he thought. Are you madder than me? Was the distance you kept so compelling, so magnetic? Your absence has entombed my family, retarded its growth. You took much of the lightness when you went and left this gravity. Are you as mad as me? as mad as my father? As the bus rattled down the duel carriageway toward Donnybrook, he thought he saw a void. He saw all their deaths. Aisling is dead. Molly will die and then Oscar and then Orla and then himself and then Siobhan and then little Keelin, the baby. And history would go on without them — or worse — as if they'd never existed. These nights drinking with his friends confirmed his decision to stay abroad even if he couldn't get treatment. The bus was skirting too close to the void: he could almost detect voices from it. More bread or I'll appear. Over the bump on Leeson Street Bridge, the canal murky and the swans asleep in the rushes. Then he dreamt Stephen's Green and he shut his eyes to wake up. Upstairs on the bus, passing Trinity College, his head leaning against the reverberating glass, Patrick was blind, his mouth open ready to roar. But between his teeth lay the enemy tongue, unable to expel a choking of native fear.

the dance of the shrimp

IT WAS THE STATION PLATFORMS that Aisling would remember in years to come. Osaka: the platform elevated and open to the city at night, the soaring commercial buildings, the neon jewelry, the pulse, the flash, Japan magnified, bending over backward, newly created, stretching itself, screaming in concentration.

Aisling taught English in Tokyo to businessmen who sat good-naturedly in orderly rows. One of them, Hiro, a middle-aged, unassuming executive, was a quick learner and a shy but chivalrous customer of the bar she hostessed in at night. It was on the twenty-eighth floor of an office building. For months he bought her drinks and paid her to sit and talk to further improve his English. Down there life cooked and steamed on the flimsy crust of earth, but here the city was the sky. Hiro drank whiskey, laughed at all her jokes, and tottered off home for the last subway to his wife and teenage kids.

One night in the elevator she bent and kissed his lips. He fled, and she thought he would never come back. Next evening in the advanced class he was attentive as usual, frowning over his verbs and sighing in relief when he conjugated correctly. He asked her after class to take the night off and took her to the huge, ultramodern Ana Hotel. They ate Japanese food in the hotel restaurant. Upstairs, in a plush room on the thirtieth floor, she strode across the room and yanked open the blinds. Ribbons of car lights interlaced through the crossroads of Akusaka, Roppongi, Toranomon, and Kasumigaseki. The sky was greenish black, and the moon, half obscured by clouds and oddly shaped, protruded like a buck tooth from the closed mouth of the night. She asked if he had seen the film *Tokyo Decadence,* and he shook his head. Then she stood on the low, wide windowsill, her body pressed against the chilling condensation of the giant plate of thick glass. A few lights were still on in the skyscraper opposite. Standing frozen by the mirror, he watched her peel her clothes off slowly. When she was naked she opened her arms wide and rubbed great wings for herself in the wet window. A trinity of shaggy red bushes beneath her arms and between her legs, breasts hanging massively, pink nipples the size of his clenched fists. She turned to face the city at night. Her back dripped with cold window water; her spine was a smooth valley rising from her ass to her neck. Legs apart, she pressed her cheek, breasts, and belly against the cool smeared glass, her eyes open, her lips parted. Hiro approached hesitantly, in his suit and tie, gasping in tiny breaths, brown gnawing eyes, hands unclenching, reaching upward to her.

He left that night to catch the last subway. Aisling took a bath and peeled the covers off the untouched bed, the sheets starched, cool, and soft to the touch. They had fucked against the window, aware of figures moving about in the opposite building; then he had taken a shower and, when he was dressed, extracted forty thousand in crisp yen from his wallet and placed it discreetly on the dresser. With a hint of apology he bowed, put on his elegant beige coat, and took his leave. In the morning, furious light came gobbling into the room and woke her prematurely. She rolled in the king-size bed, stretching her long body, and got up to shut the curtains, unwilling to be taken so raw into the empty belly of the new day. Tokyo was still half-asleep below. When she checked out at noon she stuffed into her bag two fluffy robes, razors, shampoos, soaps, toothbrushes, combs, shower caps, all the tea bags and snacks, and then pocketed the money. With a purposeful stride she walked to the subway for Ginza, where she gave a private piano lesson to a rich little girl.

On the evening of December twenty-sixth, Keelin and Siobhan arrived in Tokyo. Toru promised them they would stay with friends, but after several fruitless phone calls in Tokyo Station, he announced that they would have to stay in a hotel for one night. Keelin consulted her guidebook and they took the Marunouchi line to Shinjuku. The three backpackers made their way through a forest of neon, rows of restaurants and bars, and packs of drunken businessmen supporting each other, vomiting, stumbling, and shrieking.

"I thought the Japanese were meant to be reserved," Siobhan marveled. "Tokyo makes Dublin look like Kansas."

After they checked into a western-style room in the Sunlite Hotel, Toru spent an hour in the bathroom and then emerged as a woman.

"I'm going to Goruden Gai district. I will be back."

"What about Aisling?" Keelin said.

"I will find her, bring her back, but I have to be alone now. I can't bring *gaijin* with me. You go to Roppongi — plenty of foreigners there."

As he skipped down the corridor, Keelin stared dubiously in his wake. "Hmm. Our little Madame Butterfly is more reliable when he's a caterpillar. I don't think he's going to get her tonight. He's out for fun and games."

"Out to hustle some money, I'd say," Siobhan said.

"Let's follow him, just in case he finds her and she doesn't want to see us. Take the guidebook with you." Siobhan obediently grabbed her coat.

The two women trailed Toru's wiggling ass as he pressed eastward to a place of narrow streets and miniature bars. They lost him as he slipped into a hole-in-the-wall. Two transvestites blocked their entry, shaking their painted and bewigged heads gently but firmly. No bar wanted them as *gaijin* or women, both being anathema in this closed world. Back in Shinjuku, they stopped in a *yakitori-ya* and ate chicken balls, tofu, and green peppers on wooden skewers and watched the street thugs. A gangster fell asleep at the counter, and his pretty mistress ordered more food and drink and winked at them.

Everyone nodded and smiled when the sisters left the bar; even the gangster emerged from his torpor of slumber to wave and bow. He grinned at them, his gold and silver teeth catching the light, a degenerate magpie nest of a mouth, the fat tongue pulsating amidst the glitter.

Was Aisling alive? Keelin wondered. Could she peep through holes in the earth and whisper, say something? Because nothing was a lousy lead. Hadn't she read the fairy stories? Wasn't she afraid of witches? She should have known to leave pebbles, not bread crumbs. But she didn't leave bread crumbs; she left only doubts. If it was pride that prevented her from walking through that door, then she shouldn't have been afraid: they had all failed. The steps were too steep, and she had lost her legs. She had burst an eardrum and could no longer call. Was it sex? Had sex turned Aisling inside out until she saw nothing but her own red, blue, throbbing, slippery chaos of tripe and organs?

Toru did not come back the next night or the next. Keelin paced back and forth at the hotel and called Oscar for advice.

"You're so close. Wait a few nights."

"I don't even know if I'm close. She could be dead for all I know."

"Come on, Keelin. You've done well so far. A real little detective."

"I have a life, too. I'm being swallowed by her. Toru said she taught English and took tai chi lessons in the same place, some kind of center for night classes. I'm going to try to find out which one."

"Tai chi? I thought that was Chinese."

"So it is. He could be making it up. The man's a lunatic."

"Look. I understand your frustration. I think you're a topper. Try the night school. Do you need more money?"

Keelin hesitated. "Yes. I'm sorry. We're trying to be frugal. It's very expensive. I'm trying to keep Siobhan from every temple and kabuki show. I wish this was all over. I hadn't counted on it being so convoluted."

"The money's not a problem. Don't worry. Anything to do with Aisling would be complicated."

"Yeah, well, say a prayer for us."

"Sure. Sure I will." She turned to the sleepy Siobhan and said, "Do you think he's a bank robber? Priests don't make that kind of money."

"Maybe he's selling indulgences."

"Or his soul to the devil, more like." Keelin began to undress. "Did you find anything in the phone book under English classes?"

"It's all in Japanese, strangely enough."

"Oh, Siobhan." Keelin raised her voice. "Did you even look?"

"Let's ask at the desk. They'll know."

"You spend hours looking in the mirror or deciding which tourist attraction you want to visit next. I'm doing all the work. I brought you with me to help, you know. You're behaving as if we're on holidays. I don't think you even care about finding Aisling."

"Don't get your knickers in a knot." Siobhan climbed under the covers and turned her back. "And don't get all high and mighty either. I haven't seen you refuse to come to one temple, so don't blame it all on me. We might as well milk Oscar. God knows, nobody ever gave us anything in our lives." She flipped over and faced Keelin. "We lived our whole lives with Molly, and it never even occurred to her to take us to the seaside or a fun fair or a circus or anything. It was Aisling who used to take us in to see Santa in town. She used be there at sports day and swimming galas to see us lose. When I came in last in my swimming race, I got to the end and realized everybody was waiting for me. I was mortified getting out of that pool. It was Aisling who was sitting in the audience clapping loudly and cheering anyway, not Mammy. She told me I was the best swimmer stylistically and speed did not matter in real life but *style* did."

"Molly was busy, Siobhan."

"She loved only Aisling."

"That's not true and you know it. You should have seen how excited she was every Christmas when yiz all came home. And I used to go drinking with her on Thursdays. Just the two of us. I loved those evenings."

"She only did that so's you'd go look for Aisling for her."

"Bullshit."

"She got rid of you too."

A few nights later there was a knock on their door. Keelin put on a robe and opened it. Toru smiled coyly at her, then walked past and flopped on the bed. With no makeup and his curly hair dirty and messy, he looked uncharacteristically shabby. He still wore the tight red dress and heels, but his stockings had runs and sagged at the knees. Siobhan seemed genuinely pleased to see him; she gave him a hearty hug and pushed his hair off his face. He had a bruise beneath his eye and his lip was swollen.

"What happened?"

"I fell over a straw and a hen pecked me." Toru smiled at her shyly.

"Oh, I know who taught you that. That's a real Irish one." Siobhan laughed.

Keelin sat on Siobhan's bed opposite them. "Toru. We were relying on you."

"I look Aisling for you."

Keelin stared at him. "What happened to your grammar? You almost sounded Japanese, not Irish, for a minute."

"I can't find Aisling," he blubbered. Tears swelled in his blood-shot eyes and oozed onto his bruised cheeks. "My Aisling."

"She's not your Aisling — she's *our* Aisling," Keelin said coldly. "What's the matter, you were so bloody sure of yourself before?"

"She's not in the bar," he sniveled. "She was hostess. Men would pay money to drink with her. She always was there. None of her friends know. She's gone."

"Was she a whore?" Siobhan asked lightly.

"Let's just sit down and get the chronology in order for a minute," Keelin said in exasperation. "We got a card in 1986 with an address in Tokyo. My mother wrote back but the letter was returned. That was eight years ago. We can assume she has been here since? No?"

"Aisling could pass for a man." Toru nodded somberly. "She wore a mustache and beard and a suit and tie. Her hair she put back in a ponytail or a hat. She was tall — a giant among Japanese. She was beautiful. We would go out as a couple. There is no one like her in the world. She has powers."

"Powers?" Siobhan's eyes widened. Toru nodded gravely.

"Toru." Keelin's lips whitened. "If you don't tell the fucking truth I'm going to beat you harder than the last person who apparently got his hands on you, so help me God. I've had it up to fucking here. Enough! For Christ's sake."

Siobhan turned to Keelin. "Stop behaving like such a bully. Toru will tell us in his own way. Won't you, Toru? Maybe she *was* his Aisling, not ours. I haven't seen her in fifteen years. I don't know her. Toru, hop in the shower and get some rest. You can have my bed. I'll sleep with Keelin." She took him by the hand and gave him a towel and a robe. "Don't you mind her, Toru. She doesn't even believe in horoscopes. Hey! What's your sun sign?"

"Gemini," Toru said meekly.

"See!" Siobhan looked at Keelin significantly. Keelin glowered at them.

The next night they went to the bar where Aisling had worked. They learned the name of the evening school and were advised to go on the evenings she had taught, hoping to meet some of her pupils. Toru brought them to a friend of his, and she said they could stay in her apartment. She had bleached blond hair, one eyebrow pierced, and a plain, studious face with almond shaped eyes and no lashes. Her name was Michiko. The place was tiny. They felt her trepidation.

"We all sleep floor; no shoes in house," she told them.

The town was Kokobunji, thirty minutes outside Tokyo by

train. Michiko was a ceramic artist. She also worked at Kentucky Fried Chicken a few days a week for extra cash.

"I think picture of Aisling," she said, flipping through a myriad of albums on her shelves. "Ah, yes. You look."

A snapshot of Aisling, Michiko, and a black woman with narrow dreadlocks down to her waist. The three were sitting around a wooden table covered with brown clay pots. All were smiling. Keelin and Siobhan stood shoulder to shoulder, gazing at the photo for minutes.

"Fatima. African. Very good artist."

"Look how old Aisling is. When was this taken?"

Michiko cocked her head puzzled.

"When photo?" Keelin modified the question.

"Ah . . . lass year, I think. No, summer, May. Before Fatima go. This year."

Siobhan shook her head. "I thought we were looking for a young girl."

Keelin continued to stare at the photo. "She's thirty-six now, I guess. I never thought of that." She sat on the floor, perturbed. "She was only twenty when she took the boat."

"What is Fatima like?" Siobhan asked.

"She hard work. Came Japan make ceramics want to learn Japanese way. Like Japanese art very much. She know much on it. She with Sadao. I not know him. They both go United States. I not see Aisling after photo. Take it if you like it."

Keelin looked at Aisling's freckled face, with its small features, her curly red hair tied back. Fatima had a high forehead, sharp cheekbones, and full lips. She looked formidable.

"They were in love?" Keelin asked.

Michiko sighed. "I . . . they fight and, yes, love, but Fatima tired and love Sadao. Always on, always off. Aisling wild, big power. Sadao slow, easy, quiet. Fatima love two maybe. Aisling love everybody she want."

"So Aisling's a big dyke," Siobhan mused. "Mammy'll be pleased to hear all the progress we're making."

Keelin sucked in her cheeks and raised her eyebrows. "And engaging in priapic commerce."

"What's that?"

"A whore."

"I knew you were freaking out over that. I could feel it. Picking on poor Toru. You're so sheltered and sanctimonious, you know. Ms. little Irish *muinteoir*, living with Mammy all your life. We all left, the rest of us. Life is hard out here."

"Moontore?" Michiko said.

"*Muinteoir*. It means teacher. I was a teacher in Ireland."

"Yes? Very nice."

"It was nice, yes." Keelin turned to Siobhan. "Listen. You think Ireland is a doddle, you little stick insect. I think, for a wee Irish muinteoir who arrives in London to find her anorexic sister stalked by some lout, arrives in Japan to run around with a spaced-out transvestite, discovers her other sister is a cross-dressing bull dyke — I think I'm taking it all very well, thank you very much."

"Did you fuck Toru? That night I heard you."

"Then why ask?"

"You didn't even have a condom, did you?"

"I don't want to discuss it. It didn't go that far. I was drunk."

Michiko looked from one to the other, bewildered.

"And I'm not anorexic. So stop saying that."

"This small place," Michiko said, frowning. "Please no fight."

Hiro took only one English class a week now. This new teacher was an earnest Canadian man, the class was not exactly dull, but he thought he might give it up altogether and find some other way to maintain his English. Recently, to come to these rooms and corridors without Aisling filled him with dread.

Hiro was a compact man, always impeccably dressed. He was in his mid-fifties, but other than a fan of lines around each eye his face remained supple and tight. He had risen to a top position in his company and had an attentive wife and studious children. When he was a child, his father, a scientist, had taken the family to live in New Jersey for five years. These days he had the opportunity to travel frequently to the West on business. London, New York, Los Angeles, Paris — cities familiar to a man of his stature. Once a year he went to Hawaii with his family, and once a year to a famous shrine in Japan. He had climbed Mount Fuji. He loved his country: the startling natural beauty, the refined customs, the exquisite arts and crafts, the grace and gentility of the people, the isolated complexity of its history. He had once met the emperor at a function. Proud of Japan's economic success and democratic tradition since World War II, he was unfailingly courteous toward foreigners.

Now his fingers fucked the wool-lined, suede gloves. He pulled them on tightly, almost giving himself an erection in the process. Aisling had awakened something in him, left him at a point where everything was sexualized. His equilibrium had been upset. As he wrapped his silk scarf around his neck and exited the classroom, vowing to never return, to spend his time in the company of males, he halted in his tracks in the corridor. Aisling had come back, come to put a lid on his shocking yearning, or to release the last of what he had left in him.

"Aisling, you have grown so small. Down to my size." He smiled broadly. "To fit me now."

Keelin's mouth dropped open. Siobhan giggled. "She's not Aisling. We're her sisters. We've come to find her."

Toru, wearing jeans and a coat, spoke to him in English. "Do you know if she is in Tokyo?"

Hiro looked about. "I have to go. My wife is expecting me."

"Wait. Do you know anything about her?" Keelin pleaded. "The other teachers say she just disappeared without a trace. She never turned up for class in November and they haven't heard anything since. Any information might help."

Hiro thought for a moment, staring at Keelin. "Tomorrow, seven-thirty. Meet me at the entrance here and I shall bring you to dinner."

"What about me?" Siobhan said.

"Please, we have so little time," Keelin said. "Tell us what you know now."

He walked out, bowing to them. "Tomorrow, you and your sister." He disappeared into the crowd.

"And what about me?" Toru said, flicking his head back. "I knew I should have worn my dress."

"You come anyway," Siobhan said. "It's New Year's Eve, after all."

"For God's sake, you two," Keelin told them. "This is business."

"It's been a hoot so far," Siobhan said.

Hiro took them in a taxi to a restaurant somewhere in Tokyo. Toru wore a beaded white gown, his hair piled up, one corkscrew lock draped coyly over the side of his face. He looked exquisite, and Hiro reluctantly allowed him to join them. They sat for two and a half hours consuming an elaborate affair of tiny, beautifully arranged dishes.

"This puffer fish, great delicacy," Hiro told the women. "Many amateurs die trying to prepare poisonous fish as this. Juices can make people zombies, living dead. In Haiti it is voodoo fish. People buried alive believed to be dead and then smuggled to Dominican Republic to work as slaves." He laughed. "Your sister told me this information. She talked of the world as her village, and it was."

"I know Aisling very well," Toru sniffed. "Very political. Knew everything about workers and poor people in every country."

Hiro nodded. "This is dancing shrimp. Great delicacy. Skin peeled away alive and lemon squeezed. They in pain and dance in agony in mouth. You must try."

Siobhan ate some and smiled. "Ooooh!"

"Still move about in tummy, no?" he said gleefully.

The kimono-clad waitress brought plate after plate. "Now we switch to sake," Hiro announced imperiously, signaling the waitress. They had been drinking beer. "This snapper is cut on table lengthwise; we slice sideways so we can eat in strips. If you eat with eyes rolling in head, this is expensive, because still living."

Siobhan devoured two slices of the fish. Hiro smiled appreciatively. "Your sister has quite an appetite."

It was true. Siobhan was eating every tiny bite-size portion put in front of her. Keelin declined to eat the more graphic foods. "I see cruelty is a spice," she remarked.

Hiro shook his head, holding his chopsticks aloft. "No, no. Freshness. Freshness, not cruelty. These are only fish, after all. You have to kill the food to eat it. Do you think they give it anesthetic in kitchen?"

Toru said, "Aisling was a vegetarian."

"But she ate fish," Hiro countered, and the two men glared at each other.

"Well, that's hypocritical. Just cause fish aren't mammals. They feel pain," Keelin said. She poured sake into little cups.

"Don't pour your own drink." Hiro put his hand lightly on the bottle. "In Japan, always companion pour drinks for one another."

"Oh? That's a new one on me. I guess to stop you drinking alone." Siobhan deftly picked up some ginger with her chopsticks and ate it to cleanse her palate in preparation for the next tasty torture.

"Aisling understood contradiction. She held opposing ideas quite easily in her mind," Hiro said.

"Not when it came to big business and greedy capitalists." Toru smiled sweetly at Hiro, fluttering his false lashes so that they looked like spider legs doing the cancan. He reached over and poured his own sake. They had not yet spoken one word of Japanese.

"If you cut out meat and fish," Siobhan said, "there would be nothing left.

"And you'd be a pain in the arse to travel with," Keelin said. "I always detected a note of Puritanism in vegetarians. Them and idiots who won't have TVs on point of principle."

"Aisling would not eat meat or fish by herself," Toru said. "But if she went out in company or visited one's home she ate what was put before her."

"Good manners," Hiro agreed.

"Well, Mammy would be proud," Keelin said sarcastically.

"You are hostile to your sister," Hiro said. The waitress set down yet more tiny plates.

"No. She was a mother to Siobhan and me growing up." Keelin drained another sake and Hiro refilled her glass. She looked at her plate and sighed. "O.K., Hiro, what's this and is it going to start wrestling with my tongue?"

Outside the restaurant, Hiro pulled Keelin aside. "Come with me. I can take you to Aisling."

"What about the others?"

"No, only two of us allowed. Special place."

"What's going on?" Siobhan asked. "What are you two conspiring about?" Keelin told her, and Siobhan shrugged. "Go ahead. It's worth a try. Toru wants to take me to a club for New Year's. We can ask there. People knew her at this place."

Toru shook his head. "The girls come with me, Hiro-san."

Hiro took him aside and slipped him a bank note. Toru grabbed it and demanded his business card. Hiro warily handed him one.

"We know where you work, so be careful with her or I come and make a scene. And believe you me, salaryman, I can make a scene. Go, Keelin. It's O.K. Here is a pass for the club. The address is on the pass."

"He seems harmless enough," Siobhan said. "We'll see you at the club later."

"Harmless?" Keelin said. "Ask any fish that same question."

When Hiro and Keelin left in a taxi, Siobhan bit her lip. "Did you just sell Keelin?"

"I know who he is — she can handle him. Come, let's party." Toru flashed the bank note. "My treat for once. You pay for everything so far."

Siobhan was suddenly sober. "Aisling disappeared from that school and he was her pupil. She disappeared from the bar and he was a client."

In the Ana Hotel, Keelin stood by the fountain in the expansive marble lobby. Hiro came with a key. His face was now grave and meditative. They said nothing in the lift. Keelin went straight to the window in the thirtieth-floor room and opened the blinds. Her sister was down there, devoured by the foaming neon mouth of modern Japan.

"So what's the story?" Keelin said. "Where's my sister? Where's this special place? I see nothing here."

Hiro sat on a chair, looking past her to the window, concentrating. "Stand on the windowsill," he whispered. "Take your clothes off."

"Is that what you paid Aisling to do?"

"You are so like her."

"I look like her."

"No. Your expressions, everything," he said softly. "It's like having her back with me."

Keelin sat on the sill looking at the office building that towered opposite, "What was she to you, Hiro-san?"

"She took me somewhere and I paid her well. Every Wednesday. I paid for all the pillows, towels, robes, drinks she stole. She opened the night and showed me worms of light." He wiggled his ten fingers graphically.

Keelin looked down, her hair rubbing a patch in the condensation. "It's so quiet here. Like watching a silent screen. The city is seething and our heads are numb to it."

He walked to the window and stood by her. "She was tall and had such strength. Every Wednesday we make sex at window. Such sex. Hours and hours. In bath, in corridor, on chair. She had appetite. The English word is insatiable. And a teacher too. Listen to Toru speak better grammar than I. She, only she, could teach that gutter child. Words, so much words. Your sister had genius."

"What a waste," Keelin said, taking her head from the pane and wiping her wet forehead. She turned to Hiro. His cock was erect in his hand and he was rubbing it. Keelin leapt up.

"Aisling."

"Fuck off. I'm not standing in for her. Excuse me, I've to get the last train to Kokobunji."

"There's time. I'll pay for taxi. You can sleep here. I will go."

"No thanks." She tried to push past.

"Forgive me. I will tell you where she is. What I've done to her."

Keelin sat down warily. "Tell me."

He took out a thick wad of yen from his wallet, his cock tucked away but obviously erect in his trousers.

"Sit in your underwear." He offered the money.

"No. I don't need your dick or your money. Where's my sister?"

"Aisling was wiser than you. She always took any money I offered. She knew what she was worth. There was no shame."

"She was worth more than you could pay her." Keelin sat back on the windowsill, pulling her winter coat around her.

"What does your name mean?"

"It's from the Irish Caoilfhionn, meaning tall and fair." Keelin shrugged. "It doesn't fit."

"Aisling means dream."

"That I know."

He took off his coat and jacket and sat on the bed. "Have you ever thought she does not exist? You are chasing a dream?"

"Is she dead?"

"I am dead." He took his tie off. "Chasing a nightmare."

"Did you kill her?"

"She killed me. Skinned me alive. Made me feel touch. Now everything hurts. I lay on the floor in that bathroom and she would piss on me. Like squeezing lemon. She tied me up. Once she led me through the street blindfolded. She beat me with a belt. . . . Now I am left to dance this dance. You understand. I loved her. More than my children, more than my wife. More than my parents. More than Japan. I wanted to leave and live with her, be a slave."

"When did you last see her?"

"Ha! Like everyone else, November. I don't know more than the fools in the school. In the end it must have been just money for her. Money to go chase after that black bitch. Aisling, you left me nothing. Skinned alive, these silks and cottons scrape my body like knives." He took his shirt off. Keelin stood slowly, nervously. He approached her, wild-eyed. She climbed onto the sill and he slid his hands up her thighs under her dress. He pulled her tights down and buried his head between her legs, lapping like a cat at a milk bowl. She might have stopped him but it felt nice. She rolled her eyes in their sockets, as if they were dials that would tune in her sister, that would reach through the vein-patterned kaleidoscope and find Aisling's throat and grab it. She came sputtering into his fish-obsessed mouth, and he pulled her toward him.

"Aisling. So clever," he whispered. "You send your sister to join me to you. I will take care of you, Keelin. You I can live my life with. You earth and she sky. I can keep all I've worked for and stay in Tokyo. She takes care of those she chooses. It was not just money."

Keelin pulled away. "No, Hiro. I have to go. You can't tell me anything, so I'm back to square one. I know it mightn't look like it, but it's for my mother."

"Beat me!"

"I'm not going to squeeze any lemon on you, Hiro."

Hiro sat sheepishly on the bed, rubbing his face. Then he got up to go to the bathroom. "Wait for me. Let me get dressed, and I'll see you to a taxi."

Keelin hurried out the door, closing it quietly. Watching the door as she waited for the lift, she pressed the button continuously. Come on. Come on.

On the dance floor, Siobhan waved her thin arms above her head wiggling and shaking, biting her bottom lip in concentration. Toru spotted Keelin and left his group to run to her. She grabbed him and hugged him. Pleased, he led her by the hand to the table and handed her a drink with a paper umbrella. "Take this," he said, pressing a small white pill in her hand. She swallowed, washing it down with the frozen cocktail. Siobhan came over and kissed her.

"Keelin, are you all right? I felt as if I'd lost my arm." She squeezed in beside them in the booth.

"Is it midnight yet?" Keelin asked.

"Oh yes. An hour ago. Don't tell me you didn't notice." Toru gasped dramatically. "Nineteen ninety-five, stay alive!"

They ordered drinks and went back onto the dance floor. Keelin sat alone in the booth and worried until Siobhan and Toru came back to her and dragged her up. The rave music throbbed, Keelin felt the pill take effect, and she danced hard. Siobhan hugged her and she hugged Siobhan and Siobhan put her slender arm out and pulled Toru toward them and the three embraced in a trinity full of love and booze and drugs. The anorexic, the teacher, and the beautiful transvestite, high in the sky in Tokyo.

Hiro sat naked at the windowsill all night. He drew with his finger Aisling's outline in the condensation, licking the water off his hand sadly. Here the city was the sky. He slashed his skin with razors he took from the bathroom and lay upright into the traced figure on the glass, mixing blood and water. At five in the morning, two shocked hotel porters ran to him as he stumbled, naked and bleeding, into the pristine lobby. Bloody footprints on the marble, cheeks sliced open like floppy gills. His eyes rolling in his head.

Keelin and Siobhan had to leap, duck, and maneuver to avoid the carts rattling through the narrow aisles of the fish market. Toru, agile in his stilettos and white gown, sashayed among the boxes and gutty slush. "I'll ruin my best gown," he fretted, hiking it up over his knees. "This was meant to be my wedding dress."

"Don't worry — the bride should stink of fish," Keelin said as they weaved in single file through the chaotic ballet. Tentacles, suction cups, scales, legs, gills, fins, color. Red, white, purple, blue, silver. Gray tuna the size of cows. Carcasses stacked in rows were pushed through buzz saws. Eels lying in pools of blood in silver tins. Shipped from Africa, from Alaska, from everywhere. Fish on scales, on carts, on tables. Cut, halved, gutted, packed. Yellow eyes, jelly eyes. It was their silence that made this massacre a celebration.

A young man in a black rubber suit and apron rammed a wire down a fish throat and wiggled it about.

"Did you see that fish's eyes?" Siobhan asked her younger sister.

"Fishicide?" Keelin stared at the man in the rubber suit.

As Toru spoke to the young man, he grew grave. He turned to Keelin. "He wants to talk to you. He says his brother knew Aisling. He himself has met her."

The man said more to Toru, his soft eyes flickering from the fish to the resplendent beaded gown.

"His brother was gay. The family had hopes for Aisling, even though she was *gaijin*. At least she was woman. He says they are in Hawaii on some cult farm."

The man looked around nervously and, grabbing a flipping fish by the tail, shoved the wire down its throat.

"He says they got a postcard from Hawaii from the two."

"Can we see that card?" Keelin asked.

"It's at his parent's house in Ise. He goes there next week. You will have to wait."

"All right," Keelin rooted for pen and paper in her bag. "It is our only lead at the moment, and waiting is something I'm well used to by now. Arrange a meeting. What's his name?"

"Yasuyuki is his brother's name. His name is Yoshitada."

"Ya and Yo!" Siobhan exclaimed.

Toru gave the man their number and made a date. Then they left the market to walk by the water. Seagulls whirled around the riverbanks as the ships pulled out. Bloody fish heads were piled behind a wooden crate, their mouths wide open and eyes gone.

Keelin walked through the streets of Kokobunji and up the stairs to Michiko's tiny apartment, where her sister waited.

"We're going to Hawaii," she pronounced grimly.

"Yahoo!" Siobhan leapt up and hugged her. Then drew back. "When?"

"We have to get a ticket. I bargained with dear Uncle Oscar. He's going to send some money."

"I'd like a few more days with Yoshitada."

"That good, eh?" Keelin sighed and slumped onto the floor. "I'm weary, I am."

Siobhan sat beside Keelin and stroked her hair. "It's amazing, you know. We can't speak a word to each other but the sex is wonderful."

"Yeah? Do you make him wear his rubber apron?"

"Maybe he will come to Hawaii with us. I could get Toru to ask him."

"Why on earth would he do that?" Keelin sat up abruptly.

"To get his brother."

"Not everyone wants their siblings back."

Toru left Tokyo before they did. Siobhan permed his hair, and they drank a good-bye sake with Michiko in her apartment. His brother had requested his presence in Kobe — the family was making another vain attempt to sort Toru out. "It happens every so often." Toru delicately held a tiny sake cup, plastic rollers in his hair. "I go to Kobe and my brother tries to get me an office job. One day I'll go to Kobe as a woman and meet him off the train. One day, but not today." He patted the curlers nervously.

"When you leave?" Michiko asked Keelin.

"Oh, I'm sorry," Keelin said. "My uncle's money is taking some time to get through. We leave on the twentieth, for sure. You have been so kind. We're going to take you and Toru to dinner tonight. For all you've done."

Michiko smiled in relief. "Can I see plane tickets?"

After finishing the sake, they went to a small bar. Yoshitada sat against the wall, Siobhan leaning back on his chest. Michiko and her girlfriend sat opposite, with Toru and Keelin at the end of the table.

"Aisling sang when we come here," Toru said. "I love Irish songs. All the sad ones."

"You are wonderful," Siobhan said, grabbing his hand. "Sing us a sad song — go on."

He perked up instantly. "'Danny Boy'?"

"Oh God!" Keelin and Siobhan groaned in unison.

"That's my mother's song," Keelin told Michiko. "It's pretty dreadful. Everything I hate about home. I can't believe Aisling would teach him that."

Toru stood for the occasion and straightened his bunched skirt. He cleared his throat and bowed to the table.

"Oh Danny boy, the pipes, the pipes are calling, from glen to glen and down the mountainside." As he sang he held his arms out melodramatically and moved around the table. Leaning down he cupped his hands around Siobhan's face. "And when ye come and all the flowers are dying . . ." He swung his hips seductively. "If I am dead, as dead I may well be . . ." His voice was shaky but held the tune. He ran his hands through Yoshitada's thick hair, and Yoshitada pulled his head away roughly. "And I shall hear tho' soft you tread above me . . ." Toru winked at Michiko and her girlfriend, who giggled. "And all my grave will warmer sweeter be." He moved back to Keelin, reaching his arms toward her. "If you will bend and tell me that you love me, then I shall sleep in peace until you come to me." Keelin, shaking her head in amusement, joined in the chorus. She sang in an overblown manner to counter Toru's pitiful sincerity: "But come ye back when summer's in the meadow, or when the valley's hushed and white with snow. 'Tis I'll be there in sunshine or in shadow, oh Danny boy, oh Danny boy, I love you so."

Toru wiped his eyes. "That and 'Scarlet Ribbons' and 'The Last Rose of Summer' always make me cry."

Keelin poured him a drink. "You're a sentimentalist, Toru."

"Your sister, she taught me. Maybe she'll never come to take me home with her."

"You can come visit us," Siobhan said. "And bring my rubber man." She patted Yoshitada's arm. He wore civilian clothes, but was still beautiful while not killing fish. Yoshitada kissed her neck.

"Sing us a happy one now," Michiko pleaded, and Keelin sang "Dicey Reilly," while the Japanese clapped along, uncomprehending.

The day after Toru went to Kobe, the earthquake struck. Michiko telephoned his mother and aunt in Hiroshima. Toru's brother's house had collapsed, killing everyone inside, including his wife and baby girl. His mother had not known Toru had gone to Kobe. She cried now, thinking he was dead as well. Japan was in chaos.

Siobhan and Keelin clung to each other like limpets. "We have to find Aisling now," Siobhan murmured. "It's so easy to die."

"Toru left his camera," Keelin said. "With the film still in it."

"That's good. Maybe we can start to record our family history."

"How can someone so ridiculous be seriously dead?" Keelin asked. "Maybe he never even got that train. Maybe he's in the golden-boy district. He was right, though — Aisling never came back for him."

Michiko watched them, her face frozen, her hands crossed on her lap. "Yes, girls. Time to leave Japan. Time to go."

Aisling had prowled the streets, a hat on her head. Toru held her hand and they slid through Tokyo's alleys and bars. Now he wore a low-cut green silk gown and a black lamb's wool cloak. Aisling wore a beautifully cut designer suit that Hiro had bought for her and a fake mustache.

In one bar they found a man they were both attracted to and took him behind a curtain. Aisling had a plastic penis strapped on. She sodomized the stranger while Toru held the man's head and tenderly kissed his oblivious lips. He put his cock in the man's mouth and the man moaned happily. A true cultural exchange.

On the crowded subway she put her hands under Toru's cloak and tickled his stomach. He shrieked and squirmed like a child, but she gripped him tighter. Her fingers wiggled, prodded, and played his muscles like piano keys. Struggling to escape, he howled in awful mirth as the drunk businessmen watched. What did they see? A pretty Japanese girl in an elegant gown playing with a Western man, red hair in a long plait snaking out from a black hat. A bohemian couple breaking taboos. Japan was breaking apart, but for now the businessmen, heading home to their families, were not afraid of the changing shapes. Laughter rocked the carriage as it slinked under the riotous, hungry, attentive city.

Gliding up the escalators in tender embrace, they pierced Tokyo's throbbing heart, the neon lights calling from street to street and down the building's sides. Aisling talked all night of revolution, and Toru, who did not care much for the content, politics being insubstantial to such a fleeting eel as he, begged her instead for more songs. She understood but lectured all the same, for his edification, her best and brightest pupil. She saved the treat for last, when they were good and drunk and Toru's gown had slipped a little, exposing his flat chest and one budlike nipple. She held him in her arms and sang. He purred with satisfaction, listening breathlessly to all the words she had given him.

> The summer's gone and all the roses dying,
> 'Tis you must go and I must bide.

Aisling mocked his easily shed tears and pinched his cheek so hard she left two purple marks on his adoring, gullible face.

three

the old goat in the temple

OSCAR WAS A PRIEST in North Carolina when he first came to the States, and Gerry was a pest who loitered by the church so often that Oscar made him an altar boy. Gerry was fourteen years old, tall, gangly, and incapable of slow motion. If he was asked to cross the room, he would bolt within the space of a few meters. His coarse sandy hair stood out at all angles, and he had a long, reedy face, punctured with gray tinfoil eyes. A middle-aged couple who owned a convenience store and two petrol pumps by the side of the road adopted him at two weeks old. Gerry adored his mother, played with dolls, ignored boys, and trailed after his sister and her girlfriends. "I was the classic gay stereotype," he would say, years later, to anyone who'd listen. "When I was five I used to sleep with my grandfather on the farm. As he slept I tried to stick my toe into the slit in his long johns. Making passes at smelly old Gramps at five — now that's deeply gay."

When Oscar came to the parish, Gerry proceeded to stalk the young priest. Oscar had a bookish demeanor. He was courteous and easygoing with the congregation. If his sermons lacked conviction and passion, they were at least brief. Gerry smoked cigarettes in the garden of the little house beside the church, and Oscar eyed him nervously from his kitchen window as he dried the dishes. Altar boy was not a vocation for which Gerry was suited: he enjoyed wearing the robes and parading about the altar, but he rattled the bells whenever it suited him, failing to coincide with the appropriate parts of the liturgy. He served naked under the white robe and pulled it over his head to change in the tiny sacristy. Oscar knew Gerry was trouble.

One summer night Oscar sat on his porch nursing a whiskey in a crystal glass. Besides books, he had brought a few pieces of crystal — a decanter, fruit bowl, and glasses — as the only mementos from home. The thickness of the heat compressed and dehumanized him. Gasping for cool air and life on the peeling wooden swing, he felt himself reduced to caricature. This was not his home; this bed with brass posts and patchwork quilt had him choking on his dreams, lathered in homesickness. Loneliness rang in his ears; frustration welled his features into an uneven shape. At moments like this — the crickets bloated and thunderous, the heat from the stars as hot as the sun, the swamp of a black night sunk around him — he was his own god. Self-created with a mutilated soul. Alone in an emptied universe. Molly's letters were his sole contact with home, yet his Irishness was his only root in this weedlike, celibate life of a country priest in the wrong country. There was a sudden movement in the grass, and he almost cried out in supplication. Gerry was the last thing he wanted to face, this mutant, sly, gooselike boy. Limbs all jerks and affected spasms, face perpetually jeering and unsolemnly coy, bursts of laughter misplaced and too loud. Oscar wanted to hurl a rock but instead sat like a rat in a trap on the porch.

"My mom baked some Irish soda bread for you at the shop." Gerry slyly left the brown packet at the priest's feet like an offering.

"Thank your mother for me," Oscar said thinly. "Now run along like a good wee boy."

"Can I have some whiskey?" The boy's face was slippery and pale, lit by starlight. Oscar shut his eyes. Sweat trickled down his back and his muscles went taut against the unpleasant sensation.

"Gerry, would you ever stop acting the maggot and just go."

The boy peacocked up the steps and grabbed the glass from

him, but it slipped and broke; the whiskey seethed about the crystal and seeped into the wooden boards. Gerry shrieked in fright and ran into the grass. He yelped, tumbled, jumped, and jiggled in diagonals, ovals, and pentagons, looping wildly through the garden, calling out in gargles and whoops. The crickets rose to his cartwheel of choruses as the boy leapt through the waist-high grass, tearing at the paralysis of the night. The priest sat on the porch watching.

A week later, Gerry arrived at the door dressed in a crisp white shirt, his hair slicked back, and wearing long trousers for the first time. Oscar had noticed he was the only fourteen-year-old in the area still in short pants. He presented the priest with a bunch of wildflowers. When he accepted the flowers, Oscar had a W. B. Yeats book in his hand.

"Come in."

The boy was uncharacteristically deferential; he even bowed slightly as he passed Oscar in the hall.

"What are you up to now, eh?" Oscar said. "Are these from your mother too?"

"I picked them myself for you, Father," the boy drawled.

Oscar closed the door slowly. "Would you like to hear some poetry?"

The boy looked at the book and grinned. "Folks around here are starting to think Mr. Yeats was one of the lost apostles." Oscar blushed. He had a tendency to quote more from Irish poetry than the Bible in his snippets of sermons.

Gerry sipped a lemonade in the living room while Oscar read from the small blue book of verse.

"I'd prefer to hear a song, Father," Gerry said politely after the fourth poem in the collection.

Oscar gulped his whiskey and nodded. "You've been a good listener. I can do that much for you."

> 'Tis the last rose of summer left blooming all alone,
> All her lovely companions are faded and gone
> No flower of her kindred, no rosebud is neigh,
> To reflect back her blushes and give sigh for sigh.

Gerry gazed into his empty lemonade cup and Oscar stopped singing, self-conscious. He cleared his throat. "Who knows you're here?"

Gerry's eyes darted up in surprise. "No one."

"You have the fingers of an Ethiopian."

"What's that?" Gerry did not look at his long fingers.

"I spent six months in Africa, but I wasn't suited for the missions. I got malaria the third week."

"Did you see elephants and tigers?"

"Ireland has a lot of contact with Africa. Seems like everyone does a stint there for some reason or other. Who's going to save Africa from the Irish . . . ?" his voice trailed off. Gerry stood. Oscar eyed him. "You best be off then, boy."

Gerry was almost as tall as the priest. His hair shone with grease. In his gaunt, wily face, the eyes were nonreflective. As they paused in the hall, Oscar could see the boyish freckles fading into manhood. They leaned toward each other, Gerry straining slightly, and their lips brushed dryly.

"There are no tigers in Africa, Gerry." Oscar kissed him again.

For three risky years they were lovers in the little wooden church house with the unkempt garden. Many days, practicing the tin whistle on the porch while the boy lounged about the house, Oscar expected a group of gentlemen in hoods to appear on the lawn at any minute. But the boy was the only respite for him in those southern, sultry days when he itched to move in a more sophisticated sphere, making odd trips to New York to the opera and ballet. He might have been snookered forever in North Carolina, but he met a powerful Jesuit who offered salvation.

The young priest was staying in a cheap Manhattan hotel and eating in diners. He could afford only standing-room tickets for the opera. He stood alone at the lobby bar, pretending to study his program. He could breathe here, and the thought of returning to North Carolina churned sourly in his stomach. Leo, impeccably groomed, tall, and urbane, stood before him with an extended manicured hand. They introduced themselves, talked a little Wagner, and Leo invited him to come for dinner on the next Friday.

Leo's family had emigrated from Sicily at the turn of the century. He was born into poverty in 1917 in Brooklyn. By the 1930s his family had accumulated a vast fortune, and he was educated in the finest schools, studied medicine at Harvard, and became a Jesuit. Gynecology was his profession, if not his vocation. Few of his patients ever knew he was a priest. Always mysteriously above the rules, Leo did not live in the Jesuit house but in a sprawling apartment overlooking Central Park on the Upper East Side. Young Oscar, still a little rough around the edges, was smoothed and neatly packaged by the worldly forty-two-year-old priest. They took their vacations over the years in Italy, France, Germany, and Austria, staying in the most exclusive hotels without their white collars, eating at four-star restaurants. After the first two years together, Leo groomed Oscar for a position in an Upper East Side parish; the rich needed saving just as the poor did, and it had to be done by someone who understood the rich and their special needs. Separate seating arrangements in heaven was a given.

After meeting Leo, Oscar returned to North Carolina and packed his meager belongings. Gerry sulked.

"You can come visit me."

"You have someone else."

"That's politics, Gerry." Oscar winked. "And you're almost eighteen now, off to college in Atlanta. All those pretty boys there. You might just forget this old priest."

"You're only thirty-one," Gerry said, pouting. "That's not that old. I love you, Oscar. Do you love me?"

"Yes, yes." Oscar was exasperated. "Of course."

"Then let me come with you."

"Go to college, Gerry. It's for the best. We both need to escape this place. Now hand me those books, like a good lad, so I can seal this box."

Gerry joined the Communist Party at college; he organized

meetings on campus, went on marches, became a student leader and a civil rights activist, married a beautiful woman, worked as a parole officer after graduating with a degree in sociology, and began shooting heroin. Six-foot-five, handsome, black shades, short hair, sharp clothes . . . he cruised the park in Atlanta at night but always returned to his adoring young wife.

He sometimes visited Oscar in New York, staying a few weeks with him when his marriage broke up, and when he lost his job, and when he got out of jail. He moved to San Francisco in the late sixties, let his hair and beard grow. Oscar was aghast.

"You can't come in and out of my building looking like that."

"Better than the other company you keep. Christ, Oscar, you've become some kind of a shaved poodle for a gay Jesuit gangster gynecologist." Gerry sniffed. "Honey, if I were a woman I'd never put my legs in stirrups again."

Always restless, Gerry moved to L.A. in the seventies and traded his beard for sideburns. Oscar paid for a few stints in rehab centers, where Gerry finally kicked heroin and took to shooting speed instead. He used his good looks to hustle money and took Oscar on a tour of San Francisco sex clubs when he came to visit. The younger man shot them both up with speed and they hit the bathhouses, screwing joyously and randomly for hours. Oscar scurried back home, sipping whiskeys nervously on first class, fingering through his designer sleeves the spot where the needle had penetrated his soft Irish veins. Beads of sweat clustered on his forehead like unconfessed sins. Back to Leo, back to saving the rich Christians from the poor ones. Leo the magnificent — charming but never flippant, stern but courteous, ardent patron of the arts, patron saint of fine dining and gracious living, president of every club he joined, black eyes, pupil merged with iris, eyes of a Doberman pinscher. He was a bottom (like Gerry) and Oscar was a top. This was Oscar's advantage in life, Gerry assured him — to be a hot top in a world of bottoms.

Their bodies cupped naked, pressing against each other; Oscar dreamt he touched Aisling's ass, and there at the end of the pelvic bone was a stubby tail, one inch long, half the size of a thumb. It was soft, with a light down, and the skin smooth and warm around the cartilage within. Wagging back and forth, it thumped gently between his fingers with a certain glee. He nuzzled into the thick flesh on the back of her neck, his face lost in her shiny red hair, delighted to feel her tail wag into his touch. Aisling.

He woke and leapt up like a man forty years younger when he heard the key in the door. He ran into the hall. Patrick stood there, surprised, the key still in the door, a surgical-gloved hand on the key.

"Oscar," he faltered, "I thought you'd be at work." Oscar stood rooted, his face reddening.

"Otherwise I'd have rang the bell," Patrick explained, embarrassed.

The old priest blocked his entrance.

"Can I come in?"

Oscar's shoulders slumped. He looked disapprovingly at his nephew's backpack. "Go to the living room," he said brusquely. "We'll discuss this quickly."

Patrick shuffled by him and sat sheepishly on the couch. "Bad timing, eh?" He eyed a pair of worn leather sandals by the television and makeup scattered across a table.

"Did Orla throw you out?" Oscar said, still standing.

"Something happened that I want no part of, and there were personal habits of mine that got on her nerves."

"That I can well believe," Oscar said dryly. "Patrick, you can't move back in here. It didn't work the first time around."

"Is there somebody else in the spare room?" Patrick inquired. "Just for tonight?"

"No room in the inn. You have to leave." Oscar rooted in his pocket. "I'll give you some money. Surely you have friends somewhere."

"I could sleep on the couch," Patrick pleaded. He picked up a hairbrush; it was crammed with long red hairs.

Oscar snatched the brush away from him, and Patrick could smell the alcohol on his breath.

"I don't care what you do, Oscar. Honestly, I'm not judgmental."

Oscar sank into a black leather chair and poured two whiskeys. "Have a drink and get out, Paddy." He handed him a crystal glass. "I've had all I can handle from you kids. I've done my best. I'm financing two of your sisters' world tours. You've taken hundreds of dollars from me for courses I know right well you haven't signed up for. I found a place for Orla's child. None of you ever call me or visit unless you need something."

Patrick drew a long red hair from the couch and, holding either end, tested its strength. "It's that bastard baby that I'd watch out for, Oscar." He wound the hair around a rubber finger; his skin formed tiny red ridges and whitened under the wiry bounds.

"The spare room is taken. The couch is taken. Did Orla go interfering again with that family in New Jersey? I had a phone call months ago saying the two of you meddlers arrived unannounced trying to see the boy. I swear, Patrick, there's a want in you."

"They know your phone number?" Patrick sat up.

"Of course they do," Oscar frowned.

"Shite!"

"Patrick, you have to leave. Get up. We'll go to a bar and discuss this." Oscar strode to the hall closet to get his coat. Patrick hauled himself reluctantly from the couch. He noticed a leaflet on the television, a flyer for tai chi classes on the West Side Highway. He pocketed it and walked into the hall.

"Get your bag," Oscar said, sighing. Patrick returned to the living room for his backpack.

His uncle took him by the arm and walked him briskly down the corridor. "Give me your key."

Patrick slapped it into his hand as they waited for the elevator.

"Oscar, is Keelin back from Japan?" He rubbed the strand of hair, which unwound slowly from his finger.

"Keelin? No, no, of course not." Distractedly, Oscar hit the elevator button several times. They descended facing the door.

"I take it I can be expecting another phone call from New Jersey?"

"Maybe from them." Patrick shrugged. "Maybe from the police. Shawn ran away from home."

"Life imitating talk shows, is it?"

The doorman nodded to Oscar and opened the glass door.

"Where's the boy?"

"Shawn arrived in the Bronx and Orla is hiding him," Patrick said. "Listen, could I have some money? I'll pay you back this time. I've a job bartending in the Village."

Oscar fretted, glancing nervously up and down the street. "I don't want to know," he said, walking briskly into Central Park. "This is a bad time for anything to happen. For me to be under scrutiny. Things are complicated, Patrick. I haven't exactly been a saint in my life or even a good priest. The shit is coming down the pipes. No one will want to know me when it leaks out. No one would want to be involved. I'm in no position to sort anything out. Do you understand? I'm not thinking straight. I need you all to get out of my hair. Patrick, I'm going to pay you off for once and for all. You're a drifter and a waster and a sponger and you are mentally ill. My money is running out. We're going to have a quick whiskey in the Stanhope and then go to the bank."

"The pipes the pipes are calling, eh?"

"Yes, Patrick, and they're full of shit."

"Where are my sisters again?"

"Hawaii."

"Hawaii? I've always wanted to go there. Jesus, where do you get your money?" Patrick had to trot to keep up with his manic uncle.

"Money?" Oscar panted and scurried along, mopping his forehead with a silk hanky. "Christ! Patrick, that's the most mundane story of them all."

Slyly, the peacock hopped up the temple steps and fanned its dark, gorgeous tail. In the gardens of this Buddhist temple, in a graveyard on the island of Oahu, there lived a very old Japanese man who told the sisters that the volcanic mountain's silhouette was Abraham Lincoln reclining, nose tipped to the clouds. This was not the information Keelin and Siobhan sought, but they looked to the mountain range, following his pointing finger.

Siobhan had been reading aloud from a leaflet, telling Keelin about the fish in the pond.

"Don't believe that. All is lies," a voice had called to her, and the old man had approached them smiling. "Pond too shallow for fish. Fish very unhappy, die quickly. No privacy."

"Why didn't they make it deeper?" Siobhan had asked.

"Because they don't want all the drunks falling in and drowning."

"Drunks in a graveyard?" Keelin said.

The man looked from one to the other, stroking his white beard. "I give you tour." He shooed the peacock from the steps and walked in without removing his shoes, much to the consternation of a middle-aged Japanese businessman.

"Shouldn't we take off our shoes?" Siobhan asked.

"If you want; if they hurt your feet." He shrugged. "This temple built by Americans to make money," he told them cheerily. "Painted red because Chinese like red." He patted a red pillar. "This cement, very special. Not wood like in Japan and China. Wood easy can be carved but to make it from cement very special, huh?"

"Does Yakiyuka work here?"

"Oh, you are pretty girls. If I was young I would grab you, but I am old and am afraid you would scream."

Keelin laughed. "Listen, you old goat, we came to speak to Yakiyuka. We were told he worked here."

"He is a fool." He sighed. "But he is a young fool, so a lucky fool for now. He thinks he is a mystic. Gone to find himself at a waterfall. Better to go to Honolulu and chase sailor boys."

"Was he with a big redheaded Irish girl?" Keelin asked.

He shook his head. "No big red Irish girl would have young fool, or old."

*

Hiking the north coast of the island of Kauai, the girls had lost the path. After hours of climbing and pushing through the jungle, they saw a faded red ribbon tied to a tree on the other side of the river. "The path must have been over there," Keelin hissed. Mountains soared, cloaked in heavy forests, and hot, humid air clamped their hair to their heads. With relief they saw a waterfall in the distance, trailing eerily, silently, down a stiff mountain.

"We've come so far now," Siobhan said. But it was yet another hour before they arrived at the waterfall, which thundered into a pool, black rocks rising on either side. A Japanese boy was crouched naked on a blanket at the foot of the semicircular cliff.

"Yakiyuka, I presume," Siobhan said in relief. "We've brought you food." She swung her small backpack to the ground and rooted for plums and bread and chocolate. Without asking who they were, he devoured their offerings savagely, red plum juice running down his chin and chest. They scrutinized him with sinking hearts, then introduced themselves. He told them that the cult was on the Big Island. Mostly middle-class American dropouts living in tents and fighting with each other, subsisting on trust funds and a wheatless, meatless, grainless, fishless, yeastless, dairyless diet that made them ill-tempered. He had left for Oahu and sold tiny little Buddhas in the temple gift shop with the shallow pond and the finicky peacocks. Then he heard Kauai was the most beautiful island of them all. He found this waterfall off the tracks in the middle of the jungle and decided it was suited for meditation. He ate off the tourists who hiked to the beach or came inland to the falls.

To assuage his parents' anxiety about his being gay, he had Aisling write a postcard with him in Tokyo and sent it from Oahu — then they'd think she was his girlfriend. Aisling had never been to Hawaii.

"Have you found yourself?" Keelin asked caustically.

"I am hungry. I am not here." He shook his head cheerfully.

Keelin stripped naked, then plunged her muddy body into the cold pool. Keelin — soft, overripe, her legs threading the water fluidly. Siobhan followed, her vertebrae like a snake skeleton sliding between her jutting sternum. The two sisters swam around each other, watching each other, while the boy on the banks devoured more plums and drank the beer. When Yaki-yuka saw their camera, he asked them to take a photo. He stood naked with a large stick raised in both hands, feet apart in some sort of deranged Samurai pose. Siobhan snapped the photo and Keelin looked nervously at the sky.

"Another photo," he cried, and clambered onto a rock.

"O.K., but it's late, and it'll take us four or five hours to get back."

They soon lost the trail, if there was a trail — bits of beaten paths would disappear as soon as they ran onto them; there were no red ribbons tied to the trees. Sinking again in swamps, they beat on toward the sea, the branches snapping back from their hands, the river rushing over great brown slabs. When they reached the halfway beach the sun shimmered small and light yellow in the pale sky. Gradually it sank as they sprinted up the hills, skidding and falling, breathlessly aware of the fragile light.

Siobhan twisted her ankle crossing a stream. The dusk fizzled and dissolved. "How far have we to go?" she implored. Her heart hammered through her skin as she limped along in a loping gate, her face twisted in pain.

"Keep going," Keelin shouted back. "We can't sleep in the jungle; we don't even have a torch."

The red mud path was only a few inches wide in places, and the wooded cliffs dropped directly by the side of their feet. Turn after turn, more mountains brooded, and yet no sign of the final beach. It was now dark. They stumbled along, groping with their hands, crouched close to the ground. When their footsteps fell, animals bolted unseen under the dense foliage. A car horn honked.

"Hear that?" Siobhan gasped.

"Sweeter than any bird."

They came to a parking lot and were immediately devoured

by a cloud of fierce, malevolent insects. They struggled to open the doors of their car and flung themselves in. Keelin took a few moments to collect herself, then turned the headlights against the impenetrable edge of the jungle and reversed. "I keep forgetting just because we're tourists doesn't mean we can't die," she said. As they drove through the dark silence, Keelin grew increasingly agitated. Siobhan was distant, massaging her thighs; her ankle had swollen and disappeared traceless into her leg.

"It's over, isn't it?" Siobhan said gloomily.

"We really sidetracked here. Took a wrong turn."

"It seems a shame to give up just like — "

"Give up what, for Christ's sake?" Keelin snapped. "Were we even looking for her, or was it just an excuse to travel and have lots of weird sex?"

"Nothing wrong with that."

The next morning, the Dutch woman who ran the hotel told them there was a man looking for them and that he'd gone to Barking Sands. Baffled, they got back into the car. Driving through fields of sugar cane toward the foot of the hills, they came to a dead end. There was a car parked by the army gates and a sign that told them the beach was closed for military use. Patrick stood, a frail figure, dark sunglasses, red thinning hair, a loose T-shirt over camouflage trousers. Smiling, he approached the car, his hands in his pockets. The sisters gaped at this apparition of their older brother on the mountain road, the canes rising high above his head on either side. Siobhan flew, flinging her long bony limbs about her brother. Keelin cautiously got out of the car. She noticed that Patrick was wearing surgical gloves.

After they greeted and embraced, they walked to the gate and rattled it. "The army's requisitioned the beach — can you believe that?" Patrick said. "I wanted to see the beach because of the name Barking Sands."

"If you slide hard down the dunes the sands squeak, making a barking noise," Keelin said. "At least that's what the guidebook says."

"Not at all. My guidebook says different." Patrick shook his head. "A man had fifteen or twenty dogs and he would tie them to sticks in the dunes where they watched him go fishing every day. One time there was a huge storm; the dogs barked and barked. The man was drowned and the dogs, tied to the stakes, were smothered in the sand."

"Tragic," Keelin said. "Come on! Let's get out of here; we all need to talk."

As they got into their respective cars, he shouted over, "Oh, and by the way, I think I've found Aisling."

"Youse lot were having all the fun and then Oscar gave me a big lump sum," Patrick said later. "I intend to go to Vegas after this and parlay it into an immense fortune."

"Well, I'm glad one of us has a viable plan for the future," Keelin sighed. They sat in a restaurant with flowery plastic tablecloths and plants, parrots, and greenery everywhere. They ate a Chinese-style meal and drank muddy brown mai tais.

"If you're right, Paddy," Keelin said, "and Aisling *is* at Oscar's . . . but what's she doing there? Maybe she'd just got there — I haven't rung him since Japan. Anyone can have long red hair. The hairs were in a brush?"

"Who else could it be? Enough about Aisling." Patrick slurped noisily at the ice with his straw. "That's all we've talked about since we got here. Tell me about Japan, you lucky bastards."

"Japan was gas craic," Siobhan said, nodding through a mouthful of rice.

"What kind of a family are we?" Keelin cried. "We can't just hop around the world like fleas on a dog while our mother is sick at home."

"Sure she doesn't want us to stay there," Patrick said. "Orla offered and she refused."

"She doesn't want us to stay and do nothing with our lives."

"She made you leave and you had a teaching job," Siobhan said.

"The idea of teaching in the same school I went to for the rest of my life . . . Shite, at least Aisling has some grand passion with Fatima. The rest of us, what do we have?"

Siobhan was engrossed in the intricate act of peeling the batter from the tiny balls of chicken. Patrick ordered three more mai tais. "Chill baby, chill. We're in paradise."

As they watched the waitress walk off, Keelin sighed. "Paradise my arse! I've read the history in the back of the guidebook. These Hawaiians, they lost it all, bulldozed by the Brits and now the Americans."

"Just like home." Siobhan smiled and raised her glass close to her eye as if to study the murky contents.

"Anyway," Patrick said, leaning back in his chair and stroking his chest with rubber hands through the flimsy T-shirt, "wait till yiz hear about Orla."

On the brink of Waimea Canyon, they stood. A fog filled the world. They could see the ends of black branches that fingered through from the edge, but it was hard to believe an immense canyon gaped only a meter from their feet. Patrick leaned on the rail of the observation point and howled. The fog stood his red hair on end. A wall of white, whose density had swallowed Earth, stolen the view, and all the future with it.

Cornbread, grits, biscuits, and gravy — Gerry baked and Aisling ate. In Georgia, he explained, there was a town that called itself the Grits Capital of the World, and every year it chose a Grits Festival Queen. Aisling sat with Gerry after work and listened. She had read Gerry's accumulated unanswered letters to Oscar in New York and, on impulse, had flown out to see him. Gerry let her stay and gave her a waitressing job at Fish Alley, his restaurant on the wharf. He had been a waiter there, on and off, when he came to California decades ago. Now he had AIDS. They leafed through Gerry's photo albums, all kittens and sunsets on the covers and a risky history on the pages within. He talked for hours in his southern accent, sometimes the same stories over and over again, and then, exhausted, would ask her to help him to bed.

The albums were the keeper of Gerry, a handsome man —
San Francisco, Los Angeles, North Carolina, New York with
Oscar. Oscar somewhere in all the photo albums, even in the
childhood one, a young priest with a bunch of schoolchildren.
Oscar with mustache, without mustache. Hair dyed brown.
"He's bald now," Aisling told him. Gerry stiffened in his chair.

"Haven't seen him in the last few years, three years it must be.
Before we'd make it a point to hook up at least once a year and
always talked on the phone. The motherfucker. He never re-
turns any of my calls."

Aisling carefully licked the surface of another person's life.
Her raw tongue, cracked and discolored, rasped along the bitter
fluff, crumbs, disappointments, dust, dreams.

"Oscar," she said, almost to herself, as Gerry proudly showed
her the wicker coasters he'd made in the last rehab center.

"He paid for most of my rehabs. I've been sober four years
now. He sends me money still, a postal order with no letter. I tell
him to keep his money and come see me, for Christ's sake."

"Why don't you phone him again?"

"I can't take more rejection."

"We'll call Oscar," Aisling said finally, "and I'll tell you what
to say that will make him come visit."

Gerry smiled in gratitude and relief. She got into the bed with
him and hugged him, looking closely at his face — the Grits
Festival Queen about to die.

"Oscar," she said, sighing.

Aisling knew she fit into a mold in the off-white, shimmering
pulp of Oscar's brain. His hands had followed her as a child.
She had felt him watching her grow, smiling knowingly in his
assumptions. But she went wild. Wilder than the air, the air that
chilled him. Something snapped, and the fluid that ran was bile,
not blood, because she would noʋ bleed for him. She thought
her bones would break, but they grew big and she swelled up on
the world like a bloated shadow. If she spat in his face he would
open his mouth and catch. He pulled her in, but she had gone
wild. Her need was long past the contents of his pockets. She

kept flattening the earth where she walked, like the water tearing through the land. If she got one thing from him then that was her price. She thought she saw him all the time, a priest's figure discreet in corners of cafés, behind first-class windows on moving trains.

the act of the maggot

WHEN ARE YOU going to stop acting the maggot and sort out this mess?" Keelin asked Oscar after several frazzled days in New York.

"You're the only maggot here." He lay on the couch drunk and disheveled.

"Oscar," Keelin said. She fingered a notebook. On the first page she saw a list of words. "Who wrote in this?"

"Aisling, I suppose." Oscar unbuttoned his shirt. His chest was red, somewhat caved in, and gray-haired. Keelin read the list: *Kataract, Koncrete, Kat, Komb, Koon, Kunt, Kusp, Komfort, Kaul, Kut, Kup, Kurse . . .*

"My name starts with a K. Did she know I was coming after her?"

"She was my little girl, that's what Molly would say. No fear of death or the streets . . . She lived completely in the present. Let's go to the living room, Keelin. Come on! Let's listen to Wagner. You're scared of everything, aren't you? But she was brilliant."

"Was?" Keelin said. *Korrupt, Krutch, Koot, Kall.* "Oscar, why don't you sleep it off. We'll talk again tomorrow."

"As for that slip of a girl, Siobhan." He laughed, an hysterical hiccup of a laugh, his hand sweeping by his head as if brushing off an imaginary fly. "Aisling rang me from Japan. She needed money . . . what else? I was a whore for you all; now you are whores for me."

Keelin wrote at the top of the list, *"Monster, monster, fall from grace, I will find you in this space."* She would not let Aisling die alone. She expected all this from her. Was she forcing Aisling to run so she could run too?

"What did she need money for?" Keelin was relentless. She had been badgering him all week, and now he seemed so fragile and demented, finally telling the truth.

"Fatima had left her and she was too poor to follow. It was love. Obsessive. Aisling is crazy, you know. She's no future. She'll be some mad woman with cats. I offered her money, but she had to come and get it. You were in London pretending to look for her but getting comfortable —"

"What did you want with her? How long was she here?"

"But I sent you to Japan. And off you went." He made flapping motions with his hands, getting up and wavering unsteadily into the living room, Keelin on his heels. "Kirsten Flagstaff, listen to this — German, of course. Marvelous voice, just magnificent. Oh yes, you went. Got you out of the way. You see, you might have found her if you decided to come over here."

"I was thinking of coming to New York, all right. I was comfortable in London — that's true — but Siobhan was being stalked, so I felt I had to get her out. I told Patrick I was coming here. You were getting me out of the way so."

"Yes, Patrick told me you were on your way. Siobhan stalked? It's amazing that that dribble of a creature could incite a spark of passion in anyone. I panicked when you were at large. Silly, really. I know you better now."

"What did you want with her?"

"You wouldn't have come without my money, sure you wouldn't? Leeches. You and your brood are grub worms. Maggots. Ah yes, hear that voice? Good God!" He sat on an armchair in front of the stereo. His eyes were closed in rapturous concentration and his face was tightened like a prune. Keelin shook her head. Patrick and Siobhan were staying in the East Village with Patrick's junkie friend Cian from Dublin . . . maybe she should stay there too. She fiddled with the CD, pretending to study the cover. Aisling, I'm sorry that the obstacles proved I was fascinated by distractions. You are my prey. A scab I cannot leave alone.

Ariane, ma soeur, de quel amour blessée
Vous mourûtes aux bords où vous fûtes laissée!

Our mother's inheritance was breasts like time bombs. Our father gave us the doubting disease. If I am to be a teacher, then I want to find you first. Aren't you me? Genetically cursed? Breasts big, bulky, and ticking, whether in my sensible or your sexy bras. Brains subject to constant imbalance, unease, and ritual. You grew too big, I not at all. Had you taken my light? Before I return to my pattern, I need to rattle into the plagued world and catch you.

Tears were flowing down Oscar's crinkled cheeks as the Flagstaff CD played on. Suddenly he opened his watery eyes and squinted at Keelin. "What a kraut!" he exclaimed admiringly.

Patrick was a bartender at Nightingale on Second Avenue. There were no windows, a checkerboard floor, and some old black men sitting separately from one another at the bar, watching *The Six Million Dollar Man* on TV. Some young men played pool quietly, their voices barely rising above a murmur. Siobhan and Keelin sipped their cranberry and vodkas. Since her arrival in New York Siobhan had dyed her hair blue, got her eyebrow, lip, and belly button pierced, and had a bar code tattooed on her thin upper arm. She wore her leather pants and a tiny woolen sweater with short sleeves that displayed her new adornments.

"I've worked out a health plan," Siobhan said. "Cranberry and vodka for my bladder, red wine for cholesterol, hot whiskey for my colds, and Guinness because it's good for you."

"And what will keep you thin?" Patrick asked.

"Heroin."

"I called Molly." Keelin flicked a cockroach off the bar.

"And?" Patrick left to take a beer to one of the old men.

"Well, what was I meant to say? That Patrick guessed right,

that Aisling was with Oscar all the time? I'm hunting her; she's hunting Fatima. Fatima was with Sadao; Fatima has a brother in New York. I don't know if they all hooked up. Aisling stayed a month, I think . . . She was here since November, and then found letters from Oscar's friend Gerry, who's dying in San Francisco. He wanted to see Oscar before he died. Molly is sick and wants to see Aisling. Aisling went to Gerry instead. The story is overlapping. So that's where we are now. Aisling buggered off to San Francisco after Christmas —"

"Bugger being the operative word." Patrick cleared his throat.

"She and Gerry are blackmailing Oscar. I don't know . . . it's not easy up there. I'm sort of taking care of him. Cooking his dinners. He's taken a sabbatical from the church and he's on a bender. He's cracking up. The police were around, he thought it was for him, went ballistic. But it was about Orla. My head is addled. I've had to sit through five fucking ring cycles to get this information, such as it is."

"Blackmailing him for what? Patrick, can I've another?" Siobhan rooted in her pockets and took out a cut straw.

"Oh, I don't know. For molesting him as an altar boy . . . the usual. But it would fuck Oscar up with his sponsor Leo, who apparently would not be pleased with any publicity."

"Sponsor? Please!" Siobhan shook her head.

"The guy's about eighty," Keelin added. "Have any of you heard from Orla?"

"Nope. She's moved out of the old place, that I know. In hiding somewhere. Orla the fugitive," Patrick said. "I bet still in the Bronx, in the Irish ghetto though. Wild horses wouldn't drag her from all the bog men up there."

"Oh! Well excuse me! She's not a hipster like you two down here." Keelin threw her eyes up to heaven. "You Manhattan Irish sitting in your trendy little bars in the Village, feeling superior to the Bronx and Queens Irish, and the natives to boot."

"The only difference between that shower and us," Patrick said, "is that they don't want to be here and we do."

Patrick gave them two more drinks. "What did Molly say to all this? . . . I mean, you didn't tell her everything, did you?" He was looking at Siobhan's closed fist.

"I told her the gist of it," Keelin said. "Oh, you know Molly, vague as ever. Something about 'I knew he shouldn't have started hanging around with all them Jesuits.' More tests have come back and she has to have a hysterectomy. Siobhan, you better go back and look after her."

"What about you?" Siobhan was indignant.

"I'm going after Aisling."

"Why?" Patrick took a tiny plastic bag from his jeans pocket.

"Because."

"I'm staying here," Siobhan said. "Cian is cool. He's going to get me a job in his restaurant. Want to do a line?" Keelin shook her head. Siobhan and Patrick went into the toilet together. Keelin sat at the bar and watched the Six Million Dollar Man jump onto a roof.

"Didn't they have a bionic dog too?" One of the old men asked out loud to no one in particular.

Another man snorted. "Six million dollars for a dog, that's plain crazy."

A distinguished middle-aged man in a dark suit sat with his arm around his distraught, blond wife. She wore a pearl necklace, pearl stud earrings, and a beige blouse fastened with a Cambay brooch. The TV announcer was younger and blonder and wore a look of concern and pity, shaking her head sadly and wisely every time the camera was on her.

"He's sick. Very sick, you see," the woman sobbed. Her husband tightened his grip and looked beseechingly at the announcer, who nodded sadly and wisely.

"Our son suffers from a specific disorder called OCD," the man explained.

"Obsessive-compulsive disorder," the announcer said, her face almost cracking with concerned gravity.

"Yes, yes." The man shifted uncomfortably. "And it is unlikely he ran away. He didn't have much of a social life because of his condition, you understand. He was quite acute . . ." His wife shook with sobs in his arms. The camera zoomed in abruptly on the tears.

"It was his birth mother." Her face was taut.

"Dear, we don't know that." His voice was strained and long suffering.

"She came to call last fall, looking for him. He was upstairs in his room. I refused to let her see him. He's my son. We had him in behavioral therapy and it cannot be interrupted. I took care of him, bathed him, cared for him when he was sick. Brought him to every specialist in New York —"

Orla turned off the television. She felt her stomach lining loosen and her legs shake. "Jaysus. For fuck's sake!" She hauled her ample body off the couch. "The fuckers have gone public on me. They think I've done a TV thing." Her son, Shawn, was sleeping in the other room. She went to the phone and rang Oscar's number. Keelin answered.

Orla relaxed when she heard the note of kindness. "Keelin, it's you."

When Keelin finally put the phone down, she glanced at Oscar, who was slouched in an operatic torpor on the couch. He caught her eye and sat up straight.

"Turn the stupid woman in. She's no rights to that child."

Keelin nodded gravely. "I know."

Oscar hummed, slapping some cologne on his red neck. He straightened his tie, swept his shoulders briskly, and went to the front closet for his black cashmere overcoat.

"Leo and I are going to a Friendly Son's function. Did you get me the ticket to San Francisco?"

"Yes," Keelin said.

"Well, since you're Miss Organized, you can also think about going home to your mother. You've been here two weeks. I'm not throwing you out — this place is always open to you kids — but Molly is sick. If you're right and all Gerry wants is to see me, then I will just visit for a few days and maybe join you afterwards in Ireland."

"You look good, Oscar."

Keelin went downtown and walked along Avenue C to Cian's apartment. The Latino dealers were bundled up in hats and hoods, stamping their feet, their shoulders curled in against the February meanness. The door downstairs was covered in graffiti. A sign on the cracked glass window read DEALERS KEEP OUT. She was buzzed in and made her way up the narrow, crooked stairs to the fourth floor. A dog barked behind a door on the third floor. Cian opened the door and looked her up and down. He had a finely sculpted face, jet black hair flopping over one side. He wore a tatty leather jacket with a tight top beneath. His jeans were baggy and he wore motorcycle boots.

"You're Siobhan's sister?"

"We don't look alike."

"Thank God for that!"

Patrick was sitting on the couch rolling a joint, and he leapt up and kissed her. "What's up?"

"I just bought tickets for myself, Orla, Shawn, and Oscar on a flight to San Francisco tomorrow."

"Jesus, how did he agree to that?"

"He will."

Patrick laughed. "You've got some bottle! Hear that, Cian? No flies on her." Cian sighed, taking the joint from Patrick.

"Shawn doesn't have a passport: I can't take him out of the country. Did you see him in the newspapers?"

"Why are you getting involved in that mess?"

"Ah, Orla needs her day."

"Orla's a pain in the ass. You've met Orla, Cian?"

"She's the fat one?"

"Yep, that's our Orla. Queen of the Bronx. It's scary up there, like going to the Appalachians or something." Cian laughed cynically. He passed the joint to Keelin.

"I called Molly," Keelin said. "She's going in in two weeks for the hysterectomy. She told me she was feeling fine. She's back to the golf."

"Poor Mammy — I hate the idea of a hysterectomy," Patrick said. "I had always counted on going back to the womb as an option."

Cian snorted.

"I'm serious. It's like the door from where I came into the world has been bricked up."

"Maybe I'll ask her to keep it pickled in a jar for you," Keelin said dryly, "so you can return at your own convenience."

Siobhan walked out of the bathroom wearing thigh-high leather boots with a short leopard-skin skirt and glittery tights. There was a new stud beneath her lower lip.

"Wow, you've punctured yourself again?" Keelin gasped. She got up to kiss her, but there was an awkwardness between them now.

"Don't you think it matches her nose, eyebrow, belly, and lip rings?" Patrick asked in mock sincerity.

"Siobhan, Molly had a phone call from Japan."

"Japan?" Siobhan took the joint out of her hand and flopped on the couch beside Cian.

"Toru wants his camera back."

"Toru? He survived?"

"He never got to Kobe. Met some woman on the train and fell in love for a month, went off to Osaka."

"That's wonderful, but he's not getting the camera. I want to do some photography here, so he can come and get it. Hey! I'm getting another tattoo. My zodiac sign, Gemini. Two faces on my shoulder."

Keelin nodded. It wasn't the reaction she expected. She thought all the neon nights would light up between herself and Siobhan once she mentioned Toru.

"Keelin." Siobhan sighed. "I told you we were going to a club."

"I'm not dressed right, am I?"

"This is the East Village," Patrick protested. "Nobody gives a shit. That's what's good about it. She looks grand. Jesus, Siobhan, not everyone can have your glamour and sophistication."

Keelin glanced down at herself — denim jeans, brown flat

shoes, a plain blouse, and a woolly cardigan with embroidered flowers. Her hair in a fuzzy red mop down her back.

"It'll do. She looks ravenous. Come on — I need a drink," Cian said, shivering on the couch.

"Ravishing," Siobhan said. "I'm not down on you, Keelin, but a little style in your life wouldn't go amiss. Remember the Japanese? Style, style, style."

"I'm not getting a zodiac tattoo."

Siobhan took her little sister by the hand. She rooted through piles of clothes on the floor in the tiny bedroom and fired some at her — black tights with silver stars, blue velvet miniskirt, silver top.

"I don't have your figure," Keelin whined. "Or lack thereof. I can't wear these."

"We have the same size feet: here's some platforms. I've never seen you in heels."

"I can't walk in heels."

"There's more to clothes than function." Siobhan grabbed Keelin's hair and then let it go. "Well, the hair is hopeless. Wait — maybe if I put it in a bun. I can put some makeup on. And not your usual pink lipstick and blue eyeshadow. You have an all right figure. You're not even thirty — too young to give up like that."

"Give up?" Keelin struggled into the tight-fitting clothes. Siobhan applied ivory foundation, blusher, dark lipstick, gold and bronze eyeshadow, then stood back. She raised her eyebrows and laughed.

"I feel like Toru," Keelin said.

"He's not getting the camera back."

"We should write to him or something."

"He was along for the ride." Siobhan shrugged. "Now he's not. Attend to yourself."

"Are youse two coming or what?" Patrick said, appearing in the doorway. "Wow! You look great. How do you feel?"

"Vulnerable!" Keelin tottered on the platform boots toward the door.

A transvestite danced on the bar at the Pyramid Club on Avenue A, stepping around their drinks. "Patrick said you were going to San Francisco," Siobhan shouted above the music.

"I'm sorry I didn't get you a ticket, but I'm chancing my arm with Oscar as it is. Aisling is out there, and I need to buy time for Orla to be with Shawn. So she'll let him go back home."

"He's fifteen; he must want to be with her."

"I don't know what's going on. She doesn't trust me yet. I've only spoken to her on the phone."

"Well, I like it here. I've got a job and all that."

Keelin smiled and wanted to kiss her. Siobhan looked up the dancer's skirt as he wiggled in front of her. "Just your type," Siobhan said.

Keelin blushed. Patrick, who was listening in, looked at Keelin in amusement. "Is there something I don't know? Just wait till you bring him home to Mammy. You couldn't bring Siobhan to San Francisco anyway; she'd never get through the airport metal detector." Siobhan made a face at him, and he finished his drink and jumped into the slam-dancing crowd. Cian, who sat beside Siobhan, was nodding into his beer.

"He's tired," Siobhan explained to her sister. "You know, Patrick is driving us crazy. I think Cian is going to ask him to leave. He's in a bad way. All these rituals and stuff — he's destroyed the bathroom. Some days he just lies in bed staring straight ahead like he's paralyzed. And he stands on his head against the wall . . . I thought it was yoga, but he said he does it because he feels his organs are getting moldy —"

"Oh, God!" Keelin interrupted. "I can only save one sibling at a time."

"If you wanted to save Orla, you'd turn her in and tell her to stop stuffing her fat face and maybe she'd get laid."

Orla saw the disgust of the priest when she arrived. Shawn was quiet and sullen. Although he was dressed in a sweatshirt, ultra-baggy jeans, and baseball cap like a normal American teenager, his face twitched. Oscar was in first class, larruping down the whiskeys, and they sat behind the curtain in the galley. Keelin had played on his guilt about Aisling. He had had sex with her, he'd claimed in a tearful, drunken state during act 1, scene 3 of *Die Walkure*. And he had paid her. Keelin swore to keep it a secret, having no desire to tell the family and realizing it gave her new leverage with Oscar. Orla and Shawn wore earphones and watched the movie. Orla had brought a big bag of Cheez-Its, and she munched them methodically. The toxic orange crumbs stuck to the flesh around her mouth. Keelin almost missed Siobhan.

"Have you ever been to California, Shawn?" she asked him.

"I've been to London and Paris and the Bahamas and Hawaii."

"I've been to Hawaii too." He didn't seem interested and continued to watch the movie. Something with Kevin Costner in green tights. Keelin opened a Paul Durcan book she'd gotten at Oscar's and read through the familiar poems. Shawn began dethreading the blanket as he looked at the screen. The plane routinely droned along, as if fueled by the crunching of Cheez-Its.

When the film was over, Orla watched her son pick the lint from his clothes. She had a child and she lost it alive. Sporkin Reilly was a mean little weasel who once lived in Cootehill. She had been feisty as a girl, but it was unfair for Molly to have called her that name every time she pushed against the dictatorship of parenthood. Recently she looked in the mirror every morning, and what did she see? A bloated weasel who had broken the codes. There will be no TV audience forgiveness.

Her son had cocked his head like a bird when they played Scrabble, Monopoly, and cards in the Bronx. She let him build his nests when no others would. Cloth, lint, threads, crumbs, scraps of paper, his own hair plucked newly from his head, and hers from the bathtub, scabs from the sores he maintained in his ears and nostrils, potato peels, and rubber bands. He fashioned them into clumps, snowballing bigger and bigger, and rested his head on the tangled bunches to sleep. She knew how simple she was. She had woken in the night to feel him staring at her, perched on the other side of the room. And it confused her. What's wrong? What's wrong, my cold little egg? Red hair and speckled and hatched alone. She didn't keep him in a cage, she left the windows open — she will plead with the audience after the commercial breaks — but he never flew. He must have liked it there; he went often to the park and collected stones, tiny pebbles, clay, blades of grass, twigs, Coke can ring tops, crack vials, cigarette butts, leaves, real feathers. He bagged them all and came home to sculpt his mounds. My son, what have I done? She won't stop him or scold him; she kept all those fuzzy clumps, big and small, some the size of the television they watch all day. He put one on top and they liked it there — TV hair. She wondered what they were, what he had invested in them. Precious pillows supporting his dreams.

She rehearsed her talk-show case: "Mother Who Stole Adopted Bird-Nest Son." He would squirm on his chair like any teenager in an uncomfortable situation while the audience howled in laughter at his habits. "Son Left to Rot at Birth in Leafy Suburb." How could they have really loved him? She saw no nests in their house. The audience would crucify her, though — the fat, foreign, redheaded, baker mother who went into hiding in the Bronx with her meager savings. The host would raise finely plucked eyebrows, roll surgical eyes, and croon with the blond, svelte, silky mother who cooked him lasagna and bathed him and took his temperature and helped him with his homework. The family unit intact, father home from work in suit and tie, his quiet car rolling smoothly into the driveway, cheeks pecked. She never had a father, only a mother's brother, a Catholic priest. Wrong people, wrong lineage. They would tear her to pieces. She had no husband, but she had a son who pecked about the room, absorbed in his mania. This is his home; he is building it.

Aisling, Patrick, Siobhan, Keelin. Her brothers and sisters, fragile shells so casually hatched — now tatty feathers and matchstick yellow feet, they sat in their aviaries, on their swings and perches, nudging little mirrors that dangled from the top wires, shitting on the seeded floor, squawking for the jungle they knew before they were stacked in solitary dark boxes with small breath holes and taken abroad.

the average gazelle

SHAWN HAD WOVEN as if from nowhere a big, soft ball of lint and threads by the time they checked into the hotel in San Francisco. The child horrified Oscar, the bovine mother repelled him, and he was baffled as to how he had come under the thumb of the plain, redheaded schoolteacher. This tiny woman was bleeding him dry, and he sensed a ruthlessness and determination in her that froze his responses. His suitcase was littered with a myriad of plastic pill containers. He hurled a selection down his throat and, thus fortified, put on his best suit and collar and took a taxi to Gerry's.

A skeletal Gerry in blue cotton pajama bottoms stooped over him at the door. If he was surprised to see Oscar he did not show any emotion. He wore a T-shirt picturing Elizabeth Taylor's bloated face at its worst. It read "I'm Mother Courage." He turned and padded back to bed. "Been through it all, Baby," the shirt said on the back. The priest followed him into the apartment, closing the door behind him. In the bedroom, Oscar sat in a chair at the foot of the bed.

"I see you've come as a priest."

"Gerry, how are you?"

"Why just dandy, girl."

Oscar winced. Gerry saw this immediately and laughed weakly. "Please. What do you expect me to call you? Father?"

"Gerry, why are you blackmailing me?"

Gerry sunk in the bed, a gray creeping over his bone of a face. "For your soul, Oscar."

"It was Aisling's idea, wasn't it?"

"Aisling?" Gerry perked up. "It was a lucky break to get to know her so close to the end of my life. She made me laugh."

"I was generous." Oscar sighed. "Without my money, you might have been long dead."

"Oscar, you've compromised all your life. You've acquired every material thing, lived in great luxury. If I destroy your life with Leo, then you can start living. Look at you; I'm not one to talk, but you're doped to the gills, to the gills, girl. Hello — I mean, how miserable are you? Oh Oscar, do you love me?" His voice had grown shrill but now it sank. "Why did you do that to Aisling? Such an innocent. Don't sneer, in her way she was. A pure spirit. No bullshit. I'm so tired. I'm tired of dying, but it's not going to go away. In the long grass in North Carolina I was only a child. You will live longer than me — is that fair?"

"We lived differently."

"You're a corrupt old bastard, Oscar, and Aisling and I are honest souls; we never hid anything. Oscar, do you love her? She loved you, and we felt our demands could only help you. You want more than you need, you hoard, you only mingle with the super-rich, for God's sake! You cry at the opera, but when you see a schizophrenic Jesus Christ with a begging sign around his neck you push a button and raise the window on your Mercedes."

"The rich need their guidance also. They deserve compassion too."

"*Ye poor take heart. Ye rich take warning.* So much struggle, so many centuries. Nothing changed. My life will not stretch over into the next millennium. I'm stuck in the present, my thoughts don't even scrape beyond it."

"You sound like Aisling all of a sudden."

"We talked, and boy could she talk. You need an Aisling in both millennia. I'm glad she will live. You have grown old, your hair is gone. Oscar, I'm in such pain."

"I never met a man who didn't deserve to die."

"God, you'd make a terrible priest."

"You idealize my job, Gerry. It's just a job, you know, a big company. I rose and did well. I never made it to bishop or any of that — too much drink. *The love that dare not speak its name.* They don't care about that — sex — but about indiscretion. I've suffered my setbacks. You can't judge me."

"Honey, in this town it's the love that won't shut up." Gerry turned his head with effort and stared at the wall. One side of his face was splashed with red blotches. On the wall hung several framed diplomas: high school, university, three different rehab centers. The photo albums were on the shelf beneath.

"Get me my albums, Oscar."

"I didn't come here to look at pictures."

Gerry sighed. "Some days I was so sick. I had to work anyway. Waiting for the toilet to be free to go in and rupture my intestines and then come out to grab the plates and run to the bar for strawberry daiquiris, so help me God! There were nights when I'd get a taxi and cry in the back all the way home."

"I'm sorry."

"Why didn't you come see me? You were all I had."

"As I get older, Gerry, I need less and less. People fade, there's no longer a future. We had gone as far as we ever would with each other. Places — now that's different for some reason. Paris, Salzburg, Vienna, Milan, Naples. I only wanted to see places and hear music. Eternal things. People are fading for me. Often it's a relief when they die."

"That Irish family is all that makes you human, you motherfucker. You know Aisling." Gerry smiled, reminiscing. "She saw all the injustice. Nothing escaped her. She would even rave on about zoos, of all things — she's worse than me. How the animals are shipped around willy nilly, the whole money racket, how it's all right if you are a big attraction, a lion or a tiger or a giraffe, but if you're just an average gazelle . . ." He sat up in the bed, his eyes burning.

"An average gazelle?"

"Oscar, I'm going to turn you in. I know Leo would drop you after all these decades like a ton of hot bricks at the mere hint of a scandal, and then that vow of poverty you took would kick in thirty years later. You'd have to sober up or go live on the streets as the drunk you are. Sing, Oscar, for me, the average gazelle you tried to shunt away."

"Fuck you, Gerry." Oscar's voice was resigned as he stood and walked to the head of the bed. "You know, kid, you think I'm so hard. I brought the tin whistle — remember how I used play you tunes on that yoke? It is a gift." He took the whistle out of his inside pocket and placed it carefully, with finality, on the bedside table. "You want a song, Gerry?"

Gerry nodded. Oscar, now sixty-four, opened his small, mouselike mouth and sang "The Last Rose of Summer" to the boy who was fifty-one years old. The priest's voice now rolled in the gravel of pills and age.

> I'll not leave thee, thou lone one! to pine on the stem
> Since the lovely are sleeping, go sleep thou with them.

"Do you love me, Oscar?" Gerry whispered.

"Of course I do." The priest was exasperated. "'Thus kindly I scatter thy leaves o'er thy bed / Where thy mates of the garden lie scentless and dead.' Gerry, you're not going to make that phone call."

"I will too. I loved what I could of you Oscar, all the poetry for the North Carolina congregation. You were a missionary then, bringing moisture to me. Infusions of Yeats right up my ass. That's how I see you, before Leo. If only we had loved each other like Aisling loves Fatima. We were both whores, girl. *But one man loved the pilgrim soul in you.* See? I was listening."

Oscar was looming over him. His shadow monstrous on the flesh pink wall. A black figure with an embroidered rehab pillow in his hand.

> When true hearts lie wither'd and fond ones are flown,
> Oh! Who would inhabit this bleak world alone!

"You can't kill me, Oscar." The red blotches on Gerry's face seemed to come alive and deepen. "Isn't that the stereotype? The only end for gay love affairs? Aisling raged about that. Murder, death, suicide. Every film, every book —"

"We're not in a book now, Gerry."

Chinatown's staunch dragons stood guard as Keelin, Orla, and Shawn snuck through. In his oversize denim jeans and padded black jacket, Shawn was cagey, and his face ticked. Orla waddled, quite content, behind him, overprotective, treating him more like a five-year-old than a teenager. Keelin thought about Oscar and Gerry. At a newsstand, Orla picked up a magazine and flicked through: the blond mother and businessman father sat with Shawn in the centerfold.

"We're everywhere," she gloated.

"We'd better disguise you more," Keelin said. Shawn seemed pleased, but as he read his face dropped.

"What's wrong?" Keelin looked at him closely. Shawn shrugged and slouched on, his baseball cap pulled down low.

"He's been on holiday long enough, Orla. He should go home. They can help him. He's sick."

"They won't let him make his nests. It's all he wants to do. He needs me."

"It's all he's compelled to do. He doesn't want to do it any-more than Patrick wants to wear rubber gloves and get thrown out of every place he stays."

Shawn had gone into a shop full of Chinese junk. They followed him in and found him looking at some dolls. Keelin picked up a seashell and held it to her ear. "What do you know? I can hear the sea. Here, have a go."

Shawn took it and, placing it to his ear, smiled. "Me too."

"That's not really the sea, you know," Orla said.

Keelin raised her eyebrows. "I think we know that, Orla. Shawn, listen, do you want to go back to your parents?"

"I'm his parent," Orla protested.

Keelin ignored her. Shawn shook his head.

"O.K., we won't make you. But anytime you want, just say the word. Do you want to see a doctor?"

"They'll turn me in," Shawn said. "I hate doctors. I want to go back to the hotel. Has Oscar finished murdering the blackmailer?"

"What?"

"Orla told me the story."

"Murder?" Keelin said. "What gives you that idea?"

"The way he was acting. It's his only way out. The guy is dying anyway, what difference does it make?" Shawn shrugged and turned to Orla. "Can we buy this shell?"

The door to Gerry's apartment was ajar. Keelin quietly slipped in. The living room was tidy and tastefully decorated; she had expected something wilder. Vermeer's kitchen maid was framed over the mantel, and an arrangement of dried flowers in the grate of the blocked-up fireplace below.

"Hello?" she called nervously. "Hello?" Silence spun a web of dread across the dark rectangular gap leading to the bedroom. Gerry was still in the bed. She approached him cautiously, and his lids slid back, revealing his flat eyes.

"Aisling, you've come back," he groaned.

"No, I'm looking for Aisling. I'm her sister, Keelin."

"Oh, she's gone, honey, gone. In Mexico with Fatima. She left when Oscar said he was coming." He shifted groggily in the rumpled bed. "Is this an apparition? I'm finally getting dementia. Shit. I was hoping it would be more fun than this. I wanted to hallucinate young boys, not more relatives of Oscar. How did you get in?"

"The door was open."

"Jesus. He hadn't the guts to do it himself, so he was hoping to leave it to one of the neighbors —"

"Oscar? Where is Oscar?"

"He came to kill me — with my own cushion, for Christ's sake. A pillow from the rehab they made me shave my head in. He knelt by the bed and . . . and then he kissed me: it sounds like a song. A man who couldn't bear to look at the poor and wretched. What does the Bible say? Bring me your poor and huddled masses?"

"I think that's the Statue of Liberty." Keelin sat carefully on the chair at the end of the bed.

"Yeah, well, whatever. You should look after your uncle, child. He's a mess. The smell of alcohol on his breath nearly ruined my sobriety record, I'll tell you that now. And honey, he was doped up. Uppers, downers, inners, and outers."

"Where did he go?"

"I don't know. He left in a hurry — quite rude, after all these years, when you think of it. Didn't have the guts to do what he came to do. He wore me out. I don't even know how long I've been sleeping."

"Are you still going to accuse him of molesting you?"

"I will if he leaves me to die alone."

"Is there anything I can do for you?"

Gerry propped himself up by the elbows. Keelin put the pillows behind him. His eyes had an imperious glint. "Get me a drink from the fridge, a fruit juice. I have to take my medication. And get me new pajamas from the top drawer, over there, to the right, second drawer down. That's a girl. Now bring me those albums — no — those. We'll start with the blue one. I want to show you some pictures."

Gerry is young and handsome in the first photo he showed her. He is wearing a suit, his wife in a white dress and veil. "Cheryl, she was a beauty, look at her. My! I'm sorry for her, for what I did. The heroin, the cruising . . . had to find out eventually, I suppose, and I did love her. I went down on her every time. For a queer, that's responsibility."

His long Ethiopian fingers moved down to the next photo: his blond niece and nephew in a paddling pool in the garden in North Carolina, his sister's heavy legs and waist guarding them. "Chip grew up to be a tear-away just like his uncle Gerry. I love him, that boy. Held up liquor stores, the little rascal. I told him when I die he's to scatter my ashes in the lake back in North Carolina."

After a pilgrimage through the whole blue album, Keelin walked home through the steep San Francisco streets, trying to clear her head of Gerry — the soft, soggy, mushroomy smell of his illness, the photos and raving stories of his life. A life lived purely in the present, just like Aisling's. The wind cut through her; she felt so stiff and brittle crouching up the blustery hills that she thought she'd snap in two. Slipping the plastic card key into the slot on the door, she waited for the green flashing lights and then entered. Orla and Shawn were glued to the TV, sitting on the separate king-size beds. Orla was munching peanuts; Shawn was drinking a beer.

"Don't eat or drink from the wet bar; it's very expensive."

"He has money to burn." Orla shrugged, and Shawn smiled slyly.

"If he did, we wouldn't all be in the same room." Keelin flopped on Orla's bed. "Shawn, do your parents let you drink?"

Shawn cupped the beer protectively and looked at Orla.

"Saint fucking Keelin. There were pubs in Dublin we wouldn't go to at fifteen because the crowd was too young."

Keelin smiled, taking a handful of peanuts. "Any sign of Oscar?" she asked.

"Nope."

"What would you think of going to Mexico?"

"To hide Shawn? It would be perfect."

Shawn swigged his beer and nodded his approval. "Just like in the movies."

Oscar was missing for thirteen days. Keelin rang the front desk and was informed the booking was for one month. She spent part of the day forcing the disguised Orla and Shawn on walks around the city. Orla was lazy, more content to sit in the hotel ordering room service and watching TV. "I've never had cable before," she would whine to her impatient little sister. Shawn would look at her with a marked air of superiority. "Never? Cable's the best." They had to hide his nests, which were building up at a remarkable rate. Gerry waited for Keelin in the afternoons. She changed his sheets, washed him, fed him, and helped him to the living room to get a bit of light and change of scene. He talked frantically, guiding her through his albums, as if he could talk his way out of death by ceaselessly renewing his life.

"I won't leave till Oscar comes back," she promised him. And he was relieved. When he was cantankerous or acutely repetitive she wished he'd hurry up and die. She did not understand his craving to prolong his life as he poured over medical books. When the doctor came, Gerry would needle him for the minutest biological detail. He even asked him about the possibility of a cure developing, if he could just hang on.

From the album: an old couple. Dumpy woman in a floral dress, bald thin man with his glasses crooked on his nose, arm awkwardly around the woman: "My father killed himself, just like his father. Did I ever tell you —? Yeah, I did. My mother got Alzheimer's. It was awful. My niece took care of her. I was glad when she died. When I went home last I had to dress her — she couldn't even dress herself. Didn't recognize me. Although my niece took care of her, she left all the money and property to me. The whole inheritance. Generations worked for that farm and then the little shop, quite a sum it came to. I put it all up my arm, honey. I enjoyed every minute. God bless you, Mama."

Orla and Shawn went to a movie, their only outing on their own initative. They were in a good mood, a little drunk, having snuck some cans of beer into the cinema. Back in the hotel they switched on the TV. Keelin had been enjoying the peace and quiet, reading her book.

"*Seinfeld* is on," Orla protested, seeing her little sister's expression.

"We're not missing *Seinfeld*." Shawn flung himself on the bed, his limbs sprawled.

"All right, all right," Keelin said. "Maybe afterward you and I can go out on the town. I feel like blowing off some steam. All the day with Gerry is too much."

"Why are you doing it, then? It's Oscar's responsibility, or somebody's. I don't know why you're so indispensable to this fella all of a sudden. Who did he have before you?"

"Aisling, actually."

Orla smirked. "She left when he got really sick, though." Keelin looked over at Shawn, who was riveted by a car commercial.

On the thirteenth day, Keelin came walking back through the sloping city. San Francisco was sad. Every lost soul she talked to seemed to have just been hit on the head with a brick. Crystals, astrology, reincarnation, the I Ching, conspiracy theories — each had a gimmick. Aisling may have loved it as Gerry said, but then she would. Keelin felt the whole place was doomed — the nasty cracks in the buildings, the unnerving earth tremors, the unease of the ghettos, the burnt-out snotty hippies, the homeless Vietnam vets with their shopping carts on the windy avenues. Not her cup of tea. What's with all the coffee shops, she thought as she walked past. Go have a fucking beer. Many evenings she dragged Orla out to search the bars for Oscar. She suggested to Gerry that he might have committed suicide.

"No way, Jose! He's probably back in New York with Leo the Lion-Hearted," Gerry pouted. "And if so, I will make those phone calls. The cheek of him, shunting me into your hands."

"Thanks!"

"I don't mean it like that, girl." Gerry took a pencil out of her shirt pocket to mark down the medications he had just taken. As he put it back he prodded her breast with it.

"What'd you do that for?" Keelin was baffled.

"Just checking. You have huge tits."

"What? You thought I was padding?" Keelin turned up her nose in mock horror.

More pictures: a woman in early middle-age, deep lines in her face, heavy and still quite handsome. A man, hairy arms and a beard. A baseball cap with an MIA insignia. He's holding a beer. They are sitting on the grass leaning into each other. "My sister Mary was watching the TV with a Bible on her knee. Her husband was cleaning his hunting rifle in the kitchen. The gun went off and blew a hole through the wall of the living room, through the armchair, and she was killed. What are the odds of that? They buried her with the Bible still clutched in her hand. Should have put the TV in too."

The miles she traced on foot each day and night ribboned through her until she was tangled up and stalled. She loved Gerry now and did not want to leave him. She began hoping for a cure, taking an interest in his T-cell count. He flirted with her like he flirted with everyone, and she flirted back.

Tonight Madonna and child were slouched on their separate beds watching *Entertainment Tonight*. Orla jumped up when Keelin walked in. "Oscar was here. He threw out all the nests in a rage."

"He looked like a bum," Shawn said.

"Where is he now?" Keelin turned off the TV.

"He was shouting for you, cursing you. Where is that little bitch? If Molly heard him talk like that! She doesn't know him at all. Come to think of it, neither do I. He's a maniac."

"He wrote you a note," Shawn said, getting off the bed and walking to the mirror. He picked up a crumpled scrap of paper and handed it to Keelin. She looked in dismay at the spider scrawl: "*You you you were supposed to be heer I have flies in my heart.*"

"Look at his spelling." Shawn snorted in disdain, his face twitching.

"Flies in my heart?"

"Maybe he meant butterflies in his stomach. He was like a madman." Orla turned the telly back on. The phone rang. Orla reached for it, but Keelin ran and snatched it out of her hand.

"I'm down at the Blue Lamp in the Tenderloin. Come join me." He sounded calm. "And come on your own. I don't want those freaks anywhere near me."

When Keelin arrived at the Blue Lamp, there was a black man at the bar with his palms raised, saying, "This is not America!"

Oscar motioned to her from a table.

"I called Gerry," he said. "He said you'd been taking care of him." Oscar looked worn out.

"Where've you been, Oscar?"

Keelin quickly went to the bar and returned with a beer.

"I've been fucking up." He laughed without any joy. "You look different, Keelin. More sophisticated. Prettier."

"Really?" When she set down her beer, the table wobbled. She grabbed some napkins and ducked under the table to fix it. Oscar watched this with interest; he had been sitting at this table the entire afternoon and evening irritated by the wobble. Now this little girl came in and fixed it without a thought.

"So Gerry told you everything?"

"Just about."

"It was news to me, too. I can assure you. I'm sure she'll get an abortion. She's a sensible girl."

"What?"

"Aisling." The priest winced and clutched his heart. "He didn't tell you, then." He took out a bottle of pink stomach mixture and drank it, washing it down with whiskey. "I'm too old to be a father. Although I've been called it all my life." He coughed miserably. "I went to the desert. I tried to look into my heart —"

"You have flies in your heart," Keelin said, her eyes narrowing.

"I took some books and went to the desert. Yes, yes, I tried to look into my heart. I went to the wilderness. *Who can tear from the veins the bad seed, the curse? The race is welded to its ruin.* What kind of child would we make, your sister and I?"

"It's none of my business," Keelin said, drained and nauseated.

"I thought to myself in the desert that I needed help. I never asked for help in my life, for anything. You are the one to help me." He took her hand in his. "You know, Keelin, I had a first love. Do you remember your first love? Mine was a university professor in Maynooth when I was in the seminary in the fifties. Wonderful. I wanted to be like him — charming, warm, erudite. He had no money, but what little he had was spent in a lofty way. Leo is a cultured man, but in no way does he have the vitality of this man I loved. I was seventeen. I think he was the only man I have loved. Our affair lasted six months. He was a bad alcoholic and wasn't he walking home in Dublin one foggy night when he fell into the canal and drowned."

"Just like the triplets."

"Just like my brothers. Yes, yes. I'd never made that connection, but there you have it! *Where will it end? Where will it sink to sleep and rest, this murderous hate, this fury?*"

"I see you've forsaken Yeats, Oscar. You're with the Greeks now."

"Ah, that's right. You've a master's in English, don't you? You'll be all right. Molly and I are so proud of you, you know that? I was reading in the wilderness. America is so huge and empty. I came to this country to escape history. My history and Ireland's history. Now I'm close to ruin. This is what happens when women are allowed to run around without control. When women aren't contained. Chaos." He made an exploding gesture with his hands.

"There was another history here you blundered into. A whole history of native dispossession. The same old story as home. And it's not the women doing all the damage in this particular case, Oscar," Keelin said. "It's you."

"I'll do my penance. I'm going to stay and take care of him. You go after Aisling and help her with whatever she needs. Tell her I'll give her as much money as she wants, but she's never to come near me again."

"Last time he said you wanted to murder him."

"I did. It was the easiest way out." Oscar rubbed his stubble. He appeared unusually shabby, Keelin noticed. "That will be fitting punishment, to have to listen to Gerry talk all day long in his dementia."

"Listen, Oscar, I won't say a word of all this to anyone, but when you go back to New York, you have to get Patrick to a doctor. He has no health insurance. I had no idea Patrick was in such a state."

"I'll have to call Leo," Oscar said, collecting himself and suddenly looking at his dirty hands. "He must be wondering where I've disappeared to. I'll tell him I'm helping an old friend die. That would sound reasonable, a priestly duty, and it's the truth."

"The truth," Keelin said, sighing. "I'll do what you want only if you help Patrick."

"That's a deal. I'm going to sober up." Oscar leaned over to her conspiratorially. "It will be horrible. You'll have to take care of Gerry for another week or so while I'm recovering."

"How will you do it?"

"I have antidepressants and other tranquilizers. When I'm not drinking I take those." He smiled crookedly, and he moved as if in discomfort, holding his chest. "I function in a highly controlled state of insanity at all times."

"Not so controlled."

"No, not when I'm drinking. It's a safety valve, Keelin, to let off a bit of steam. You'd need one, too, if you had a stronger personality."

When they were on the way back to the hotel, Oscar put his arm around Keelin and said, "Do you forgive me? Do you forgive me?"

Keelin hesitated and Oscar withdrew his arm to flag a taxi for them both. As the cab came to a stop, he turned to her.

"Well, the important thing is, I forgive myself."

It had taken Oscar weeks to be able to function without the alcohol. He'd sent them to a cheaper hotel and kept their room himself, choosing to remain very much alone. Keelin visited him every few days to give him reports, and each time he looked like a different man. One night he was wearing a toupee. "I didn't like being bald one little bit," he told her. She noticed a sun lamp in the room, and he got browner and browner until he finally turned orange. In late April, Keelin sat with Gerry for the last time before she left with Orla and Shawn for Mexico. Aisling had told Gerry that Fatima and Sadao were in Mérida, in the Yucatán peninsula.

"Did I ever show you my FBI file?" Gerry said. "It's over on the bookshelf. Half of it's blacked out, but they let you have all the useless stuff."

"Yes, you've shown it to me," Keelin said.

"What is Oscar doing? He said he'd be here half an hour ago."

"Poor Oscar. I suppose he's not a bad old skin. He said he went into the wilderness. Went to the desert to look into his heart."

Gerry opened his eyes suddenly and looked at her in disbelief. "Sure he did, honey. Palm Springs."

"What?"

"He checked into the Riviera Hotel in Palm Springs and read Greek tragedies by the pool. He told me about it. You don't know your uncle as well as I do, my dear."

"What's this?" Keelin picked up a glass crystal from the bed-side table.

"It's a crystal Aisling gave me when she left. I forget what it was supposed to do. Nothing very good, judging by the state of me now."

"I didn't know Aisling was into all this crystal crap."

"Crystals, tai chi . . . she was interested in it all. Not in a flashy way, but I saw her consult the *I Ching* when she needed to make a decision."

"Pah!" Keelin snorted. "That explains a lot."

"Yes, you look like her but you're pragmatic. She wasn't quite connected to anything. Though she lives like I lived, you and I are more alike. She even hung around those feminist witch shops. You know — spells and all that good shit."

Keelin smiled at him, wondering what he thought an old, gay revolutionary and a young Irish woman had in common. "I've seen those shops here. It was the kind of stuff Siobhan would love, too. I miss Siobhan — she'd be a lot more fun in Mexico than Orla and Shawn. At least she'd want to see a few pyramids."

"I've never been out of America, you know . . . never even out of the United States. I would have liked to visit Cuba." His voice was faint. "Or China, or Russia."

"I love you, Gerry." Keelin kissed him on the mouth.

"I hate to leave the country like this. Nineteen forty-three to nineteen ninety-five — my life is contained rather neatly in the last half of this century, don't you think? Grim years. All the evil done in the name of capital. I hope I did my best for my half century. You and Aisling must take care of the next."

"All by ourselves?" Keelin smiled at him, stroking his thin gray hair. She went to the shelf and took out an album, the first one. "These old pictures are my favorite. Look at this one."

Gerry followed her with his eyes and a smile crept to the corners of his mouth. Nineteen forty-eight, the father in a short sleeve shirt, the mother in a floral dress, smiling. Both her hands rest on Gerry's shoulders. He is five years old. Grinning and twisting. Awkwardly holding his sister's hand. She is seven, a bow in her blond hair, her father's fingers tenderly by her cheek. They pose proudly in front of their little country store. Nearby, a truck is parked under a weeping willow tree. The petrol pumps stand behind like two sentry guards. The gateway of the future.

Gerry was too weak to talk. He looked at her, his silver eyes grown dark.

"The real plague is in our hearts," she told him.

the doubting disease

PATRICK WORRIED that he had swallowed the fog after the scream at the canyon had created a void in his belly. This fog was now an unfurling, contaminated weight, and he couldn't be sure, but maybe he could dispel it by tapping on his teeth, seven times a tooth with each fingernail. Should the thumb be involved? Were his hands clean enough? He wasn't certain, but just in case, once more; once is never enough.

These organs spongy and ill, rotting inside of him, suspended in a sodden lump by his spine. Every day now he hooked his feet off the rafters and hung upside down to release his belly mass from its clump. Deep breathing mopped it up a bit, but he never became quite squeaky clean. Never quite free of doubt. Increasingly he was paralyzed by repeated action and thoughts that were incessantly renewed without direction. Perhaps he was blind, but he saw the past duplicated until the future had to be discarded.

Doubt was a disease. A curse in the DNA. A poisoned parcel handed generation to generation exploded in his face. He ran from the wideness of the world, searching for a small, clean place.

"Grasp the sparrow's tail." Morningdew's arms swam in the air, his students tracing his moves in Riverside Park. Patrick waited until the man stopped speaking and then approached him gingerly.

"Excuse me." Patrick hesitated. "I need to ask you a question."

Morningdew smiled. "Sure. Just a few minutes."

Patrick sat on the grass and observed the lesson. Morningdew, a slim, gray-haired man in his mid-forties, was telling his students to visit the Museum of Natural History.

"I want you to look at the video of the lemur. One type of lemur is the sifaka from Madagascar. The sifaka, in particular, is the best dancer in the animal kingdom. You can learn tai chi from the lemur." He began hopping sideways in giant, loping, diagonal steps, his arms widely cupping the air. The students looked on in astonishment as he bounded past them and then jogged back. "Of course, I don't have a tail, and the dance is all in the tail." He wiped the sweat from his forehead and told them to do pushing hands. As they paired themselves off he walked over to Patrick.

"Did you know my sister Aisling?" Patrick clutched a worn flyer.

"Aisling?" the teacher said. "Of course! I told her she could be a master herself if she'd iron out a thing or two. We only had her for a few weeks, though. How is she?"

"That's the problem. I have an urgent message to give her. Our mother's sick and I don't know where she is."

"Hmm. I can't help you there. She was like an angel; she came and graced us and left without a word."

Patrick turned in despair to the river.

"But you know who might know? A Nigerian guy, Abraham. She brought him along with her when I was appearing as John F. Kennedy's ghost in the Village."

Patrick looked baffled. "My friends were playing in a band and I did a guest appearance to educate the public about what really happened in Dallas. Abraham . . . now let me see. He sells watches on the corner of Fifth and Fifty-seventh." Morningdew pointed to Patrick's feet. "You shouldn't stand or walk with your feet pointing outward. Point them in the direction you are going. It's logical; otherwise you're heading toward gravitational collapse. And put 70 percent of the weight on the ball of your foot. Nijinsky, Michael Jordan, Mick Jagger — they all tiptoe. Ever notice that?"

Patrick turned his feet inward. Morningdew made slight alterations with his own foot, his hand firmly on Patrick's shoulder.

"Thanks." Patrick stared dubiously at his new feet. "What did happen to JFK? The Mob?"

"The KKK. That's not even JFK buried beside Jackie in Arlington — it's Tippit, a cop."

"What happened to his body, then?"

"He was dismembered by Scottish Celtic druids and thrown in a lake in Texas."

"Wow!"

"Stay for the lesson, if you want."

"No, I have to work. Maybe some other time."

Morningdew smiled and walked back to his class. Patrick suddenly turned and ran back to him. "Where should I put my tongue?"

"The tongue should go on the roof of the mouth," Morningdew said gravely and with authority. "The tip almost touching the back of the top teeth."

"That's brilliant," Patrick said, enthused. "I'll definitely try it." As he left he listened to the teacher speak to his students, who had gathered in rows behind him. "Embrace the tiger, return to mountain." The group stepped and turned, hands reaching out in perfect synchronicity.

With his tongue flattened against the roof of his mouth, Patrick walked past the Plaza Hotel enjoying the smell of horse shit from the tourist carriages. There were many foreigners selling scarves, bags, and watches, all with fake designer labels. If the tai chi teacher was right, there was Abraham, standing outside the Warner Brothers building with a briefcase full of watches. He was deeply black, wearing a brown leather jacket, a white shirt, and a tie. Chubby fingers held the case open for passersby. Abraham was strangely dwarfed by a giant Bugs

Bunny statue, glamorous in a tuxedo, holding out a victory carrot.

"Abraham?" Patrick said, more to the looming Bugs Bunny than to Patrick.

Abraham was immediately suspicious.

"I'm Aisling's brother, Patrick." Patrick's gaze moved from the fright of the bunny.

Abraham's shoulders relaxed and he grinned, revealing big blocks of widely spaced white teeth, like tombstones planted on a pink, gummy ridge.

Oscar sat with Gerry as Gerry stubbornly refused to die. He was in the hospital now, but his condition had not deteriorated. As Gerry sat up in bed with a photo album, Oscar read a book and tried to ignore his friend's convoluted excursions down the self-induced, catastrophic, syringe-strewn memory lane.

"My grandfather, the one who I used to try and molest, hung himself, poor Gramps. My father shot himself with a rifle. Put the barrel in his mouth and pulled the trigger with his toe —"

"Hanged." Oscar did not look up.

"I beg your pardon?"

"Hanged. A human is hanged. Not hung. Clothes are hung."

Gerry stared at Oscar for an instant and pushed his feet yet harder against the frame of death's door.

When Oscar returned to the hotel that evening, he saw a red flashing light on his phone. He listened to the message: "Oscar, it's me, Patrick. I'm in San Francisco with Fatima's brother Abraham. We're going to Vegas, but we were wondering if you could let us crash at your place tonight. Just for one night, I swear. We'll be very good. See you at ten."

Oscar lay on the bed, kicked off his shoes, and sighed heavily before opening the top drawer of the bedside table and un-screwing the lid of a pill bottle. "Childproof," the label read. I wish, Oscar thought.

That night Abraham wore a little black velvet Muslim cap with colorful beads sewn in geometric patterns. His clothes were neat, a line pressed in his beige trousers. Energy was an element of all his movements, each gesture deliberate but dynamic. His stocky frame moved neatly and cautiously, his arms in a horseshoe shape, as if driving himself by invisible gears. He was soft-spoken and patient, and he listened thoughtfully before replying with a voice that was deep and melodious. Patrick led Abraham into the luxurious lobby of the big hotel. They smiled approvingly at each other.

"Not bad. Not bad." Abraham playfully punched Patrick in the arm.

"Yeah! Pity Oscar has to be here." Patrick rocked back and forth on his newly turned-in feet.

When Abraham's older sister Fatima was ten, Mozambique became independent and the children were finally sent to schools. Their Nigerian father came home from the South Africa mines forever. He worked as a clerk in the local court and dealt in the black market on the side. Fatima joined the women's movement when she was fifteen and trained to become a health worker.

Independence brought floods, cyclones, a South African–funded civil war, drought, and famine. Armed bandits destroyed villages and farms. The beachfront in Maputo was heavily mined. Grimly, Fatima plowed ahead with her studies and work in the ruined economy. Once, in a refugee center in the countryside, she saw a huddle of people on the horizon making a hesitant approach. They stalled and gathered motionless in the distance. Fatima got on a bicycle and rode out to them, only to realize they were all naked, with only the semblance of clothes painted on, to replace the ones the bandits stole.

Several men wanted to marry her and approached her father with offers, but she refused, preferring to live alone in her own cane shack. Her father told her that everyone would think she was a prostitute. The first time he came looking for her she chased him out of her shack with a broom, but he came back.

When she refused again, he beat her to the ground with an iron bar, sedated her, and smuggled her to Nigeria with her brother.

Abraham, in terror of his father, looked at his older sister on the airplane. Completely veiled, her half-closed and swollen eyes flickered numbly through a grille in the material. She was to be concealed within the sealed skull of their paternal family home in Lagos. The family was unusually fundamentalist for Lagos. Abraham's father took him to the mosque and told him he would be sent to the university as soon as he could speak English, but Fatima was imprisoned in their home under the unblinking eyes of the women who spoke only Yoruba and left the house heavily veiled. At night she forced Abraham to teach her the English he had learned, and instead of praying she practiced woodcarving in the Yoruba style. The family mocked her for her efforts, and her father, laughing with them, arranged a marriage for her. First, however, he needed to make sure she wouldn't try to run. She was not made to wear a veil in the house, but he shaved her head. In an upstairs room the beatings were systematic, frequent, and emotionless. After each session, one of the women would take her to the bathroom, wash her down, and dress her wounds.

Meanwhile, Abraham took English lessons from Aisling, who was passing through Lagos. Abraham was lonely, and he clung to her easy presence as a soothing balm after the wasps' nest of a house.

One day, Aisling fainted in the street. Abraham took her into a house with blue, peeling walls, where some women gave her tap water as she slumped in a chair. Not wanting to leave her, he brought her to his family's house. His father was back in Mozambique but would be returning to Nigeria for the imminent wedding. For three days and nights Aisling lay in the bed beside the kitchen, nursed by Fatima, an unsmiling person. Fatima dragged her up the stairs, where she sat on a toilet bowl in agony, shame, and fever, as chickens pecked about the straw at her feet and cocked their heads at her from the yellowing enamel bath. One night the grandfather told Aisling he would write to her father imploring him to take her back and forgive her. A woman traveling the world on her own must have done something awful for the men in the family to let her go. His own daughters and granddaughters were escorted by their brothers or male relatives everywhere they went. Otherwise they worked ceaselessly at home, washing, cleaning, cooking, and taking care of the men and children. In the damp lull of evening they hung around the house like the chickens, waiting passively.

That night, Fatima sat by Aisling's bed. When Fatima pulled her blouse over her head, Aisling saw welted valleys cut across the brown plane of her back, and she saw animals stumbling in famine herds across the drought-ridden plane, knees buckling at the red watering holes that were bloated with blood and flies. Fatima lay in the bed beside her patient, and she cried angrily and quietly at this redheaded free woman who would vanish as soon as she could keep some fluid in her intestines. Only amoebas kept this woman here; creatures unseen to the eye. As she lay beside Aisling's burning body, the damp, white hands of fever stroked Fatima's small breasts. Half lucid but loathe to miss any opportunity, Aisling tried her best to make Fatima come, and Fatima swelled up into the room in a putrid gasp, her eyes turned inward to the vacuum of her future. Pain was the air that moved invisible against her skin, and oxygen razored into her mouth until she was afraid both lungs would be breathed out in shreds, her insides emptying all hope onto the floor. She would soon be a vacant smear in some man's house. *To go*, she said, thickly accented. Togo, Aisling heard. *No, no, to go.* Fatima stuffed with ideas and agonies and thoughts and aspirations. *To go.* To be kept intact. Full. Anything but to live within the barred teeth of a family, her brain hollowed into a dull cavity by the knife of tradition and kin. *To go. I, I. I go.*

Abraham cringed on the stairs. His English was better than his sister's, and he wanted to help her tell the story, but now he was swallowed by a huge dread. Fatima choked on her grief, and Aisling gaped in uncomprehending pity. I don't understand. *To go. To go.* With me? Where? *Yes. Yes. You. Yes.* All the relations were breathing heavily upstairs, thick snores that wove ropes out of the air. Abraham felt the ropes slide on the floors, wrapping about his ankles like blind snakes.

The next morning the fever broke. Aisling morosely sipped more tap water, which she believed had made her sick in the first place. Her legs shook and silver dots tingled before her eyes when she moved too quickly. Abraham whispered their story to her, and she kept glancing at Fatima, who sat grimly beside, her eyes fixed on Aisling. Aisling had some money, but they had none. She knew some men who could fix papers and told Fatima she would come back. Abraham translated, and Fatima shook her head vehemently — there was no time, her father would be back anytime now. She had all her papers in order and she knew where they were kept.

In the dead of night the three stole out to the unlit, empty street. With curiosity, Fatima looked at her surroundings; she had never been outside the house and had been drugged during the ride from the airport. That house crouching behind her was once the whole horrible world. Fatima and Abraham supported Aisling to a taxi stand; then they checked into a hotel on the other side of town. Fatima smiled for the first time. It seemed to Aisling, as she was carried up the stairs, that they were helping her escape rather than she helping Fatima. Abraham stood by the door, reluctant to leave the women, unable to take his eyes off his sister. But he returned home, coming to his street and moving mechanically toward the house that leaned blankly in the dark. This street spun sudden terror all around him. It struck him that the house was a head and their lives were just ideas inside that head. Four men suddenly gathered around him with belts, and he was thrashed by his uncles and his grandfather. He would not let the women wash him, but sat shivering in the dry bathtub, naked and appalled.

Abraham never got to university but married a cousin and became a taxi driver. Lagos was a sprawling, wild, dangerous city, and his quiet manner was drowned in all its bustle. He felt like a tiny pea rolling noiselessly through the roar of the universe. One day, mauled by the August noon heat, he received a letter from his mother, Lina, who was still in Mozambique. He read with amazement her instructions to go to a specified address to pick up a package from Japan. He drove his taxi to the address, and a woman with tight clothes and braided hair greeted him and gave him a bubble-wrapped ceramic globe. Instructions, written in Portuguese, ordered him to smash it. He ran down the stairs and broke it on the curb, finding inside a steel container holding four thousand American dollars and a note. Fatima had become an artist in Japan. She'd sold a piece for this amount and she felt he should have it.

Abraham's wife had family in America, and they used the money to fly to New York. Shortly after their arrival, his wife took another lover. Abraham moved to a tiny studio apartment in Brooklyn and lived a quiet life alone, only venturing out to sell his watches and to go to the mosque on Fridays. When he and Patrick went for lunch after meeting on Fifth Avenue, Patrick mentioned his penchant for gambling. Abraham enthusiastically agreed to accompany him to Vegas, jumping at the chance to fulfill a desire in a life where desire was maintained gravely, at a distance.

Oscar removed his contact lenses and put on his spare pair of glasses to inspect his uninvited guests. The Nigerian seemed shy and embarrassed by the invasion; Patrick was defensively cocky and nonchalant.

"Calm down, Patrick. Sit down, will you?" Oscar was irritated. He noted Patrick's surgical gloves.

"We wanted to tell Keelin the latest. Where Aisling and Fatima are."

"The telephone was invented for such information-conveying purposes," Oscar said.

Patrick shrugged. "I don't have a telephone and I don't use public phones and me and Abe are going to Vegas, so we thought we might as well check out San Francisco."

"Perish the thought one of you might have a life." Oscar

winced and poured himself some pink stomach medicine into a small glass by the bed. "And you used the telephone to ring me this evening."

"Hotel lobby phones are different, obviously. We can stay with Keelin. I thought she was here, to tell the truth. I was missing out on all the craic as usual."

"Crack?" Abraham looked up.

"Not that kind." Patrick smiled. "The Irish kind. Where are Keelin and Orla, anyway?"

"They went to Mexico weeks ago," Oscar said. When Patrick and Abraham looked at each other, he added, "Aisling's not there, is she?"

Abraham clasped his hands in front of him and looked at Patrick before he spoke. "Aisling, I believe, is in Guatemala. Fatima was there, but I recently got a letter from her saying she was in Honduras. Aisling does not know that. But she's looking for her and might find her."

They ate at the hotel restaurant. Abraham was quiet and polite and very deferential toward Oscar. When he went to the men's room, Oscar turned to Patrick. "Where did you find him?"

"Well, as you keep saying, I have no life. I thought I'd try my hand at some detective work, since everyone else seems to be making a hames of it. I saw a tai chi flyer in your apartment that time and went up to the class."

"That chancer? Morningdump, or whatever he was called?"

"Yep. That's him. He told me where I could find Abe."

"He seems like a nice, serious young man. A pleasant change from all those artsy Irish junkies you hang out with. Listen, Patrick. Talking of that time in my apartment. I paid you a sum of money in January. Then you used it to go to Hawaii and spill the beans. Am I right? Consequently I have that viper little sister of yours on my back. I thought we had an understanding."

"I didn't know that was hush money." Patrick shifted awkwardly in his seat.

"Well, it wasn't your shagging birthday."

"I'm sorry. But you and Aisling? I still don't get it."

"I paid you off, Patrick. Remember I said, 'I'm paying you off for once and for all'? That's not exactly subtle, now is it?"

"I wasn't blackmailing you. You just thought I was, so I took the dosh."

"Everyone's blackmailing me."

Abraham returned to the table and the waiter came with the food. Patrick watched the waitstaff swish around the restaurant in their pink stripy aprons, balancing great silver trays over their heads. "They all look like gay butchers," he said.

"I noticed that the corridors have mint green stripes," Abraham added.

"Like pajamas," Patrick said. "And did you see the getup the bellboys have to wear? They look like lion tamers."

"Now he's complaining about the decor!" Oscar shook his head. "I didn't know you had such an easily bruised aesthetic sense."

"No, no." Abraham was appalled. "It's beautiful, Padre, beautiful."

"Padre?" Patrick snorted. "What's with Padre? You're a Muslim."

Abraham flushed. "It's a term of respect."

Oscar patted his hand. "I appreciate it, Abraham. I only hope some of your manners rub off on my nephew."

"Jesus, Oscar," Patrick said. "You know, when you're sober you're so fucking pious."

Patrick and Abraham spent three days and two nights in San Francisco. Oscar was glad of their company and the fact that they sat with Gerry, giving him a break. Gerry was delighted with the two young men. As pathetic as he knew he was, he tried to sit in a chair, wearing not his hospital gown but his purple turtleneck and denim overalls. He showed them his pictures; they listened to his diarrhea of stories.

"He doesn't seem like he's dying," Abraham told Oscar in the evening. Oscar looked at him in horror.

"Come on, Patrick, or we'll miss the bus," Abraham said.

"You know, Padre, we missed the plane coming here because he insisted on going back to the apartment to make sure he'd put out his cigarette."

"I had this awful feeling I'd started a fire. I always do that." Oscar frowned and looked at Patrick.

"I suppose there's no chance of a wee loan," Patrick said, grinning.

"I paid you off in bulk. It was up to you to do what you wanted with it."

"I know — only messing," Patrick said. "I'm going to parlay it into a cool million." He waved his *How to Win in Las Vegas* in the air and swung his pack onto his back. Abraham was waiting for him by the elevator. Oscar and Patrick hugged each other, then Oscar watched him trundle down the green-striped corridor. A phobic nephew disappearing down the pajama leg of a giant.

Gerry was released from the hospital and let home to die. Oscar hired a nurse for him but stayed most of the day by his side, reading to him and watching videos.

"Vienna, Paris, all that shit," Gerry said from his bed. "You're so unsophisticated, Oscar. How come you never went anywhere really interesting? Never out of Europe."

"For the simple reason that I'm not interested in anything outside Europe. All history and culture is there. Who else had Dante, da Vinci, Mozart, Shakespeare, Wagner, Joyce? What else is there? I don't care to look at primitive masks and all that rubbish. Say what you will about white people, but we made it to the moon."

"Christ! You're so different from Aisling. I don't understand. What did you want with her?"

Oscar thought awhile before answering. "Aisling has no doubt. She lives like a tiger. Since she was a child I watched her. I went back every year. Those kids looked up to me. I bought them all the latest stuff from America. They were the first Irish kids with Walkmans, and those candy rocks that explode in your mouth — what were they called again? Aisling was the eldest and the brightest. Ah . . . I was mesmerized by her, that's the God's truth. I saw her learn to walk and talk and her little titties grow. She was unlike anyone. I suppose I saw her as part of the new generation in Ireland. We had grown up in the shadows, but here were Catholics raised with surety as the new dominant class. I don't know what happened to her. Why she didn't want anything. Why she ignored history."

"I don't think those kids are as obsessed with being Irish as you are," Gerry said. "I always tired of that nationalist bent with you. You remind me of the Danes. Every time I see a Dane, they're covered in little red flags. I don't see what's so extraordinary about Denmark, do you?"

"They did invent Lego." Oscar raised his eyebrows. "Listen to me, will you? Nothing is more cruel than being caught out by history. To be visiting Hiroshima on that very day. To have been Irish for eight hundred years. Gerry, you of all people know that we, as average gazelles, have to live our lives against history. We should take advantage when its currents run our way, but we can't run from it. Like white people, we're having our millennium. You think any other race would behave differently? I don't. To tell the truth, I don't understand Aisling but I thought of her every day of my life. She was more of a man than any man I have met. In fact, Gerry, she was my ideal man, and I saw it from the first, from the days she was skipping rope. From the time I taught her to dance the jig and sing songs in the kitchen. I played the tin whistle, and all the while I wanted to touch her. I'm afraid I might have. I had this dream of her, you see. This vision. She possessed conviction and cunning and grace —" Oscar paused and looked at Gerry. "Gerry, can I play you a tune?" He gestured toward his tin whistle on the bedside table. Gerry looked at it suspiciously. "You can. But *ER* is on soon, and I'm not missing all those handsome doctors to hear you play that damn flute."

Oscar reached over and dusted off the whistle. "I played this for you as a child, and then for Aisling."

"Tell me, Pied Piper." Gerry scrutinized Oscar. "Are you drinking again?"

*

He had an uncle, a spry carcass of a man, who was told to help him. But for all his vocation, he missed soothing his nephew's whirling brain. The priest doled out bread and the sinner was not hungry; he poured whiskey when he was not thirsty; he gave him money that he knew he'd fritter away. But he never asked what was needed — the soothing light of medicated salvation.

Oscar dozed at Gerry's deathbed midafternoon, *The Odyssey* on his knee. Gerry drifted in and out of consciousness, half-watching a talk show. Humans surprising other humans. Long-lost mothers, huge creatures stumbling to the stage to grab ruined adult children. Too late! Their day is done. Nothing left but a long road of disappointments to tread down. Twins reunited, staring at each other in delayed shock. Am I you? Are you me? Too late.

Oscar jolted awake, his overtanned face rumpled in fright.

"What was Aisling?" Oscar gulped. "Some barbarian peacocking out of Asia?"

"What's wrong?" Gerry managed to whisper.

"Keelin asked me to take care of her brother. Patrick's a grown man. I let him go. And I saw him creep around the bloody hotel room as if he were in Hiroshima, protecting his hands, moving things with his elbows."

Gerry reached out his stick arm and let Oscar crawl into his deathbed. Lie in his needle-thin arms. His eyelashes, hard and white as toothbrush bristles, scratched the priest's skin.

"Poor Oscar." Gerry sighed. "Too late."

Patrick and Abraham reached Las Vegas on the bus from Chinatown, full of awe and jubilation. They meandered up the strip, pointing and exclaiming before entering any casino.

"It's like an evil Disneyland," Patrick said.

Abraham shook his head in wonder at the desert sky shattered with lights. "Hold on now, Patrick. Before we hit the town we have to find a place to sleep."

The first week they stayed in a big casino, but then the weekend rates forced them to a motel. Abraham found a job as soon as he ran out of money and told Patrick he was going to settle.

"I feel truly happy here," he said with his usual sad, pensive expression. "All the pretty lights — how could anyone ever feel bad?"

"That's sick!" Patrick was aghast. "You know, this is not a city to work regularly in, Abe. Money, money. Haven't you seen how money loses its value here? How can you work for the minimum wage when you see people win the jackpot in an instant?"

"I kept losing. In the end you lose. I'm lucky to get this job. I have no green card."

"Neither do I, but shit . . ."

Abraham moved into a cinder-block house with two African-American men on the fringes of town. Patrick lost all his money playing blackjack and slept on their couch. The desert waited hungrily outside. During the day he straggled in shorts and stained T-shirt through the flashing lights and clanging noise of the casinos, sweeping his hand inside the metal bottoms of the slot machines for overlooked quarters. He found a few and pushed them into a slot. He lost. Then the next day he won five bucks and traded it in for a gambling chip. By the end of the week he bought himself some good clothes in the mall and was staying in a suite at the Mirage.

"I have a system," he told the three men in the cement house.

He was counting cards, learning the formulas from a book. The trick was not only to count cards but to disguise that fact from the trained eye of the dealer and the pit boss, who prowled like a caged animal amidst the tables. Soon he was thrown out of a few casinos, and it was becoming increasingly difficult to find places where he could count, since most casinos dealt the cards from a shoe, not double-deck. Broke again after two weeks, he deposited himself once again on Abraham's couch. One day he was walking on the strip when he noticed a package on the sidewalk. It was a sealed box of hair dye with a woman's smiling face on the front.

"What's all this shit?" Bill, one of the men in the house, screamed from the bathroom, holding a blackened towel and glaring at the black spatters that covered the white tiles. Patrick sat sheepishly on the couch, his red hair now jet black. Abraham came home and stared at him in fright. "Are you in trouble?" Abraham asked.

Patrick shook his head. "I just found it on the road. I thought it might be lucky."

"He's in trouble," Bill glowered. "He's in trouble for sure."

A long day's silence between Oscar and Gerry was broken.

"I just want to say thank you. You may have been blackmailed, but you've come through for me. I needed you here. I couldn't die alone."

"We are born alone and we die alone. Each to our own separate graves."

"But what about after?"

"Don't tell me you're going to make a clamorous deathbed conversion."

"But is there an afterlife?"

"We'll plead our lonely lives before our private gods, and none of us will be saved."

"Will everyone be there?"

"We'll sit in silence between the strangers with whom we shared our lives."

"Will we be scared?"

"Only afraid that we might have to live again."

"How can you say that?"

"I know nothing about death. I know a good wine. How can there be an eternity in paradise without good wine?"

"So now I know what hell is. A restaurant where all your parishioners are in heaven, seated around the tables, and I'm their waiter. Do you know anything about life?"

"I know the strongest dreams may yet be the ones we built from sand."

"Do you love me? What do you see when you see me?"

"I see the skeletons dance on the hillside."

"Did you love me as a boy?"

"Shh! Listen. Can't you hear them? *Con legno.*"

"Fuck you, Father!"

Patrick was rich again and checked into the Stardust. He rented a car when Abraham had two days off and they drove to the Grand Canyon. Patrick assured him he had packed provisions in a small backpack, and they followed a footpath down into the earth. After an hour's hiking, Abraham asked for water.

"Catch." Patrick threw him a beer.

"I need water."

"I didn't bring any. Just beer."

Abraham sighed and opened the can of warm beer. They sat on a rock and admired the view. "You'd better stay where you are. The guys say you can't come back."

"I figured it would come to this." Patrick lit a cigarette.

"I'm sorry."

"I'm used to it."

"Why don't you get a job like me?"

Patrick laughed. "If I start cleaning I might never stop."

The next afternoon, at a traffic light in Vegas, a prostitute approached their red convertible. She was plump and as deeply black as Abraham, but with long blond and copper red extensions in her hair. She wore a red leather miniskirt, a low-cut, tight pink top, and tall white boots. Abraham and Patrick looked at each other and smiled.

"Hop in!" Abraham nodded to the back seat, and the woman smiled and clambered into the car.

"Yahoo!" Patrick whooped and accelerated.

"What's your name?" Abraham shouted over the noise of the car.

"Raven."

"That's pretty." Abraham nodded. "Very nice. Very nice."

Patrick winked at Raven through the overhead mirror and she smiled back, the sun glinting off her gold front tooth.

As the three lay naked in the hotel room watching cartoons, Abraham dozed off with his hand cupped over his genitals.

"Do you know where we could get some coke?" Patrick asked Raven.

"Sure. Want to come with me for a ride in your nice car?"

They dressed and crept out, leaving Abraham asleep as Wile E. Coyote fell down a canyon to his doom, a boulder landing on his head.

A row of squat cement houses was sliced by a dusty dirt road. The air was sweetened by sewage, and there was no sidewalk. Just dirt right up to the door. The windows of the houses were glassless square holes. Warily, Patrick followed Raven through an open door. As Patrick's eyes adjusted to the light, he saw several African-Americans in the room eyeing him suspiciously. A tall man stood at the door. There was a gun on the table beside him. Under the table, a skinny dog scratched its side with a dirty, bandaged hind leg.

"He's cool," Raven told them. "We just came to get high."

Patrick sat, suddenly self-conscious of his scrawny, fish white body and his mop of jet black hair. After smoking some crack, the men loosened up a bit. Patrick was relieved when he noticed there were two women in the corner. When they left, the man at the door, whom Patrick realized was only about fifteen years old, came out in the sun to admire his car.

When they got back to the room, Abraham refused to do any coke. "No, not for me. I've got to get going. I have to work early in the morning."

"Come around tonight after work," Patrick said. "We'll be here, or you can page us in the casino." Abraham could barely look at Raven; he averted his eyes when she kissed him good-bye.

"He's cute," she said, when Abraham was gone. "A little square. Hey, can I call some of my friends over?"

"No sense in wasting a suite," Patrick said, closing the door, opening it and closing it again, opening it once more before closing it finally.

Abraham returned that night to find the living room full of women. There was a mirror on the table with several white powder lines. When Patrick saw him, he jumped up and pulled his robe together.

Abraham took him aside. "Patrick, when you get a whore, you're just meant to have sex and that's it."

"Really? I'm a novice. I never read the rule book."

"It was my first time, too. But I know they should leave."

Patrick shrugged. "No. This is the most fun and sex I've had in years. Relax, Abe. They're all pretty cool."

"I'm going to leave. I can't stay."

"Suit yourself." Patrick patted his friend on the back. "You enjoyed yourself yesterday, huh?"

"It was a good trip. The last bit made me feel dirty all day."

Patrick nodded, as if he sympathized.

"I don't understand you. You wear rubber gloves but you pick packages off the street and spend all this time with these women?"

"Some things are contaminated, some not. I have a system," Patrick said. "It's too complicated to explain."

"And not logical."

Patrick frowned. "I wouldn't go that far."

When Abraham left, Patrick did a line of coke and dangled his car keys drunkenly in the air, his white robe falling open. "Which of you lovely young ladies wants to go cruising?"

Abraham showed the letter to Patrick a few days later as they watched a magician perform an act with his wife and young daughter in Circus Circus. Each member of the magic family wore a loose-fitting Ali Baba costume. The turbanned magician put his wife in a box and sawed her to pieces in front of the numb, overstimulated crowd gorging itself on popcorn and hot dogs. The drums rolled, and he took his veiled daughter by the hand and proceeded to hypnotize her.

"Fatima is in Honduras, as I thought. Here's her address. She says it's on the coast and she'll be there for a while."

"No mention of Aisling."

"She hasn't mentioned your sister to me since the night I left them in the hotel in Lagos."

"Not even in New York?" Patrick looked at the letter. "I'm going to take this address and send it to Keelin. Oscar must know where she is . . . Jesus, come to think of it, nobody really knows where anybody is."

"Your sister wants something from my sister. I don't know what."

The daughter, wearing multicolored satins and a ruby stud in her belly button, was suspended horizontally in mid-air. With a flourish, the father swept a large plastic hoop about the levitating girl. The mother, smiling, held out a sword on a red cushion.

Patrick looked at Abraham in amusement. "They were girlfriends, Abe."

"Fatima was with Sadao," Abraham said. "She wasn't like that. And Aisling was with me in New York."

The father held the sword under his daughter's back. With a clash of the cymbals, he shoved her down onto the blade until it stuck out of her belly — without a drop of blood shed. And she never even opened her eyes.

"From what I've heard of Aisling, she'll sleep with animal, vegetable, or mineral." Patrick shoved the last bite of a hot dog into his mouth and again examined the Portuguese in the letter.

"Where can I contact you?" Abraham stood, then reached for the letter.

"Just page me. I'm usually in the Mirage or Barbary Coast."

"How's it going?"

"Well, I'm up two grand again. I get by. I've worked out a new poker system. They won't allow me play blackjack anymore. I'm crashing with this Persian guy, Amir, in a motel at the moment. He helped me out once or twice when I was skint, so I look after his father for him."

Amir's father was dying. He lay in the cot beside the window while Amir gambled all through the night. Every morning Amir came and shook Patrick awake in the main bedroom. Patrick stumbled into the grotesque red jangle of the casinos to play poker with the tourists, hardcore professionals, big white men in cowboy hats, and Chinese in yellow shirts with flyaway collars. He ate at the casino buffets alone, occasionally meeting Raven to get high or take her to dinner. Sometimes his obsessions would grow so loud and hurt so much that he'd have to find a place in an empty corridor to sit and focus on one point in front of his eyes to sever the growing anxiety, the unrelievable panic. At nine each night he walked to the Budget Suites behind the Stardust. Alone, the old man would stare at him, a certain steady horror in his gaze. He spoke no English and had lost his only other son in the Iran-Iraq War. It was hard to lose a child, especially the wrong one. One day, as Patrick changed the bed, Amir standing with his father draped limply in his arms, he found a shell-less hard-boiled egg in the dirty sheets. He picked it up carefully between two fingers and turned to Amir, who remained stoic. The father gazed unflinchingly. Patrick placed the egg with reverence on the windowsill and finished making the bed. That night Patrick dreamed that he was carrying the egg down the stairs of the motel when it hatched, and the old man's own father was born. The father died the next day, and Amir returned to Los Angeles with the body. Patrick never saw him again.

Oscar stood by the living room window. Gerry lay dead in the bedroom behind him. Oscar absently twirled the tin whistle in his hand and spoke out loud to the street below. As if Gerry was more likely to be there than in the long slender corpse on the bed.

"You weren't a lion, Gerry, but you weren't an average gazelle, either. At the very least, you might have been a giraffe." And he tapped his whistle twice off the window, then put it to his mouth and inhaled, as if calmly withdrawing all music from the world.

Aces and eights — a plague bell in a card hand. When he cashed in, a fifty-dollar bill came sliming from behind glass, like a frog in his hand, and so he ran. Green as the boggy hills that spawned him, croaking for mercy in the crimson-gloom corridor of a desert hotel. Then he hopped back to the grand halls, where there was money in the machines. Not greed. He didn't play to accumulate. He played to control the panic of the still world breathing. His greenish freckled hands webbed with a fan of cards. Aces and eights — dead man's hand moaning out like a foghorn in the casino zinc rain. This ghost of the foghorn; as a child, a wee quivering tadpole, he had lain in his bed and worried with it through the night. He is a man now in a parched inland town.

Often Raven and Patrick would wander around the casinos trying to spot the most hideous apparition among all the flotsam of Vegas humanity. There were legions of old, unsmiling ladies in jogging suits sitting by the slot machines, their stuffed ashtrays trailing thin toxic lines into the broken air. The disabled sourly losing, shifting hopelessly in their wheelchairs and rooting for more change. This city was serious. There was not a glimmer of humor in all its flash and glitter.

"I have to show you something," Patrick told Raven one night at the bar. "I've found a real specimen."

"Patrick, we need to talk," Raven said urgently, following him as he marched through the aisles in his striped shorts and Donald Duck T-shirt.

"There." Patrick pointed to a woman sitting under a display car with a bucket of quarters and a grim look of determination on her face. She was an obese Native American and she had a cleft head. Her hairline was midway on her scalp, behind the split. The skull rose in two huge bald bumps. One of her eyes was an empty slit and her left hand had only two curled fingers that mechanically put the coins into the slot.

"Pretty good," Raven nodded. "Pretty damn good."

"Probably the result of some nuclear testing in the desert," Patrick said as they hid behind a row of poker slots, observing.

"Probably." Raven grabbed Patrick's arm. "Listen, sugar, I've just been on a job and the guy is connected with the casino or something. But he had a briefcase full of fifty-dollar bills. Can you imagine how much that is?"

"No, not really."

"Patrick, I know someone who works at the desk. I could get a spare key. You go up there and get the money."

"You're joking, right?" Patrick straightened up.

"He wants me to meet him and go for a drink."

"I'm meeting Abe in a few minutes."

"Then take him, babe. You want to live in Vegas forever? We could get a house somewhere. Picture it, honey — your own house. I'm telling you, the money is in the briefcase on the table, for the taking. The man is a fool. I'm going to talk to my friend. Where are you meeting your little friend?"

"Back at the bar here." Patrick scowled. "This sounds like a cinch. Too fucking easy. Are they Mob? No — don't answer that."

"I'll see you in half an hour at the bar." Raven kissed him and walked off.

Abraham wiped the sweat from his brow after hearing Patrick's plan. "Oh my goodness."

"Abraham, come on. You'll never get anywhere. We're just a pair of eejits. There's no future for us. Take a risk. We've nothing to lose."

"Nothing to lose," Abraham repeated slowly. "Nothing."

"Here she comes." Patrick slapped Abraham on the back.

"O.K., boys! Here's the deal. Me and him are going for a drink and a show. The money's still on the table in a brown leather briefcase. These are the keys to my car, it's parked outside my apartment. Don't head toward L.A."

"Where'll we meet up?" Abraham asked.

"I know," Patrick said. "There's a town on the way to the Grand Canyon. Chloride. It's a tiny, weird place. There wasn't a soul there when we stopped off. The only person we saw was a woman on a horse riding down the street."

"Fine. Chloride. I can remember that name. But where in the town?"

"The cemetery. They had a graveyard with a big sign. Chloride Cemetery. Where all the action is."

"What kind of place you taking me to? Some hippie shit?" Raven said.

"I don't know, but it's Bumblefuck, Arizona, and they'll never find us there," Patrick said.

"I'll be there tonight or tomorrow morning. Wait for me. And man, don't screw me over on this one."

"We won't," Abraham said. "You have our word."

"Hey, Mr. Righteous is coming too? Well I'll be damned."

"Nothing to lose," Abraham said, shrugging.

"Vegas gets everyone in the end." Patrick grinned. "It's the sound of the money."

She gave them the key and they walked to the elevators. Patrick put his hand on her plump ass and she brushed it off. "Be serious, Patrick. This is heavy shit. No fucking up. Don't get into one of your funks."

"I'm cool," Patrick said. "No shenanigans." He laughed. "Look at Abe. So sad."

"The room is empty now. Room 7888. On the seventh floor."

"See you in Chloride." Patrick waved as the elevator door closed.

They slipped the key card through the slot and pressed down on the handle. On the table were a champagne bucket and some gambling chips. Patrick grabbed the briefcase and, turning nervously, dropped his wallet. He scooped it up with a matchbook that had fallen with it. Keelin's address in Mexico was written on the inside.

"Jesus." He stared at the address. "Wouldn't want to leave this here."

"Come on!" Abraham urged, pushing Patrick out the door.

They legged it down the endless, garish corridor to the elevator.

"I should get rid of this in case they catch me." Patrick threw the matchbook into a trash bin downstairs.

Vegas vanished behind them as they drove into the desert.

"Say bye-bye!" Patrick said.

"Bye-bye!" Abraham laughed and waved from the front seat. "Should we open it?"

"Yeah, go on!" Patrick's hands were clammy inside his gloves as he gripped the wheel.

Abraham popped it open to find wads and wads of green notes. "Close it," Patrick whispered in awe. "Jesus tonight!"

Five minutes later Patrick was paralyzed at the wheel, his eyes wide open in terror. "I have to go back."

"What?" Abraham turned sharply toward Patrick.

"The matchbook. I dropped it in the room. It had Keelin's Mexico address in it. Oscar gave it to me just three days ago."

"You threw it out in the lobby. I saw you. Don't you have her address somewhere else?"

"I have it in my address book too. I already sent her a letter. But are you sure I picked up the matchbook from the floor?"

"I saw you." Abraham breathed deeply. "Patrick, you've done this before, but for stupid stuff. This is serious."

"You're right. You're right." He nodded slowly, in a daze. "Absolutely."

Abraham covered his face with his hands, and later, when he lifted them, he saw the sun's rays through dark thunderclouds. He turned to Patrick, who was now riven in panic.

"I'm going back. I have to check. I left it on the floor. I know I did."

"No."

"They're going to a show. It'll take hours. I'll knock first, pretend I'm looking for someone."

"I'm not going back with you, Patrick. No way! Let me out here."

Patrick pulled over, and Abraham got out in a rage.

"Come on, Abe. Get back in. You won't have to come in with me."

"You're crazy — I've known that. You do crazy things all the time. But now you're a fool. I'll hitch to Chloride and meet you there whenever."

Patrick nodded distractedly, then screeched around and headed back toward Vegas. In the distance, clouds rained on the mountains. The air was tight. Abraham stood alone on the empty desert road with a briefcase full of money.

*

Patrick knocked loudly on the door. No answer. He pressed his ear to the wood and listened. He pounded the door with his fists. Nothing. Sweeping the key swiftly through the slot, he pushed the door and dashed in. Three men stood about him and caught him by the arms.

"Jaysus, wrong room. I was looking for my friend Paddy. What's up, lads?"

He was led through the casino with a bloody face and T-shirt. Though his eyes appealed in wild fright to everyone he saw, the faces he met were those of a dazed species. The sound of the money in the machines set like hot molten iron in his ear and the ring-ding-ting of the slots glowed with him as they led him to the parking lot. In the car they pressed him once more for the money. He would give no names, no places. Shook his head and blubbered. Now he was in a movie as they drove toward the desert; he could see the wide camera shot of the car splice through the neon fizz, and a close-up of himself, his plastic gloves torn off, his fingernails bloody and sliced. His balls twisted and shrunk after they were wrung like wet, raw sausage.

"Oh Jesus and Mary and sweet Saint Joseph," he sniveled in the car.

They told him they'd let him go if he gave the name and location, but he shook his head, blood bubbling out of his nose.

The car was freed from the city and sped onto the highway. He tried to think of good things. The night before the pope's visit, when Uncle Oscar, so suave and debonair, visited with the two priests, and Aisling sat at the table with them. Two men now sandwiched him in the back seat, and the man in the front shouted at them to push him down so he wouldn't be seen. They grabbed his hair and plunged him down, as if baptizing him in a river, but they didn't pull him up. He looked at the fuzzy floor, the blood rushing to his head. Molly was at the piano all night and they all sang songs, rebel songs, famine songs, drinking songs, sad songs. Folded over like a collapsible deck chair, Patrick focused on his limbs because they looked different. The fingers seemed more angular, his hands were like flat blocks, and his bare, hairy legs merely paper apparitions. If he could only reach his finger out and touch each toe through the man's scuffed brown shoe, then he would be safe. The index finger stretched and stroked the left foot and then the right. "What the fuck?" the man kicked him in the chin and Patrick's tongue was snapped in between his teeth until his mouth swelled with blood. The car turned off the main road and jolted up a bumpy track for miles. They stopped and pulled him out where there was no road to be seen. They were in the middle of the desert.

"Don't hurt me. I don't know where it is or what you want."

Why torture him here? Just for the scenery? And it was so beautiful. The yellow earth for miles and the buckled yellow mountains. The sky reaching in an arc of bright blue from one vast horizon to the other. They were shouting among themselves. Just leave the little shit. Shoot him, shoot him. Why? I haven't done a thing. Why would you shoot me for money? They grabbed him and sat on his chest. Money? Where's the fucking money? He was hauled up by his bloody Donald Duck T-shirt and flung onto the ground. He knelt like a dog, spitting a tooth onto the earth. The place was teaming with ants. As the men fought, these ants surrounded the tooth and rocked it back and forth. So much life in the desert. Lizards and snakes and rats and . . . clear exploding shots pinned through the iron ring and ding of money pounding in his ear, and he lay flat down. Now he could hear so clearly, could even hear the ants lift the tooth, but the fantastic blue of the sky was fading, and a fog was rising behind his eyes, blotting out the world. *Glory O! Glory O!* The music came swinging over the desert plains, sung by priests and mothers and missing children, and it settled in the sands and it seeped into the rough earth. And Patrick is smiling. Aisling is turning to him, accepting a drink, her face is flushed and her eyes so bright. Oscar's missionary friend has his eyes tightly clenched through the whole song, Molly's rubbery hands spider over the keys: *Glory O! Glory O! to her brave sons who died, For the cause of down-trodden man!*

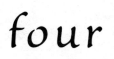

four

the magpie of mexico city

I N A RENTED ROOM in Mexico City, Keelin's mind was unraveling under Shawn's tyranny. Rules were arbitrary but absolute. She was being oppressed by nests. There were parts of the room where neither Keelin nor Orla could walk. Since Keelin had been so close to AIDS, she was contaminated and there was nothing they could touch mutually. Her outcast cup and spoon were kept apart. Her towel segregated. Floor sweeping was not tolerated. Doors had to be opened slowly; no sudden movements were permitted anywhere, as dust could rise from the floor. Her skin was in the air, and he could not let this contaminated air rise to his mouth. The nests grew bigger. There was one near the window as big as a table, made of leaves, stones, lint, and threads. Clothes were being plucked apart, blankets dethreaded and feathers stolen from the pillows. When Keelin entered the room, she slid along the wall as Shawn eyed her, his terror readily transformed into rage. His face a pinball machine of tics. Worried, Orla met two other fifteen-year-olds in a disco and brought them home. But Shawn could not let them in. He peered through a crack in the door and said he'd see them outside at the sandwich bar, and then he didn't go. Keelin realized he was not mobile and postponed the search for Aisling until after she had decided what to do about him.

Keelin went to Trotsky's house and took a picture of the toilet. She studied the bullets in the wall and later, in the garden, thought of the ice pick. Crude instrument. Ancient almost. In the rain, standing outside the blue-painted *farmacia,* she pictured those assassins. They came so far to kill. Lonely and at a loss, she still didn't want to return to Shawn and Orla. There were cockroaches that waited on the wall, not changing position for hours. The nests were full of them, moving with them, rocking at night. She thought she could hear them scratch around inside. Placing roach motels in the corners, she bided her time, but they checked in and dined with impunity. Some were now deformed, new mutants moving with the same old rapidity. Assassin. Crunching them with her shoe. The boy wouldn't leave his nests alone with the sisters anymore. He was afraid for them now that they were alive. Orla pleaded with Keelin to keep her company at home but was too lazy to join her sister in jaunts around the giant city. While Orla sat at the corner café eating cakes, Keelin was standing on top of pyramids one day and being groped on underground carriages the next. One afternoon Keelin was sheltering from the May heat in a cinema when she got a nosebleed. In the bathroom, she grimaced in the mirror while mopping up the blood. The brown skin of popcorn kernels stuck out from between her teeth like cockroach wings.

Later she ran into Orla at the sandwich bar. Orla had a weekend bag in her hand.

"Remember those fifteen-year-olds?" Orla asked excitedly.

"What about them?" Keelin paid for a sandwich and began to unwrap it.

"Well, they want to take us to Acapulco. Shawn won't come, but I packed a few things for you. They've a car. We'd be down there tonight and back tomorrow evening."

Keelin took a big bite of the sandwich and shrugged. "I don't know."

"Please, Keelin. It's a chance to see Acapulco."

"Where is Acapulco?"

"It's on the coast, down south."

"You won't go anywhere in the city with me but you want to drag me all over creation. What's up your sleeve?"

"I've packed your swimsuit and a pair of knickers." Orla dangled the bag in the air. "And an extra pair of leggings in case you wet yourself."

"How thoughtful."

"Come on."

Keelin thought of returning to Shawn without Orla as a buffer.

"What the hell."

"We have to hurry. We're meeting them beside the cathedral."

Keelin took a last bite of her sandwich and warily followed her sister. "All my worst decisions start with a 'what the hell.'"

The boy Quique leapt out of a battered car when he saw them. Quique was short and fair-skinned, and his light brown hair hung in his eyes. His arms were muscled; he'd told them before that he was training to be a matador. As they approached, Keelin stalled. Three middle-aged Mexican men eyed them from inside the car.

"They're not fifteen," she said as Orla clambered into the front with Quique. One of the men got out, and Keelin got in back between them.

"This is my papa," Quique said, introducing the man in the driver's seat. His father, Jorge, was a big man with a beard. The two galoots in the back had no English but barely grunted a word in Spanish, either. One had a bunched-up face and a wobbly mouth that looked as if it was perpetually trying to smile but could never muster the requisite emotion. Tattooed hands rested over the other's big belly; he was tall and European-looking, a wide cartoon scar across his throat.

The battered car wove through the traffic under the polluted slate sky and headed south out of the city. When it grew dark they discovered the headlights didn't work. Quique rolled joints and passed them around, and a cooler of beer was almost empty by the time they hit the highway. Keelin refused nothing.

"I might as well be numb for my rape and murder," she leaned up to tell Orla.

"Relax!" Orla pushed her back between the two unsavory specimens. The boy rested his head against Orla's ample shoulder in the front seat. Unlit, the car hurtled through canyons, Mexican music blaring from the radio, lightning forking through the air and providing green flashes of illumination.

"My behavior will not stand up in court," Keelin told the uncomprehending man beside her. The father put his hand behind him and squeezed her leg.

They reached Acapulco the next afternoon. It was full of American fast-food restaurants and white tourists. As they checked into the Hilton, Mexican Indians worked invisibly to make it all shine.

Jorge paid for Orla to be flown like a kite from a parachute over the bay as the rest sat eating tostadas and drinking margaritas on the beach.

"You want a go too?" he asked Keelin.

Orla was a small dot on the horizon.

"My life is difficult enough without dangling myself above Acapulco in a parachute." She took a photo of him and his buddies. "For the police," she told them pointedly.

Orla skidded through the blue sky. When they roped her down onto the sand, her skirt blew up above her ears, exposing her giant thighs and lack of underwear.

"Dress up, girls; we're taking you out." Back in the hotel room, Jorge clapped his hands together. The two other men lay on beds, scratching their balls and watching cable.

"This does not look like the local gringo joint," Keelin grumbled when they arrived at a club and giant executioners with hoods and bare chests lifted their axes and let them walk under.

Inside there was a boxing ring with stripping women. Busboys walked around dressed in prisoner stripes and dragging balls and chains, and naked women climbed stairs to a glasswalled shower. Drinks were imbibed out of mugs shaped like breasts, the milky tequila spewing out of the ceramic nipple. A bishop floated by with menus.

"Maybe you don't like me," Jorge said to Keelin. "Which one

do you like?" He made a gesture toward his friends, who stared at a Madonna video on the TV screens. Keelin pointed at a slim, tiny girl with cropped black hair. Jorge smiled knowingly and called her over. Casually, the girl climbed up on the table and began to dance for them. She pulled down her knickers with a jolt. Not teasing at all. She was completely shaved. Keelin was mesmerized. Without that line, the world ends. For now it was a coin slot, but that girl carried the sea in her, just there, the last remnants of a fishy past. A trail of flesh and change from sea to trees to strip bars.

"Are you pretending to be a lesbian now?" Orla threw her eyes up to heaven.

Keelin rose with dignity from the table and crunched over the stony floor. In the black-walled restroom, a short Spiderman mopped the floor. His dark Mayan eyes burned out at her from behind the costume, his lips red and frowning through the slit.

"I'm leaving now, Orla," Keelin said upon returning to the table. "This is not my scene. I don't know what I'm doing here. What if poor Molly saw us now?"

"Relax, Keelin, would ye? You're not Miss Marple. We're Irish; we do everything in a roundabout way that involves lots of drinking and bonking."

The sisters sat and ate in the bus station. "I'm staying here for a wee bit with Quique," Orla said.

"What about Shawn?"

"You can check on him. He's fifteen, almost sixteen. He's not a child."

"He's ill. He won't let me come near him."

"The poor wee gossin. Don't be so hard on him." Orla sighed. "Why are you so mad at me, Keelin?" She mopped up her huevos rancheros with some tortilla. "Because I'm fat?"

"What?"

"I see you stare at me. I can feel your disgust."

"No." Keelin squirmed. "Well, you weren't always so fat. I just wonder why."

"Molly is fat. You don't hate her for it."

"I don't hate you. Jesus."

"You expect me to lose weight until I look like you, and you aren't even happy with your own body."

"That's true. I do need to lose ten pounds."

"Aisling once told me that there are two types of bodies. Good bodies and bad bodies. A good body is not a body that is healthy, it's a body that's used to sell a product." Orla pointed to the Budweiser ad with two women in bikinis. "See? Good bodies are everywhere." She tapped the table with an eggy finger. "We all feel we have bad bodies because we cannot be used to sell."

Keelin applauded lightly with her fingers on her palm. "Bravo."

Orla wiped her mouth and grinned. "That's the one thing Aisling knew that the rest of yiz hadn't a clue about. You all think I'm stupid, but I'm not."

"I better go look for Aisling in Mérida. We kind of got stuck in Mexico City, since we can't abandon the shagging nests."

"Tell Shawn I'll be there soon. To wait for me."

Keelin drained her Coke. "Orla, do you ever see animals out of the corner of your eye though you know they're not there? Sort of a trick of the eye? Like a cat walking by the open door and you turn quickly, just to like check, you know, though you know there is no cat?"

"Nope." Orla stood. "I'm going back before they sleep without me."

Orla patted Keelin on the back. "Take it easy, love. Aisling is living her own life. Enjoy Mexico. You'll be back with Molly before you know it. Relax."

Keelin felt a sweat break out and sparks fly before her eyes. "Relax?" She rubbed her brow despairingly with one hand. "I just went out to get a sandwich and ended up in Acapulco."

When Keelin got back, she found that Shawn had used red and blue masking tape to mark the floor in complicated patterns, surrounding his nests like angular Saturn rings. Dirty red hair hung over his gaunt, old-man face.

"Have you eaten?" Keelin stood at the door, opening it inch by inch. It was dark inside. Shawn saw her eye the floor.

"I've worked out a system."

"I'm going to go and get you food. Want to come?"

"No, get Orla to do it."

"Let me in, Shawn."

He reluctantly stepped away from the door. An immense nest blocked the window. It was made of branches, clothes, lint, mud, food cartons, shredded comic books, newspapers, and it was tied with belts and tape.

"I marked the parts where you can walk in red and the parts where Orla can in blue."

Keelin approached the huge nest in awe.

"Keep in the red, I said!" he howled. She looked at her feet and stepped into the red path.

"It's ginormous," she croaked.

"Stay away from it. It's not finished."

"How come my red path doesn't go to the toilet, Shawn?"

"I hadn't finished."

"Why did you come with Orla, Shawn?"

He hesitated, caught off guard. "I was driving my family crazy. My dad hates me, and they would fight about it all the time."

"When did you start making nests?"

"When I was nine."

Keelin let her bag slip onto the floor, causing Shawn to freak out.

"Keelin, I told you to stay between the red lines! Now you've raised God knows what dust. Slapping things about."

Keelin lay carefully on the bed, mindful not to make a commotion. "You made this in the last two days, huh? What else did you do?"

"I read," he said defensively. "You read all the time."

She looked at a pile of comic books by his bed. "Do you know what happens to superheroes?"

"What would you know?"

"Oh, I know. I just ran into Spiderman. They end up cleaning toilets in strip bars in Acapulco."

He was puzzled. Keelin sighed. "A few months ago as a schoolteacher I'd have tried to whip you into shape. Now I'm at a loss. What will we do with you at all — at all?"

In the night that was darker than ever, Keelin's dreams were pursued by animals. She stirred throughout the chase and turned in the bed toward the blocked window. There was a rustling inside the giant nest. Rats, she thought.

"It's not rats," Shawn said in the morning. "The center is wire and has plastic bags tied to it. I left the window open. It's air, I swear." There was a trail of dry blood from his ear. His pillow was dotted with red spots.

"I'm surprised you don't put bells on it," she said. "And wheels."

He laughed, and when he laughed he looked like Patrick.

Shawn had scabs inside his nostrils and he scrunched his nose to stretch them, testing the momentary pain. Then he fingered one and it felt satisfyingly monstrous in scale to his nostril wall. An alien terrain, offering depth and possibility. But when he held Keelin's hand mirror to his face and pulled at his nose to look, all mystery vanished. The scab was small and banal, lacked complication. He kept more in his ears. If he didn't pick them for two days they would be gone, and it was painful to start from scratch. He laughed at the pun. Keelin peered over her book at him.

"You said Orla would be back days ago." Now he looked at his ears in the mirror.

"That's what she told me. I've to get going, but I can't leave you."

"Go. You both left me before," he sniffed in disgust.

The next day Shawn came back with an old broken bicycle pump and some branches.

"Where's my hand mirror?" she asked.

He placed his new booty in a pile beside the largest nest and brushed himself off carefully. "It's in one of the nests." He had his back to her.

"Which one?" Her tone was strained.

"I can't remember."

"I'll tear the whole shagging lot apart."

"You know the laws."

"Laws? Jesus, Shawn, find it. I want it. I'm going out and I expect it to be there when I come back, you hear?"

Keelin left and walked through town. Earthquake cracks forked through the buildings like shadows of lightning. She halted in front of a Ferris wheel that spun almost empty in a cramped fairground full of rubble. Every half-hour she had to pee, and it burnt. That very morning she had spotted a minuscule green worm in her pants. A womb teaming with worms? A bladder devoured? She might have been mistaken. Lately animals were all around. Cockroaches on the wall, rats in the nests; at night she was afraid to sit on the toilet in the dark in case there was a frog inside. In the morning, a definite aftertaste of feathers and fur in her mouth. Finally she stood at a fruit juice counter scouring her dictionary for words. Her phrase book was full of strange sayings that had the poignant distinction of being selected as the bare minimum for scraping by. The bitter bones of communication. She was struck by their pathos when read at random. *¿Podria limpiarme el parabrisas? ¿Le importa que fuma? Me está esperando. ¿Comprende usted? Cubrale. ¿Queda muy lejos? ¿Puede ayudarme? ¿Quieres bailar? Prefiero el esquí acuático.* Under the Making Friends section was Spanish: "I have wall-to-wall carpeting in my house back in Canada." The dictionary at the back had too many misprints and omissions. She looked up orange, but they didn't have it. They had "magpie." *Manzana* was house corner, but *manzana* was apple in the shop. Maybe both, but wouldn't apple be more important? Shouldn't oranges take precedence over magpies? Nothing was certain now for her. Unable to make a decision about what to get, she headed back home.

Shawn had salvaged the mirror and almost threw it at her

before curling up on the bed, his shoulders shaking. She took it to the bathroom and squatted naked over it. No sign of the worms. His weeping crept like a shadow over her, peeling away her apathy with its black nails. He was not an injured bird but a child. And he was sick. She had assumed herself to be a teacher. A roach ran in a senseless pattern, avoiding invisible obstacles in the gray filthy tub.

"You're over the line! Over the line, you bitch!" he screamed, then recoiled as she tried to comfort him with a hand's touch.

"You are going home, child of grace." She was firm but patient.

He hurled himself into the bathroom and closed the door. Water ran and splashed. After ten minutes he emerged soaked. Soap bubbles on his chin.

"Orla would be sorry." He did not look at her.

"I know, but she doesn't know best."

"My dad hates my guts. He hates the nests."

"The nests are bad, Shawn. Don't you hate the nests?"

"Orla told me I'm like an artist. They're sculptures."

"An artist might have a choice."

Shawn sat on the bed, a bubble shimmering and clinging tenaciously to his chin. "I've no papers, remember? They waved us through on the bus, but it's not like that getting out."

"We'll go to the embassy."

"I want to stay here." He closed his eyes.

"No you don't."

"I could get you in trouble."

"No you won't."

"I want to find Aisling too."

Keelin laughed. "You're a right chancer, you are."

Keelin knew he could throttle her, but he was a passive creature, doomed to the monotony of hoarding. Constructing useless monstrosities that transferred the blockages in his brain to shambolic obstructions in the room. He was not the arbitrary dictator in this totalitarian space, merely a puppet. Our obsessions keep us as slaves, she thought, as she felt the same tingling in her ass. An itchy colony of worms? She grabbed the mirror once more to check. Squinting from the light in the bathroom, she cursed her leaky brain as she squatted again over the magnified side of the mirror to reassure herself. But this time they were there.

Keelin scrubbed her body raw in the shower and wept for herself. Her face contorted and repulsed. In the morning her period came heavily, and she was doubled over the side of her bed with cramps. Shawn observed her with surprise, then went to splash about the bathroom. Not able to pull the shower curtain, since she also touched it, he flooded the floor each day. He came back and sat on the bed, watching her closely, worrying that her volatility might lead her to stray from the paths he had assigned. Impatient under his gaze, she went into the bathroom and slipped in all the water, landing with a bump on the dirty tiles.

"For fuck's sake!" Keelin exclaimed.

"Careful," he whispered to himself. She came out looking ghostly, stumbled, fainted. Painstakingly avoiding the red marked path, he peered over her fallen body. He wanted to pick her up. He should pick her up. His thin, white arms reached out, but he was afraid to get too close. He was frozen helpless when she stirred and whimpered.

"Shawn, I feel so weak. Give me a hand." Keelin groaned and shifted onto her side.

"I can't."

With much effort she hauled herself up and dragged her infested body to the bed. He sat on his bed, morosely picking at his nose.

"The boy magpie," she taunted. He winced and took his finger out of his nose.

Orla came tottering home later that night, through the nests, her feet squashed into a new pair of high heels, her face painted, her head sprouting that burning bush of red hair.

"Shawn's going home," Keelin said, sitting up on her elbows.

Orla looked at Shawn. He nodded, eyes cast down. "I guess I am."

"Suit yourself." Orla glared at Keelin. "What's wrong with you?"

"Thanks for the sympathy." Keelin lay back.

"What has she been saying about me?"

Keelin snorted in exasperation. "Would you ever cop on? He's ill. Maybe there's a cure, a treatment."

"Since when have you become a medical expert?" Orla went to touch Shawn, but he shriveled away from her on the bed. "Do you want to go?"

Shawn shut his eyes and sunk his head between his knees.

"We can't disappear forever," Keelin groaned. "Once I find Aisling, Oscar won't give me any more money."

"Screw Oscar! I've been offered a job in that sandwich bar downstairs. I like Mexico better than America."

"It *is* America," Shawn snapped. "Meso America."

"Whatever." Orla made a face.

Keelin shifted in the bed. "Ooooh. Would somebody take pity on me and get me some painkillers? I've got killer cramps."

"You don't look good." Orla inspected her sister.

"I feel dizzy when I stand."

"Serves you right for interfering," Orla said, narrowing her eyes.

Shawn went to the embassy and identified himself. They proved eager to take him home. One official had read about his story in a magazine, but Shawn said he had run away alone. He came back to the room for the last time with a box full of paper clips and some foam from an embassy cushion. He spread the foam in the big nest and hung the clips all over it.

"And he never even called me mother," Orla sniveled on the bed.

"Get a grip, woman." Keelin kicked her sister's fat rump with her bare heel. "You've been watching too many soap operas."

Shawn laughed as he took his suitcase in one hand. He and Orla embraced. She squeezed him hard, her gosling, her cold egg. It had been too late, of course.

"Write to me here and maybe I'll visit you." She squelched a kiss on his cheek.

"I'm sure his parents would love that," Keelin said.

Approaching Keelin, Shawn halted halfway and waved. She waved back from her sickbed.

"Sorry," he said.

"What are you sorry for her for?" Orla grabbed him again.

"Good luck, Shawn," Keelin said. "If you ever manage to hatch anything in one of your nests, be careful of it."

"I'll come with you to the embassy." Orla grabbed her handbag.

"You're staying here," Keelin ordered. "I don't want any trouble at this stage."

Shawn closed the door slowly and softly behind him.

Orla, without saying a word, dragged the nests into the hall and bagged them. She broke each apart with dread, afraid of finding awful things inside. Were these homes that bloated with overattentiveness? Sanctuaries that choked the light? She untied the many belts and tore at the big one beside the window. The sun that had pierced through the tiny gaps, causing spotty shadows, now drove into the room with a blinding surge. Orla blinked with loss. She took the nests downstairs, black bags full of them, and came up to sweep away the scattered remnants. The floor was littered with leaves and lint and wood. My son, she thought, and blubbered as Keelin stumbled out of bed on wobbly legs and took her two hands.

"You called him a magpie," Orla said.

"I was disgusted."

"Why a magpie?"

"Magpies are collectors."

"I thought it was to do with the rhyme."

"*One for sorrow*," Keelin quoted.

"If you saw a single magpie, you had to touch wood or spit or salute."

"I used to do all three." Keelin had to lie flat with her feet still on the floor.

"It reminds me of Shawn. He's doing it all to keep trouble at bay, I think."

Keelin nodded. "When we enter a church we have to dip our

fingers in the holy water and genuflect before sitting. You see the Jews completely caught up in tying things about their wrists in a particular manner and bowing a certain amount of times, and the Muslims having to face Mecca. Hindus exhaust themselves with handcrafted offerings. All religions have their rites to ward off evil spirits."

"What Shawn did was no more than all those shenanigans."

"Oh no, Orla," Keelin said. "If your habits are all your own you're mad, but if you ritualize in a group you're close to God."

On the back of the bus to the Yucatán peninsula, Keelin chewed on a dubious cocktail of painkillers and some worming tablets for dogs that Orla had gotten her with her flawed Spanish, washing it all down with pink diarrhea syrup. Her long hair brushed off her arm and she nearly leapt out of her seat, convinced there were cockroaches crawling on her. Gerry had said Aisling was in Mérida. That was the weakest clue so far, but then none of the others had worked out either.

On reaching Mérida, she checked into a run-down, colonial-style hotel. There was a central courtyard and several Mexican families lived on the ground floor, their washing lines strung up like parade bunting. On the upstairs floor, transient backpackers stayed in huge rooms with bolted saloon doors. Her room had an old three-piece mirror and oak dresser. Large windows faced a narrow, bustling street. The toilets squatted in an insalubrious row, with only filthy, plastic curtains as doors and no toilet seats. Keelin collapsed on the bed, exhausted after the twenty-hour bus journey. The traffic outside scoured her head until it was raw and flaky. Small processions — virgin statues raised above dark heads — floated under her shuttered window. The sun went down and everywhere she could hear music playing. Patches of jangling melodies and voices with no center. Mosquitoes buzzed in her ear. She was too terrified to unzip her backpack because she had a feeling a mouse had jumped in in Mexico City. She was almost able to feel its rodent presence burrowed into her sealed crumple of clothes. It was after dark that the she-worms would crawl out of her and lay eggs in her ass, returning inside in the morning. A fan whirred on the stained ceiling high above her phobic head. As she approached the tarnished mirror she was stalled by a face ready to disappear. Possessed by animals. The hotel proprietor told another Irish guest that he was worried about *la pocina pelliroja,* since she slept all day and went back and forth to the toilet. This middle-aged Irish woman in a white linen suit nervously pushed through the saloon doors. Motionless, Keelin stared at her from the brass bed.

"Are you all right?"

Keelin heard the English words in her own accent and breathed heavily, shaking her head.

"Will I bring you to a doctor?"

Keelin nodded. The woman helped her out of the bed and down the stairs. There was a mariachi festival in town. On each corner were three little men in colorful hats and spangled costumes, dueling it out with the competition. The town square sparkled with them.

"Just my luck I hit town at this moment," Keelin said. They were the first words she spoke to this stranger.

"Ach, sure the place is infested with them," the woman agreed. "You can't sit down without being serenaded."

"I have three who come out of me every evening and play in my ass."

The woman looked astonished and remained silent until they reached a one-story house down a side street.

Wearing a bowtie and waistcoat, the doctor sat behind a big wooden desk. Keelin had forgotten her dictionary, although "dysentery" was translated in it as "woodlouse." He frowned, listened to her heart, tested her reflexes.

"Abra la boca." He pulled her jaw open and shone a light in. *"¿Cuánto tiempo hace que se siente así?"*

She shook her head. "Oh, how long? Is that it? Emm, *una semana. Tengo diarrea y . . ."* She did not know how to say worms. She wiggled her finger at him and he put his hands on his hips and looked puzzled. He brought her to a side room and inserted a glucose drip. *"Acuestese ahí, por favor."* He pointed to a couch and she lay and let the glucose slide into her. *"¿Debe quedarse en cama durante cinco días, entiende?"* She nodded, not understanding at all. The Irish woman entered and told her she had to get the bus to Belize tonight and needed to pack. Keelin thanked her and wondered how she kept her linen clothes so white. Abandoning angel. Come back, bundle me up, and take me home. I'm lost now for sure. Too late for everything. Becoming unrecognizable, even in those three images of herself in the triple mirror. Which one was her? The doctor removed the drip and she placidly stared at the hole in her arm, expecting a little green worm to peek out and inspect its surroundings. Refusing to take any money, the doctor gave her a bottle of pills that had been sitting on his desk when she came in. Keelin streeled through town, supporting herself occasionally by the yellow walls, weaving through the mariachis' strumming and the hiss of castanets. In Japan, at a Buddhist shrine, a little plastic Mickey Mouse mariachi had been stuck in the soil, holding two green castanets. Now that the circle of images was closed, her journey must be almost over. There was a notice back in the hotel: $300 for ten days in Cuba, flight and hotel included. Rebelling finally against her quest, Keelin counted her money and fled Mexico and its festive streets the next evening.

When the plane took off, she felt a surge of freedom. "This is the business," she said jubilantly. "Screw Aisling and Molly. I'm going to Havana." Soaring without gravity, her temperature blazing, her ass still tingling, urinary tract burning, bowels rumbling, and mosquito bites swelling and oozing all over her body.

the worship of worms

KEELIN FELT the end of her tether, strained on it, and heard it snap. She had found herself on a Mexican singles tour without Spanish, sharing a room with a dark young Mayan woman who had no English. An irritated tour guide visited and told her she shouldn't have come if she was so sick. She protested that she was all right, she didn't hold anyone responsible, and she would be O.K. if just left alone with her memories and hallucinations. *One for sorrow, two for joy.* Cockroaches as big as men walked upright behind the door. She understood immediately when she heard the sporadic needling of legs spindle by on the carpet. With a jerky, spasmodic gait, they trembled down the corridor outside, two at a time, immense figures, ready at any moment to open her door.

In the schoolyard in the west Irish mountains, they had spread stories of spiders abroad who bit on your arms and, when you returned home, millions of baby spiders would break out of your sores. The partition opened between the two classrooms, and they joined together in the late afternoon for singing. *There was an old woman and she lived in the woods, weile weile waile.* Rows of children's voices pressing on toward harmony. *She had a baby three months old, weile weile waile.* Stories whispered in the yard of unfaithful wives whose husbands plucked out their pubic hair one by one. *Diarrhea custard, diarrhea pie, all mixed up in a dead man's eye.* They found horror to play with and now here it was, unfolded. *Snot on toast ten feet thick, all washed down with a cup full of sick.* Her body turning inside out in a hotel room. Aisling was the most popular girl in the school but bold as brass. The partition opened; Keelin saw her older sisters. Siobhan ignored her, but Aisling would wink. Keelin, good as gold. They had been close enough in age to play with each other in the yard. Siobhan, her head cocked to the side, standing with a handful of marbles she never wanted to use in case she lost. *She stuck the penknife in the baby's heart, weile weile waile.* Patrick's knobby legs blue from the cold, holes in his socks. Aisling would shout fiercely at the teachers when he was kept in during break to finish work he couldn't finish — rubbing out words over and over again. Endless corrections that wore through the page. Filling the holes in the letters. Polka dot copy pages. The o's and a's and circles in the p's. One time Aisling marched in and dragged him out to play, and they never kept him in again. They must have been afraid. And in the schoolyard the girls would say that the husband pulled and pulled on the last pubic hair, but he couldn't get it out — *come out you black bastard,* he roared, and the milkman in the wardrobe jumped out, thinking he was caught. No blacks in Ireland, though, so those jokes must have come from England. Keelin would pretend to laugh. Aisling took pleasure in putting on her younger sisters' coats and walking them home. Bending to tie their shoes. She had no tales of warning or repulsion to tell. *They hanged the woman who killed the babe down by the river Saile.* With all that loomed, Keelin had felt it was only love that would secure her mind from the fear she lay wide open to now. A giant roach leg brushed across the door with a thin rasp. *Would you rather run a mile, suck a boil, or eat a barrel of snot?* Mammy, I love you. Help me. Oscar, if you knew I was here, would you bail me out? The highlight of the year was your visits, your gifts, your walks on the cliffs. The plague was in Keelin's heart. Darkness swirled about the world. A miasma of human failure, methodically plotted, evolved from grim games in the schoolyard to the solitude of the last sickness before death. Pain and the end of hope, well anticipated in bright voices ritualizing on the slopes back home.

Outside the window hovered the remote figure of Sive. Sive the madwoman, kept in the upstairs room of her parents' shop. Keelin sat bolt upright in the bed because she could hear her now, though she had never heard her before. Hear her cry like the mad daughter and the spooker of children she was. Feed her and she will stay out of sight. Once held in your arms, now shut in her room, scaring children with her matinee and evening appearances at the glass. Some of those children have futures already behind them. Faces so protean she could reach out and squash them into the likeness of something worse than her. She was chained to her misbehavior, her crockery breaking, her skirt hoisting, her angry choir of demented voices.

The wretched face pressed close to the hotel window and Keelin held her breath, afraid that the glass might break. Between the creatures outside the door and this ghost by her window, she was cornered. *You have no choice but to remember me. More bread or I'll appear. My warrior cry, my signature tune, my leitmotif. Echoing in the shrinking bounds of your adult life. You never knew I could follow you. Are you as lonely now as I was always?*

A Cuban doctor came and cured her. Gave her pills for the worms and injections for dysentery and tablets for the urinary tract infection that turned her piss orange. When Keelin cried in gratitude, the doctor, a slim, brown-haired woman of forty, took her to her cousin's beach house just outside Havana. She placed her in the tender hands of four generations of the one family for convalescence. An uncle spoke some English and a brother named Enrique spoke French to her. Lean and bearded, Enrique made little ceramic pigs and mice for the tourists, though he had a Ph.D. in chemistry. Keelin watched him play soccer on the beach while a toddler straddled her knee. Patient and playful, with a huge tattoo on his right thigh, he drank through the afternoons and, just as he edged into a restless moroseness, he would switch, drinking water from eight on and playing the guitar. He paid close attention to her from the first moment of her arrival, entertaining her with little gifts and flowers and songs as she recovered. He held her in the sea, peeling down the cups of her swimsuit and stroking her breasts. At night they stole out of the crowded beach house and had sex on a blanket in the sand. After dancing all evening at a local cabaret they walked home with his friend, a young Russian woman. They guzzled rum with mint leaves back at her Spartan apartment and, drunk and pliable, the woman joined them in her bed. Keelin closed her eyes as Enrique held her and let his friend touch her. She was knitting back her sanity with sex. She woke that night after a dream in which Aisling died, and she was startled at the depth of her grief for the abstract sibling. Usually there was a membrane around her psyche that protected her from the ultimate certainty of death, but tonight she felt death raw and looming. Though the worms had gone, she was paranoid and she felt them again. My asshole is haunted by worm ghosts, she thought. The two naked bodies stirred beside her. Sive came to the window and said, "The old gods have been on our backs so long we've begun to worship worms."

Havana was in tatters. The walls crumbling, the colors faded. Police stopped to question her companions, and she stood apart as they scrutinized her. On one dead street, a black man stared intently from a wrought-iron balcony. Her friends told her to be quiet, not to open her mouth, to pretend to be Cuban. They taught her a Spanish song. "La Cucaracha." One morning one of the boys at the beach house came running through the palms in the yard. He had found a body washed up on the beach. A cluster of men now gathered around the rotted trunk of a corpse at the water's edge.

Aisling raged by the bottomless lake in Panahachel, Guatemala. The authorities had filled the lake with bass so the tourists could fish, but the bass ate all the indigenous fish and went far from the surface, where only deep-sea divers could reach them. The ancient fishing communities on the lake were now destitute. As more Indians were exterminated, the evangelists flooded in, painting wordless targets on squat walls in muddy towns. Aisling ignored the signs flapping on buildings everywhere, warning of a cholera epidemic. *The hunger is on us, it is the will of God, let the will of God be done.* Her great-grandmother had died in the workhouse outside Cootehill one winter, leaving her own grandmother orphaned. Aisling would run forever to keep from winters like those. She walked from sullen town to sullen town, around a somber lake necklaced by seven volcanoes. Two tiny girls in embroidered clothes hauled a giant rice bag between them, backs bent. She could have offered to help but hesitated; the last thing these tiny things needed was more help. She could see the way they looked at her, as if she were a ghost by this lake.

By the time she reached the last town, a dreary pageant straggled down a steep mountain street. The flat music barely scraped the hollow evening as a group of nuns herded the men and women under the low, muddy sky. The town watched in stunned boredom, faces piled on top of one another and elbows hanging out of glassless windows in the stone houses. Aisling couldn't wait for the ferry to arrive and take her away. She stood studying the rippled surface, no fish left but the imported bass lurking far below. The boat arrived and had a big sticker of Snoopy straddling a missile with a U.S. flag on it. She leaned toward the water and saw a drowned man looking up.

Keelin was on a deck chair, listening without comprehension to the frenzied Spanish. A boy shimmied up a tree and got a coconut, sliding down again. He took a silver machete and cut the top off. Then he slopped a dose of rum into the shell, extracted a straw from a jam jar on the table, and handed her the drink. Her skin smelt pleasantly of salt and sweat. When she closed her eyes, her inside lids were imprinted with the round stains of the sun. Even when she faced the ground, the glow of the discs did not diminish. One burn for each pupil. Aisling's eyes pierced into Keelin's. The long-lost sisters stared in surprise at each other.

"Where are you?" Aisling asked.

"The shore of an outcast Caribbean island. You . . . I've been searching for you for almost a year — everywhere in the world. Where are you?"

"Central America. You're getting hot."

"Are you there now?" Keelin asked.

"I've moved a bit from where I am now. You are lagging behind a few months, but the gap is closing in. By now I have found what I was looking for."

"I've had a good year at your expense, Aisling, but it's time for me to draw it to a close. When I open my eyes, I will come after you."

"Why are you looking for me, Keelin?"

"I will ask you this now, and if you answer I promise I will never ask you the same in the flesh. Why did you leave our family? You've all but destroyed us with your absence."

"I scoured the earth. Continent to continent. Everywhere, families grasping at one another for meaning. I was looking for something else and I found it."

"Tell me, where are you now?"

"Now I am crossing a bottomless lake surrounded by volcanoes. But I am long gone."

Laughter swelled, and the boy who found the drowned man was trying to impress his girlfriend, who had just arrived. She was skinny, with a curved face, her chin and forehead protruding. She shook her head and brushed him off, much to the others' delight. Keelin was told to go upstairs and hide there while the police came and bagged the body. When she emerged they were debating whether to go into town with her or rent mopeds to drive into the jungle. The boy asked her to accompany him to the bar on the beach to get some more bottles of rum. Salsa music blared from the radio, and the grandfather dragged the reluctant grandmother up to dance. Once up, she rolled her hips, and the children squealed in delight.

Keelin walked briskly with the boy on the beach; he was trying to act out the discovery of the body for her. It was the third he had found in two months, she thought he said. Next year, he said, he would try to get to North America himself and make lots of money. His family would be sad, but all the young men were going to come with him; they were attempting to build a raft as he spoke, but none of the rafts had held so far. His parents did not know of the scheme. The United States would be his new father, he said, shaking his fist in the air, North Americans his new brothers and sisters. Then he taught her a line of Spanish, and they raced down the beach shrieking it: "*Yo camino a la playa por comprar ron.*" Over and over, they sang this phrase, ankle-deep in the warm water, swift feet sinking softly in hot sand. Aisling ran just behind them, but they never looked back. She herself had seen and heard the children in North Africa running barefoot and in rags through the mud towns, playing and singing a rhyme of family terror: "My father's wife she took my life, my father ate me for his dinner."

embrace the tiger

MOLLY TOOK A DECK CHAIR from the shed and opened it in the overgrown garden. The sun was out but there was still a chill wind from the sea. Bundled in a coat, she looked hopefully at the sky. She was just out of the hospital, so the chill might have been her imagination. Everyone was claiming it was the best summer ever. All those who booked holidays in Spain were raging, so the neighbor said. Apart from her sister, a golfing companion had been her only visitor after the hysterectomy. The solitude was beginning to fray her privacy. Sometimes she stayed at the club after nine holes to have a few gin and tonics and see who turned up. She had begun to talk to people about her kids and her brother in America. A cloud moved over the sun and Molly closed her eyes rather than look at the old house in shadow. It must be a hot summer — all the grass was scorched. Not a spot of green anywhere. The farmers would be complaining, and the tourists. Forty shades of yellow. She wondered if all lives end up so quietly. *I am the woman forgotten in the light. The old hound who hungered for a second chance at life.* The phone rang. She hauled herself up off the chair in a lather of sweat and walked through the musty kitchen toward the machine's insistent demand.

Orla looked pleased to see Keelin and grinned broadly from behind the counter in the Mexico City sandwich bar.

"My shift is over in a jiffy; we'll go upstairs together. Oh — hold on a tick." Orla handed her a photo. "You left your disposable camera, so I finished the film and developed it. What's this?"

Keelin looked at the photo for a minute, puzzled, and then yelped in delight. "Trotsky's toilet."

In a restaurant that night they sat opposite each other over a plate of food and drank beer. "I almost don't want to tell you this, but Patrick will have my guts for garters if I don't," Orla said.

"What?" Keelin asked.

"He got our Mexican address from Oscar and sent a note giving us Fatima's address in Honduras. He bets Aisling is with her."

"When was this?"

"End of June. Just last week." Orla drank some beer thoughtfully and then frowned. "I think send her a letter but leave it at that. Tell her Molly's sick. Don't waste any more of your time."

"I can't go back now and get a job for September. I might as well try. It's only two countries away. You know, when I came back from Cuba I stopped two days in Mérida and went to see the pyramids. I've got pyramid psychosis. I want to see the ones in Guatemala and Honduras, too. So it's not all for her."

"Whatever. If you ask me, you have the same obsessive shite as the rest of us. Patrick had a cryptic message for you and all. What the hell was it? Oh yeah. He wrote, 'A word to Keelin. Embrace the tiger, return to mountain.'"

"He's taking the piss," Keelin said.

"Or eating too many fortune cookies."

"The tiger is Aisling." Keelin narrowed her eyes dramatically. "The mountain is Molly."

They both laughed.

"Maybe she has her reasons, Keelin," Orla said carefully. "For not wanting anything to do with us. God knows, I've felt it at times. Belittled by yiz all, so I was. Molly had her in the bed till she was twenty; no wonder she got out, for fuck's sake. She thought she'd get away at university, but Molly moved the whole lot of us up to Dublin. And Oscar pawing after her her whole life — Jesus, when I think of it. It's disgusting."

"Oscar? Not when she was a child."

"All those nights in the kitchen and him teaching her songs and dances. I saw the way he looked at her."

"I never saw that."

"I was older than you," Orla said. "He's such a slimy bastard. Uncle Toad, Aisling and I used to call him. Yuck!"

Keelin laughed. "I never knew all that."

"Uncle Toad." Orla nodded, pleased.

"I want to wait and call Molly when I have some good news. I sent her a postcard from Cuba. We should all be together this Christmas."

"The highlight of my year," Orla said with a sneer.

"Let's go dancing." Keelin signaled for the check.

"Saints preserve us! You want to go dancing! It must be that holiday in Cuba. You did more than get rid of your worms. Did you get laid?"

"As a matter of fact, I did," Keelin stuck her chest out.

"Go girl, go!" Orla got up and thumped her on the back.

When Keelin was leaving Mexico City, she and Orla said their good-byes in the room, and they both cried. Keelin waited for a taxi across from the sandwich shop and watched her sister working behind the counter with a net over her hair and a green uniform. Orla had always got on Molly's nerves. Siobhan and Patrick thought she was a culchie. Oscar was repulsed by her weight and lack of grace. The nuns had described her as feisty when she was a teenager. She might have played it straight and been happy. She was always the one with boyfriends, even if they were the heavy-metal types. Here she was now, at thirty-three, with a net over her hair, working in a sandwich shop with no family of her own. Something Keelin knew she would have liked. But maybe people's lives are not so bad when they are inside of them looking out. The little yellow VW taxi came and Keelin climbed in, craning over her shoulder for a last glimpse of her big sister behind the counter. Or maybe they are worse. What had Molly told them all their lives? Orla was handing a sandwich and a drink to a businessman. She wore pink lipstick and she was smiling. And in the end, life will break your heart.

Oscar was driving drunk in North Carolina. He nodded over the wheel, his eyes closed. Braille driving. Waking occasionally when the car hit the curb, which guided him along miraculously. When Gerry's nephew came to the door, Oscar said he had to lie down. "Could I have a drink? A whiskey."

There were children crawling everywhere and toys scattered all over the floor. He pushed some big coloring books off the couch as he flumped down. The bearded nephew handed him a whiskey in a mug. Oscar gulped it down.

"The urn is in the trunk." He handed him the keys. "He said he wanted his ashes in the lake out by the woods where he used to play. I forget the name of it, some local place."

"I know where that is." The nephew nodded and went out to the car. When he returned Oscar was passed out cold, with vomit on his shirt and chin.

"It weren't in the trunk; I found it in the front seat." The nephew tried to rouse the comatose priest. He took off his baseball cap and ran his hand through his long hair. "Shit. He's just like Gerry said he'd be. Drunk as a coot. Randy, help me get this goddamned whiskey priest into the bed in the den." An older boy got up from the video game and took Oscar by the shoulders. Randy stepped on a dog in the hall and it yelped grievously. Oscar did not stir.

At dawn a rumpled Oscar sat huddled and bleary at one end of a little row boat while the nephew and Randy rowed and three other little kids pulled at the dog's ears. The lake was still and there was a small island in the middle with one fishing shack. A light morning mist skimmed the bumpy surface. The nephew wore a T-shirt that read "Kill 'Em All, Let God Sort Them Out" and was decorated with a giant bald eagle over the American flag. They all kept calling him sir, and he felt it was only to mock him. They would have been Catholics, so they knew to call him Father. The sooner this was all over with, the better. Randy took the urn out of the bag.

"Where did you get that?" Oscar sat up, suddenly aghast. They all turned and looked at him as if he were mad. The boat rocked.

"Steady on, old chap," Randy said, and the others giggled.

They were as mean as weasels, as mean as Gerry had been when he first hounded him. *I was innocent when you were crouched in the grass.*

"Want to do the honors?" The nephew relented somewhat, offering him the urn.

"No, God no." Oscar closed his eyes. The dog's tail kept thumping on his black Gucci shoes.

The nephew shrugged. "Me, me, me!" the children said, grabbing for the urn. The nephew shook his head at his litter and nodded toward the priest, winking. "Say good-bye to your great-uncle Gerry, kids."

"Good-bye, Uncle Gerry," they all chimed raucously.

Oscar opened his eyes as the man opened the urn and watched as the contents were emptied into the mist.

"Jesus, Mary, and sweet Saint Joseph," Oscar muttered. "Have pity on me."

"Do you want to say a prayer, sir?" the nephew asked.

"For whom?" Oscar said thinly, averting his eyes from the unsavory family as the last foggy traces dissolved and the flames of the morning sun began to burn.

Black vultures circled over the canals in Belize City. They swung above Keelin's head as she made her way to the bus station between the piles of rubbish at the side of the streets.

"Polio," a German backpacker said as they stopped for refreshments on the road to Tikal. He stared casually at a boy with shrunken limbs and a huge head lolling to one side. Flies crawled inside the child's mouth as he lay in a small wheelbarrow under a tree.

At Tikal a howler monkey threw a branch at her when she hiked through the jungle on the way to the pyramids. Bats flew from stony openings in the ruins. Rats teemed on the streets of

Guatemala City as she ate chicken chow mein at a café counter. They ran in packs, so many that some were crawling over the other's backs. Down here, the cockroaches had wings. Keelin was beginning to feel that she could not share the planet with other species. She knew that when she was old they would be all that was left to her. When everything was whittled away, it would be the creatures of the earth and the birds of the sky and all those fucking fish in the sea.

On the border to Honduras, she was the only gringo. Sullen men with machetes and Panama hats eyed her steadily. There were cholera warnings pasted on the walls of the bathroom; she scrubbed her hands raw. As she sat in the hot station, a lizard fell from the roof and landed on her arm.

A young boy threw her backpack on the roof and she got on the bus. A tall hippie with a beard and a long gray ponytail spied her as he mounted the steps, and he sat beside her.

"Are you a traveler or a tourist?" he asked, staring down at her freckled face.

"Tourist," she said.

"I hate tourists." He wrinkled his nose.

"I hate that distinction." Keelin turned to look out the window as the packed bus pulled onto the road.

"A traveler doesn't just see the sights — he explores the culture, talks to the people," the man pontificated loudly. "I've lived down here ten years. First Guatemala, now Honduras. My mother died and left me a sum of five hundred a month. Can't do dick with that in California. So what do I do? I come down here and live like a king for the rest of my life." Lasciviously he eyed her sticky cleavage. "Stick with me, baby. I know these people. These are border towns. No place for a pretty little thing like you. Hey, I bet the mosquitoes love you. Try some of this." He squirted lotion on her arm and rubbed it in. She pulled her arm away. "I'm buying this in Guatemala and I'm going to sell it to the gringos on the beach at Tela —"

"Tela?" Keelin said. "I have to see someone there. Do you know —?"

He brushed off her inquiry. "I don't mix with gringos. I drink the water from the tap. The sand flies are a bitch. It might be paradise without them, but it ain't. One more step down and you're officially on Mosquito Coast. They'll eat you alive. Unless, of course, you have this lotion potion. I don't live in Tela — too touristy. You couldn't handle the place where I live. I'm not kidding, babe — you wouldn't last a day. Runaway slaves escaped there and founded a town. The people are black, not Latino, and they speak Garifuno. That's a mix of African and a few other languages. A mongrel tongue. I speak a few words myself now. The best way to reach the settlement is to walk through the sea. There's no road, no path. These jungle bunnies live like savages. A little girl like you, you wouldn't last a minute. Straight into a pot."

"What's it called?"

"Ensenada. Take a walk through the sea and turn right. Ha! Don't even entertain the notion."

"So you think I'd be out of my depth, do you?"

"Baby, you look as if you'd be out of your depth in a parking lot puddle."

Keelin reached into her pocket. "Let me buy some of that stuff."

"Sit back. Hold tight. We have only seventeen more hours to go, and the road disappears pretty soon. Cling to me if you have to. I can see you scare easily."

Keelin couldn't figure out which was more excruciating, the rocky mountain road or the belligerent hippie who talked into her ear the whole way. They got to the border and the official took one look at her passport and shook his head sadly.

"Where is special stamp?"

"No, I checked in Mexico City. I don't need a visa."

"Yes. Sorry. You have to go back to Guatemala City, to embassy."

"Can't I get it here?"

The official looked at her and rubbed his stubbly double chin. "Fifty U.S. dollars."

"I've only got twenty in U.S. But I've got a student card." She handed him the note and a fake student card Orla had gotten for her in Mexico City, and he took it and waved her through. She marveled that she had just gotten a student discount on a bribe. As she walked up the jungle road she saw the hippie gesticulating and beckoning.

"Come on, shortie, you'll miss the bus."

"You don't speak Spanish after ten years?" Keelin had discovered this about him as the bus rattled with just the two of them toward Copan. She was incredulous.

"Communication is not all about language," he said, somewhat rankled. "These are my people. We have reached a plateau of higher understanding."

"I'm sure they feel just as warmly towards you."

He leaned toward her and snarled, "Border towns are rough places. Watch your step. Do as I tell you and you might survive."

"Veinte," the bus driver said when they stopped in a pretty town square. Keelin paid and got off.

"Veinte? You must be joking, buddy," the hippie hollered at the bewildered driver. "It was only quince the last time, you bastard. And that's all you're getting. I pay my taxes. Here's quince, and you're not getting any more from me until you fix your damn roads. Comprende, amigo?"

He hopped off the bus.

"I can see you have a special rapport with the natives," Keelin said.

"You better believe it, kiddo." He swung his bag over his shoulder and fingered his beaded necklace. "What are you up to now? How 'bout you and me get a room?"

Keelin waved a guidebook. "I'll see you around. I'm going to the pyramids tomorrow and then up to Tela.

"At seven there's a gringo happy hour in that watering hole over there."

Keelin walked into the dark bar at seven, having nothing else to do. Two white women sat at a table and beamed at her. She smiled back tentatively.

"Hello, Keelin. We heard you were coming."

Keelin was startled, but just then the hippie came to the table with four beers. "Fellow Irish." He grinned. "I found you some compatriots."

Keelin stayed and got drunk with the schoolteachers from County Kerry, who spent the summer months traveling. "You should go to El Salvador," they told her. "It's free in."

"Is that a club?" she asked.

"No, the country. No border tax. Now Nicaragua — they charge."

The hippie got angry with her when she wouldn't take her hair out of a bun and show him how long it was. He challenged her to a fight. "Come on outside!" He danced with his fists in the air.

"Maybe you'd better go back home," Keelin told him. "I'm sure you're depriving some village of its idiot." The hippie snarled, brandished a beer bottle, and proceeded to break it over his own head.

"Good shot, Keelin," one of the sisters said.

Keelin raised her palms. "Look, no hands."

The locals seemed used to him and turfed him gently through the saloon doors.

"Here was I all nervous about a Honduran border town." Keelin shook her head. "All those quiet guys with machetes staring at me and I find myself in a bar brawl the first night with a violent hippie from California."

"*Estoy buscando a mi hermana,*" Keelin told the man at the hotel in Tela the next night. The dark lobby had a tinge of sewage smell. It opened onto a sea that dragged over the strewn shore in darkness. Broken pieces of wood lay scattered on the sand — trunks of trees rotted and smashed. The night porter remembered them, but their names were not on the register. He said they had probably gone. Outside the vultures sat on the broken trunks; perhaps they had been circling over her head all the way from Belize.

"*Entonces, me he perdido,*" she said sadly to the sea as he gave her a key.

Her room had no window but it had a TV. She watched a bit of *Charlie's Angels,* which she left on as she strolled down the unlit stone corridor and onto a balcony. The salty sea washed into the great wound of darkness and the wooden debris on the sand took on shapes of unnamable animals. Among these apparitions vultures walked like brooding prison guards.

"More bread? If it were withdrawn, Aisling, would you really appear? Whose bread? Oscar's? Not even Oscar's; it's Leo's. We don't know him, and he propelled us all over the globe. He got me here. Siobhan, with a junkie in New York, Patrick gambling in Vegas, and Orla selling sandwiches in Mexico. Leo's whores. Charlie's angels. *Ariane, ma soeur.* Wounded by such a love. *Vous mourûtes aux bords où vous fûtes laissée.* You died on the shores where you were left. *¿Que desea usted?* The sea, the sea, *a gra geal mo chroi.* No entiendo. I'm fluent in Garufuno. Runaway slaves. *¿Ensenada?* I can handle it, you lousy hippie. *For I have gone about the world like wind.* And I bet if she's anywhere close, she's there."

Keelin slammed her fists on the balcony rail.

At dawn she put on a swimsuit and a T-shirt and walked into the sea. She waded along the rim of the coast, waist-deep, the water lapping the border of jungle. Along the way she saw a hammock strung up between two palms on a narrow beach. The violent hippie reclined, reading *The Firm.* He grinned at her like the Cheshire cat.

"You came."

"Yep." Keelin stood to her thighs in the water. "How much farther is the town?"

"Not long. You can walk through the jungle for this part, but it's quicker by sea. Man, I thought you were someone else. You Irish all look alike. Come on, babe, I know your game. Jump on up here; I've a snake you might just want to meet."

"See you later so." Keelin waved and kept walking.

"Wait," he called. "You think it's so great to be young? You think I'm jealous of you 'cause I'm fifty-five? Well, at least in my lifetime I've seen clean beaches."

"We'll all be the same age when the millennium turns, hippie, twentieth-century slaves trying to escape. We're both as good as dead."

"Watch out for syringes washed up on shore," he shouted, as she moved away through the small waves.

Aisling was on the beach. Her hands reaching out, her body turning slowly, trancelike. She was doing tai chi. Grasping the sparrow's tail, she stepped and faced the ocean and saw Keelin walk out of the sea. Her arms dropped to her huge belly and her broad, freckled face cracked open into a smile and a shout. Keelin shyly walked to her immense sister. *Am I you? Are you me?* She was engulfed in Aisling's torso, a breast at either ear, the stomach pressing her chest, something kicking inside.

"I'd forgotten you were pregnant," Keelin gasped happily.

"Seven months." Aisling grabbed her belly.

"Molly has been worried all these years."

"I called her. She's all alone and just out of hospital. Actually, she's worried about you." Aisling took her by the hand and they walked to a bench under a palm roof. Flies jumped off the sand away from their feet. An enormous black woman with a machete cut them each some coconuts, and Aisling chose two fish from a blue bucket. The woman cooked the fish in a big iron pan over a fire.

"Hungry?" Aisling asked. Keelin was stamping her feet to prevent the sand flies from biting her legs. "Listen, Keelin." Aisling rubbed her sister's ears. "Wow! I still have to get you some earrings. Remember? They haven't closed up, have they?"

Keelin nodded and shook her head. She kept touching Aisling and smiling. The woman put two plates of fish and rice and plantains in front of them, and Keelin ate ravenously.

"Keelin, pet." Aisling poured some rum into the coconuts and handed her one. Her face was torn in sorrow as she touched the fish head on her plate. Keelin remembered that her sister was a vegetarian.

"Patrick is dead," Aisling said.

The angry sun blocked the horizon and cooked the rotting jungle. Patrick, poor Patrick. A shadow on a stone. A face in the window. Keelin crawled on the sand, blubbering. "There must be some cliché that can salvage the rest of my life. If I could only turn back the clock. Time is a great healer. We will meet again. I told Oscar to help him. He promised."

"Oscar has no money of his own. Leo mightn't leave him a dime in the end."

"But he promised me."

Fatima joined them, telling Keelin that her brother Abraham had waited in a cemetery in a town called Chloride for two days. He gave half the money in a briefcase to Patrick's girlfriend and handed in his half to the police in Vegas. He told them the story, and they got the guys that shot Patrick.

"Abraham?" Salvation is in the details. The puzzle distracted.

"My brother. He got deported. They sent him back to Nigeria."

"He was killed? With a gun? By some guys? He had a girlfriend? Why did he get shot and the others didn't? He went back? Why would you go back? Suicide?"

Fatima was as tall as Aisling. They seemed to fit. Aisling broad and white, Fatima black and bone thin.

"Abraham," Keelin repeated the name. "Wasn't he a bit too eager to kill his son?"

"I hope not. I got Abraham to make me pregnant."

"I thought it was Oscar's."

"Oscar?"

"Uncle Toad."

"I only sleep with men for money unless I'm dressed as a man. I do the fucking if I'm not charging."

A year ago Keelin would have been shocked, but now she only asked, "Abraham?"

"I wanted a baby that would look like Fatima. That would be a part of Fatima genetically."

"Genetics? We have bad genes. *Ariane, ma soeur . . .*"

245

"*Phèdre*?" Aisling lit up. "Now there was a fucked-up family. I have Racine here, but I left all my Greek books with Oscar —"

"She was genetically doomed. Patrick was, and maybe all of us except Orla."

"Speak for yourself."

"Who's that?" Keelin said, and Fatima and Aisling turned around. With his long hair, bare chest, and dark, high cheeks, Sadao strode down the beach, looking more like a Native American warrior than a middle-class Japanese boy.

"Sadao." Aisling smiled, looking at the expression on her little sister's face.

"Is she O.K.?" Sadao asked.

"How does he know who I am?" Keelin asked sharply.

"Willy told us you were coming to Tela."

"Willy? The hippie? You could have left a note at the hotel, then."

Keelin began to cry again. "Today's one thing. But what happens after the shock of it subsides and the fact sinks in? When we just have to live with a dead brother. When we get older and have no photos. We have no photos. You'd think Molly would have taken one fucking photo. When he's just a name we tell to new friends. Just a story. Maybe it's not true. Maybe Oscar is just acting the bollocks, playing games with me again."

"Oscar had him cremated. He saw the body. Gerry, too. Poor Oscar."

"Together? Patrick and Gerry?"

"Not in the one pot," Aisling said.

"So Gerry finally died. God love him."

"You knew Gerry? Christ, you really did follow me."

"Sometimes I thought I saw you everywhere," Keelin said, her face rumpling pathetically.

"Where did you see me, bundle?" Aisling put her arms around Keelin, who cried into her chest.

"London. Japan. Hawaii. New York. San Francisco. Mérida. But then in Cuba I had these dreams. That you were dead and then that I talked to you. Was that the night Patrick died?"

"Shh," Aisling whispered, rocking her.

"We all missed you so much when you left home. Mammy sat down at the kitchen table every Friday to write. Patrick was so good, wasn't he? He was so nice. He had horrible friends in Dublin, so he did. Will they be at the funeral? We have to go home now, not Christmas. Molly needs us."

"Give her another drink, Aisling. Maybe she could sleep." Fatima stroked Keelin's long red hair in one curt movement and walked off with Sadao.

"No. Then I'd wake up and it would be night."

"That's fine. I'll stay with you; don't worry."

Keelin looked down at her own hairy legs. "I need a shave, that's for sure. And these flies are eating me alive."

"Trouble in paradise," Aisling smiled.

"Is this paradise?"

"What do you think?"

"Paradise is the fire at home at Christmas, with us lot all telling stories and getting drunk. You were missing, but at least you were alive."

"What? No palm trees?"

Keelin slept drunk in their hut and woke at night. She stood out under the thin palms. Stars dropped like an abundance of overripe fruit. Patrick had been gouged from the earth by stupid violent men. More stars fell. The world was ending. Insects crept into the mouths of inert children. Evil had wings down here, and the devil could fly, and reptiles slipped from roofs, raining down like iron knives. What creature had ever harmed her? Even when the worms lived inside her, they never really hurt her. But she was spooked by all that crawled and flew. Behind her, in a hut on three hammocks, Aisling, Fatima, and Sadao swung through a long, blissful sleep. *They have come so far. Assassins.* Keelin lay on the sand and thought of Patrick. Poor wee gossin. Why did he go back to his death? It was the disease, wasn't it? The doubting disease. The doubt made him a slave, but he was not mad. Her own conscience was wide open and sick for what it saw. Did Aisling have it? Then Keelin cried for Molly, all alone in Ireland. It was summer, and she would be trying to drag her deck chair around the garden to get some sun between patches of clouds. Her grief reached from one horizon to the other and smothered the earth.

"There's no need to go to Ireland, babe. The funeral is over."

"What?" Keelin looked up. The hippie stood close by.

"That's what your sister said, chickpea. You never called home to check?"

Keelin impatiently stomped past the hippie up to the hut. Aisling was inside, wearing a sarong, her shoulders freckled and bare, swinging in a hammock. She smiled at Keelin.

"Where are the others?" Keelin asked.

Aisling shrugged and peeled a banana.

"How are you today?" She lay belly-up, swinging vigorously from side to side.

"Does Orla know about Patrick?"

"No. Siobhan knows. Maybe Molly wrote to Orla by now."

"I've got to call Molly today. When's the funeral?"

"It's over, Keelin. I told you, Oscar —"

"He's already buried? That was fast. Does the devil know he's dead?"

"I said he cremated him."

"Oh."

Oscar opened the little side gate of the Middle Chapel and Molly went into the graveyard. They climbed the hill to their family plot. All their kin were buried here in graves now overgrown, the stone cross tilted. Weeds grew from the cement among colored chips of stones, and beetles lived among artificial flowers in a plastic dome, foggy with condensation. Molly scattered the ashes over the grave.

"Odd without a body though, and him being away so long. I suppose it's a good job you had him cremated because it's full here now. Everybody is being buried closer to town. But I love this place and he belongs with his family."

The tiny whitewashed church was sealed in a quietness that merged with all the lost memories and stained-glass ghosts, names unspoken in so long, lives choked by the vegetation of racing years. Many small hills encircled the graveyard. Their rounded presence cushioned the twins' mourning, their grief rising and falling, cut by twisting lanes. A farmhouse stood on a distant hill as a place to rest their thoughts before looking back. Oscar put his arm around Molly.

"We'll have his name put under all the other names."

Molly nodded and gazed out over the scorched land.

"I've never seen the fields so burnt. They were always green in the old days."

"Have you contacted his father in Wexford?"

"After all these years, call him in the asylum to tell him his son is dead? Now what, in God's name, would be the use of that?"

They stood slightly apart. The ashes blew out of her hands into the bright air and settled among the weeds and stones. *Are youse the family that ate the grass?*

"What happened to those children of yours, Molly?" Oscar's face was ruined in sorrow. Molly sighed. Their bodies were too heavy, so she turned them to ash. The earth was full, so she had to scatter them on the hillside. There was no place in the land, so she threw them into the sky.

"*Arra*, they all left in the end. Our family is over in this country," Molly said. "We should have waited for the others maybe. Poor Keelin would have liked to have been here. She was very fond of Patrick, so she was. Maybe you could have said a mass."

"No, no." Oscar shook his head. "It's for the best. I can always say a mass at a later date, but you're going to visit Aisling and it wouldn't be right to put the ashes in storage."

Molly brushed her hands together with finality. "I remember the day he was born and all. A boy after the two girls. There was a gentleness to him. Sure God love him. Never stood a chance. The poor bundle never even had a bed of his own growing up, and now he can't have a grave."

Oscar smiled weakly at his old sister. She sat down stiffly at the side of the grave, closing her eyes to pray aloud. *And thoughts of youth, this solemn hour, have brought me, in my last step, a childlike wavering.* Oscar remembered a walk on the cliff and Patrick straying too close to the edge. He could not bring himself to talk to God. Doubts collected in his mind like lichen on tombstones. He bent down to take the urn and saw there were ashes left, so he shook them onto the earth as Molly prayed. *Begin once more, O sweet celestial strain. Tears dim my eyes: earth's child I am again.* Good-bye, Gerry, he thought. At that moment two crows bolted out of a tree and spun into the blue sky. An old ragged farmer drove a herd of cows with heavy udders down the road. May God have mercy. He had been so drunk he must have put Gerry's ashes in the back seat before he had gone into the nephew's house. Patrick's urn was on the front seat. Poor Patrick, now sunk in a small, misty lake in North Carolina. And now Gerry dispersed in this remote County Cavan graveyard outside Cootehill. Their ghosts commingled, meeting, confused. No spirit recognition of the land, a wild ghost scared from a disconnecting family tree. This gravesite seizing up in rejection like a body with an alien liver. Oscar put his hand abruptly to his chest. He had flies in his heart.

"Jumping Jaysus, now that takes the biscuit! You followed me to Hiroshima and threw Toru a lay?" Aisling lay on the beach in shorts and a halter top, her pregnant belly in the air. Thighs and calves spread out like continental maps. North America, South America.

"Patrick asked me had I seen the marked step in the Hiroshima museum. The shadow on the stone. He'd seen it in the bomb book you sent Oscar for his birthday."

"Molly and Oscar were born that day, on the sixth of August."

"I'd never made the connection." Keelin watched Fatima and Sadao in the sea.

"You took to my life like a duck to water, child of grace."

"Not really." Keelin played with the sand. "I feel I need roots.

I can't wait to get back to Ireland. You know I almost lost my mind."

Aisling nodded, as if she had been the one to arrange it. Then she recited,

*You are to know the bitter taste
of others' bread, how salt it is, and know
how hard a path it is for one who goes
descending and ascending others' stairs.*

Keelin blinked into the sun. "I thought our meeting would be different. I thought you'd love me more. My memories of childhood are all memories of you. You loved me when I was a child. You took such good care of me."

Aisling rubbed her belly and sighed. "Somebody had to. God knows Molly was a bit batty. Orla and I used say when we'd see her, 'Here comes Molly, the big cheese, not the full shilling.' I'm kind of complimented, but why did you follow me? Didn't you have a life of your own?"

"A small one," Keelin said, shrugging. "But I felt panicked. That I should live out the last years of the century more fully. And I wanted to find you."

"Our lives straddle both millennia, Keelin. You'll be thirty-three and I'll be forty. Half of your life in each century."

"But as soon as it turns, there will be such an ending. The last part of my life will start. My life just a tiny clasp around a great mountain of events."

"Jesus woman," Aisling laughed. "It's only the Roman calendar. And the pope changed the calendar in the Middle Ages, so about ten days are missing from the millennium anyway."

"I could do with those ten days."

"Apply to the Vatican. None of it means that much. Just a big party in a few years."

"I won't be going to any party that night. I'm going to charge you a fortune for babysitting." Keelin lay back on the sand.

"There is the sea and who will drain it dry?" Aisling spoke words Keelin recognized. They had the same body of knowledge.

"That was a sly one, giving Oscar the Greeks. They almost drove him mad."

"I thought it was appropriate. Seeing as they all sleep with their mothers, kill their fathers, and eat their children."

"Yes, but they had unity of time, place, and action. Something our family never mastered."

"You can say that again. I had a difficult time in New York, trying to get pregnant with Abe and coping with Oscar at his most manic."

"So you gave him the Greeks."

"Do you remember the time Oscar took us for a walk on the cliffs? On the train he had us all singing 'I see the sea, the sea sees me.' He wasn't a bad aul' sort, sure he wasn't?" Aisling stood with her arms outstretched and sang, "I saw the sea, the sea saws me. Remember I kept singing that instead? And he corrected me everytime for fun. You little kids thought it was for real."

Aisling remained quiet, watching Fatima and Sadao embrace in the water. Who was it that hurt you? Keelin thought, Did he have the weight of the world on his side? You were so little, your arms reaching out — one for affection, one for information, a seesaw woman. Were you, so little, shot into the air? Your voice now teaming with imbalance? Aisling only reminded her of her own plague. There were swarms in her brain, swarms without hives.

Fatima got out of the water. She was staring at the sisters lying on the sand. Fatima's face was serious, her hair long and in dreads down her back. Sadao had to reach up to dry her head with a towel, but she didn't take her eyes off the women on the beach.

"Fatima wanted a child," Aisling confided. "She and Sadao can't. But my baby comes soon, and it belongs by blood to her. She likes that, but she thinks I have to tell Abraham."

"You're not going to?" Keelin rolled closer to Aisling in the sand. Fatima was approaching.

"Frankly, I'm not impressed with the male role in reproduction." Aisling kissed Fatima on the lips, and Fatima finally smiled.

"You must tell her now," Fatima said, as Sadao plonked down cross-legged by the group.

"Yeah, yeah! Hold your horses. I was about to thank you very much. Keelin, pet, we're moving on soon." Aisling took her sister's hand. "Molly is going to come join me. She needs a break. Away from all the reminders."

Keelin sat up erect in the sand. "For how long?"

"We're going back to Mozambique," Fatima said. "I have a position there, rehabilitating children who were recruited to fight the war."

Keelin's head swiveled from one woman to the other. "Mozambique? That's insane. It's the poorest country in the world —"

"Exactly. No better place," Aisling said. "Fatima still has money from Japan. Her art sells for a fortune there. She's the breadwinner. Hey, the weather is good, it's cheap, the war is over, and the children have to be taught not to kill. And if we don't like it, we can always go to Madagascar. I've had my eye on Madagascar for quite some time. To see those lemurs, the sifakas. Have you ever seen tapes of them dance?"

"All of you?" Keelin's face was agog.

"Hai!" Sadao nodded.

"You have a bizarre family," Keelin said to Aisling.

"It's who you share your life with, not what branch of the family tree you're perched on."

"Then why did you trick Abraham into a baby if blood ties don't matter?" Keelin got up angrily. "And what about Christmas?"

"Maybe, but I doubt it. The house is rented so she'll give it up."

"What about my stuff in Ireland?"

"Call Molly and discuss it."

"I intend to." Keelin stomped off in fury.

Fatima had caught some fish and was gutting them outside

the hut that evening. Sadao was drinking with some local men around a burning metal drum.

"Where's Aisling?" Keelin asked Fatima.

"I don't know," Fatima said, putting the fish in a bucket. "Are you staying for dinner?"

"I found a phone in one of those empty resort houses and I broke in and called Molly. No answer. So I called Oscar and he said she's going to join youse lot. He thinks its a grand idea. She's on her way. And guess what? He gave her the money. He's shredded this family with Leo's money. I'll never ask him again for anything as long as I live. My stuff is now with my aunt Mary in Dublin. Two cardboard boxes is all I amount to when Molly was done. I didn't even know she was in contact with Mary. I thought she avoided her because her children were so successful and she lorded it over Molly. Back home, that was the biggest game in town — your kids' exam results and careers. I worked so hard to be the one Molly could be proud of. Jesus!"

"Sit down, Keelin. You're making me nervous." Fatima rinsed her hands in another bucket. Her accent was a strange hybrid of Irish and African. "Your mother is welcome to join us in Mozambique. I'm sure she won't stay forever, but it makes more sense than us all going to Ireland. My mother, Lina, is old now too. She's eking a living selling snuff in the cane town outside Maputo. I have to go back. And then there's Abraham —"

"What about me?" A red liquid sun melted into the whole sky and the sea turned the color of watery blood. Palm trees stabbed the shoreline as proof of paradise. The jungle around them was beginning to expand with the nightly noise. Keelin tied her hair in a bun and crouched beside Fatima, helping her to pick up fish junk from the dirt. "I feel like such a pest. It wasn't how I wanted to be. I wanted to save her. I thought Molly would never forget what I did for the family."

Aisling came back through the tiny cluster of huts with the old hippie. She was holding a small gray monkey. Her red hair was washed and combed, her eyes blue. The same blue as Oscar's. Keelin was quite struck by her. *A giantess; and as she walked the villages burned.*

"I wanted things too from your sister that I never got," Fatima said.

"That's why you have Sadao?"

Fatima nodded. "Loyalty. He's faithful. Your sister is wild."

"But he's a man."

"There are more than two sexes, Keelin."

The hippie took the monkey and put it on his shoulder. "We were back in town, dudes. There's a party at the brothel."

"I'm going to play piano for them again." Aisling grabbed Fatima and kissed her neck and shoulders from behind, and Fatima smiled and leaned back into her. Keelin nodded a greeting at Aisling, her eyes full of tears. Aisling grabbed her and pulled her into the hug.

"Can I come?" Keelin whispered to Aisling.

"To the whorehouse? Eric Satie isn't quite their style." She squeezed Keelin's shoulders and wiped her tears with big blocks of fingers not unlike Molly's.

"No. To Mozambique."

After devouring Fatima's fish and rice, Aisling talked up a storm, her belly laugh booming through the village.

"Toru said you were a vegetarian and now you're eating fish."

"There's nothing else to eat here, Keelin."

"Toru thought you were trying to save the world," Keelin said sulkily.

"I was trying to work it out. Hiroshima, Nagasaki. It made me think. We mammals, especially Homo sapiens, did so well out of that meteorite that hit just around here sixty-five million years ago. It had the impact of one hundred atom bombs and we blossomed after it. It's in our blood."

"What, like a genetic memory?"

"I see how the people gather by the shore. Humans love a beach. Are we longing to go back to where we came from?

From where we never meant to leave? We didn't crawl out of the sea to become us. We clambered to reach other waters when we were trapped in dried-up pools. We aren't seeking to evolve, but forces of environment challenge us and develop us beyond our plain of dreams. Life is infinite when perceived as a continuum, hollow and brutal when we take it in chunks. In one lifetime nothing can be achieved. You're frightening yourself with historical thinking, Keelin, when peace will only come geologically. Hope is not in the millennia, it's in the billennia."

"But then our individual lives mean so little." Keelin glumly prodded the fish eye.

"We will always exist, if not as us, so don't get so attached to or upset by the limitations of your form. Don't fret in the mirror, Keelin."

"But who are your family?"

"Hominidae."

"That's one hell of an extended family." Keelin sighed as she squished the burst eye with her fingernail. "I love you. What does that mean?"

"Jaysus, you're really running out of arguments now, aren't you? Love is a protective instinct needed for group survival."

"What if love is a phenomenon, Aisling? A seed planted in our dreams." Keelin ripped the skin off the fish's face and wondered if Fatima and Sadao, who were leaning against each other, were even listening. Had they heard it all before? "And when I look at the scenery around here I think it's beautiful. So what is beauty, then?"

"If we look at the earth we are moved to love it; this is to protect the earth," Aisling said, grinning indulgently at her poor ignorant pupil, "not to grow strange fruit in our dreams."

"And to think Toru was relying on you for the revolution."

Fatima laughed. "She believes in evolution, not revolution."

"There has been a mutation in our DNA, Aisling. I think you know that." Keelin plucked the flesh out of the fish's cheek and ate it. "This mutation manifests itself in different ways. It's making me nervous of every other species on earth. It devoured

Patrick. Orla seems fine, but I lived with that nesting bird boy in Mexico City. What about your child? Weren't you afraid to get pregnant?"

"My molecular clock was ticking."

Fatima sat up. "What's wrong with you all? What is this? Our child is in danger? Aisling?"

"What's family to you, Keelin?" Aisling asked sharply.

"You know what I see now when I see our family?" Keelin said. "I see Goya's Saturn devouring his sons. I see life shrinking, the big bang sucking us into a vacuum. I see evolution, our brains growing bigger than our hearts."

Aisling smiled. "You're a wild one. Can't you see we are peas in a pod? We're indistinguishable."

"Gerry thought I was like him. I must have an insipid reflective personality."

"None of us are special."

"If you are me, then who are you?"

"I'm the sister you never wanted, unwilling to be your friend. Go away alone, by yourself, and live. You can achieve nothing in a lifetime. There are no good ideas. When the sun burns up, then all of it, all the pain and frantic grasping, will have been pointless."

Fatima and Sadao started clearing up the plates, and Keelin jumped up to help. Aisling walked through the sea back to town. The hippie combed his hair and followed closely behind. Keelin stood at the shore. Aisling carried a light, and the light moved smoothly with her through the dark water. In the new leftover quiet, Fatima and Sadao meditated behind the hut in front of a wooden laughing Buddha.

At dawn the village children prodded Keelin awake. She looked down the still coast, then went to the hut.

Aisling was back dangling in a hammock, reading a battered yellow copy of *The Magic Mountain* and drinking a beer. "Whoa, the flies must have got you last night."

"I was waiting for you. You must have seen me sleeping on the shore."

"I did. In fact I stepped over you," Aisling said, raising her bottle. "Grab a beer. Willy and I had a ball. The craic was mighty."

"Are you a Buddhist?" Keelin asked.

"You must be joking. I was never inclined toward religion. I don't have any spiritual aspirations."

"I imagined something different. Gerry let on you were into crystals and witchcraft and New Age stuff."

"All that's crap. Those fucking gobshites who think that they're so politically correct with their crystal shit. They're using the earth for their own ends, like everyone else. Bravo once more for the performing earth! And as for spells and witchcraft, Jaysus. As if burning eggshells in a cup will make any difference in this shitty world."

"But Gerry said you hung out at those New Age spell shops."

"That was just to sniff out some fresh snatch."

"What about your politics? I thought you were obsessed with the underdog. The Native American and all that."

"Yeah, yeah, whatever. Protectors of the land. They sold the land for a few beads. Some protectors."

"Aisling, are you taking the piss? You know who you sound like? You sound like Oscar."

"I worship Fatima's pussy. That's my altar."

She attempted to get out of the hammock, but fell to the floor over all the bottles. Fatima woke and ran to pick her up. They argued in rapid Japanese for a minute, until Aisling brushed herself off and waddled out of the hut, holding a beer and clutching her batik sarong around her with one hand. Keelin trailed after her. The village women filling buckets of water from the central tap took a moment to stare.

"TEETH SHALL BE PROVIDED," Aisling roared at them, and they turned back to their task. "Do you remember the sermon Ian Paisley gave? In hell there will be wailing and gnashing of teeth? And this old woman says, 'But Reverend, I have no teeth,' and he roars at her, 'TEETH SHALL BE PROVIDED.'"

"You used to be a real republican — you and Oscar, all for the IRA," Keelin said.

258

"Yeah, well, that's before I saw Bora Bora, baby. I combed a lot of pretty islands and wondered who the hell would care about anywhere as godforsaken as Northern Ireland. Why would you stay there? Who gives a fuck about land that doesn't belong to you, anyway? The poor Catholic's enemy is not the poor Protestant or the poor Brit. They have the same enemy. They're all in their grotty little council flats, killing and dying for the land. What shagging land will any of those poor bastards ever be given except six foot under, with no elbow room? And the weather is shite to boot. But that's my motto, for what it's worth. Teeth shall be provided. What's yours, Keelin?"

"More bread or I'll appear."

Aisling fell on the ground laughing. Keelin smiled from ear to ear, pleased. "I'm going to come with you and Molly, but I have to go back to the hotel in Tela. I left my stuff there with the manager. Come with me through the sea."

"Get lost in somebody else's life." Aisling rolled naked in the dirt, her sarong undone, her stretched belly smeared with dirt. Keelin dropped to the ground and closed her sister's sprawled legs, pulling the sarong over her, glancing at the villagers who stared with disapproval.

"Come back to the hut. You're making a show of yourself," she urged.

"Oh, fuck off. I'm on mushrooms. I have to go into the jungle and dance." Aisling stood up, leaving the sarong in a puddle in the dirt. She swung around and raised her fist in salute to her sister. "TEETH SHALL BE PROVIDED," she yelled, and then disappeared, her flesh jiggling into the green density of the tropics. Keelin walked in embarrassment through a cluster of women and children and waded into an empty sea.

Keelin later returned to the settlement with her bag that she carried through the sea. The hut was bare. No hammocks, no notes, a plastic bucket with dirty, fishy water in the corner. The ground and walls and mud floor was all that was left. Keelin ran around the back to look for Buddha, but he was gone too. Just the upturned wooden crate of an altar without any flowers. Outside the hippie's hut the gray monkey was tied to a red

Coca-Cola crate. A mother hen waddled by him with several chicks in her wake. The monkey picked up one of the chicks and rooted through its feathers. The mother hen ignored him. He turned the chick upside down and shook it and sat for a while, holding it to his chest, frowning. Keelin observed the proceedings closely. The monkey sniffed at the chick and then bit between its barely wriggling legs. Keelin gasped in horror.

"Haven't you ever seen a monkey with a chicken before, sweetheart?" The hippie had come up behind her. She swung around and grabbed him by the arm. "Where have they gone?"

"Who?"

"How were they when they left?"

"I didn't see anyone leave."

"Aisling, Fatima, and Sadao, for Christ's sake?"

"I don't remember them. That hut's been empty as far as I know."

He released himself from her grip in annoyance. "People come, people go. I'm not a cop. I don't keep track of every gringo. I have a Bible with lovely light paper pages. I use it to roll my grass."

"How could they have taken all their stuff through the sea? Did they get a boat?"

"If you want to get out of here, a taxi is your best bet. Come inside for a toke. You look as if you could use a doobie."

"Taxi? Through the sea?"

"There is a road out of here too, you know. You never did explore this place, sweetie, did you?" he said dismissively. "Never even talked to the natives. You thought yours was the most interesting story here. Wrong."

The studious monkey, who now held the chicken upright, opened the wings like a fan, sticking his fingers searchingly through the soft, grubby feathers. Keelin smoked a biblical joint and spaced out while the hippie ranted and raved, full of hippie venom. "I've just about finished this book." He picked up the depleted hardcover Bible and showed it to her. "All except the maps. The maps are no use to me."

He juggled conspiracy theories like balls in the air — plane crashes, the Oklahoma City bombing, aliens, JFK. Suddenly it was frogs — deformed frogs found all over the United States. Three legs, eyes in their throats, double sets of webbed hands. He said it was the pollution, and if the frogs couldn't handle it, neither could the humans. The frog would be the first to usher in the end. Patrick's ghost appeared to her at the straw door — Patrick the frog finder, with only one eye down his throat, seeing nothing in the darkness.

"I don't know if you should go to New York and become a schoolteacher," the hippie said with satisfaction. "The kids shoot 'em there."

Fed up, Keelin left. The world she had walked through was big, and they were all only linked to a few threads of humanity. Those threads were so hard to handle, spindling out into the haywire universe at an unholy tangle. Molly, Oscar, Aisling, Orla, Siobhan, Shawn, and Patrick's ghost, a severed thread. Only now and then could she reel them in for a kiss. She watched the shore in case they were coming back. In case they had forgotten something.

Alone, Keelin sat by the sea until the sun sank like lead below the horizon, dragging the day away with it. Aisling, my sister. But it had been herself who was wounded by such a love. Herself who had been left on the shore. No note. Had they gone to meet Molly in some far-off place? A plane ride away. Which airport? Which hemisphere had she darted to now? Keelin, her back hunched and her hands clasping her ankles, spoke out into the sea. "This story is not true. I am not Keelin? You are not my sister. We never crossed ways. So restore my sight; I am blind by these waters. And you are disappeared."

Her bag on top of her head, Keelin struggled, grunting through the sea. As she waded, the current pulled her away from the shore. The water reached her chin and she swallowed it in panic. The land seemed shadowed and steep at that point, the jungle farther away than it should be. It was getting dark, and she groped inside the bag for her waterproof passport and wallet holder. The big bag sank quickly, with a slurp of a splash. She had to swim, as the water was above her mouth. She was frightened and her will to live was not strong. She considered letting herself sink and disappear. Would Siobhan or Orla come looking for her? Would Oscar give them money to find her? Her legs spun against the sea bed but found no floor to the world. They do not love me. They do not love you.

In the dim hotel lobby in Tela, Keelin rang Orla in the sandwich shop in Mexico City. Molly had written to Orla, so she knew about Patrick, but not the details of Molly's trip. Keelin was clingy and mournful.

"Aisling told me to get lost."

"She was kind to you to the end so," Orla said.

"Come back to Ireland with me."

"There's nothing there now. No family. Look, maybe someday. I got to go, I'll get in trouble."

She wanted to go home. How many years do people live? Her mother was old. Fifteen more years, and she would only see her fifteen more times, fifteen Christmases. Fifteen winter fortnights. But nobody was left there. The world had snapped shut, the future had been submerged, and home was over forever. She fumbled for money and rang Siobhan.

"Come here," Siobhan said. "New York is cool. Give it a lash anyway. I'd like it if you did. We can apply for the green card lottery together. Once you get papers you can teach. Cian won't mind if you stay with us."

"I want to go back to Ireland and teach."

"Why go back?" Siobhan echoed Orla. "What's there?"

It was irrefutable. A mad father in a country asylum, a gravesite up on a hill, without the last name filled in. Two cardboard boxes of clothes, books, and God knows what, in an aunt's house. She didn't want to go home to stand alone at a grave. Poor Patrick, locked away now in a room in her head, his memory hovering at the stairs, his ghost waiting to be fed.

"I can't emulate Aisling, who has no country, no religion, no sex. Aisling is history's escapee."

"Chill out, Keelin. You're taking yourself too seriously."

"I was thinking of becoming a junkie too, actually."

"Listen, about my little habit — don't even think about it. I just need a break from thinking about food. This shit helps me, honestly. I'm not ready to feel again. You have an M.A. Go become a teacher. You only took a year off."

"But look what that year has done. It was ten missing medieval years all in one."

She had not been discarded. She had been launched. Remember the game? One metal ball lobbed through the air to hit the other. But she had not been metal and she shattered on impact. The steel ball unmoved. One beloved child . . . There really had been only one beloved child.

"I feel bad, Siobhan. I think about it. About Toru. It makes me stop dead in the street and put my hand to my face in horror."

"What, that you fucked him?"

"No no no. That he was gone for days and when he came back he'd been beaten up. Remember? He came straight to us after the beating. Maybe Aisling and Toru went to each other after their beatings. She passed sometimes as a man, but sometimes she got burnt. Aisling was scared, Siobhan. It wasn't easy for her. Toru came with his bruises and his blood and his stockings torn, and I screamed at him, and I told him she wasn't his Aisling, she was ours, but I couldn't see I was wrong."

"You were always too judgmental," Siobhan said.

"And you say I should teach. I must have been having delusions of adequacy."

"Oh, come on. You'll be a better teacher now than you would have been if you lived forever with Molly. Which is what you would have been doing if Aisling wasn't in either of your lives."

"Why did they leave Ensenada with no forwarding address? Maybe something awful happened."

"Molly happened! I mean, come on, she was using you. If it makes you feel better, maybe those freaks were run out of town. Aisling pissed everyone off eventually."

"I love Molly. I just can't picture her bolting out of Ireland."

"Yeah, well she didn't bring her womb."

"True. Or her breasts. But still, I can't condemn her to inaction, like her own mother did and the old lady she worked for. And everyone else."

"Can you picture her in Mozambique with her African daughter-in-law and her Japanese son-in-law?" Siobhan raised her eyebrows in New York, and Keelin laughed in Honduras.

"Oh, to be a fly on the wall," Keelin said. The fly who sees all. Who watches us through our lives and settles on our wounds, inside our mouths, when we lie down to die. Black legs wading on our open eyes. Finding its likeness in our lashes. Poised with the worms of the ground and the vultures of the sky to release us back into the earth and on to what we are so reluctant to become. "Send the camera back to Toru. You're not using it."

"I took half a roll by myself. You know, I think Patrick is in one of the pictures."

"We have a photo?" Keelin was thrilled.

"Well, I warn you, he was standing on his head when I took it. To purify his organs, he said. But you could flip it over."

"That would look kind of strange."

Keelin stood on the same balcony in Tela that she'd stood on a week before and watched the vultures strut the sand among the broken trees. This revolutionary year was over, and now came the long exile of the rest of her life without a family. "I had been so presumptuous to have come to carry you home, and you took my home away," she said aloud. "Now that the lesson is neatly learned, do I get a reward for my understanding and acceptance? Do I get something in return for the huge love I still feel for you? I ascended and descended others' stairs, but at my own I only stood at the top and called. More bread, more bread. I threatened you. Cured my hunger. But every day the hunger begins again, and we do anything to satisfy this, our huge need.

"Are you still naked in the jungle? Monster, monster. The cunt that ate the world. Your insatiable cunt. You are the animal the other animals were trying to warn me about, the black, hunched bird of prey. There was something not quite right, couldn't put my finger on it. I will miss you. I'm jealous of your love for Fatima, and that she never even noticed me. Never even saw a resemblance between us. I am cautious, but I ran wild in your shoes for one year. You were kind in the end. Please, one day come back to me. I might care for your child like you cared for me. You warmed my clothes at the stove, you undressed me, bathed me, walked me to and from school, bought me sweets with your pocket money, talked to me, played with me. Were you my mother, or did you take my mother away?"

She turned to see a man, a fellow guest, listening to her ravings. It had been so long since she had been around her own language that she took it for granted no one would be able to understand her. But this guy looked like an American. He had long blond hair and a surfboard by his chair. They probably did share a language. She smiled slightly at him and he pointed to her feet.

"Dude, your clodhoppers are tweaked!" he said.

She stared uncomprehending to where he pointed: the shoes that she had worn around the world were split at the seams and the sole slobbered apart like a ravenous tongue.

That night she dreamt of empty water. When she awoke she recalled a dream she had the first night in Japan. Aisling swam naked and close to her. A cockroach sat midway on the opposite wall, digesting the darkness around it. "Aisling," she said, "take care of Molly for me." She felt the sea inside her head. The tide pulling back, leaving a drenched, bereft floor.

In her underwear she walked the damp windowless leg of the tiled corridor and down to the shore — the cruel shore that drew the line, the split in the world. The sand was chilled beneath her feet. Light vibrated behind the membrane of darkness, ready to claw through and drain the night to day. Her arms outstretched, she waded into the gigantic ocean. She felt the longing to go back, to not become us, to undo what we became, to unbirth the species. The last born. The bartered child left on the shore. There must be other homes to be had. Safe places in the world. Safer than her own home had been. The bruised sky healed from black to mottled purple to speckled yellow, and morning shone. She swam backward out of the sea, and when her arms struck the sand she dragged herself to the shore, scraping through the smashed shale and shingles and small white shells. Bright currency of the sea offered to the land. Nothing can be achieved in a lifetime, and there were no good ideas. But we didn't crawl out of the sea to become us. There was something beyond our plane of dreams. She sat under the warm sun, half in the water and half out. A stark and sudden evolution of hope. The face in the window was gone. Keelin had been a delicate growth — sentimental and dependent, attached, territorial, committed to remaining indigenous. Was that the greatest lesson of them all? The crash course in severation? Aisling was history's hag, dethreading its pockets, discarding its loose change. Aisling was a great teacher. But more than that, Keelin now knew. The triumphant mad. Aisling was Sive escaped, well fed, and dancing like a sifaka through the jungle.

epilogue

Epilogue

unclean cages

"MY HAIR IS FALLING OUT and I have no bones," Oscar told Leo. "Just soft yellow sticks, warped and smelling slightly of sulfur." He lifted his arm to his nose and sniffed.

Leo and Oscar sat under a white canopy on the grounds of the Grand Wailea Resort in Maui. Leo had convinced Oscar that a quick nip and tuck would do wonders for his flagging spirits. They had gone to Leo's plastic surgeon in Palm Springs, and Leo brought Oscar to convalesce in Maui. Oscar's face was bandaged. Leo wore swimming trunks. He was in his eighties but still lean and agile, with a head of thick white hair. His face was smooth and unwrinkled, and his expression was that of a coma victim, grown old without experience. Oscar had stubbornly worn a black shirt and white collar to the pool. Short sleeves were his only concession to leisure. He and Leo were looking for a retirement house in Hawaii. The pool stretched for seeming miles of slides and lava bars, overhanging flowers and waterfalls. Children were forbidden in the section where they reclined. A beautiful blond waiter came and took their order. A mai tai for Leo, an Irish whiskey for Oscar. They caught each other staring at the waiter as he wound away through sun-soaking bodies and laughed.

"Oh," Oscar groaned. "It hurts to laugh. I mustn't be healed yet." He grew frightened at the thought of what he would look like when the bandages came off. When the young waiter came back, Leo signed for the drinks and flashed a saintly smile.

"Darn. I forgot my book. Oscar, did you bring the paper?" Oscar slurped some whiskey and rooted in his bag. He extracted a Bible, much to Leo's surprise.

"Surely you didn't steal that from the hotel room?"

"How long since you read this book? Bet you've even forgotten the ending."

Leo took the book suspiciously. "It's a Protestant Bible."

"See if they end the same way. That book has us badly trained to expect paradise, fall, apocalypse, and redemption in every story."

"What part do you have a problem with?"

"Redemption." Oscar leaned back on his chair. "Read me Revelation 18:2."

Leo looked at Oscar, impressed. "I see you've stayed in many hotels recently."

"I was sorting out my family."

"Indeed! I'm glad that's all over. My money isn't infinite."

"They're all grand." Oscar waved his hand dismissively.

"You're a good man, Oscar. Many others wouldn't have given so much of themselves."

"Those kids were a disappointing bunch. Didn't amount to much." Oscar sighed. "I wonder if Molly had her life over would she have any children at all."

"You did your best for them. And that poor young hemophiliac altar boy you mentored over the years. It was a very Christian thing you did, nursing him." Leo patted Oscar's leg sympathetically. "More than duty called for."

"Read it, Leo," Oscar said. "I want to hear it aloud. It was one of my mother's favorite bits."

Somewhat embarrassed, Leo cleared his throat and flinched before reading softly, above the sound of blue waves stroking the beach and children playing happily in the distant pools. *"And he cried mightily with a strong voice, saying, Babylon the great is fallen, and is become the habitation of devils, and the hold of every foul spirit, and a cage of every unclean and hateful bird."*

Leo closed the book and put it under the towel. "Enough of

this, Oscar. As the Irish would say, you need to be taken out of yourself. When the bandages come off you'll be a new man. Am I mistaken, but do I sound Irish after all these years with you? Now that's one for the books. What a thought. Maybe we should go there next summer. Take a trip around Connamara. A few of my patients could recommend some fine restaurants in the region. We could stay in a castle, and you could show me your roots." Leo nodded thoughtfully at his lover. He stood and stretched contentedly.

"How come, Leo, you never seem to grow old?" Oscar asked, envious, his own face butchered and in swaddling. Awaiting a new, uncertain birth. "Is it a Jesuit thing? or a Wilde thing? A hideous picture in the attic. And that innocence you've projected all your life — is that an act too? I sometimes think you are the devil himself."

"Money, darling, money. Look here, cheer up, you're a good man, Oscar. I made the right choice all those years ago at the opera. I'm never wrong. Perhaps we should have an anniversary party this year. Invite all the right people. We've had our ups and downs, but this is redemption right here, and paradise. Don't occupy yourself with that palaver about foul birds and unclean cages or whatever. That's not for the likes of us, for goodness sake." He stepped up to the pool and dove in, his long, ancient body spearing the water gracefully. Death's sure arrow. Oscar turned his head stiffly toward the sea and grimaced at the other islands as a gentle breeze blew his drink napkin off the table. A glittering sea wrapped around a beautiful island, a whiskey priest drunk and bandaged in paradise. He might trickle over into the next millennium, but nothing belonged to him. They had all stolen a brief existence from an indifferent history, and in the end these borrowed lives would break their hearts. A sweet-scented wind got caught up suddenly in the trees. When he leaned over to sip his whiskey, the blood rushed to his muzzled features, just as the wind retreated from the leaves. Oscar lay back on the white chair. He closed his eyes and whispered, "Oh, how I loved those dirty birds."

acknowledgments

While the actual writing of a book is a solitary act, the support I received from many people was invaluable. In this matter I will limit myself to those who worked on the text itself. I would like to acknowledge my former editor, Lenora Todaro, for hunting me down and serving breakfast to America, and Pat Strachan, for kindly inheriting this new book. I'd like to thank Jenny Shute, who never did get that restraining order against me. I am grateful to all my fellow Hunter College students for their advice and opinions on the manuscript, especially Anna Van Lenten, Marta Koziorzebska, and Erik Johnson, who ate my hummus and drank all my beer on the roof. And, above all, I'd like to thank Afshin, for everything.